ONCE UPON A TIME

A TIME

❧NEW FAIRY TALES❧

ONCE UPON
A TIME
❖ NEW FAIRY TALES ❖

EDITED BY PAULA GURAN

PRIME BOOKS

*For Ellen Datlow and Terri Windling—
without whom so many wonderful new fairy tales for both children
and adults would never have been written.*

❦ CONTENTS ❦

EVER AFTER

Where did it start for you? When did you first discover fairy tales?

For me, it was a book titled *Fifty Famous Fairy Stories*: no author or editor listed, only the illustrator, Bruno Frost. Published by the Whitman Publishing Company as part of their Famous Classics series, the copyright dates are 1946 and 1954. I think the first version was a traditional hardcover with a dust jacket. My edition is printed on cheap pulp paper—286 pages total—and its "hardcover" is printed in vivid color with a shiny cellophane-like coating over cardboard. Frost's line drawings are enhanced with spot color of either aqua or pink. I still have it: spine replaced with packing tape and pages crumbling.

I have no idea where the book came from or when, but I know my mother read its stories to me before I could read myself. Then I later read them myself, over and over. The tales are, of course, sanitized versions, but decently written in straightforward, never condescending prose. The selections are a hodgepodge—probably heavily influenced by Andrew Lang's fairy tale books of various colors—of English and Scandinavian folktales, Charles Perrault, the Brothers Grimm, Hans Christian Andersen, Madame d'Aulnoy, Arabic literature, and maybe other sources.

I don't care to analyze the origins of the contents or even ponder why these fifty were selected—this is a holy book to me. It was both magical and very real—it took me away from "real life" but it also was pertinent to my life in many ways—and it was even revelatory.

Far from turning me into the sort of girl who expected some prince to save her, fairy tales were examples of people, animals, even beasts becoming who and what they *really* were. Bad things happened to all kinds of people, but if you were clever and showed others your value, you'd triumph in the end.

I also remember being deeply outraged at foolishness. As much as I loved the story "Rapunzel," for instance, I thought the mother—who so desired rampion she endangered her husband and lost her child—to be idiotic. Rapunzel herself was a complete lamebrain for thoughtlessly exclaiming, "Good mother, how is it you are so much heavier to draw up than the King's son? He takes but a moment to climb up to me."

In my teens, I discovered that wasn't the question the girl posed when the tale was first retold by the Grimms. Rapunzel's query was: "Why it is that my clothes are all too tight? They no longer fit me." After living nightly with the prince "in joy and pleasure for a long time," Rapunzel was pregnant. If you lock a girl up in a tower and don't tell her anything about birth control, pregnancy is a natural consequence of "joy and pleasure." What a relief! She wasn't stupid, just ignorant.

Nor did I see the prince as a rapist or a victimizer. He was so devoted to Rapunzel he threw himself off the tower when he thought he had lost her forever. And Rapunzel turned out to be damned resourceful; after giving birth to twins and living through great misery, she healed the prince's blindness and saved the man she loved . . . and possibly a whole kingdom. The way I saw it, they'd lived through hard times in the unsafe, brutal world outside isolating towers and unprotected by royal entitlement. Rulers with such experience would be a good bet to reign well and serve their people.

I also eventually learned my *Fifty Famous*/Andrew Lang/Brothers Grimm version of "Rapunzel" was not the only traditional story about a maiden locked in a tower. There are similar tales to be found in many cultures. The Grimms weren't even correct in calling it a folk tale. Their source may or may not have known it was a retelling of a story published by Friedrich Schultz in 1790, who had—in turn—

translated it from "Persinette," a 1698 French story by Charlotte-Rose de La Force. "Persinette" was evidently inspired by Giambattista Basile's "Petrosinella," published in 1634 in the first volume of his *Lo cunto de li cunti.*

I came to view the vegetable-craving mother-to-be in a different light too. The cravings of a pregnant woman can indicate dangerous vitamin deficiencies, and in many folk traditions fulfilling an expectant mother's desires for certain foods is of tantamount importance. Perhaps it *did* amount to a matter of having to have the rampion or dying.

The witch? Maybe she was a wise woman or herbalist who had knowledge that could save both mother and child. Demanding custody of the child in return seems an extremely unequal deal, but it may have been in the infant's best interests if the mother was weak or ill.

Or perhaps the father was thinking only of saving his own skin or his wife's life. He might have doubted the chances the child would even be born.

As for shutting a child reaching puberty away from the world—many parents wish they could do that very thing. Some even attempt to do so—sometimes with similar outcomes as far as pregnancy.

I have many more—often conflicting—ideas about the meaning of the story now. And I'm not a scholar or expert in folklore and fairy tales—I'm sure they have even more to say.

But, at the very least, the story said something about how we all have to grow up and break out of whatever towers we are imprisoned in. We all wander lost and blind at times; we all hope for a happy ending or, at least, that our suffering will be worth its cost.

That is part of the wonder of fairy tales: they are simple, intimate stories that are, at the same time, complex and broadly applicable. We experience them and understand them one way as children, other interpretations arise as we become adults, still more thoughts as we mature further. As children we feel the darkness in the woods and fear what lurks in its shadows. As adults we begin to understand that there is no light without the dark; that without the dangers of life, the risks, the difficulties, the hardships, and the monsters, we cannot grow. If we never go into the woods, we'll never really understand the "ever after" of our lives.

The old stories were intended for adults or an "all ages" audience that included children. They began as folk tales told aloud; later they were literary works authored by individuals (although often inspired by or based on the older oral traditions). Eventually shaped into what was considered a more suitable form for children, adults then disdained them as nursery stories.

Then in the late twentieth century, while still existing in versions intended for the youngsters, fairy tales re-emerged in literary retellings as stories for adults, .

"Rapunzel," my randomly chosen example, has directly inspired contemporary authors such as Anne Bishop, Emma Donoghue, Esther Friesner, Gregory Frost, Louise Hawes, Tanith Lee (twice), Elizabeth Lynn, Robin McKinley, Lois Metzger, Richard Parks, Lisa Russ Spaar, and others. There are several beautiful picture book versions in print, and it has been expanded into novels for children with books like *Golden* by Cameron Dokey (2006), *The Stone Cage* by Nicholas Stuart Gray (1963), and *Letters from Rapunzel* by Sara Holmes (2007). *Zel* by Donna Jo Napoli (1996) and *The Tower Room* by Adèle Geras (1992) are novels intended for young adults; for adults there is *Bitter Greens* by Kate Forsyth (2012).

"Rapunzel" has been adapted into graphic novels and for dance, stage (including incorporation into a Broadway musical), television, video, had its eponymous protagonist turned into a Barbie doll, and—with *Tangled* (2010)—animated by Disney and consequently into inestimable Disney Princess merchandise.

And that's just *one* fairy tale, not even a story considered among the very best known, most popular, or most beloved.

Fairy tales evolve. This mutability is one of the many reasons fairy tales have endured and continue to both reflect and effect culture.

In the last few years, the idea of fairy tales being more than "kid's stuff" has found a broader audience. What had been (re)established among scholars and in genre and mainstream literature for decades has, through television and film, now truly reached the masses. Although far from the first fairy-tale-based television series, *Grimm* debuted on NBC in fall 2011. The premise: dangerous fairy-tale creatures exist in the "real" world; only a cop descended from a line of "guardians," the "Grimms," can defeat the monsters. ABC introduced series *Once Upon a Time* in October 2011. In it, fairy-tale characters have been brought into "our" world by a curse. A spin-off, *Once Upon a Time in Wonderland* will hit small screens fall 2013. The CW premiered *Beauty and the Beast* on October 11, 2012—loosely based on the Ron Koslow-created 1987-1990 CBS series—which was, of course, an updating of the fairy tale.

In 2012 there were two Hollywood versions of Snow White's story: *Mirror Mirror* and *Snow White and the Huntsman*. This year, 2013, has already seen releases of *Jack the Giant Slayer*, *Oz the Great and Powerful*, and *Hansel & Gretel: Witch Hunters*—none of which were spectacular successes. Will that stem the cinematic tide? Probably not. You can still expect *Frozen*, a Disney-animated film of Hans Christian Andersen's "The Snow Queen," to open late in 2013. *Maleficent*, starring Angelina Jolie as the villainess from Disney's *Sleeping Beauty* is due out 2014, as is a live-action *Cinderella* directed by Kenneth Branagh. Also scheduled for 2014: a film version of Steven Sondheim's fairy tale mash-up musical *Into the Woods*. In March 2013, the *Boston Globe* estimated the number of fairy-tale slated to be released between 2012 and 2014 at twenty.

Unless intended specifically for children, these twenty-first century revampings often go back to the darker roots of the stories. Heroines are seldom passive victims and inequality in general is often battled along with other evils; some are extremely violent and overtly sexual.

There are probably more theories of why fairy tales are enjoying their current resurgence as there are fairy tales resurging: it's merely a public-domain path for the entertainment industry to capitalize on the post-Harry Potter boom in fantasy; fairy tales offer an escape from our economic doldrums and unsettled times; they aren't an escape at all, but horrific confrontations; most movies are reworkings of fairy-tale tropes anyway, so this is really nothing new; pop culture has a tendency to infantilize (as with superheroes), this is another way to do it; fairy tales provide both heroes and heroines, villains and villainesses and provide a focus on a female, but with plenty of room for violence and SFX that appeals to the male demographic; they are iconic, we have a built-in nostalgia for them, and familiarity breeds easy marketability; when Disney played with and cleverly twisted its own concept with *Enchanted*, it made Hollywood reconsider the trope (and, yes, there are rumors of an *Enchanted 2*) . . .

Who knows what makes a trend? After all, for the last four decades or so there have been myriad academic theories, explanations, and not always civil debate about fairy tales themselves.

Nowadays fairy tales are assiduously studied, interpreted according to differing philosophies, mined for inner meaning, psychoanalyzed through various filters, and hotly debated. Fairy tales can be seen in many—often antithetical—ways. There are those who consider them morally deficient, others as means to enforce traditional morality. They are seen as sexist or feminist; timeless or products of a specific time and event; nationalistic or universal; hegemonic or subversive; eternally relevant and totally irrelevant; metaphoric or allegorical; considered as art or dismissed as tawdry entertainment; too scary and violent or a safe way to deal with primal fears; they appeal to us because they give us hope or they validate what is real . . . ad infinitum.

This anthology, however, has no agenda other than to present new fairy tales written by some talented authors. I gave the writers no definitions or boundaries. I simply stated that traditional stories often started with the phrase used as the title—"once upon a time"— but fairy tales have always resonated with the reader's own time and place. They have power and meaning for today and tomorrow. Contributions could be new interpretations of the old or an original story inspired by earlier fairy tales.

I also invited each author to say something about the writing of their story and/or what fairy tales meant to them. I think you'll find the comments introducing each story far more illuminating than what I have provided here.

For the last few months, I've been keeping this treasury of wonder, if not locked up in a tower, at least all to myself. Now it is time to allow you to experience these wonderful new fairy stories and their marvelously varied ever afters.

Paula Guran

June 2013

Online Sources for Fairy Tales Old and New

Cabinet des Fées (www.cabinetdesfees.com) celebrates fairy tales in all of their manifestations: in print, in film, in academia, and on the web. Also hosts two fiction zines.

Endicott Studio (endicottstudio.typepad.com) is an interdisciplinary organization dedicated to the creation and support of mythic art. Their *Journal of Mythic Arts* appeared online from 1997 to 2008. Site includes essays, stories, and musings on folklore, modern magical fiction, and related topics.

SurLaLune Fairy Tales (www.surlalunefairytales.com) features forty-nine annotated fairy tales, including their histories, similar tales across cultures, modern interpretations and over 1,500 illustrations..

Fairy Tale Review (digitalcommons.wayne.edu/fairytalereview) is an annual literary journal dedicated to publishing new fairy-tale fiction, nonfiction, and poetry. The journal seeks to expand the conversation about fairy tales among practitioners, scholars, and general readers.

This story was originally written in exchange for a donation to help survivors of Hurricane Katrina. I was broke then, but I could write, and I found someone who was interested in having a story written to a prompt of their choosing. At the time I'd never been to Louisiana, so I instead wrote about a watery setting. I grew up with Korean folktales of the Dragon King Under the Sea, which I remember more from the illustrations in the children's books than the stories themselves, and I have often thought that they are the closest thing that Korean lore has to Faerie.

Incidentally, the treasures in this story owe something in spirit to a certain fantastic table owned by my grandmother, which my cousins and sister and I would often marvel over: a hollowed out bowl of wood with a glass top, within which were souvenirs gathered from the many places my grandparents traveled to when they were younger.

Yoon Ha Lee

The Coin of Heart's Desire

Yoon Ha Lee

In an empire at the wide sea's boundaries, where the clouds were the color of alabaster and mother-of-pearl, and the winds bore the smells of salt and faraway fruits, the young and old of every caste gathered for their empress's funeral. In life she had gone by the name Beryl-Beneath-the-Storm. Now that she was dead, the court historians were already calling her Weave-the-Storm, for she had been a fearsome naval commander.

The embalmers had anointed Weave-the-Storm in fragrant oils and hidden her face, as was proper, with a mask carved from white jade. In one hand they had placed a small banner sewn with the empire's sword-and-anchor emblem in dark blue; in the other, a sharp, unsheathed knife whose enameled hilt winked white and gold and blue. She had been dressed in heavy silk robes that had only been worn once before, at the last harvest moon festival. The empire's people believed in supplying their ruler well for the life in the sea-to-come, so that she would intercede with the dragon spirits for them.

The empress had left behind a single daughter. She was only thirteen years old, so the old empress's advisors had named her Early-Tern-Journeying. Tern had a gravity beyond her years. Even at the funeral, dressed in the white-and-gray robes of mourning, she was nearly impassive. If her eyes glistened when the priests chanted their blessings for the road-into-sunset, that was only to be expected.

Before nightfall, the old empress's bier was placed upon a funeral boat painted red to guide her sunward. One priest cut the boat loose while the empress's guard set it ablaze with fire arrows.

Tern's oldest advisor, a sage who had visited many foreign shrines in his youth, turned to her and said over the crackling flames and the lapping water, "You must rest well tonight, my liege. Tomorrow you will hold court before the Twenty-Seven Great Families. They must see in you your mother's commanding presence, for all your tender years."

Tern knew perfectly well, as did he, that no matter how steely her composure, the Great Families would see her as an easy mark. But she merely nodded and retired to the meditation chamber.

She did not sleep that night, although no one would have blamed her if she had. Instead, she thought long and hard about the problem before her. At times, as she inhaled the sweet incense, she wanted desperately to call her mother back from the funeral ship and ask her advice. But the advice her mother had already passed down to her during the years of her life would have to suffice.

Two hours before dawn, she rang a silver bell to summon her servants. "Wake up the chancellor of the exchequer," she said to them. "I need his advice."

The chancellor was not pleased to be roused from his sleep, and even less pleased when Tern explained her intent. "Buy off the Families?" he said. "It's a bad precedent."

"We're not buying them off," Tern said severely. "We are displaying a bounty they cannot hope to equal. They will ask themselves, if the imperial house can afford to give away such treasures, what greater might is it concealing?"

The chancellor grumbled and muttered, but accompanied Tern to the first treasury. The treasury's walls were hung with silk scrolls painted with exquisite landscapes and piled high with illuminated books. The shapes of cranes and playful cats were stamped onto the books' covers in gold leaf. Tiny ivory figurines no larger than a thumbnail were arrayed like vigilant armies, if not for the curious fact that each one had the head of an extinct bird. Swords rested on polished stands, cabochons of opal and aquamarine gleaming from their gold-washed scabbards, their pale tassels decorated with knots sacred to the compass winds. There were crowns of braided wire cradling fossils inscribed with fractured prophecies, some still tangled with the hair of long-dead sovereigns, and twisted ropes of pearls perfectly graduated in size and color, from shimmering white to violet-gray to lustrous black.

"None of these will do," Tern said. "These are quotidian treasures, fit for rewarding captains, but not for impressing the Twenty-Seven Great Families."

The chancellor blanched. "Surely you don't mean—"

But the young empress had swept past him and was heading toward the second treasury. She drew out her heaviest key and opened the doors, which swung with deceptive ease on their hinges. The guards at the door eyed her nervously.

The smell of salt water and kelp was suddenly strong. A dragon's single, heavy-lidded eye opened in the darkness beyond the doors. "Who desires to drown?" asked the dragon spirit in a low, resonant voice. It sounded hopeful. Most people knew better than to disturb the guardian spirit.

"I am Weave-the-Storm's daughter," Tern said. "They call me Early-Tern-Journeying."

The eye slitted. "So you are," the dragon said, less threateningly. "I've never understood your dynasty's need to change names at random intervals. It's dreadfully confusing."

"Does the tradition trouble you?" Tern asked. "It would be difficult to change, but—"

The light from the hallway glinted on the dragon's long teeth. "Don't trouble yourself on my account," it said. Musingly, it added, "It's remarkable how you resemble her around the eyes. Come in, then."

"This is unwise," the chancellor said. "Anything guarded by a dragon is locked away for a reason."

"Treasures hidden forever do no good," Tern said. She entered the treasury, leaving the chancellor behind. The door swung quietly shut behind her.

Despite the dragon's protection, it was difficult to breathe through the dream of ocean, and difficult to move. Even the color of the light was like that of rain and lightning and foam mixed together. The smell of salt grew stronger, interspersed curiously with the fragrance of chrysanthemums. But then, it was better than drowning.

"What brings you here?" asked the dragon, swimming alongside her. Its coils revealed themselves in pearlescent flashes.

"I must select twenty-seven gifts for the Twenty-Seven Great Families to impress them with the dynasty's might," Tern said. "I don't know what to give them."

"Is that all?" the dragon said, sounding disappointed. "There are suits of armor here for woman and man, horse and elephant. Give one to the head of each family—although I presume none of them are elephants—and if they should plot treachery, the ghosts that live in the armor will strike down your enemies. Unless you've invented gunpowder yet? The armor's no good against decent guns. It's so easy to lose track of time while drowsing here."

Tern craned her head to look at the indistinct shapes of skeleton and coral. "Gunpowder?" she asked.

"Don't trouble yourself about it. It's not important. Shall I show you the armor?" The undulating light revealed finely wrought armor paired with demon-faced masks or impressively spiked chanfrons. She could almost see her face, distorted, in the polished breastplates.

"That's no true gift," Tern said, "practical though it is."

The dragon sighed gustily. "An idealist. Well, then. What about this?"

As though they stood to either side of a brook, a flotilla of paper boats bobbed toward them. Tern knelt to examine the boats and half a verse was written on one's sail.

"Go ahead," the dragon said, "unfold it."

She did. "That's almost a poem by Crescent-Sword-Descending," she said: one of the empire's most celebrated admirals, who had turned back the Irrilesh invasion 349 years ago. "But it's less elegant than the version my tutors taught me."

"That's because Crescent was a mediocre poet, for all her victories at sea," the dragon said. "Her empress had one of the court poets discreetly rewrite everything." Its tone of voice implied that it didn't understand this human undertaking, either. "In any case, each of the boats is inscribed with verses by some hero or admiral. If you float them in the sea on the night of a gravid moon, they will grow into fine warships. To restore them to their paper form—useful for avoiding docking fees—recite their verses on a new moon. And they're loyal, if that's a concern. They won't sail against you."

Tern considered it. "It's an impressive gift, but not quite right." She envisioned her subjects warring with each other.

"These, then," the dragon said, knotting and unknotting itself. A cold current rushed through the room, and the boats scattered, vanishing into dark corners.

When the chill abated, twenty-seven fine coats were arrayed before them. Some were sewn with baroque pearls and star sapphires, others embroidered with gold and silver thread. Some had ruffs lined with lace finer than foam, others sleeves decorated with fantastic flowers of wire and stiff dyed silk. One was white and pale blue and silver, like the moon on a snowy night; another was deep orange and decorated with amber in which trapped insects spelled out liturgies in brittle characters; yet another was black fading into smoke-gray at the hems, with several translucent capes fluttering down from the collar like moth wings, each hung with tiny, clapperless glass bells.

"They're marvelous indeed," Tern said. She peered more closely: each coat, however different, had a glittering crest at its breast. "Are those dragons' scales?"

"Indeed they are," the dragon said. "There are dragons of every kind of storm imaginable: ion storms, solar flares, the quantum froth of the emptiest vacuum . . . in any case, have you never wondered what it's like to view the world from a dragon's perspective?"

"Not especially," Tern said. In her daydreams she had roved the imperial gardens, pretending she could understand the language of carp and cat, or could sleep among the mothering branches of the willow; that she could run away. But dutiful child that she was, she had never done so in truth.

"Each year at the Festival of Dragons," the dragon said, "those who wear the coats will have the opportunity to take on a dragon's shape. It's not terribly useful for insurrection, if that's what the expression in your eyes means. But dragons love to dance, and sometimes people so transformed choose never to abandon that dance. At festival's end, whoever stands in a dragon's skin remains in that dragon's skin."

Tern walked among the coats, careful not to touch them even with the hem of her gown. The dragon rippled as it watched her, but forbore comment.

"Yes," she said at last. "This will do." The coats were wondrous, but they offered their wearers an honest choice, or so she hoped.

"What of something for yourself?" the dragon asked.

Some undercurrent in the dragon's tone made her look at it sharply. "It's one thing to use the treasury for a matter of state," she said, "and another to pillage it for my own pleasure."

"You're the empress, aren't you?"

"Which makes it all the more important that I behave responsibly." Tern tilted her chin up to meet the dragon's dispassionate gaze. "The treasury isn't the only reason you're here, is it."

"Ah, so you've figured it out." The dragon's smile showed no teeth. It extended a hand with eight clawed fingers. Dangling from the smallest claw, which was still longer than Tern's hand, was a disc rather like a coin, except it was made of dull green stone with specks in it like blood clots, and the hole drilled through the center was circular rather than a square. The most interesting thing was the snake carved into the surface, with every scale polished and distinct.

"Is it watching me?" Tern asked, disconcerted by the way the snake's eyes were a brighter red than the flecks in the rest of the stone. "What is it called?"

"That is the Coin of Heart's Desire," the dragon said with no particular inflection.

"Nothing with such a name can possibly bring good fortune," she said.

"It never harmed your mother."

Then why had she never heard of it? "In all the transactions I have ever witnessed," Tern said, "a coin must be spent to be used."

The dragon's smile displayed the full length of its jagged teeth. "You're not wrong."

Tern inspected the coin again. She was certain that the snake had changed position. "How many of my ancestors have spent the coin?"

"I lost count," the dragon said. "This business of reign-names and funeral-names makes it difficult to keep track. But some never spent it at all."

"Why isn't it mentioned in the histories?"

The dragon's eyelid dipped. "Because I like to eat historians. Their bones whisper the most delicious secrets."

There was a saying in the empire: Never sing before an empty shrine; never dance with ghosts at low tide; never cross jests with a dragon. Tern said slowly, "Yet the empire has prospered, if those historians are to be believed. We can't all have failed this test."

The dragon did not deny that it was, indeed, a test.

Tern looked over her shoulder at the door. Its outline was visible only as an intersection of shadow and murky light. "There's no other way out of this treasury." When the dragon remained silent, she touched the coin with her fingertip. It was warm, as if it had lain in the eye of a hidden sun. She half-expected to feel the rasp of scales as the snake moved again.

The dragon withdrew its hand suddenly. The coin dropped, and Tern caught it reflexively. "I'm afraid not," it said. "But that's not to say that you won't receive some benefit on your way out. The question is, what do you want?"

"What did my mother trade it for?"

"She asked to leave the treasury and never return," the dragon said. "Two days and two nights she spent in here, contemplating her options, and that was what she came up with. She didn't trust the treasury's temptations. Of course, she thought she had been here much longer. Time moves differently underwater, after all."

Tern tried to imagine her mother as a young woman, newly crowned empress, hazy with sleeplessness and desperate to escape this test. "How long have I been here?" she asked.

"Not long as humans reckon time," the dragon said. Its cheerfulness was not reassuring.

"The gifts for the Twenty-Seven Families," Tern said. "Whatever becomes of me, will they be delivered to the court?"

The dragon waved a hand. "They're yours to dispose of as you see fit. I'm done looking at them, so I don't see why not."

Tern glanced around again. She might be here for a very long time if this went wrong. "I know what I want," she said.

The dragon drifted closer.

Her voice quavered in spite of herself, but she looked the dragon full in the eye. "I don't know what bargain has bound you here all these years, but I want no more of it. Let this coin purchase your freedom."

The dragon was silent for a long time. At last it said, "Dragons are unpredictable allies, you know."

"I will take that chance," Tern said. Was this reckless? Perhaps. But as she saw it, the empresses of her line were as much prisoners as the dragon was. Best to let the dragon pursue its own destiny.

"Someone needs to guard the treasury, you know." The dragon canted its head. "You don't seem to have a spare dragon."

So this was the real price. "I will stay," Tern whispered.

"A determined thief would make mince of you in minutes, you realize."

Tern frowned. "I thought you'd want to leave."

"I do," the dragon said, "but I take my duty seriously. There's only one thing to be done, then. Pass me the coin, will you?"

Not sure whether she was more bemused or bewildered, Tern did so. She felt a curious pang as the coin left her hand.

"The guardian of a dragon's treasure," the dragon said, "should have a dragon's own defenses."

With that, the dragon slipped out of its skin, so subtly that at first Tern did not realize what was happening. Scales sparkled deep blue and kelp-green, piling up in irregular coils around the dragon's legs. The dragon itself took on the shape of a woman perhaps ten years older than Tern. Her black hair drifted around her face; her eyes were brown. Indeed, she could have been one of Tern's people.

"The skin is yours," the dragon said in much the same voice as before, "to use or discard as you please. Don't tell me that I never gave you choices."

"At least wear something," Tern said, appalled at the thought of the dragon surprising the chancellor while not wearing any human clothes.

"Your empire won't thank you for giving it to a dragon to rule," the dragon said, although it did, at least, choose for itself a plain robe of wool.

"You will rule with a dragon's sense of justice," Tern said, "which is more than I can expect from the women and men out there who are hungering after a child's throne." She handed over the keys of her office.

The dragon's smile was respectful. "We'll see." And, pausing at the threshold: "I won't forget you."

The door closed, and Tern was left with the coin and the dragon skin.

It was not until many generations later, when one of the dragon's descendants braved the second treasury, that Tern learned that she had been given a dragon-name. Not a reign-name, for she was done with that, and not a funeral-name, for she was far from dead. The empire she had ceded was now calling her Devourer-of-Bargains. After all this time, she had come around to the dragon's own opinion on this matter. It was a confusing human practice, but she wasn't in any position to argue.

A number of generations after that, when a different empress braved the treasury, Tern asked what had become of the Dragon Empress from so many years ago.

The empress said, "According to the records, she disappeared after a sixty-year reign, leaving only a note that said, 'I'm looking for another coin.'"

The empress was looking wistfully at a particularly lovely beryl set in silver filigree. Eventually she returned her attention to Tern, but she kept glancing back at it. The woman's face looked oddly familiar, but Tern couldn't place it. Probably a trick of her imagination.

The rest of the conversation was fairly predictable, but Tern contemplated the dragon's sense of justice once the empress had gone. Time moved differently underwater, after all. She could wait.

—

Yoon Ha Lee's first collection of short fiction, *Conservation of Shadows*, was published earlier this year. She lives in Louisiana with her family and has not yet been eaten by gators. She has been fortunate enough to avoid entanglements with dragons. It's the tigers you really have to watch out for. Or maybe the foxes.

—

Fairy tales and folk tales have always been important—as a blueprint for expecting the worst, or as a suggestion that you might make it after all; some wolves can be killed. To look at a tale is to look at the story itself, the hidden stories behind it, the world in which it was written, the ways it's changed and why. One of the reasons that fairy tales continue to fascinate us is because to examine any aspect of that story is to be retelling it already—asking questions, looking for more.

"The Lenten Rose" is a retelling of Hans Christian Andersen's "The Snow Queen," which has always been a favorite of mine, largely for the things it doesn't tell us, the little dark places waiting for a light. Particularly, it leaves Kay and Gerda sitting on the balcony as their journey vanishes from their minds, leaving them, the story suggests, essentially unchanged from the children they were when they began it. But of course that's not how journeys go; that's where my story starts.

Genevieve Valentine

THE LENTEN ROSE

GENEVIEVE VALENTINE

*The roses out on the roof were in full bloom . . . and Kay and
Gerda seated themselves each on their own chair, and held each
other by the hand, while the cold empty grandeur of the Snow
Queen's palace vanished from their memories like a painful
dream . . . And they both sat there, grown up, yet children at
heart; and it was summer—warm, beautiful summer.*
—"The Snow Queen," Hans Christian Andersen

Two strangers are living in a house.

It's summer; warm, beautiful summer.

The house is choked by roses—white, always white, nothing must be
red any more.

Every window has heavy curtains. He closes the curtains at the
first frost, every year, and doesn't open them again until the roses
bloom.

She's tried to kill the roses, a hundred times.

When Ensio found Gerda, back on the day when Kay went missing,
she was walking home from the shop, across the bridge toward the
other side of the river, where her grandmother's house was pressed
in the center of a little row of houses (from her garret window she
could see the water until the bend, where the trees closed over it).

He reached her at the very center of the bridge.

"Kay's mother's had a telegram," he said.

She sat on the wall, and when Ensio tried to hold her she turned so her legs dangled off the edge, and when he asked, "Gerda, what can I do?" she said, "Find my grandmother, she'll know," and he set off running like he loved her.

She cried until her jacket split up the back; she cried until her new red shoes fell one by one into the water.

A pair of crows was circling.

She thought, like a dreamer thinks, I can find him if they can't.

When she dropped, there was an empty boat waiting, pointed north.

In school, when Kay was still a little boy, the teacher showed that Finland was shaped like a woman, arms reaching upward.

She's beautiful, the teacher promised, the most beautiful woman of all; the guardian of a nation.

It was good to know. Gerda was lovely sometimes, when they were playing in the snow and she looked at him and laughed, but now Kay knew it wasn't serious.

There was real beauty, somewhere far away. It felt like a brave thing to think.

If Kay saw a face sometimes, when he looked out the window in winter—two lines of frost shining off her high wide cheekbones, lips the color of milk ice, sharp black eyes rimmed just at the edge of the iris with blue—wasn't it just the Finnish Maiden?

(It was a lie, of course, the sort of lie children tell themselves when they're trying to be patriots.

Some stories are older than others; those your grandmother tells before any school can reach you.

It was the Snow Queen.

Once, she smiled at him.

He pressed his hands to the glass. Around her white hair, everything was winter and dark.)

~

At home, Gerda tended the roses that grew along the garret and the balcony rail. The winters turned them into witch's fingers, but every spring they bloomed thicker, and by summer they were all awake, deep red, with burn-black centers.

The roses spanned both garret windows together, and on summer nights they sat among the thorns and watched the river, and when Kay asked, "Shall we be always together?" Gerda said, "I promise."

(He was hers when things were warm and green; why he changed in the cold, she never knew.)

He saw the Snow Queen everywhere, in winter.

The dry flakes blowing across the cobbles got caught in the wind and became her slim, welcoming hands. Frost against the branches in the shadowed forest was the Queen in glittering robes, turning to greet him.

When he saw her, his heart beat faster; when water moved under the ice, it sounded like she was calling him.

He remembers the shards of mirror that entered his heart and his eye.

He thinks that even without them, he would have gone with the Queen.

They were racing home across the bridge, when the mirror shards struck Kay.

It was after school; they always started from the fountain at the square, and ran all the way home.

(That year, the boys had started to tease him about losing to Gerda. Sometimes he started before time, so if they were watching, they'd see him ahead.)

She remembers that as they crossed the bridge he stumbled (he never stumbled), and when she turned back to help him he shoved her hand away, snapped, "I'm fine—my feet got heavy, that's all. Took you long enough. Trying to win by cheating?"

"Kay, that's mean."

"Stop sniveling," he said, picking up his schoolbooks. "It doesn't do you any favors."

She walked home behind him, watching his back.

She didn't think that anything was wrong. Boys got this way eventually. His child's face was gone. He had cheekbones, now, and deep blue eyes, a down-turned mouth the girls in school said marked him as romantic.

The other romantic boys were awful, too.

(She had waited, though, before she doubled back; for those five breaths, she had been running free of him, and her feet had dug sprays of snow from the ground.)

At seventeen, she worked in Mr. Vatanen's curio shop.

Sometimes Kay waited for her, walked her home.

They took the bridge quietly, moving closer to the tangle of empty thorns around their windows.

One day he said, "I'm too smart to grow old here. I'm joining the army. We're fighting the Reds, you know."

As they walked across the open field, dry snow scudded across the path; he looked at it like a man in love.

The walls of the house are painted blue-green.

It's safest. White's too like winter; yellow too like spring.

It drains you—he's looked sick in it, ever since he came back—but you live with your choices.

She has a red dress. She puts it on (only ever in the house) when she needs to feel color. When she's alone.

She never wears it long; red makes you remember things.

The first days she was adrift, she fell ill.

The pair of crows had called out when it wasn't safe to land, and at last Gerda had come ashore where the Lady of Spring kept a greenhouse more than a mile by a mile.

As she rested from her fever, the lady taught her to garden; to coax a flower from a seed; to make remedies and poisons.

"You never know what you need," said the Lady of Spring. "War's everywhere, and a woman has reasons."

(She had forgotten some of home, in the fever. But she must have studied, once; she listened to the remedies, and memorized the poisons.)

"Is there a red flower missing?" she asked once. She was picking blooms from a patch of the Lenten rose—its true name was hellebore, she knew now, and it could poison you through.

The Lady said, "A flower missing! Well, I never. What's one flower in a gardenful? Come inside, and I'll teach you another trick with those."

"All right," said Gerda, so bright the Lady laughed.

It was weeks before Gerda was well enough to walk the greenhouse alone, all the way to the far wall, a footstep from the bank of the river where a little boat was.

That was when she found the barren ground, and overturned the earth, and found the rose.

He was on watch, when the Snow Queen came.

His fellows were asleep, huddled trying not to freeze to death before morning, and Kay had been staring at the snow and thinking how it could bury a man so you would never find him again.

(When the Snow Queen came, he thought for a moment that the dead were rising.)

The white reindeer that drew her sledge were quiet as dreams, and inside she was sitting with the same cloak drawn about her he remembered from a dozen winters.

She wore a diadem of ice, end to end across her white brow.

When she turned to look at him, her face was like the frost in the shadowed trees, her eyes deep as the water under the river ice.

She held out her hand to him.

"A boy as clever as you shouldn't be here," she said, in a voice like the wind through silver bells.

She was right—clever boys had fallen by the hundreds and the hundreds as they all fought for nothing in the wild, but the shard of mirror had poisoned his heart to hope, and he only called, "And where should I be, then?"

"Beside me," said the queen, "and a prince in my palace of ice."

It had been a long war, and an awful war; he was doomed to die, and it's easy to be poison-hearted when your stomach's empty.

And though he didn't love the Snow Queen (he didn't love anyone, his heart had frozen through), he walked out to meet her, and when she drew him into her arms and pressed her lips to his lips, he hardly felt the cold.

Well past the towering trees, when the river grew too fast and Gerda clung to the boat prepared to drown, a Laplander woman on a reindeer crashed through the water and pulled her to shore.

Gerda was brought near the fire and wrapped up warm in a red jacket, and a cap was put onto her head. Someone was taking her book of poisons from her hands; the Laplander woman's face appeared as she knelt and said, "What dragged you so far, Southlander?"

Not a woman, Gerda thought, a girl, a girl my age. Am I still a girl? I've been on this river so long.

"I'm looking for Kay," she said. "He got lost in the snow, away from his soldiers. Crows have been calling. They told me he passed this way."

And the little robber girl said, after too long, "You had best rest here a while, then. The north is no place for the weary."

They sleep on opposite sides of the bed.

They try, sometimes, to rest in one another's arms, but it never lasts (there's not much rest to go around).

She sleeps turned to the window, looking out at the bend in the river. He sleeps nearer the fire, under extra quilts; he's never been warm, since they came home.

~

The palace of ice was never dark.

Its ceiling was cathedral-high, and its walls were curved and smooth to touch, and the floor was like the river in deepest winter.

("I can't keep hold," he said, for his feet were numb—he'd walked for days behind the sledge. His voice barked back at him until he covered his ears.)

There was nothing in the throne room, not even a chair. When he fell to his knees, nothing impeded him.

(Shadows slithered behind the walls; he saw men he knew, who had been buried under the snow and the ice.)

The Snow Queen turned to him. She was dressed not as a sovereign, but as a woman; her hair was soft as new snow, threaded with Lenten roses, and when she knelt, it brushed the ground between them.

Her gown, under her cloak, was thin as a veil, and he felt that if only the shard was pulled from his eye, he could see through it, but somehow it was only her face he saw, bright white, and sharp, and cruel.

"Now, my prince," she said, in a voice like the wind through silver bells, "are you happy?"

"No," he said. (The word came back to him—no, no.)

When she smiled and reached for him, he realized he felt no cold from her skin; he didn't feel anything. The little white flowers in her hair were frozen through.

"Then walk out and be free," she said.

He looked behind him—which way had they come?—but everything reflected light, and there was no way out.

When he turned back, the Queen had vanished.

He was alone, and it was deepest winter everywhere, and when he breathed too quickly the air made a mist as thin as a veil.

For half a summer, Gerda lived in the Sami camp, where the reindeer spent the warm months eating and shoving at one another.

The robber-girl's name was Meret, and she gave Gerda anything—a red tunic embroidered with all the colors of spring, a blue cap lined in fur, a thick sharp knife—except the book of poisons from her time with the Lady of Spring.

"None of the plants you need are here," Gerda said. "What use is it to you? Give it back."

"If I do," Meret said, "you'll only go."

Gerda said nothing.

(Underneath the love of poisons and the love of the open, there was a promise she made long ago, under a bower of roses.)

At night, in the bed beside Meret, Gerda breathed Kay's name to the crows, and each morning they said, "We saw tracks in the snow, they are his," and she thanked them, and fed them suet.

But during the days she looked across the flat wide land, without any curio shops or village squares, and she gathered plants to make remedies, and when the reindeer were herded back at night she saw Meret smiling under her red cap, two dogs running beside her, waving upraised arms to guide them home.

At night they sat by the fire and mended reins side by side, and there was singing, and sometimes the howl of a dog when it was lonely; Meret always laughed and said, "They want for winter."

She had a face like a white rose, thought Gerda, sometimes, without knowing what she meant.

One night, the crows came back and said, "Gerda, we have seen him, he is in the palace of ice."

The robber-girl already had a blade to her throat, but when Gerda said, "Meret," she went still, and moved away the blade, and said, "This way."

Meret gave her a reindeer, and tied it to a sledge.

"I'm keeping your book as payment," Meret said, looking at nothing.

"Good," said Gerda. "Look out for the Lenten rose—the white hellebore—it's poison."

"I know what poison is," Meret said. The reins knotted under her hands.

"Make him cry," Meret said. "That's the only way the shards will wash away. Then he'll be as he was."

Gerda said nothing.

"I don't care what you do," said Meret. "It's just my mother knows, that's all. She's a Laplander woman."

(The robber-girl was a Laplander woman, too; as grown as Gerda, and she had sharp eyes, nimble fingers that tied any knot you asked of her without ever looking.)

Gerda laced the red jacket tight against the cold, remembering, all the way north to the cave of ice.

Mr. Vatanen's curio shop does business enough that he can afford to stay home, and have Gerda mind the shop.

But the people who come are still wary, and before they touch something they always ask if it belonged to this family, or that one. No one wants a thing from a family who has parted with it on ill terms, or the cursed effects of a doomed soul who died badly.

Sometimes Gerda says, "I don't know who it belonged to first," and the old man who was asking will look up at her with narrowed eyes, saying, "It's not good for a shopgirl to lie, she risks losing her place."

She'll say nothing; think about the book of poisons.

She freed the reindeer, tied the unstrung reins to a boulder, held one end down the slope of ice as it twisted downward, to the cave.

It was bright, even here, and scarred in patches, white and ridged and curling in like the edges of the Lenten rose.

In the center was Kay, with a knife frozen in his hand. He had tried to dig himself out through the ground; he sat in a nest of ice. His shins were raw and bloody.

His face was all bone, and his eyes were pale and wide. He looked like no one she knew.

(She was glad; she worried, if she remembered who he had been.)

But she knelt in front of him, and said, "Kay, it's Gerda. I've come to take you home."

"I don't know you," he said, his eyes moving always just past her face.

She flinched, said, "You do, Kay. I've come to take you home. I made you a promise."

He looked her up and down. She shivered.

"I remember you tended the roses," he said, like she was a servant in a fairy tale.

"Yes," she said. "Yes, and I loved you there, once."

"I—" he stopped, as if his breath had given out. "I'm waiting for the Snow Queen. I love her. She wants me for her prince, and I'll have my reward if I can only walk out and meet her."

"Then come along, if you love her. Let me take you to her. Just stand up with me."

"No," he said, and tears were already spilling, large gasps that sounded like something breaking. "No, I don't want to go. I can't go back."

"I know," she said, after five full breaths, in and out. "But winter comes any minute, and then it will never be light here again. We have to run."

"I can't run," he said, fresh tears running over tears that had already frozen. "I've tried, my feet are too heavy."

"I've cut you free."

He was calmer, now. He wiped his eyes.

He blinked twice, hard, said, "Something is gone."

"I know," she said, after too long; held out a hand.

(She understands him, sometimes, more than he thinks.

He might think he's a coward for ever being there, for wanting to die there rather than go on.

But she hadn't known there would be a boat, when she jumped from the bridge; just that her feet were too heavy to carry her, and she was burning all over from grief.

She wanted the water. The rest was accident.)

~

It isn't that he wanted to go to the winter palace and belong to the Snow Queen.

(She was beautiful, beautiful as she had been the first time she came to his window, and if she'd only loved him he'd have left the shards in his heart, stayed clever and cruel until he rotted around them.)

He was frightened of her, and of the place she led him to. When she was gone, he screamed at the ice, and dreamed of her, and lost all sense of cold, and decided that to die wasn't such a sacrifice. Maybe, long after this, the Queen would cut the shard from his heart, place it on her tongue until it bled white.

It isn't that he wanted to stay in the palace.

It's just that he had no hopes of coming home. You forget what you have no hope of.

He recognized Gerda as soon as he saw her.
(She was in a bright jacket; he remembered, all at once, a trellis of red roses.)

He pretended not to, as long he could.

Once, she was quiet for five full breaths, and he waited to see what it meant.

He'd hoped she would leave him behind.

She didn't let go of his hand, all the long trip home.
(They walked along the reindeer trails for days, Gerda looking at every profile for Meret. Gerda never saw her, but at the village, Meret's mother, the Laplander woman, had two ponies waiting.)

As they went south, it turned slowly back to summer.

Kay said little, and whenever she took his hand he looked down, as if surprised her skin was warm.

His eyes had lost their color, in the winter palace; now they were pale as glacier ice, and he hardly brought them up to look around the plains where the reindeer had crossed it, to mark the turning season.

The silence grew, and grew, and soon they were under the shadow of the trees, and it was too late.

For those five breaths, deep in the cave with Kay pleading not to go, she had closed her eyes, thought about the plants that make a poison.

The night they reached home, after Kay was sleeping, Gerda crawled out the garret window to cut the roses out at the root.

But though the vines that wrapped the terrace were the same, the red roses were gone.

They had bled all their color. They were white as hellebore, now; white as a palace of ice.

He never asked her what she had done. Maybe he had forgotten the roses. It was just as well.

Red makes you remember things.

When he looks out the kitchen window in the mornings he seems a decade older, but even with a face made of edges, his profile is kinder than it was.

(The Laplander woman had promised; as he wept, the shards of mirror had washed away.)

Gerda had thought his heart would close again, and be whole, but that was her own foolishness. Some things leave hollows behind them no plant in the world will heal, the center burned black.

They let it be.

This is home, and autumn is already going; nothing can be done about it now.

Gerda never saw the Snow Queen. When she reached him, Kay had been a long time alone in the cave of ice.

(She had hoped; she had wanted to see the Queen. It would be worse if he had only dreamed her.)

She'd had to take her sturdy Lapland knife and smash the ice that had wrapped his ankles, before she could even speak to him, before she could ask him to stand, before she could take his hand and lead him home.

He doesn't remember it, she thinks. She doesn't know. It would mean asking him.

What's one more lie, in a gardenful?

They had passed the greenhouse garden, too, as they came home—bursting in its late-summer dress of bright golds and purples and reds.

The Lady of Spring had been working behind the glass, up to her elbows in dirt, picking flowers for a poison.

She was happy. She never raised her eyes from the ground.

Gerda took her hands off the pony's bridle, clenched them in her lap as if around a little book, until they were well clear.

Kay looked at her, said nothing.

Soon the river turned, and she saw the bridge, and the wisps of smoke from the town, and soon, soon, soon, they were home.

He waits on the main road, off the square.

(He met her at the shop, once; too many mirrors.)

When she appears he leans in and kisses her, lips cold as winter brushing her cheek.

They walk, a little apart, over the bridge.

He looks at the faces the frost makes in the trees; she looks at the bend in the river, like an outstretched arm reaching north.

Ahead of them is the little house; white roses; the rest of a year.

◆ ◆

Genevieve Valentine's first novel, *Mechanique*, won the 2012 Crawford Award and was a Nebula nominee. Her second novel is forthcoming from Atria/Simon & Schuster. Her short fiction has appeared in *Clarkesworld*, *Strange Horizons*, *Journal of Mythic Arts*, the anthologies *Federations*, *After*, *Teeth*, and more. Valentine's nonfiction has appeared at *NPR.org, The AV Club, Strange Horizons, io9.com*, and *Weird Tales*, and she's a co-author of pop-culture book *Geek Wisdom* (Quirk). Her appetite for bad movies is insatiable, a tragedy she tracks on genevievevalentine.com.

Why fairy tales? She was bitten by that bug early, having devoured the Andrew Lang color fairy books as an impressionable girl. It is why, when asked to give the Andrew Lang lecture in 2012, (past lecturers had included J. R. R. Tolkien, who gave the "On Fairie-Stories" lecture, as well as John Buchan!) she hesitated until told that—as the twenty-second lecturer since 1927, she would be the first woman to do so. At that point she signed on. They had to bring in about a hundred more seats as the hall filled up.

One of the things *Jane Yolen* enjoys doing is retelling a familiar story from the point of view of an unfamiliar narrator, and "The Spindle's Tale" is no exception. Here an innocent is coerced into doing an evil deed, and pays the price instead of the powerful enchanter. One might wish to ask if this is meant as a political fable, but Yolen always says, "I tell the story. I leave commentary and exegesis to academics and critics. And if you think I am being disingenuous, then you don't know me very well! As I wrote at the end of a recent poem: 'After the soldiers leave the field/Truth stays on, under its own banner.'"

The Spinning Wheel's Tale

Jane Yolen

I worked all my life. Indeed, I worked for every hand that touched me: spinning a thread, spinning a tale, spinning a life. Yet all I am remembered for in this kingdom is the one death that was spun of a witch's lies.

Blame her, not me, for the hundred years of devastation, the castle waiting while sleep stole breath after breath. Blame her for hedges run riot while gardeners dozed. Blame her for the loss of revenues, avenues, a major highway becoming a byway, a byway a path.

But do not blame me. I only spun what I was held to, did what I was told.

I was always a poor woman's right hand, the small business base, not something fit for palaces. Yet here I was brought, set into curse and tale. We who are the workers have no say in the production. It is an old story, but a true one.

I remember the acorn, the sprout, the single green leaf. But that never features in this tale. The story begins with spinning, spinning the wheel, spinning the curse, spinning the lies that lie at the heart of a mouth, a castle, a hedge.

And of course it all begins with a witch.

Let us call her Malara. Or Maleficient. Or Maladroit. It is all the same. She was jealous, of course, of her twelve sisters, of her position in the middle of their pack. Not the prettiest, not the fairest, not the smartest, not the sweetest, not the eldest, not the youngest. All those get special mention in any recounting. She was, so she liked to say, the median, the middle, the muddle, and the mess.

Well at least in this she was honest, if in nothing else.

Everything Malara put her hand to was a failure. A wish for a woman's fecundity produced a litter of babes too small and too early to live, and a blasted womb thereafter. A wish for a garden to produce led straight to a proliferation of weeds the likes of which had never been known in the land. A wish for the early marriage of a prince turned into an early funeral as well. She did not have a good head for wishing.

But oh, how Malara could curse.

She could cause the dead to rise, pennies on their eyes, and a death rattle in their mouths that went zero to the bone.

She could curse a man to impotence, a cuckold to impudence. She could curse a purse to poverty, a poet to prosody, a singer to a sore throat, and a hangman to his own noose. She could curse a king to catastrophe, a princess to catatonia. She was herself the queen of curses.

No wonder she ceased to be invited to royal births, royal christenings, royal engagements, royal weddings. Even funerals were forbidden to her.

She was left with nothing—nothing to do, nothing to favor—and that led to her to having everything to do with what happened ever after.

Her sisters tried an intervention, tried to teach her the lighter side of magic: how to cause the lame to dance, milk to spring from a maiden's breast. Tried to insert her as the muse in amusing histories. But as with everything Malara did, things always turned to the worst.

And there it could have stood, with her sisters loving her and wishing to help. With them worrying over her, thinking she'd been damaged somehow, that none of this was her fault.

But when at last they understood how much she reveled in her talent for cursing, even her sisters left her alone.

And that is when she found me and made the last of her curses.

O acorn, that you never had known spring. O oak, that you never had grown limbs. O limbs, that you never were sawn, planed, bended, and bowed. O wheel, that you were never made.

Malara found me in a byre, set aside after a lifetime of use. Her fingers started me awhirl again and I was pleased to be found useful. She tested the spindle, and I was delighted to feel magic. She wound wool through all my parts, and I was thrilled to be spinning anew.

I thought her no more then a solitary crone, for so she presented herself, as if touched by age, humped with it. We limped up to the forbidden tower.

There was such a sense of wonder in her touch I ignored the darkness in it. Stupid old oak.

There was warning in her songs. I thought them full of beauty. Foolish acorn child.

I dreamed that I might be the one to spin straw into gold. Silly old wheel.

Instead of slowing my rotation, instead of tangling the yarn, I held my spindle upright. My wheel made many smooth turnings. I was addled with work, in love with production.

I did not see the world coming to an end.

There was a knock on the door.

A girl fair as morning entered, the sun-gold in her hair all the riches I was ever to see.

"Grandmother," she said to the witch. "I am here for my lesson."

Malara smiled and handed her the spindle.

It pierced her finger and all the world spun down.

So why is it I, not the witch, being put to the flame?

Jane Yolen, author of over eighty-five original fairy tales, and over 335 books, is often called the Hans Christian Andersen of America—though she wonders (not entirely idly) whether she should really be called the "Hans Jewish Andersen of America." She has written a lot of fairy tale poetry as well, and has been named both Grand Master of the World Fantasy Convention and Grand Master of the Science Fiction Poetry Association. She has won two Nebulas for her short stories, and a bunch of other awards, including six honorary doctorates. One of her awards, the Skylark, given by the New England Science Fiction Association, set her good coat on fire, a warning about faunching after shiny things that she has not forgotten.

My lovely green-eyed Mother told me many traditional fairy tales when I was an infant, following these up with her own wily *re*tellings.

The influence of these can be seen in my children's collection (*Princess Hynchatti*) published in the 1970s but written by me in the 1960s. In these stories are such things as a prince who falls in love with the witch helping him to win the difficult, task-setting princess, and the prince who drives a swan nearly crazy by repeatedly kissing it—wrongly—sure it is a princess under a spell . . .

Evidently such magical twists still obsess me.

Tanith Lee

Below the Sun Beneath

Tanith Lee

I

Life drove him into death, so it had seemed. It was the choice between dying—or living and *causing* death, to be corpse or corpse-maker. Perhaps Death's own dilemma.

He had joined the army of the king because he was starving. Three days without eating had sent him there; little other work that winter. And the war-camp was bursting with food; you could see it from the road: oxen roasting over the big fire and loaves piled high and barrels of ale lined up, all a lush tapestry of red and brown and golden plenty, down in the trampled, white-snowed valley. He had fought his first battle with a full belly, and survived to fill it again and again.

Five years after that. And then another five. Roughly every sixth year, the urge came in him to do something else. But he had mislaid family, and even love. Had given up himself and found this other man that now he had become: Yannis the soldier.

And five years more. And *nearly* five . . .

The horse kicked and fell on him just as the nineteenth year was turning towards the twentieth. Poor creature, shot with an arrow it was dying, going down, the kick one last instinctive protest, maybe.

But the blow, and the collapsing weight smashed the lower bones in his right leg, and he lost it up to the knee. All but its spirit, which still ached him inside the wooden stump. Yet what more could he expect? He had put himself in the way of violences, and so finally received them.

The army paid him off.

The coins, red and brown, but *not* golden, lasted two months.

By the maturing of a new winter he was alone again, unemployed and wandering, and for three days he had not eaten anything but grass.

Yannis heard the strange rumour at the inn by the forest's edge. The innwife had taken pity on him. "My brother lost a leg like you. Proper old cripple he is now," she had cheerily announced. Yet she gave Yannis a meal and a tin cup of beer. There was a fire as well, and not much custom that evening. "Sleep on a bench, if you want. But best get off before sun-up. My husband's back tomorrow and if he catches you, we'll both get the side of his fist."

As the cold moon rose and the frosts dropped from it like chains to bind the earth, Yannis heard wolves howling along the black avenues of the pine trees.

He dozed later, but then a group of men came in, travellers, he thought. He listened perforce to their talk, making out he could not hear, in case.

"It would seem he's scared sick of them, afraid to *ask*. Even to pry."

"That's crazy talk. How *can* he be? He's a *king*. And what are they? A bunch of girls. No. There's more to it than that."

"Well, Clever Cap, it's what they say in the town market. And not even that open with it either. He wants to *know*, but won't take it on himself. Wants some daft clod to do it for him."

Yannis, as they fell silent again, willed himself asleep. In the morning, he had to get off fast.

A track ran to the town. On foot and disabled, it took him until noon.

The place was as he had expected, huts and hovel-houses and the only stone buildings crowded round the square with the well, as if they had been herded there for safety. Even so, at his third attempt he got a day's work hauling stacks of kindling. He slept that night in a barn behind the priest's house. At sunrise he heard the priest's servants gossiping.

"It's Women's Magic. That's why he's afeared."

"But he's a *king*."

"Won't matter. Our Master'll tell you. Some women still keep to the bad old ways. Worse in the city. They're *clever* there. Too clever to be Godly."

Beyond the town was another track. At last an ill-made and raddled road.

He knew by then the city was many more miles of walking-limping. And all the wolfwood round him and, after sundown, as he crouched by his makeshift fire, the wolves sang their moon-drunk songs to the freezing sky.

On the third day, a magical number he had once or twice been told, he met the old woman. She was out gathering twigs that she threw in a sack over her shoulder, and various plants and wildfruits that she put carefully in a basket in her left hand. Sometimes he noted, as he walked towards her along the path, she changed the basket to her right hand and picked with the left. She was a witch, then, perhaps even knew something about healing. There had been a woman he encountered like that, before, who brewed a drink that stopped his leg aching so much. The medicine was long gone and the full ache had come back.

"Good day, Missus," he therefore politely said, as he drew level.

She had not glanced up at his approach—that confident then, even with some ragged, burly stranger hobbling up—nor did she now. But she answered.

"Yes, then. I've been expecting you, young man. Just give me a moment and I'll have this done."

He was well over thirty in years, and no longer reckoned young at all. But she, of course, looked near one hundred: to her the average granddad would be a stripling. And she was expecting him, was she?

Oh, that was an old trick. *Naturally*, nothing could surprise *her*, given her vast supernatural gifts.

Yannis waited anyway, patiently, only shifting a little now and then to unkink the leg.

Finally she was through, and looked straight up at him.

Her eyes were bright and clear as a girl's, russet in color like those of a fox.

"This is the bargain," she said. "Some wood needs chopping, and the hens like a regular feed. You can milk a goat? Yes, I believed you could. These domestic chores you can take off my hands for two or three days. During which time I will teach you two great secrets."

He stared down at her, quite tickled by her effrontery and her style. She spoke like someone educated, and her voice, like her eyes, was young, younger far than he was. Though her hair was gray and white, there were strands of another color still in it, a faded yellow. Eighty years ago, when she was a woman of twenty, she might well have been a silken, lovely thing. But time, like life and death, was harsh.

"Two secrets, Missus?" he asked, nearly playful. "I thought it always had to be three."

"Did you, soldier? Then no doubt three it will be, for *you*. But the third one you'll have to discover yourself."

"Fair enough. Do I get my bed and board as well?"

"Sleep in the shed, eat from the cook-pot. As for your leg—don't fret. That comes included."

During that first day she was very busy inside the main hut that was her house, behind a leather curtain; at witch-work he assumed.

Outside he got on with the chores.

All was simple. Even the white goat, despite its wicked goat eyes, had a mild disposition. The shed allotted as his bedchamber was weather-proof and had a rug-bed.

As the sinking sun poured out through the western trees, she called him to eat. He thought, sitting by the hearth fire, if her witchery turned out as apt as her cooking, she might even get rid of his pain for good. Then some few minutes after eating he noticed his leg felt better.

"It was in the soup, then, the medicine?"

"Quite right," she said. "And in what I gave you at noon."

He had tasted nothing, and stupidly thought it was relief at this interval that calmed his phantom leg. He supposed she could have poisoned him too. But then, she had not.

"Great respects to you, Missus," he said. "I'm more than grateful. May I take some with me when I go?"

"You can. But I doubt you'll need it. There's another way to tackle the hurt of your wound. That's the first secret. But I won't be showing you until tomorrow's eve."

He was relaxed enough he grinned.

"What will all this cost me?"

"It will," she said, "be up to you."

At which, of course, he thought, *I'd best be careful, then. God knows what she's at, or will want.* But the fire was warm and the leg did not nag, and the stoop of dark beer, that was pleasant too. Well, she had bewitched him, in her way. He even incoherently dreamed of her that night. It was some courtly dance, the women and the men advancing to and from each other, touching hands, turning slowly about, separating and moving gracefully on . . . There was a young girl with long golden, *golden* hair, bright as the candlelight. And he was unable to join the dance, being old and crippled; but somehow he did not mind it, knowing that come the *next* evening—but *what* the next evening?

The succeeding day, at first light, he noticed the large pawmarks of wolves in the frost by the witch's door, and a tiny shred or two that indicated she had left them food. There had been no nocturnal outcry from the goat or chickens. Another bargain?

Everything went as before. Today the goat even nuzzled his hand. It was a nice goat, perhaps the only nice goat on earth. The chickens chirruped musically.

When the sun set, she called him again to eat.

She said, "We'll come now to the first secret. It's old as the world. Older, maybe. And once you know, easy as to sleep. Easier."

Probably there was more medicine in the food—his resentful leg all day had been charming in its behavior—but also tonight she must have put in some new substance.

He woke, having found he had fallen asleep as he sat by her fire, his back leaning on the handy wall.

She was whispering in his left ear.

"What?" he murmured.

But the whispering had stopped. She stood aside, and in the shadowy sinking firelight she was like a shadow herself. The shadow said, in its young, gentle and inexorable voice: "Easy as *that*, soldier. Nor will you ever forget. Whenever you have need, you or that wounded leg, then you can."

And then she slipped back and back, and away and away, and he thought, quite serenely and without any rage or alarm, *Has she done for me? Am I dying?* But it was never that.

He floated inwards, deep as into any sea or lake. And then he floated *free* . . .

Children dream of such things. Had he? No, he had had small space for dreams of any sort. Yet, somehow he knew what he did. He had done it before, must have done, since it was so familiar, so *known*, so wonderful and so blessed.

He was young. He felt twenty years of age, and full of health and vigor. He ran and bounded on two strong, eloquent legs, each whole and perfectly able. He sprang up trees—*ran* up them, impervious to pine-needles and the scratch-claws of branches, leapt from their boughs a hundred feet above and flew—wingless but certain as a floating hawk—to another tree or to the ground below. Where he wished, he walked on the *air*.

The three gray wolves, feeding on bits of meat and turnip by the witch's door, looked up and saw him; only one offered a soft sound, more like amused congratulation than dismay. Later a passing night bird veered to give him room, with a startled silvery rattle. A fox on the path below merely pattered on. Later he went drifting, careless, by three or four rough huts, where a solitary man, cooking his late supper outdoors, stared straight through him with a myopic gaze. Blind to nothing physical—he was dexterous enough with his makeshift skillet—the woodlander plainly could not detect Yannis, who hovered directly overhead. Even when Yannis, who was afterwards ashamed of himself, swooped down and pulled the man's ear, the man only twitched as if some night-bug had bothered him. A human, it seemed, was the single creature who could not see Yannis at all.

He roamed all night, or at least until the fattening moon set and the sky on the other side turned pale. Effortlessly, he found his way back to the witch's house. A faint shimmering line in the air led him. He followed it, aware it was attached to him, and of its significance, without at all understanding, until at last he found it ran in under the shed-house door, and up to the body of the man who sat propped there, so deeply asleep he seemed almost—if very peacefully, in fact, nearly *smugly—dead*—and slid in at his chest. *The cord that binds me, while I live,* he thought. *And only I, or some very great witch, could see it.*

He paused a moment, too, to regard himself from *outside*. Rather embarrassed, he reassessed his value. Aside from the leg, he was still well-made. And strong. He had—a couthness to him. And if not handsome, well, he was not an ugly fellow. He would do. He was worth quite a lot more than Yannis, since his crippling and invaliding out of the army, had reckoned. Yannis gave himself a friendly pat on the shoulder, before pursuing the cord home into his physical body, and the warm, kind blanket of sleep that waited there.

"You will never forget now," she said, next morning. "Whenever you must ease the spirit of the leg, you need only release *your* spirit. Then the leg will never fret you, no matter that its physical self is gone and it sits in a jail of wood, just as you do in the prison of flesh we all inhabit till death sets us free."

"Is it my soul you've let out, then?" he asked her. Since waking up again he had been less confident. "Isn't that going to upset God?"

She made a noise of derision and dipped her bread in the honey. "Do you think God so petty? Come soldier, God is *God*! How could we get these skills if it weren't allowed? But no, besides. It's not the soul. The soul sits deeper. It's your *earthly* spirit only you can now release, which is why it has the shape of you and is male and young and strong. And too—as you've seen—nothing human, or very few, will ever espy you in that form. You will be *invisible*. Which, when you reach the city, can render you service."

"You think I'll use the knack to do harm."

"Never," she said. "Would I unlock it for you, if I thought so?"

Yannis shook his head. "No, Mother."

"And I am your mother, now?"

He said, quietly, "She was yellow-haired and pretty. I don't insult you, Missus. And anyway, I meant . . . "

"There," she said, and she smiled at him. She had a sunny smile, and all her teeth were amazingly sound and clean, especially for such an old granny as she was. "And now, Yannis, I will give you the second secret. Which is less secret than the first."

He sat and looked warily at her as she told him. "You'll gain the city by nightfall. There is a king there, who is a coward, a dunce, and as cruel as those failings can make a man. He has twelve girls by three different wives, all of these queens now dead, and mostly due to him. But the princesses, as we must call them, as we must call him a king—for they're all the royalty we'll get in such a land as this—are at a game the king is frightened of. He wants to be sure what they do, for *un*sure he is, and to spare. And when sure, to curb them. But he dares not take on the task himself."

"This is the tale I heard elsewhere," said Yannis, who had sat forward, partly eager to forget for a while about spirits and souls and God.

"You may well have heard it, for rumors have been planted and are growing wild. Already the king has hired mercenary men to spy on the girls and catch them out. These mercenaries were of all types, high, low, and lowest of the lowest, even one, they say, a prince, but doubtless a prince in the same way of this king being a king. All fail, and then the king gladly has them murdered. That is *his* bargain. The man who spies on and renders up the princesses, him the king will make his princely heir. But fail—and off with his head."

"If it's so hard to catch his daughters, then why try?"

"Because it is never hard at all. Those who watch the girls, or would do, the princesses drug asleep, being themselves well-versed in witchcraft. Whoever wants to find out anything must not taste a bite nor swallow a sip in that house, unless it be from the common dish or jug, and sampled by others. Or if he is forced, he must only pretend. And immediately after he must feign slumber or better—slip into a trance so sleeplike, so *deathlike*, it will convince the sternest critic. Then he may follow those girls as he wishes, and learn all and everything. Providing, of course, none can see him."

Yannis said, "For example, by letting his spirit free from his body."

"Just so."

Next a silence fell. It came down the chimney and through the two little windows with the shutters, and sat with the witch and the soldier, timing them on its endless noiseless fingers to see how much longer they would be at their council.

At last Yannis said, "Two secrets, then. What is the third?"

"I said already, *son*, you must find the third secret yourself. But some call it Courage and others Arrogance, and some blind fool Madness. You must *act* on what I have taught you, that is the third secret. Now, go milk my goat, who has fallen in heart's-ease for you, and bid my chicks goodbye. Then you shall set off again, if you're to reach the city gate by sundown."

Yannis stood like a man distracted. Then he said, "Either you want my death, and so have done this. Or else you mean me to prosper. But—if that—then *why*? I'm nothing to you."

"For sure perhaps, or not," she said. "But I have been something for *you*. For even when you were a warrior in the wars, you have cared for me."

"But Missus—never ever did I meet you before . . . "

"Not me that speaks these words, but so many others—*womankind*. My sisters, my mothers, my daughters, the daughters of my daughters—all of those. For the old woman and the young woman, they the rest of the soldiers might have killed for uselessness, or put to a use that would have killed them too. Those women that you helped, that you defended, and hid, that you gave up your food to. Women young and old are dear to you, and you in the midst of turmoiled men, blood-crazed and heartless, have where able been a savior to my kind. And so, also to me, Yannis, my son."

Then Yannis hung his head, lost for words.

But she, as she turned in at the leather curtain, said to him, lightly, "I will after all tell you a third thing. It is how the old beast of a king knows his daughters are at dangerous work."

Yannis shook himself. "How, then?"

"*By the soles of their feet.*"

II

They used a different language in the city—in their buildings, their gestures. While their speech contained foreign phrases, and occasional passages in a tongue that was so unlike anything in the regions round about that it took him time to fathom it. However, he came to realize he had heard snatches of it before. It was an ancient and classic linguistic of which, racking his brains, he saw he had kept a smattering.

Most of the city was of stone. But near the center—where a wide, paved road ran through—the architecture was, like the second language, *ancient*, and some even ruinous, yet built up again. Tall, wide-girthed pillars, high as five houses stood on each other's heads. Large gateways opened on terraced yards. A granite fountain played. Yannis was surprised. But the metropolis had been there, evidently, far longer than those who possessed it now.

On a hill that rose beyond a treed parkland, a graveyard was visible, whose structures were domed like the cots of bees. He had never seen such tombs before. They filled him with a vague yet constant uncomfortable puzzlement. He did not often turn their way. And he thought this reaction too seemed apparent with the city people. Where they could, they did not look into the west.

The sun set behind the hill about an hour after he had got in the gates—he had made very good speed. But it was darkly overcast, and the sunset only flickered like a snakeskin before vanishing.

How strange their manners here.

The innkeeper that he asked for chances of work, or shelter, answered instantly, in a low, foreboding tone, "Go to the palace. There's nowhere else."

"The *palace* . . . "

"I said. Go *there*. Now off with you or I call the dogs."

And next, at a well in the strengthening rain, the women who cried out in various voices, "*Off*—go on, you. Get work at the palace! Get your bed there. There's nowhere else."

And after these—who he took for mad persons—the same type of reply, often in rougher form, as with the blacksmith in the alley who flung an iron bar.

All told, a smother of inimical elements seemed to lie over the old city, the citizens hurrying below with heads down. Maybe only the weather, the coming dark. Few spoke to any, once the sun went. It was not Yannis alone who got their colder shoulder.

The last man to push Yannis aside also furiously directed him, pointing at the dismal park, by then disappearing in night-gloom. "See, *there*. The palace. And don't come back."

To which Yannis, thrusting him off in turn, in a rush of lost patience answered, "So I'm the king's business, am I? Are you this way with any stranger who asks for anything? Go and be used and win—or die?"

But the man raised his fist. In a steely assessment of his own trained strength—which the witch's teaching had returned him to awareness of—Yannis retreated. No point in ending in the jail.

Black, the sky, and all of it falling down in icy streamings, which, even as he went on, altered to a spiteful and clattering hail. He thought of falling arrowheads. Of the horse which fell. Of the surgeon's tent . . .

At the brink of the park a black crow sat in an oak above. And Yannis was not sure it was quite real, though its eye glittered.

I am here by Something's will.

But the will of what? A king? A witch? Some unknown sorcerer? Or only those other two, Life and Death.

In the, end, all the trees seemed to have crows in them. Stumbling over roots and tangles of undergrowth, where rounded boulders and shards nestled like skulls, Yannis came out onto a flight of stony stairs. It was snowing, and the wind howled, riotously bending grasses and boughs and the mere frame of a strong man. And then a huge honey-colored lamplight massed above out of a core of towery and upcast leaden walls.

He judged, even clapped by now nearly double and blinkered by snow, that the palace was like the rest, partly ancient, its additions balancing on it, clinging and unsure. But it was well-lit, and rows of guardsmen were there. One of them, like the unwilling ones below, trudged out at him and caught him, if now in an almost friendly detaining vice. "What have we here?"

"I was *sent* here," said Yannis, speaking of Fate, or the fools in the city, not caring which.

"That's good, then. Will cheer him up, our lord. Not every day, would you suppose, some cripple on a stump can enhance the evening of a king."

His own king had once spoken to Yannis. The king had been on horseback, the men interrupted, respectfully standing in the mud, just after the sack of some town. The king had commended them for their courage. It was ritual, no more, but Yannis had been oddly struck by how the king looked not like *other* men. That was, the king was not in any way superior—more handsome, say, let alone more profound, yet *different* he was. It had not been his fine clothes, the many-hands-high horse. It perplexed Yannis. The king seemed of an alien kind—not quite human, perhaps, but nor was it glamorous.

This king was nothing like that anyway. When Yannis first saw him he was some distance off, but even over the sweep of the tall-roofed, smoky, steamy, hot-lit hall, he appeared only a man, ageing and bearded between black and gray, and drunk, possibly; he looked it.

The guardsman who brought Yannis in quickly pushed him into a seat at one of the lower tables. Here sat a cobbler, tellable by his hands, some stable grooms still rank from their duties, and so on. A lesser soldier or two was in with the rest. The guard said, "Eat your fill. Have a big drink and toast his kingship. Don't get soused. He'll be talking to you later."

The tables where the king's court sat near him lay over an area of painted floor just far enough off to indicate status. The king's own High Table was up on a platform. It faced the hall, but directly to its left side another table spread at a wide angle. The king's table was caped in white cloth-of-linen, hung with medallions of gold. It had utensils, beakers, and jugs of silver and clear gray crystal. It was crowded, the Master occupying the central carved and gilded chair. The left-hand table meanwhile had a drapery of three colors, a deep red, a plum yellow, and a chestnut shade. But no medallions hung on it. The jugs were earthenware. It was also completely empty, but having twelve plain chairs.

An armorer next to Yannis asked questions and commented. Where did Yannis come from? Oh, *there*—Oh, *that* little war? A *horse* did for his leg? What luck! Try that pie—best you've tasted, yes?

Finally Yannis asked a question. "Why is that other table empty up there?"

"Oh, they'll be in."

"Who?"

"His girls."

Yannis, cautious, casual: "His wives, you mean?"

"No wives at present. He got sick of wives. His daughters. No sons—none of those useless women of his ever made him a son. Just girl after girl. Now look. Here they come. Do as they please. Women always will, unless you curb them."

Color. Like a bright stream they rippled into the basin of the big room, flowed together across the platform.

And if this king was only human they, Yannis thought—or was the idea only the strong ale?—*they* were *not*, not quite. Nor like that other unhuman king. These women, these girls, these twelve princesses . . . like water and like fire, things which gleamed and grew and bloomed and *altered*, metals, stars, alcohol—the sun-wind in the wheat . . .

Not beautiful—it was never that, though not *un*beautiful—graceful as animals, careless as . . .

"Where are you off to?"

Yannis found he had half-risen. He sat again and said quickly to the armorer, "Pardon me, just easing my leg."

And looked away, then back to the platform and the twelve flames now settling on it like alighting birds. Because of the table's angle, he could see each of them quite well. They had no jewels, unlike their father. They wore the sort of dresses some not-badly-off merchant's brood might put on.

You could not but look. Their hair . . .

A hush had gone around the hall, and then been smothered over by an extra loudness.

Watching, very obliquely now, Yannis noted the king exchanged no words with any of these young women, not even she who sat down nearest to him.

None of them appeared particularly old. Yannis tried to guess their ages—a year, a little more or less between each one and her closest neighbor.

He had been dazzled. Enough.

Yannis took another draught of ale, and when he raised his head the armorer had shifted, and there was another man.

"Listen, and get this right. You're done dining. In a count of twenty heartbeats get up. Go out that door to the yard. Someone will meet you. You'll be going to see the king."

Then the man himself got up and went, and the armorer did not return, and Yannis counted twenty beats, rose, and moved out into the torch-scripted, black-white winter yard. The wind had dropped with the snow. Two new guards bundled him along to another entry, and up some miles of crooked steps. It was like being escorted to his own hanging. God knew, it might well be before too long.

The king stood in his chamber. He was a bloody king, lit by the galloping hearth.

The king scrutinized Yannis, unspeaking.

After which, the king spoke: "The Land of the Sun Beneath."

Yannis stared. He must be meant to—the king unsmilingly smiled: "Have you heard of such a land? No? But you're traveled. Where have you put your ears? In a bucket?"

Yannis had pondered what to do if offered a drink—in the light of the witch's advice to trust only the communal and well-patronized plate or jug, as in the hall. But this was not a hospitable king, either. It was a game-player, and—an enemy?

Something nudged Yannis's brain back to its station.

"Your Majesty means—the country into which the sun sinks at evening, in the tales . . . ? The lands beneath the world . . . "

"*In the tales*," said the king. "The sun goes under the rim of the earth. Where else can it go?"

Yannis stood there. He knew that many clever scholars had decided the earth was not flat, that the sun circled it. Others, however, remained stubbornly in the belief of a flat world with killing edges. It was, observing nature, difficult not to. And the roots of this city were ancient, primal.

"Yes, Majesty."

"Yes. The Land of the Sun Beneath, where the sun rules after darkness falls here. But there is a land beneath those lands, ever without the sun. Some call it Hell, and some the Underworld. What do you call it, Crank-Leg?"

Yannis thought the king did not anticipate a reply.

The king said, "I suppose, soldier, you'd call it death. Maybe, when they cracked your leg off, you even paid a little visit."

Yannis found he hated the king. It was a response that this king wished to foster in him. The king preferred to know how he weighed with common men, and to make men hate and fear provided an instant measure. Yannis had glimpsed traces of hate, fear, all over the court, both high and low exhibited signs. So the king knew where he was.

"Well," said the king, "you've few words. Do you know what you're to do here?"

Yannis did, of course. "No, sire."

"Then you are not like all the rest, all seven—or was it seventeen of them—those others who failed. Very well. My daughters, in my hall, those girls with their hair. Even *you* will have noticed them. On nights of the round moon they go to another place, the place we spoke of. Despite they sleep all together in their luxurious bedchamber, which every night is locked and guarded to protect and make sure of them—on those three nights they *slip through*, like water from a leaky bowl. At dawn, they come back. Do you know how this was discovered?"

Yannis heard himself say, "By the soles of their feet."

The king unsmiled. His eyes shone like scorched stones, cooling, cold. "So you *do* know."

"Only the phrase."

"Yes. The soles—not of their shoes, which are pristine as when sewn for them—but the skin of their feet. *That* is marked as if worn right through. Blemished, *black* and *red* and decorated in silver and sparkle, too. As if they'd bruised and torn them, then dipped them in rivers of moonlight and rime. You must follow these bitch-whores of mine, and see how they get out, and where they go, and if—*if*—it's to that hidden underland, and next—what goes on *there*. Things no man can see, of course, and keep his sanity. But you'll already have been there, as I said, when you lost half your leg. You'll already know. You're already partly mad. Why else are you here now?"

"And were the other men mad, sire?"

"They must have been, would you not say, old Crook-Shank?"

"Have you," said Yannis, "never yourself *asked* your daughters?"

"I?" The king stared at Yannis. "A king does not ask. He is *supplied*. Without asking. I set others to find out. And now *you* are here. If you succeed, you will be my son, and a prince, my heir, to rule after me. Any of the twelve whores you choose shall be your wife. Or all of them, if you want. I'll have someone fashion an extra large bed for the sport. If you fail, however, your head shall be slashed from your body, as the best of your leg once was. Top to toe, soldier. That's fair. And now," said the king, "since this is the first of the moon's three round nights, the servant outside will show you the way."

It was rising in the long middle window, the moon, round as the white pupil of an immense dark eye. It watched him as he entered and was closed in, but it watched them, also, all twelve. Together, they and he made thirteen beings. But the moon perhaps made fourteen. Besides, there were the animals.

Three big, wolf-like dogs sat or stood, still as statues; a strange pale cat, with a slanted yellow gaze, lay supine. Additionally, there were little cages hung up, in some of which small birds perched twittering—and as the door of every cage stood open, several others flitted to and fro, while occasionally one would let loose a skein of lunar song, or a moon-white dropping would fall, softly snow-like on the floor.

The princesses were arranged, like warriors before a skirmish, some on the richly-draped yet narrow beds, or they stood up, and two were combing their hair with plangent silking sounds, and drizzles of sparks that flew outward in the brazier-spread fire-glow. This combing and spark-making was like the playing of two harps, a musical accompaniment to the birds' descant.

A magical, part uncanny scene. It lulled Yannis, and therefore made him greatly more alert.

But he took time, as with the king, and since they stared full at him, even the dogs and the cat, and some of the birds, to study these women a while.

For a fact though, he could not properly see past their hair.

Charms they had, and they were alike, all of them to each other—and unalike, too—but the hair was still, in each one her symbol, extraordinary, unique. Three colors, every time transmuted. For *she* had hair red as amber, and *she* hair brown as tortoiseshell, and *she* gold as topaz—and *she* red as beech leaves, *she* brown as walnut wood, *she* gold as corn fields—*she* red as summer wine, *she* brown as spring beer, *she* gold as winter mead, and *she* was red as copper, and *she* was brown as bronze. But she—Yannis hesitated between two flickers of the brazier-light—*She*—the youngest, there, there in the darkest shadow of the farthest bed—*she* had hair as gold as *gold*.

"Well, here's our father's latest guest."

It was the tallest, eldest girl who spoke, with amber hair. In age, the soldier thought, she was some years his junior, but then a wealthy, cared-for woman, he knew, could often look much younger than her years, just as a poor and ill-used one could seem older.

"There is a chamber set by for you," levelly said the girl with tortoiseshell hair.

"Every comfort in it," said the girl with topaz hair.

"But we know you won't enjoy that since—" said the girl with hair like beech leaves.

"You must watch us closely and follow behind so that—" said hair like walnut wood.

"You may report to the king what we do," concluded hair like cornfields.

"A shame," said Summer Wine.

"And unkindness," said Spring Hair.

"Every inch of your tired frame must protest," said Winter Mead.

"But such is human life," said Copper, tossing her locks as she stopped her comb.

"Alas," said Bronze, also stopping hers.

Then, in the sparkless gloaming, Gold-as-Gold said this: "We know you must do it, and will never deny you have now no choice. Come, join us then in a cup of liquor for the journey, and we'll be on our way, while you shall follow, poor soldier, as best you can."

The soldier bowed very low, but he said nothing, and when they poured out the wine, each had a bright metal cup with jewels set round the rim. But the cup they gave him was of bright polished metal too.

Then the young women drank, and the soldier pretended to drink, because what the witch had told him was so firmly fixed in his brain he was by that instant like a fine actor who had learned his part to perfection. And presently he did speak, and said might he sit just for a minute, and the young women who were by then finishing putting on their cloaks and shoes for the outer world, or so it looked, nodded and said he might.

Yannis thought, *The draught came from the same pitcher. The drug must be in the cup—but no matter, I never even put my lip to it without my finger between.*

Next he plumped down the cup, spilling a drop. He let his head droop suddenly and seemed surprised. He smiled for the first, stupidly. Then he shut his eyes and thought, *God help me now*, but he had not forgotten the secret of the trance.

Another moment and Yannis himself sat upright in the chair, even as his body stretched unconscious across it. He was out of his skin. And oh, the moonlight in the chamber then, how thrillingly clear, a transparent silver mirror that he could see straight through. And the soul-cord that connected flesh and spirit, more silver yet.

He let himself drift up a wall, and hung there, and watched.

They came soon enough, and tried him, gently at first. Then they mocked, and Amber and Beech Leaves and Spring Beer slapped his face, and then Cornfields came up to him and tickled him maliciously. Walnut Wood kicked his sound ankle, and Bronze and Winter Mead spat on him. Tortoiseshell cursed him articulately, in which Summer Wine and Copper joined. Only Topaz stuck a pin into his arm and twisted it.

Sure he slept, they then turned together up the room to its darker end, where Gold yet stood, the youngest of them. She instead came down, and hesitated by him a second. Standing in air, the soldier thought, Now what will *she* do?

"Poor boy," said Gold, though her face was impassive, and she anyway half his age. "Poor boy."

"You silly," called one of the others. "Why pity him? Would he pity *us*? Hurry, so we can be off."

So Gold left him, or his body, sleeping.

But Yannis pursued all of them, unseen, up the room.

They spoke a rhyme in that ancient and angular other tongue, and then they stamped, each one, on a different part of the floor. At that, the dogs, cats, and birds—who had taken not much note of him— looked round at the far wall, which sighed and slowly shifted open. Beyond lay blackness, but there came the scent of cold stones and colder night. One by one the girls fluttered through like gorgeous moths. Yannis followed without trouble. Even though the hidden door was already closing, he strode on two strong legs straight through the wall.

III

Beginning with an enclosed stone stair, which did not impede the now-fleet-of-foot Yannis, the passage descended. Nor did the almost utter dark inconvenience him; his unbodied eyes saw better than the best. After the stair came a descent of rubble, but everything contained within the granite bastions of the palace. Here and there the accustomed steps of the princesses now did falter. Once, Yannis found to his dismay, he reached out to steady the youngest princess.

Fortunately, she seemed not to realize. But he must be wary—her compassion might have been a trap.

He had learned her name, nevertheless. The eldest girl had called her by it. Evira. That was the name of the youngest princess, Gold-as-Gold.

Ultimately, the way leveled. Then they walked on in the dark until splinters of the moon scattered through. At last full moonlight led them out onto a snow-marbled height, far above the city. They were on the western hill, where massed the houses of the dead.

Yannis knew they must soon enter some mausoleum, and next they did, after unlocking its iron gate with a key the eldest princess carried.

Yannis had lost all fear. He had no need of it.

Within the tomb lay snow and bones, and the ravages of the heartless armies of death and time.

And then there was another door, which Yannis, as now he was, saw instantly was no earthly entrance or exit. And despite his power and freedom, for an instant he did check. But the twelve maidens went directly through the door, even she did, Evira. And then so did Yannis too.

Beyond the door lay the occult country.

It was of the spirit, but whether an afterlife, or underworld below the Sun Beneath—or an else-or-otherwhere—Yannis was never, then or ever, certain.

Although it was unforgettable, naturally. In *nature*, how not?

Should the sun have sunk into a country beneath the earth, then this land, lying below the other two, had no hint of daylight. Nor was the round full moon apparent. Yet light there was. It was like the clearest glass, and the air—when you moved through it—rippled a little, like water. The smell of the air was sweet, fragrant as if with growing trees and herbs. And such there were, and drifted flowers, pale or somber, yet they glowed like lamps. Above, there was a sort of sky, which shone and glowed also, if sunlessly. Hills spread away, and before them an oval body of water softly glimmered. Orchards grouped on every side, they too glinting and iridescent. The leaves nearby were silver, but farther off they had the livelier glisten of gold.

The moment this somewhere closed around them, the women discarded their cloaks and shoes, and shook out the flaming waves of their hair. Then they ran towards the lake.

As they ran, he saw their plain garments change to silks and velvets, streams of embroidery budding at sleeves and borders like yet more flowers breaking through grass.

And he was aware of his own joy in the running, and his lion-like pursuit, his joy in the otherworld, in life and in eternity. Strong wine. Strong as—love.

He did not glance after the spirit-cord, however. He sensed he might not see it, here.

When the women reached the lake, they were laughing with excited pleasure. Some of the silver and golden leaves they had sped under had fallen into their hair—ice on fire, fire on water—he, too, had deliberately snatched a handful of each kind of leaf. But the leaves of the lake-side trees were hard with brilliancy. *They* were diamonds; they did not deign to fall. Impelled he reached out and plucked one. It gave off a spurt of razorous white—like a tinder striking—filling the air with one sharp snap.

"Someone is behind us," said the eldest princess, amber-haired.

The others frowned at her, then all about them.

Yannis thought, *Strange, Amber is the oldest of them, yet she is young like a child, too. Perhaps in knowledge, soul-wise, the youngest princess of all . . .*

And I, he thought, *What am I? Perhaps in fact I am only drugged and dream all this—*

But the youngest princess, Evira, said quietly, "Who could follow here, sisters?" Trusting, and like a child as well.

They could not see him, he knew. Not even the silver and gold and diamond hidden in the pocket of his no-longer-physical shirt.

Then what looked to him at first like a fleet of swans appeared across the lake. Soon he saw twelve gilded boats, one for each princess. Who guided these vessels?

Up in the air, Yannis stood a pillar's height high. He scanned the vessels; each rowed by itself, and was empty.

Beyond the lake a palace ascended. It resembled the palace of the king in the world above, yet it was more fantastic in its looks, its towers more slender, more burnished—a female palace rather than male, and certainly young.

In the sunmoonless dusk, its windows blazed rose-red and apricot. Music wafted over water.

Oh, he could see: this country mirrored the country of Everyday, prettier, more exotic—yet, a match. Had *they* then instinctively created this otherworld out of its own basic malleable and uncanny ingredients? And was that the answer to the riddle of *all* sorcery?

In a brief while, the fast-flying boats beached on the near shore.

Then the princesses happily exclaimed, and flung wide their arms, as if to embrace lovers. And at that—at *that*—

There they are, Yannis breathed, in his unheard phantom's whisper.

For there indeed *they* were.

Begun as shadows standing between the land and the water, gaining substance, filling up with color, youth and life. Twelve tall, young and handsome men were there, elegantly arrayed as princes. But their royal clothes no better than the panoply of their hair— one amber red, one brown as tortoiseshell, one gold as topaz, red as beech leaves, brown as walnut wood, gold as corn fields, summer wine, spring beer, winter mead; copper, bronze, and gold—*as gold.*

In God's name—could God have any hand in this? Yes, yes, Yannis's heart stammered over to him. A snatch of the ancient tongue came to him, from his own past, where he had known pieces of it—that the soul was neither male nor female, yet also it was *both* male and female. So that in every woman there dwelled some part of her that was her male other self. Just as, in every man—

The fine princes walked into the arms of their twelve princesses.

Why not? They were the male selves of each woman. Every couple was already joined, each the other, sister and brother, wife and husband, lovers for ever and a day.

Yannis stared even so as the princes rowed them all back across the lake to the palace of unearthly delights.

Invisibly, he sat in turn in every boat.

Was it heavy work for them? *No.* Yannis was lighter even than the light.

Nevertheless, they sense I am with them, he thought.

He returned to the air and landed on the other shore first.

How long, that night? Dusk till dusk—so many hours. In the world they had left, he thought at last it would be close to dawn. But here it was always and never either night or day.

In the kingly great hall that far outshone that of their father above, the young women danced the often lively dances of their world and this one, forming rhythmic lines, meeting and clasping hands with their princes, parting again to lilt away, and to return. Sometimes the young men whirled them high up in their arms, skirts swirling, hair crackling. Wheels of burning lights hung from the high ceiling, which was leafed with diamond stars. On carven tables food had been laid, and was sometimes eaten, goblets of wine were to be drunk. Somewhere musicians played unseen. There were no other guests.

The soldier watched, and sometimes—the plates and cups were communal—he ate and drank. He wondered if the food would stick to him, or leave him hungry; it seemed somehow to do neither. He himself did not dance until it grew very late.

And then, as it had happened on the shore, and as he had known it must—turning, the soldier found another woman stationed quietly at his side. She at once smiled at him. He knew her well, though never had he seen her before. She might have been his sister.

"Come now," she said, soft as the silver and golden leaves in his pocket, and firm as the single adamant.

And onto the wide floor of the hall, which seemed paved with soot and coal and frost and ice and candle beams and sparks, she went. And somehow then she was dancing with the amber prince who had partnered the amber eldest princess. So then Yannis went forward, and took the princess's hand. While his spirit's sister danced with the prince, Yannis danced with Amber, who seemed then to see, if not to remember him.

"How lightly you step," he said.

"How strongly you lead," she answered.

After this, one by one, he danced with each of them, twelve to one, as his feminine aspect engaged their princes.

"How strongly you lead," said each princess, seeing him, too.

Until he came to the youngest princess, Gold-as-Gold Evira.

"How strongly you *step*," said she.

"How *lightly* you lead," said he.

And he looked into her eyes and saw there, even on that curious dancing floor, a color and a depth he had met seldom. And Yannis thought, *This after all, the very youngest, soul-wise is the eldest—*

And she said, "By a ribbon of air."

And he said, "But I must follow you."

"You," she said, "and no other."

"Are you so sure?" he said. He thought, *What am I saying?* But he knew.

And she smiled, as his soul-sister had, and he knew also her smile. And then his inner woman returned, and coming up to him she kissed his cheek, and vanished, and he, if he had grown visible, vanished also.

From high up he watched the princesses and the princes fly towards the doorway and hurry down to the boats. As they ran he saw the naked soles of their feet, and they were worn and bruised and in some parts bloody from so much dancing, and streaked with shines and spangles.

Yannis ran before them over the lake. He ran before them up the land beyond, missing the tender farewells. He bolted across the orchards of the Otherwhere, and behind him he heard them say,

"Look, is that a hare that runs so fast it moves the grasses?" One thought it must be a wolf, or wildcat.

Then he fled to the mystic entry to the world, and unmistakenly rushed in like a west wind, and found instantly the silver spirit-cord flowing away through the mausoleum, and on. So out over the graveyard hill, and in at the secret corridor, and up inside the palace walls. Straight through the stone he dived. And stood sentry behind his body, sleeping tranced as death in the chair, until they came in.

"Look at him!"

Eleven sisters scorned and pinched him and made out he snored, the fool.

By then the Earth's own dawn was rising like a scarlet sea along the windows. It showed their dresses were plain again, and how weary they were, having danced in their physical bodies all night. But the body of Yannis the soldier had slept with profound relaxation. So in he stepped to wake it up at once.

"Never a hare, nor a cat, running. *I* ran before you, exactly as *I* followed you all night, my twelve dancing ladies." Just this said Yannis, standing lion-strong on his legs of flesh and wood, eyes bright and expression fierce. And he showed them leaves of silver, and of gold, and a diamond, taken now from his physical pocket. He told them all he had seen, and all they had done, every step and smile and sip and sigh. And he added he had not needed three nights to do this, only one. "Meanwhile, I will remind your highnesses, also, of mockery, pinches, blows—and a twisted pin."

Their faces whitened, or reddened.

But Evira Gold-as-Gold only stood back in the shadows, her cat and dogs and most of her birds about her.

"What will you do?" Eleven voices cried.

"Why, tell the king. And he will make me his heir, and you he will *curb*. Whatever that word means, to him."

Then some of them began to weep. And he said, "Hush now. Listen. What you do harms nobody. More, I believe you do good by it, keeping the gates oiled between here—and *there*. And he is a poor king, a coward and tyrant, is he not? His people sullen and afraid, his guards afraid, too, or arrogant and drunken. He's not how a king should be, his people's shepherd, who will die for them if needs must. Few kings are any good. Few men, few human things."

But still they sobbed.

Then Yannis said, "I tell you now what *I'll* do, then."

And he told them. And the crying ceased.

Down into the king's hall went Yannis, with the twelve princesses walking behind him on their bare and bruised and lovely feet.

And as he had suspected, the instant the court and soldiers saw the daughters walked meekly with him, everyone grew silent.

The king with his grayed black-iron beard and hair looked up from his gold dish of bloody meat. "Well?" he said.

"Their secret is this, sire," said Yannis, "they stay wakeful on full moon nights and do penance, treading on sharp stones, and praying for your health and long life, there in their locked room. Such things are best hidden, but now it's not, and the luck of it is broken. But so you would have it." And then he leaned to the king's ear and murmured with a terrible gentleness this, which only the king heard. "But they are, as you suspect, powerful witches, which is why you fear them; but the old gods love them, and you'd best beware. Yes, even despite all those other men you have allowed these girls to dupe, and so yourself had the fellows shorn of their heads: blood *sacrifices*, no less, to the old powers of Darkness you believe inhabit the lands below the Sun Beneath. This too shall I say aloud? Or will you give me what I'm owed?"

Then the king shuddered from head to foot. Top to toe, that was fair. And he told everyone present that the soldier had triumphed, and would now become a prince, the king's heir, and might marry too whichever of the daughters he liked.

"That's easy, then," said Yannis. "I'm not a young man; I'll take the oldest head and wisest mind among them. Your youngest girl, Evira." *And because,* he thought, *she is the golden cup that holds my heart.*

And gladly enough she came to him, and took his hand.

~

Less than half a year the iron king survived; maybe he destroyed himself by his own plotting. But by then Yannis was well-loved by the city, its soldiers loyal to him, for he had learned how to be a favorite with them, having seen other leaders do it.

Yannis, therefore, ruled as king, and his gold-haired queen at his side. Some say they had three children, some that they had none, needing none.

But it was not until after the burial of the cruel first king that Yannis said to his wife, "But did your white cat, at least, not protest?"

"At what, dear husband?"

"At your changing her, for however short a space, into a goat."

"Ah," Evira said. "Of course, you have known."

"And the dogs to wolves, and the birds—to chickens . . . "

"They were glad," said Evira, coolly, "privately to meet with you. For I had sensed you were coming towards us all, and foresaw it was the only way that you would let me tell you and warn you and teach you—and so help me to save my sisters, who trust no man easily, from our fearsome and maddened father. The way matters stand in this world, it is men who rule. So here too it must be a man. But a man who is cunning, brave, kind—and with the skills of magic woken in him, needing only the key of one lesson."

And from this they admitted to each other that Evira had disguised herself as the elderly witch in the woods, and since she was far cleverer than her sisters, none had discovered her. Though at the last, as they danced, because of the russet radiance of her eyes, Yannis did.

To the end of their lives he and she loved each other, and Evira and her sisters went on dancing in the other country below the sun, even with Yannis sometimes. But he never betrayed them. Never.

It took storytellers, alas, to do that.

——

Tanith Lee was born in the UK in 1947. After school she worked at a number of jobs, and at age twenty-five had one year at art college. Then DAW Books published her novel *The Birthgrave*. Since then she has been a professional full-time writer.

Publications so far total approximately ninety novels and collections and well over three hundred short stories. She has also written for television and radio. Lee has won several awards and in 2009 was made a Grand Master of Horror. She is married to the writer/artist John Kaiine.

—✦—

When I was a child, fairy tales were not for the faint of heart. My mother used to read to us from this massive book with a horned demon dude on the cover. Readers and writers are partners in story, and my fertile imagination contributed horrifyingly vivid details. Thus twisted (thanks, Mom!) I grew up to write two best-selling teen fantasy series: The Heir Chronicles (*The Warrior Heir, The Wizard Heir, The Dragon Heir, The Enchanter Heir*); and the Seven Realms series (*The Demon King, The Exiled Queen, The Gray Wolf Throne, The Crimson Crown.*)

"Warrior Dreams" is set in the gritty industrial landscape of the Cleveland Flats, where the crooked Cuyahoga River meets Lake Erie. The Lake Erie region boasts a rich folkloric tradition, rife with water monsters such as nixies and grindylows; zombie-like Wendigos; storm hags, ominous black dogs and the feared Nain Rouge—the Red Dwarf of Detroit. Some elements have been transplanted from the Old World, some are home-grown.

I love to marry contemporary issues (e.g., our [lack of] treatment of wounded warriors) with fantasy elements and unexpected settings.

I've discovered I can get away with a lot in a fairy tale.

Cinda Williams Chima

Warrior Dreams

Cinda Williams Chima

Russell's new home under the abandoned railroad bridge was defensible, which was always the first priority. Secluded, yet convenient to the soup kitchens downtown. It offered a dry, flat place for his sleeping bag, and some previous occupant had even built a fire ring out of the larger rocks.

The bridge deck kept the snow and sleet off, and because the bridge wasn't in use, he didn't have to deal with the rattle-bang of trains. Any kind of noise still awakened the Warrior—the dude born in Kunar Province, in Korengal, in the Swat Valley—even in places like Waziristan, where he never officially was. Any sudden noise left him sweating, heart pounding, fueled by an adrenaline rush that wouldn't dissipate for hours.

Best of all, the bridge was made of iron—a virtual fortress of iron, in fact, which should've been enough to win him a little peace. That and the bottle of Four Roses Yellow Label he'd bought with the last of this month's check.

But Russell was finding that, for an out-of-the-way place, his new crib on Canal Street was in a high-traffic area for magical creatures. The river was swarming with shellycoats—he heard the soft chiming of their bells all day long. Kappas lurked around the pillars of the bridge, poking their greenish noses out of the water, watching for unwary children. The carcasses of ashrays washed up on shore, disintegrating as soon as the sunlight hit them.

Where were they all coming from? Was there some kind of paranormal convention going on and nobody told him?

The first night, he'd awakened to the adrenaline rush and a pair of red fur boots, inches from his nose.

"Hey!" Russell said, rolling out of danger and grabbing up the iron bar he always kept close. The creature screeched and scrambled backwards, out of range. It was the size of a small child, with a long beard, burning coal eyes, and a ratty red and black fur coat. Like a garden gnome out of a nightmare.

"Listen up, gnomeling," Russell said, "you sneak up on a person, you're liable to get clobbered."

The creature struck a kind of pose, lips drawn back from rotten teeth, one hand extended toward Russell.

"Je suis le Nain Rouge de Detroit," it began.

Russell shook his head. "En Anglais, s'il vous plait. Je ne parle pas Francais."

It scratched its matted beard. "You just did."

"Did what?"

"Spoke French."

"Maybe," Russell said, "but now I'm done." He leaned back against a bridge pillar and lit a cigarette with shaking hands. At one time, he'd been fluent in five languages, but he'd forgotten a lot since the magic thing began.

The gnomeling let go a sigh of disgust. "I am the Red Dwarf of Detroit," it repeated. "Harbinger of doom and disaster."

"I hate to break it to you," Russell said. "But this isn't Detroit. It's Cleveland. Detroit's a little more to the left." He pointed with his cigarette. "Just follow the lake, you can't miss it."

The dwarf shook his head. "I may be the Red Dwarf of Detroit, but my message is for you." And then it disappeared.

Way to ruin a good night's sleep.

The second night, it was the dog. Russell woke to find it snuggled next to him, its huge, furry body like a furnace against his sleeping bag. He nearly strangled it before he realized what it was. He was definitely losing his edge. No way any animal that size should've been able to sneak up on him

"Hey," Russell said, sitting up. "Where'd you come from?" After holding out his hand for a sniff, he scratched the beast behind the ears. It was immense, probably a Newfoundland, or a mix of that and something else.

Russell liked dogs. They accepted a wide range of behavior without question, and they believed in magic, too.

The next morning, Russell shared his meager gleanings from the dumpster behind the Collision Bend Café, and the dog elected to stay with him another night. Russell's rule was, if a dog stays two nights, it gets a name.

"Is it all right if I call you Roy?" Russell asked. The dog didn't object, so Roy it was. That night Russell fell asleep, secure in the belief that old Roy had his back.

He awoke to six nixies tugging on his toes with their sinuous fingers. Yanking his feet free, he said, "Ixnay, nixies."

They swarmed back into the water and commenced to squabbling about what, if anything, they should do with him.

"He sees us!"

"He will tell!"

"We must drown him!"

"Some watchdog you are," Russell said, glaring at Roy. The Newfie stretched, shook out his long black coat, and trotted off to anoint the bridge for the hundredth time.

After shooing away the nixies, Russell kindled a fire. He hadn't lost the knack since he'd been chaptered out of the Army. Like riding a goddamn bike. He curled up and tried to go back to sleep, but he couldn't shake a sense of imminent danger. The nixies kept muttering, and that didn't help. He tossed and turned so much that Roy growled, got up, and found a spot on the other side of the fire.

It was no use. Russell sat up. As he did so, the wind stung his face, bringing with it the stench of rotten flesh.

Stick with Lieutenant MacNeely. It's like he can smell danger.

He searched the embankment that ran down to the water. There. He caught a flicker of movement along the riverbank. The lights from the bridge reflected off a pair of eyes peering out of a tangle of frozen weeds. The eyes disappeared and the weeds shifted and shook, a ribbon of motion coming toward him. Something was creeping closer, stalking him. Something big. Was it plotting with the nixies or was it here on its own?

Warrior Russell planted his feet under him, reached down and gripped his trusty iron bar.

Know your weapon.

You are the weapon.

With a roar, the creature burst from the underbrush, its claws clattering over the concrete as it bounded forward. It was incredibly tall, cadaverously thin, with long, snarled hair. Coming to his knees, Russell waited until it was nearly on top of him, then jack-knifed upward, swinging his iron bar, slamming it into the creature in mid-air. It screamed, a sound as lonely as a train whistle at night. Then burst into shards of ice that rained down on the riverbank until it looked like his campsite had been hit by a localized hailstorm.

"What the hell was that?" Russell muttered, brushing slush off his parka.

The nixies looked at each other, chattering excitedly, pointing at Russell. One of them slipped beneath the river's surface and disappeared.

"Where'd she go?" Russell demanded, glaring at them. He stood, cradling the iron bar. "If she went for reinforcements, well, then bring it. I'm Russell G. MacNeely, and I'm not giving up this crib."

The nixie reappeared a few minutes later, with reinforcements. A reinforcement, rather. The newcomer—a girl—surfaced with scarcely a ripple, regarding Russell with luminous green eyes. Her skin was ashy white, with just a hint of blue, and her long red hair was caught into a braid just past her shoulders.

She raised one pale hand, and waved at him, a tentative flutter of fingers. Russell waved back.

She flinched back, eyes wide. "So you *can* see us."

"I'll pretend I can't, if that makes you feel better," Russell said. "I'm used to it. It helps me fit in better in the world."

"You killed the Wendigo," she said, her voice the sound of moving water over stone. "I'm impressed. They aren't easy to kill, one on one."

"I killed the *what?*"

She scooped up a handful of ice. Tilting her hand, she let it fall, glittering in the lights from the bridge, clattering on the concrete.

"Uh, right. Wendigo," Russell said. "Don't they usually hang out further north?"

"Usually," she said, with a sigh. "Not these days." Sweeping bits of ice out of the way, she boosted herself onto the bank. She wore a skimpy dress of what looked like seaweed, and a necklace of water lilies and fresh-water mussel shells. She was sleek and fit, her arms and legs well-muscled, as if she worked out. Though her skin was pale as permafrost, she was probably the loveliest thing Russell had ever seen.

Just stop it. You always get like this when you're off your meds. There's just no point in that kind of thinking for someone like you.

Truth be told, he hated being on meds. He hated living in a black-and-white world, blinders over his eyes, cotton stuffed in his ears. Sleepwalking. Sitting at the bottom of a well of sadness, unable to climb out.

He needed to stay alert. He needed to be able to defend himself.

I am not a violent person, but I will defend myself.

"I'm Russell, by the way," he said. No reason he couldn't be friendly.

"I'm Laurel," she said. With nimble fingers, she unraveled her braid. Then rewove it—tighter.

Russell cast about for something else to say. "Um—you're not as green as most nixies," he said, hoping that would be taken for a compliment.

She shook her head. "I'm not a nixie. I'm a kelpie." She'd been focused on her braid, but now she raised her eyes to Russell's face, as if to assess his reaction. "A limnades kelpie, to be specific."

The word was familiar, but all he could think of was seaweed.

Kelp. The other Russell—the pre-deployment Russell—would have known. The other Russell was good with words.

"Nixies, kelpies—what's the difference?"

"I'm a shape-shifter," Laurel said.

Ah, Russell thought. A shape-shifter. In the years since the TBI, he'd become familiar with many magical creatures, but there always seemed to be more to learn.

"And a warrior," she added. "I'm the last remaining guardian of the lakes."

"A warrior." Russell resisted the temptation to roll his eyes, and bit the insides of his cheeks to keep from smiling. A small victory for the old social filters. And the new role of women in combat.

"The nixies are debating whether to kill you." She said this matter-of-factly, like she was interested in Russell's opinion on it.

"I'd like to see them try." Russell scooped up the iron bar and rested it across his knees. "I'm not a violent person, but I will defend myself."

He'd said that, over and over, in therapy.

Laurel watched him handle the iron staff with something like jealousy. "I can see that you have some skill with weapons," she said.

"I should," Russell said. "That used to be my job. Killing people." When Laurel's eyes narrowed, he added, "Don't worry. I only killed the bad guys—or at least that's what I thought. Then I got RFS'd out of the Rangers for misconduct, along with a bad case of TBI and PTSD."

"You sure have a lot of letters," Laurel observed.

"My point is, I'm not considered competent. So nobody is going to believe a thing I say. Your secrets are safe with me."

Laurel cocked her head. "What is this 'TBI' and 'PTSD'?"

"I got blown up a lot when I was in the military," Russell said, stretching out the kinks in his back. "So now, my brain doesn't work like other people's. For instance, I can see and hear you. No offense, but that ain't normal in my world, so I'm crazy. They claim I was crazy before I enlisted. Not their fault."

She thought about this for a moment. "I can see and hear *you*," she pointed out.

"I didn't make the rules," Russell said. "Anyway, what are you doing so far upriver? You're surrounded by steel mills, and it's all iron bridges and what-not. Your kind don't tolerate iron, right? You're gonna make yourself sick."

"It wasn't our idea," Laurel said, "We've been forced into the rivers, because the lake is no longer safe. But, you're right—we can't survive here for long. The rivers are cleaner than they used to be, but still not healthy enough to live in permanently. Plus, as you said, there's the metal."

"There's the metal," the nixies sang.

Laurel wrapped her arms around her knees. She was completely dry, now, and looked like any other half-naked girl you'd meet at a body-builder's convention. More at home in her body than most girls.

"Our time is up, Russell," Laurel said. "You and I—we are doomed."

"We are doomed," the nixies sang.

"You've seen the omens," Laurel continued, "both the Red Dwarf of Detroit and the Black Dog of Lake Erie."

"The black dog of—" Russell swung around. Roy was sound asleep again, snoring and farting by turns. "You mean Roy? He's just a stray."

"Call him whatever you like, a Black Dog has signaled doom on the lakes for centuries."

"So you're saying that *I'm* doomed, if he's hanging out with me?"

"I'm afraid so," the kelpie said. "I give you another day, maybe two."

Russell thought on this a moment. "Can you tell how I'm going to die?"

Laurel shook her head. "From all appearances, I'd say you'll get drunk and fall in the river." She nudged the bottle of Four Roses with her foot.

"Well, thanks for the heads up, but I don't get whether you're warning me to be careful, or telling me to do whatever the hell I want because I'll end up dead either way."

"I'm here to offer you a warrior's death," Laurel said.

The warrior? That guy's already dead, Russell wanted to say. That guy doesn't exist any more. But of course he didn't, because it wasn't true. "What do you mean?"

"I told you that I'm the last remaining guardian of the lakes. When I am gone, the lakes will run with the blood of the gifted."

Russell rubbed his stubbly chin. "What's the mission? Do you want me to slaughter all the people who're dumping crap into the lake?"

Laurel shook her head. "Pollution *is* a problem, but our immediate concern is the storm hag of the lake."

"The storm hag of the lake," the nixies sang.

"What—what—what—wait a minute," Russell said. "Storm hag?"

"You've not heard of her?" Laurel tilted her head, perplexed. "She is famous. All the Lake Erie sailors know about her."

"I don't know any sailors," Russell said. "I'm not from around here. I just came in on the bus."

"I've known a lot of sailors," she said.

Russell put up both hands. He had a feeling he didn't want to know about the sailors. "Never mind. Tell me about this hag."

"Her name is Jenny Greenteeth. She roams the lakes, riding on an enormous lake sturgeon. She foments storms, then pulls ships underneath the water and drowns the sailors."

"I can see where that's a problem for the sailors, but how is that a problem for you?"

"It's not just sailors," Laurel said, fingering her necklace. "Jenny has lived in the lakes since the dawn of history, but she has recently developed a voracious appetite for magic. We think *that* might be the result of phosphates. Or hormones. We've fought back, but none of us can stand against her. Many of us have died—not just nixies and kelpies, but grindylows and watersprites, snallygasters and selkies and hippocamps."

"No offense," Russell said. "But that sounds like a catalog of the world's most obscure magical creatures. Creatures nobody but me will even miss." Not that anybody would miss *him*, if he disappeared.

Laurel snorted softly. "Most of the original creatures of faerie are already extinct. Those that call attention to themselves were the first to go. Elves and unicorns, griffins, centaurs, and dragons—humans loved them to death. We may be all but invisible, but that's why we've survived."

That's how I survive, Russell thought. By being invisible. "I'm sorry," he said. "I didn't mean to imply that you aren't important.."

"I'm used to it," Laurel said. "Magical creatures persist in those places in the world that are hard to get to. That are still relatively free of iron and pollution. There are pockets of dryads in the deep forests of South America, sea serpents and mermaids in the great oceans of the world. Once the Great Lakes were large enough to shelter us, too. These days, not so much. Think about it—it's the tiny magics, like hexes and charms and lutins, house elves and brownies and woods sprites that add color and texture to the world. That keep it from being all metal and glass and right angles. Can we really afford to have less magic in the world?"

"Well, when you put it that way," Russell began, "I guess I—"

"With every creature she destroys, Jenny grows larger and hungrier and more dangerous. Soon the lake will be completely barren of magical creatures. Except, of course, for her. Then, I believe, she will turn her attention to the land."

"Can't you gang up on her?" he asked. "Couldn't all of you together take her down?"

"We have tried. Every time we've gone against her, we've suffered huge losses. I am the sole survivor of my squadron."

How'd it happen, MacNeely? How is it that you're the only survivor?

"What do you mean, your squadron?"

"There used to be scores of us, patrolling the Great Lakes from Superior to Ontario. Now there's just me. You see, the only weapon that works against her is iron, and none of us can wield it." She raked back her red mane of hair. "We need a champion."

"We need a champion," the nixies sang.

"A champion?" Russell frowned, perplexed.

"We need someone who can partner with us. Who can wield iron on our behalf. We need a warrior." She looked Russell in the eyes, and then down at the iron bar beside him in the snow. "We need you."

"What? No!" he said. "Oh, no. Don't look at me. You've got the wrong guy."

But she *did* look at him, a mingling of eagerness and challenge.

"Don't you get it?" Russell said, his anger rising. "I'm done with that. Heroes get killed. If they're lucky."

He should know. He was a bona fide hero, with the medals to prove it. And the wounds that nobody saw, that nobody wanted to see.

"You've proven that you can wield iron—can kill with it, if you have to. You've experienced magic, so you know what we stand to lose. You are unique in the world, Russell G. MacNeely."

"Yeah, well, you try and be unique for a while, and see how it works out for you," Russell growled.

"I *am* unique," Laurel said, "in these lakes, at least. My entire family—my mate, my birth family, and my children have been killed. I'm the only one left."

"I'm sorry to hear that," Russell blurted, as regret sluiced over him. "I know what it's like to lose a child."

"Son or daughter?" Laurel asked.

"Daughter," Russell said, wishing he hadn't brought her up.

"How did she die?" Laurel asked.

"Oh, she's not dead," Russell said. "I stay away from her. It's better that way. Safer."

Know your weapon.

I am the weapon.

Laurel cocked her head. "But if—if she's still alive, then—?"

"Look, back to business," Russell said. "Even if you found a champion, how would he hope to go after this hag? Wouldn't she just swim away? And if he swam after her, even if he caught her, he'd be too exhausted to fight."

"We have a plan," Laurel said, as if she'd just invented the wheel. "We'll set a trap."

"You have this all worked out, don't you?" Russell laughed bitterly. "Now all you have to do is find somebody to do it. Somebody else. You can't expect me to fight your magical battles for you."

"You don't understand, Russell," Laurel said. "I'm not asking you to fight for me. I'm a warrior, too. We'll fight together."

Russell looked her up and down. "Right. Now, I'm going to bed. With any luck, I'll get some sleep."

Turning his back on Laurel, Russell ducked under the bridge, took another hit of the Four Roses, and crawled into his sleeping bag.

"Whether you help me or not, your fate is sealed," she called after him.

He didn't sleep well. All night long, the nixies sang of battles and valor, invading his dreams. The soft tinkling of bells from the river told him the flow of refugees was continuing.

He dreamt he galloped through the waves astride a white horse, bursting through spray, his sword held high over his head. Just ahead, Jenny Greenteeth rose out of the waves, rose and rose and rose until she blotted out the sky. He swung his blade with a two-handed stroke and—

A faint noise woke him. Gripping his weapon, heart thumping, that metallic taste of fear on his tongue, he searched the darkness.

"It's me, Russell," Laurel said, sounding amused. "Put away the iron. I won't hurt you."

He heard a soft rustle of fabric. Then she sat down next to him, unzipped his sleeping bag, and slipped in beside him. She was very clearly naked.

"What are you doing?" Russell said, rolling on his side to face her.

"Isn't it obvious?" she said. "Please say yes." And then she kissed him, which awakened sensations he thought he'd forgotten.

With every ounce of resolve that was in him, he gripped her shoulders and pushed her to arm's length. "Why?" he demanded.

She regarded him, perplexed. "Because I want to?" She poked him playfully. "It seems you do, too."

"Why?" Russell repeated, bringing up his knees in defense.

Laurel let go an exasperated sigh. "Well, it's kind of a tradition for warriors on the eve of battle to—you know—in case it's the last time."

"I told you," Russell said. "I'm not going to fight. No matter what you—"

"Russell." Laurel put a finger over his lips. "Silly. I wasn't talking about you," she said. "I was talking about me. I just need a little cooperation."

And so, after a bit more persuasion, Russell cooperated.

After, they lay, looking up at the sky. Or they would have, if the bridge wasn't in the way. Laurel fingered Russell's dogtags. "What are these? Amulets of some kind?"

"It's ID. So, if you're killed, they can figure out who to notify."

"What about this one?" She read the inscription aloud.

"I will always place the mission first.

I will never accept defeat.

I will never quit.

I will never leave a fallen comrade."

"That's the Warrior Ethos," Russell said. "It's something they make us memorize, but they don't believe in themselves." He sighed. "All I ever wanted to be was a soldier."

In the morning, he awoke alone. Hungry and sore and worn out, like he'd been doing battle all night. Laurel was a warrior, for sure. He smiled, remembering.

"Laurel?" he said. No answer beyond the howling of the wind, blowing down the river.

He quickly yanked on his clothes, shivering in the cold. Laurel's seaweed dress still lay where she'd dropped it, dried and disintegrating.

Crawling out from under the bridge, he saw that black thunder-clouds were piling up in the northwest. An unusual sky for February. Something bad was brewing.

The area around his campsite was deserted, not a nixie nor a pixie to be seen. After the tumult all night long, it was a little unnerving. And, truth be told, a little lonely.

"That was a strange dream," he said aloud.

Roy lifted his head and whined when Russell spoke. "Guess I didn't dream you up, boy." He'd been half-convinced the dog would be gone in the morning, too. Gently, he gripped the dog's ruff to either side and looked at him, nose to nose. Roy's eyes glowed like red coals, like in all the stories about hell-hounds.

"Are you really the harbinger of doom?" Russell asked. "Is my number really up?" Would the harbinger of doom leave piss-marks all around the camp?

In answer, Roy unfurled an impossibly long tongue and licked him in the face. Pulling away, he pawed at a bundle, lying in the snow. A long bundle wrapped in seaweed, a squarish package next to it. Russell knew what it was before he ever picked it up.

"You forgot something, Laurel!" he called. "Come get this stuff! I don't want it."

Nobody answered.

He couldn't help himself. He was a warrior, after all. Picking free one edge of the seaweed shroud, he unrolled it.

It was an iron sword in a leather baldric, a massive blade with dragons on the hilt. As he drew it out, he saw that it was freshly oiled and free of rust and incredibly sharp, as Russell found out when he tried his thumb on the edge.

"Ow!" he said, sucking on his thumb. "You call this a weapon? Where's my M110?" he called out. "How 'bout an M4?" No answer.

Unwrapping the other bundle, he pulled out a circular shield and a silver helm.

He picked up the shield in his right hand, the sword in his left. Dancing around on the riverbank, thrusting and parrying, he fought an invisible opponent to surrender.

He'd taken fencing lessons, back in the day. It was an up-close, intimate dance that seemed appropriate to a warrior. His muscles remembered what his unreliable mind had forgotten.

A soft whickering drew his attention back to the river. A horse stood there, dripping wet, having just climbed out of the water. Her coat shone white with a faint tinge of blue, translucent as stillwater ice. Water streamed from her red mane and tail. She wore no saddle or bridle, only a necklace of water lilies and freshwater mussel shells. The luminous blue eyes were hauntingly familiar. Recognition pinged through Russell.

"Laurel?" he whispered.

"I told you," she said, tossing her head and pawing at the earth with her hoof. "You won't be alone. We're in this together."

He took a step back, shaking his head weakly, the tip of his massive sword dragging in the snow. "No," he said.

She came forward, twitching water from her tail, her eyes fixed on Russell. When she was close enough, she reached out and butted him gently with her head. He stroked her velvety soft nose. Pulling back her lips, she exposed fearsome sharp teeth. Gripping his parka, she dragged him forward a few steps, toward the river's edge. Then knelt, to make it easier for Russell to climb on.

Russell looked back at Roy, hoping for direction. Roy sat in the snow, his tail beating on the ground, his red-coal eyes fixed on Russell.

"Is this it, Roy?" Russell asked. "Is this how it all ends?"

Roy said nothing.

"I can't believe I'm asking advice from a dog I've only just met," Russell muttered.

He looked back at his crib under the railroad bridge, the meager campsite he'd defended like a junkyard dog, knowing it was the best he could hope for. He could stay here, and eke out a living, dumpster-diving and haunting the soup kitchens. He could go back to the world and start taking his medicine again. Or he could do this thing. He could be a warrior, one more time. It was the one thing—the only thing—he'd ever wanted to be.

Laurel had her head twisted around, looking at him.

"Where is everyone?" Russell asked.

"They're down in the harbor, waiting for you."

"You said you had a plan?" Russell said.

"The nixies will lure her inside the breakwall," Laurel said. "That will prevent her from taking advantage of the sturgeon's speed. We can either run her aground or trap her against the breakwall. Then it's up to you."

It's up to you, MacNeely. Somebody has to take out that gunner or we'll never get out of here.

Russell picked up the helm and slid it onto his head, strapped the baldric onto his back, and slid the sword into it. He retrieved his shield and strode to the kelpie's side. Swinging his leg over, he twined his fingers into her mane. "Let's do this thing," he said.

The next thing he knew, they were flying over the concrete barrier at the water's edge and plunging into the icy river. It was a good thing he was holding on tight, or he would've been pitched right off. The water was just as cold as Russell expected, but Laurel gave off heat like a furnace, warming his entire body. He could feel her muscles under him, extending and bunching, extending and bunching as she swam with the current, following the switchbacks of the crooked river toward the lake. The shoreline blurred by, faster than Russell could focus. Fleetingly, he wondered whether Laurel was in a hurry to act before he had second thoughts.

They swept under the Shoreway, under another railroad bridge, past Wendy Park on their left-hand side.

They burst out of the mouth of the river like a log out of a chute. At that point the wind hit them, a furious pounding from the northwest, whipping up whitecaps even within the breakwall. Laurel kept swimming, angling across the flow of water to a spot just inside and to the east of the passage through the break into the greater lake. There she hovered, constantly swimming just to keep from being swept out into the lake.

"We'll wait here," Laurel shouted, but Russell could barely hear her over the howling of the wind and the thunder of the waves crashing over the wall.

Just beyond the wall, the lake water seethed with swimming bodies—nixies and grindylows, watersprites, and selkies. This was the bait that was meant to lure the storm hag.

She was on her way, if the weather was any indication. Sleet hissed into the water all around them, found its way under Russell's collar, and bit into his face like a thousand tiny knives. If not for Laurel between his knees, he'd be frozen solid already. Swiping ice from his lashes, he peered into the distance, where the black horizon melted into the turbulent lake.

Then he saw it, something that looked like a massive tidal wave heading for the breakwall, higher than any other wave. Ahead of it, magical creatures peeled off to either side, desperate to escape.

"Is that something?" he asked Laurel.

"That's her," she said, and dove.

Russell clung desperately to her back, squeezing his eyes tightly shut. Pressure built in his ears until it seems like they might pop. He held his breath as long as he could, then tried to let go, so he could kick his way to the surface. He stuck to her back like a burr on Velcro, unable to free himself. He breathed in—he couldn't help it—and to his surprise, it was fine. He reached up to his neck and found gills there—deep slits on either side. He was breathing underwater.

That's when he knew he was having some kind of a major breakdown. *When you see things, MacNeely, what do you see?*

Russell's head broke the surface, and then Laurel's, and he saw she'd come up just inside the breakwall. Russell turned to look just as the storm hag burst through the passage from the lake, driving a cryptozoological menagerie before her.

Russell gaped at Jenny Greenteeth, pawing through his mental thesaurus of words for huge. Like colossal. Humongous. Statuesque. Immense. She was as tall as the thunderclouds piling up behind her, and she rode a fish the size of a freight train.

Her skin was the color of verdigris, like copper after years of exposure to seawater and sunlight. Her hair was chartreuse, with jewels, shells, pearls, and other glitterbits woven into it. She wore what looked like a fortune in bling—pearls, diamonds, opals, and other gemstones roped around her neck. She controlled her steed with reins that looked to be made of moray eels.

Her eyes were the mustard yellow of a sulfur spring, her teeth grass-green, and she wore a kind of armor made of brass plates.

"Shipbuilder's plaques," Laurel explained. "One for each ship she's foundered."

"Shit," Russell said, looking down at his puny shield, then back up at his opponent. And laughed. "She's colossal. We're totally fucked."

"Courage, Russell," Laurel said.

The sturgeon surged forward, plowing into the school of fleeing lake creatures, magical and not. The storm hag sluiced her fingers through the water on either side, straining them out. She crammed fistfuls of nixies, kelpies, carp, and walleye indiscriminately into her mouth.

Even astride the fish, she towered over buildings on the shore.

And then, she began to sing.

Come into the water, love,
Dance beneath the waves,
Where dwell the bones of sailor lads
Inside my saffron caves.

"What's that all about?" Russell asked.

"It's her thing," Laurel said briskly. "Kind of a tradition. She likes to sing before a kill. The others are going to draw her this way, into the closed end of the breakwall, so she's trapped. Then we're going in. Just be careful—her claws are deadly poisonous."

"*Now* I'm worried," Russell said, grinning. What the hell did he have to lose?

That MacNeely? He's crazy brave.

There was a time when being crazy served a soldier well.

The surviving decoys made a sharp right turn past where Laurel and Russell lurked, making speed toward a small opening in the break water at the west end—too small for the sturgeon to fit through. When Jenny saw where they were headed, she yanked her reins hard right, digging in spurs made of oyster shells. She lashed her mount with a small whip, screeching, "Don't let them get away!"

Like a lake freighter, the sturgeon made a wide turn to follow, its wake slopping over the shoreline like water sloshing out of a bathtub. It put on speed, blood staining the water from the wounds in its sides. It reached the breakwall at ramming speed just as the last of their quarry slipped through the hole. The sturgeon slammed into the opening, ramming halfway through, and then stuck there, its tail flailing, sending tidal waves onto the shore.

Outside the breakwall, the nixies cheered.

But Jenny Greenteeth wasn't done yet. Howling in fury, she stood astride the breakwall like a colossus at the gate. Truth be told, Russell thought she might indeed be a little bigger than she started out.

"Russell," Laurel said. "I think it might be time to draw your sword."

"Not yet," he said, leaning forward to whisper into Laurel's ear. "I'm going to need both hands. Bring me in close to the fish," he said.

"He'll smash you against the rocks," Laurel protested, swimming closer just the same. They followed the breakwall in, avoiding the lashing tail, until they were all but bumping up against the sturgeon's side. The eel reins were dangling in arm's reach. Russell gripped the reins and ran up the slippery side of the fish, coming up underneath Jenny's position on the wall.

Russell reached over his shoulder, gripped the dragon hilt of the sword, and pulled it, hissing, from its baldric. It was all he could do to hold the blade steady with his trembling arms. Balancing lightly atop the sturgeon, he slashed into the storm hag's ankle with a two-handed swing. Then slid down, flattening himself against the sturgeon's side, pressing his face into its leathery skin, clinging to the eel harness as if his life depended on it. Which it did.

Jenny screamed, a scream that could have been heard in Canada. Crouching, she scanned the area around her feet for the culprit.

"Hey! Greenteeth!" Laurel shouted. "Over here!"

Turning, she spotted Laurel, hovering between the sturgeon's tail and the wall. Flopping down on the sturgeon's back, she reached for Laurel while the kelpie swam furiously for open water. Seizing hold of the water horse, Jenny lifted her, dripping, while Laurel struggled in the hag's massive hand, shifting from horse to girl to slippery fish.

"What's this?" Jenny snarled. "Did you sting me?"

Russell ran lightly up the hag's spine, using the braids in her hair to climb to the top of her head.

He stood there, sword in hand, and his eyes met Laurel's. She nodded, once, then sank her razor teeth into Jenny's fleshy palm. Enraged, the storm hag flung Laurel away. The kelpie landed, broken, on the rocks of the shoreline and lay there without moving.

Russell rappelled down the front of the hag's face. Bracing his feet on either side of her nose, a hair's breadth above her gaping mouth, he plunged his sword into one of her sulfur pool eyes.

The storm hag exploded, covering Russell head to toe with yellow goo and launching him far out into the lake. He hit the water hard and sank, a helpless bag of broken bones in the churning waves. Drowning's not a bad way to go, he said to himself as he spiraled down.

Then multiple hands were supporting him, lifting him back toward the surface. He saw it coming toward him, so brilliant it hurt his eyes, and then his face broke through, into the sunlight.

Incredibly, the storm was over, the waters lapping calmly against the breakwall, the sky that brilliant blue that sometimes happens on rare days in autumn.

"Laurel," Russell gasped. "Where's Laurel?"

"Don't worry," the nixies said. "You go together."

"Good," Russell said. And closed his eyes.

An honor guard of six nixies laid the two warriors side by side in a small boat filled with water lilies and sea glass and some of the sea hag's ropes of pearls, since she wouldn't be using them any more.

Followed by a retinue of nixies and grindylows and shellycoats and water dragons and brook horses, they towed the boat far out into the lake, to a place where the sunlit waves glittered all the way to the horizons. The mourners commenced to diving, bringing up pebbles and stones from the bottom of the lake and piling them into the boat until it sank beneath the surface.

The nixies scattered flowers over the warriors' watery grave and chanted,

I will always place the mission first.
I will never accept defeat.
I will never quit.
I will never leave a fallen comrade.

Every one of them knew that a new Lake Erie legend had been born.

"This is it?" Margaret MacNeely ducked under the metal infrastructure of the bridge. "This is just as you found it?"

Sergeant Watson nodded. "Yes," she said. "Except, you know, for the personal effects we've already given you. The medals and like that. We were afraid somebody would take them, if we left them there."

There wasn't much. A sleeping bag, left unzipped, gaping open. The charred remains of a fire. A U.S. Army backpack.

Margaret knelt and poked through the backpack. A few flannel shirts, socks, underwear, an extra pair of jeans. The e-reader she'd given him last Christmas, carefully protected in a plastic bag. She flicked it on, scanning through the bookshelves. They held the books she'd pre-loaded it with, nothing more. Before his four deployments, he'd been an avid reader. These days, he had trouble concentrating long enough to read a book.

On the ground next to his sleeping bag lay some shreds of dried vegetation. It looked like seaweed.

Margaret slid the straps of the backpack over her shoulders and returned to the riverbank. "But you didn't find a body?"

"Sometimes it takes months for a body to surface, especially this time of year," Watson said. "Sometimes they never do."

Margaret walked along the rocky beach. "Why would he come

here?" she muttered, kicking driftwood out of the way, shivering in the November wind.

"Does he have friends in Cleveland?" Watson asked. "Has he ever been here before?"

Margaret shook her head. "Not that I know of. But, I guess it's possible. I haven't seen much of him since his discharge from the service." Looking down the shoreline to the west, she saw a small flotilla of boats bobbing just inside the breakwall. And more people on the wall itself.

"What's going on over there?" she said.

Watson rolled her eyes. "This giant fish got caught in the passage there. The biggest lake sturgeon anyone has ever seen. So there's a lot of talk about sea monsters and like that. *Weekly World News* has been and gone. If you ask me, it's a big stinky mess. I'm just glad they didn't give me the cleanup job."

Just then, Margaret noticed something caught in the rocks by her feet. Reaching down, she pulled it free.

It was a necklace made of fresh water mussel shells. Bits of rotting flowers fell away as she lifted it.

"What did you find?"

"Looks like somebody dropped a necklace," Margaret said. She sighed, and blotted away tears with the backs of her hand. "I appreciate your bringing me down here and all," she said. "It just helps to see where my father died."

"I'm glad to do it, ma'am. See, I was in the military myself." She paused. "They said he won the Silver Star."

"Yes. He did," Margaret said, her voice low and bitter. "And the Distinguished Service Cross."

"That's something."

"Yes," Margaret said. "That's something. Being a soldier was everything to him."

Pulling out the bag of effects they'd given her at the station house, she surfaced the velvet case that contained her father's medals. Lifting the Distinguished Service Cross from its nest, she weighed it on her palm.

"Ma'am?" Watson put her hand on Margaret's arm. "What are you doing?"

"I'm going to give it back to him," Margaret said. Cocking back her arm, she threw it. It flew in a high arc over the lake, glittering like a meteor in the sun until it disappeared into the waves.

⸻

Visit **Cinda Williams Chima** online at cindachima.com; follow her on Facebook (www.facebook.com/CindaWilliamsChima) or on Twitter @cindachima. She also blogs intermittently at cindachima. blogspot.com.

For more information on folkloric monsters, including those specific to the Lake Erie/Great Lakes region, Chima suggests:

The Storm Hag of Lake Erie:
- americanfolklore.net/folklore/2010/07/the_storm_hag.html
- www.examiner.com/article/the-lake-erie-storm-hag-demonic-siren-of-the-great-lakes

The Wraith of the Creek:
- americanfolklore.net/folklore/2011/08/wraith_in_the_creek.html

The Nain Rouge (Red Dwarf of Detroit):
- www.unknown-creatures.com/nain-rouge.html

The Black Dog of Lake Erie:
- thecabinet.com/darkdestinations/location.php?sub_id=dark_destinations&location_id=lake_erie

⸻

My favorite fairy tales are the terrifying ones. I first read *Grimms' Fairy Tales* at the age of five; no adult seemed to realize how many nightmares were in that book. I loved "Bluebeard" more than anything else, particularly the moment when Bluebeard's bride drops the key in the blood. Such a simple accident, yet with great repercussions.

I based my story, in part, on the Russian fairy tale "Sivka Burka." (You can find a version here: www.artrusse.ca/fairytales/sivka-burka. htm.) This is the premise: The father became ill, and he ordered his sons: "When I am dead, bring me bread to my grave three nights in succession." Horrifying! I tried to imagine what sort of a man would demand such a thing, and what sort of bread would be best for a dead man.

Kaaron Warren

Born and Bread

Kaaron Warren

There was once a baby born so ugly her father packed his bags in fury when he saw her.

"Who did you lie with, the baker or his dough?" he called over his shoulder as he left. Already he was planning to surprise his girlfriend who always smiled when she saw him and asked for nothing.

"Only you!" the mother called back. She held her baby in a soft brown blanket, though she had to lean against the wall for support.

The baby was as heavy as a calf and the size of the award-winning pumpkin at the fair five years earlier, a pumpkin that had never been matched before or since. Yet the baby had slid out sweetly, like dough through a piping bag.

And yes, she was pale, pasty, and fleshy.

"Don't leave her in the sun," Mrs. Crouch, the cruelest woman in the village said. "Or you'll have a loaf of bread for a daughter." (In her defense, her husband spat brown juice wherever he stood, beat her with a stick when he felt so inclined, terrified the children with ghost tales, and never, ever spent a dollar when a cent would do.)

Still, the mother loved the daughter very much, especially once she learned how to laugh. Chuckles bubbled out of her like the froth in fermenting yeast, and anybody close by couldn't help but join in. She was so gentle and sweet they called her Doe, and that suited the way she had grown to look as well, like risen dough waiting to be baked into bread or sweet rolls.

Children loved to make her laugh, because her whole body quivered with it and it was beautiful to watch.

Each night she and her mother would sit together and tell stories and jokes. Sometimes her father would visit. (Always at dinner time. Her mother was the most marvelous cook. Her pastry was like flakes of pure heaven.) And he would tell them stories of his journeys. His girlfriend was long-since departed, and he now traveled the world selling and buying clever items for the kitchen. He bought Doe's mother a gadget for lemons and one for eggs, he bought spices and seasonings that made the whole house smell delicious.

Neither of them hated him for his early desertion; he was, for the most part, a good man and they loved his stories and gifts.

Each night Doe's mother would stroke, mold, press, and kneed her flesh, stretch and smooth it. Sometimes this hurt, but it also always felt good.

By the time Doe was eighteen, she had transformed into a beautiful, lithe young woman with a sense of humor, an infectious laugh and a vast storehouse of stories.

In short, she became marriageable.

She had no interest in such a thing, though. She knew she could not have children because those parts of her were not fully formed, and she saw no other reason to tie herself to one man.

Like her father, she enjoyed journeys, explorations, and with her mother's blessings and warnings, her father's financial help, she set out for adventure.

She spent ten years exploring the world, tasting, seeing, learning, becoming, loving. She ate damper, dinkelbrot, pain de mie, bagels, sangak, roti, and pandesal. She learned how to cook each loaf, loved to watch it brown, hug it to her chest warm from the oven. And like each loaf, each lover felt different, because she could mold herself around them. Encase them. More than once a man wept after their lovemaking.

"Nothing. Ever. So beautiful." The words in gasps.

Each encounter left her dented and stretched. She could massage herself back into shape, but she missed her mother's gentle touch and the stories they shared.

One day, her mother contacted her. "Your father is buying me a wonderful gift. A bakery! I will make cakes people will want to keep forever and others they will eat while still standing at the shop counter and order another."

"Will you bake bread?" Doe asked

"If you come back, you can be the bread baker. My dear little Doe."

But Doe had changed. She felt as if all she'd eaten, smelt, and seen so much; all the men she'd loved, all the women she'd spoken with, all the stories and jokes she'd shared: all of this had altered her. Would her mother still love her?

Her mother sighed as they embraced, but there was no judgment, no disappointment. "I've missed you!" she said, and her fingers pressed and stroked until Doe felt ordinary again.

And she set to work baking the most wonderful breads for her mother's bakery.

All this is to explain how it came to be that Doe helped to fulfill the awful Mr. Crouch's dying wishes and thus lay his cruel ghost to rest.

As he lay on his deathbed he said to Mrs. Crouch, "You have been a bad wife. Only this many times have we had relations." There is some dissention as to how many fingers he held up. "You owe me three more. After my death, you will lie with me three nights, or this village will suffer the consequences."

He lay back, then, and demanded bread. He loved Doe's tiger bread and chose that as his last meal.

Doe walked into his sick room. Even though she'd been warned, the stench was overwhelming. She knew the odor of yeast left to ferment too long, but that was nothing compared to this. She'd smelt dead animals in the roof drains and the worst toilets any nightmare could dredge up. She'd smelt a man who hadn't bathed for twenty years.

Nothing came close to the stench of this room.

She pinched her nose and squeezed to close her nostrils.

"Here she is, the beautiful baker," Mr. Crouch said. "Come and knead me, darling. I am ready for you," and he weakly tugged away the covers to reveal his naked body."

She placed the tray of bread beside him and left the room.

It is said he choked on a crust; that was not Doe's doing.

They buried him three nights later. Fearful of his curse, the women of the town went to Mrs. Crouch, to help prepare her to go to his grave.

She said, "He was repulsive alive. I cannot lie with him dead. And you know he was a cruel man; he means to damage me. Destroy me."

She refused to go that first night. The next day ten fields were found withered.

She refused to go that second night and the next day the clinic for the unwell was burnt down. Many would have been lost were it not for the early-rising Doe and her mother, who sounded the alarm.

The villagers went to Mrs. Crouch to beg her to lie with her dead husband. "He will take the children next. You know he will," they said.

She refused. "He means to destroy me. Mar me for life, haunt me into eternity, kill me."

They turned from her, distraught but not surprised. She was selfish and cruel and didn't care about the rest of them.

"I am driven by bad fortune! All my life!" she called after them, as if that made a difference.

Doe had led a blessed life, really. Full of good fortune and windfalls.

She went to Mrs. Crouch, who sneered at her as she always did.

"My deepest sympathies," Doe said, and she held Mrs. Crouch close, squeezing until the woman made an imprint in Doe's soft body.

In the bakery, she mixed dough, let it rise, punched it down, shaped it, let it rise again.

She baked this bread hard and brown. She baked Mrs. Crouch with her eyes closed.

As the moon rose high, she carried the bread lady to the cemetery. It was light, as good bread should be.

She laid it on Mr. Crouch's grave. "Darling," she called out. "Darling, I'm here."

Then she tripped away to hide.

At first, there was stillness, a terrible quiet that made her doubt her ears. Then a disturbance in the dirt, a writhing, then four nubs appeared, then eight, like pink growing tendrils of an unpleasant plant.

He rose up naked and fully erect.

He fell upon his bread lady, roaring, biting, thrusting, filled with lust and fury. Doe looked away and she thought, *I will tell her I understand. What woman could lie with this man and ever feel clean again?*

He fell upon his dough-wife, the Lady Bread, and his sweat, his juice, the dampness of the air, helped to dissolve the bread into a pale mush. He did not seem to care. He stood up, shook himself like a dog, then nodded and sank into his grave.

All at once, sound returned; the rustling leaves, the howling dogs, and Doe felt that she could leave.

In the morning, the only tragedy found was Mrs. Crouch, strangled with her own hands clenched around her neck, her eyes wide, tears dried in a map across both cheeks.

There was reward to be had though.

On clearing the Crouch's house, their secret fortune was found, and this was shared amongst them all. Not only that, but for a dozen years to come the crops grew tall and golden and brought good fortune to them all.

As for Doe . . . as her mother aged, they looked for a baker to take her place. One day he came to them, and Doe felt soft on the inside as she had never felt before.

His hands were warm and she could feel her flesh shift at his touch. He could mold dough like an artist and needed only four hours sleep a night.

All the village was happy for their Doe.

And that is all to explain why, each year on December the twenty-first, the villagers all buy the perfect Lady Bread, thus bringing good luck upon themselves and upon the village and all who pass through her.

＊＊＊

Shirley Jackson Award-winning author **Kaaron Warren** has lived in Melbourne, Sydney, Canberra, and Fiji, She's sold many short stories, three novels (the multi-award-winning *Slights*, *Walking the Tree*, and *Mistification*) and four short story collections. Two of her collections have won the ACT Publishers' and Writers' Award for fiction, and her most recent collection, *Through Splintered Walls*, won a Canberra Critic's Circle Award for Fiction, two Ditmar Awards, two Australian Shadows Awards, an Aurealis Award, and a Shirley Jackson Award. Her stories have appeared in Australia, the U.S., the UK, and elsewhere in Europe, and have been selected for both Ellen Datlow's and Paula Guran's "year's best" anthologies.

You can find her at kaaronwarren.wordpress.com and she tweets @KaaronWarren.

＊＊＊

The story "Tales That Fairies Tell" seemed like a natural for me. The invitation to contribute to this anthology came as I was working on a collection of modern, feminist-centered fairy tales—*The Queen, the Cambion and Seven Others*: eight fairy tales generously illustrated with art by Arthur Rackham and Gustave Doré. Recently published by Aqueduct Press, it also includes my essay, "A Secret History of Small Books," tracing the path of literary fairy tales back to the late seventeenth century and Charles Perrault's *Histoires ou contes du temps passé*, in which Puss—featured in this story—makes a memorable first appearance.

Richard Bowes

Tales That Fairies Tell

Richard Bowes

1.

"In the old world years ago," said the Cat, "monarchs were plentiful, Mortals and Fairies co-mingled, dragons flew and animals spoke; witches, ogres, dragons, a host of magic creatures roamed the countryside, and a cat could stare at a king."

The Cat spoke to Julian in the midst of a mad collage of a dream. He'd had a few of these recently and would wake up trying to grab some of the details. This one began in his stepmother's loveless suburban kitchen in New Hope. But instead of his father and stepmother with their respective despair and hostility he saw the figure everyone in New York (the Big Arena as it was called) desired or at least wanted to be seen with at that moment.

The artist/couturier Clemenso sat naked and looked right past Julian as everybody did. Clemenso's Crisis Fashion Show was also in the dream. Models covered head to toe in bullet-resistant fabrics filed past his fridge.

There was more. But during it all, only the Cat—better known as Puss—spoke. He sat on the lap of the infamous and beautiful Veronessa who, in turn, sat under a basketball net suspended from a gold hoop at the gym-themed Park Avenue High and delivered his little speech.

Always after these dreams Julian would awake wanting to grab and preserve details and always they evaporated at his touch.

This time they stuck, even made a certain sense when Julian awoke in the dark. Not many hours before he had seen Puss and Veronessa in just that pose and place. Veronessa was tall, with a cloud of pale red hair. Her blog, *Tales That Fairies Tell* (*TTFT*), was the hottest tip and scandal site in the Big Arena. It featured a running commentary on Fairy Godmothers, who had them and who didn't.

Everyone said Puss was her pet. A few hinted it was the opposite way around. But none disputed that she wore clothes better than anyone else in the Arena and could command a spotlight. Her costume that evening at Park Avenue combined a lightweight bomb fragment-resistant jacket—its blue matched her eyes—and gray/black city camouflage slacks.

Julian wore a class of 1958 U.S. High School gym uniform, the prescribed outfit for waiters at Park Avenue High—1958 had been last autumn's discovery and was tired. It was easy to know what was passé but those said to have zeitgeist antenna, who could sense the next new thing, were treated as sacred prophets.

Julian was waiting on one said to possess that skill. Jack Reynard, an impresario also known as "the Fox," was there with a party. About Reynard someone had said, "Cold whimsy is his style: he works with a chuckle and a blade between the ribs." His current project—Macabre Dance, ballets about the famous deaths and mutilations of dancers—had the aura of a sure thing.

Julian saw no way he could be part of that scene. He was not graceful and members of Reynard's party seemed amused by even the sight of his bare knees. So his attention was fixed on Puss.

Julian had heard stories of Veronessa bringing the Cat right into places that didn't admit pets because she was Veronessa and he was extraordinary. So the first sighting of what seemed a plain black and gray tabby was a disappointment. Puss looked as if he owned the place. But what cat doesn't?

In the dream Puss was much larger and stared right at Julian. In real life he hadn't deigned to do that. Nor had he spoken.

Julian opened his eyes and immediately looked at his palm

(as everyone did on waking) to see if there were messages in his implanted feed. There were none. Julian gazed around the two-room studio on the twenty-fourth floor of a Chelsea high/low (high floor/low rent) with uncertain heat, hot water, air conditioning, and elevator service. He shared the place with a waitress/composer, a pedicab driver/dancer, and a tour guide/filmmaker. All four had come from various bankrupted suburban towns or small wrecked cities hoping to snatch a crown out of the gutter.

Lack of success and poverty had not united them. None of his roommates were close enough to Julian that he could wake any of them up and tell them his dream.

Then, suddenly, the Cat was back, ears twitching. Julian realized that what he was seeing wasn't a dream but a kind of vision that was being sent to him somehow. Puss said, "My tale was born around fires in caves, given form before the hearth and came of age in palaces without an unscented breath of air. It has entertained sophisticated adults and small children for centuries."

The tabby's tail switched back and forth. "In the past I've swallowed monsters whole to help certain mortals whom I loved. Who knows what wonders are yet to unfold?"

The pedicab driver snored in the background as Julian watched Puss who regarded him through slitted eyes. "Whatever shall I do with this one?" he asked.

Veronessa was no larger than the Cat who sat beside her. "He's nothing special," she replied, propped on a pile of gosling down pillows and seemingly amused. "Okay-looking but not compelling. He isn't someone who'd succeed without a lot of help. The simplest way would be what you do most easily: a quick pounce, a bit of play, and done."

The Cat ignored her. "It's easy to get attached to the memory of one's first pet. Mine was a wonderful young oaf without an idea or plan. His imagining he was my owner was what charmed me most. I get sentimental about those who remind me of him."

Veronessa shrugged. Puss stretched and bared his claws. "Cardinal Richelieu had a litter of kittens in a basket in his study at all times.

He found their antics amusing, and a distraction from the bloody murder of running France. When the kittens grew up he gave them as presents to favorites who cherished them."

"As a pet," she said, "everyone will say that this one seems an odd and boring choice."

"They said that about me when we first went out in public," he replied. "And will say the same about you when they know me a little better."

2.

Next morning, Julian woke up late and alone. His roommates were all at work. As he showered and shaved he remembered the Cat and Veronessa clearly. He wondered if he was crazy and if the insanity could be used artistically.

He left the apartment, descended in an unreliable elevator. As New York approached the mid-twenty-first century, artists were abundant and some were even talented. Though much of the city's wealth was lost, most of its towers remained and the classier neighborhoods still blazed with nighttime light. In those enclaves the beautiful and desperate mingled with the famous and wealthy.

The city was, as always, restless, hard to please, and easy to bore. Painters, chefs, comedians, dancers, actors, and even writers were each worshipped in their turn and then abandoned.

Julian hurried to work hoping he could get a coffee and roll out of the kitchen before his afternoon shift. Instead, when he came in the door, the maître d' immediately sent him to the manager's office.

The manager, a brute of a woman, said, "Don't bother changing into uniform." When he asked why, she answered, "Customer complaint from last night. You ignored a request so he had to ask twice. That's once too often and one complaint to many."

"I don't remember there being another one," he said.

She replied, "Precisely." He started to argue, but the large blank-faced man who escorted unimportant guests out the door when they misbehaved did the same for Julian.

He walked home in a dull panic. Thinking about the night before, he could imagine only one incident that could have produced a complaint. Jack Reynard had snapped his fingers to get Julian's attention away from Veronessa and Puss. The Fox had been irritated. He had gestured across the gym floor where a three-on-three basketball game was taking place. These were regular, staged events: shirts vs. skins. This time two of the skins were female one was male.

"One of my guests prefers the skins be all boys," said Reynard.

It took Julian a few long moments to realize this was a command not an idle wish. Only then did he bow and go to find the maitre d' with the Fox's orders.

It had cost him his job. He was broke and alone.

Julian had been on the lookout for the next cutting-edge phenomenon since coming to the city. BIG, at the moment, was Crisis Fashion with its respirators built into collars and tops so silken it was impossible to believe they stopped bullets. But its hold was shaky.

Julian was an artist, but he had discovered he was no designer; he lacked both the instinct needed to tell him how far to go and the nerve to go an inch or two farther. Nor could he model clothes to any effect. "Buyers don't really see you and they certainly don't see what you're wearing," a very thin and bald agent once told him.

No Exit Comedy had been THE thing before Crisis Fashion. It took place in cellars with locked, guarded doors and standup comics with faces like vultures. Patrons, once they found they were not the evening's entertainment, would laugh with glee and join the comics in lashing out at the ones fated to be the victims of savage ridicule.

Julian had tried to find a place there. But as a comic he wasn't vicious enough to excite the crowd. And planted among the audience as a victim, he wasn't strange or vulnerable enough to bring out the crowd's bloodlust.

"If there's something you won't do for a laugh," a four-hundred pound comedienne told him, "you got nothing to live for in this business."

There were many things Julian would not do for a laugh. He decided to stick to his art.

The apartment was empty when he returned, which was the only good thing that had happened all day. Julian lay on his futon, put his hands over his eyes, and tried not to cry. He was a failure. His father and stepmother lived in a tiny apartment since they'd lost their house and wouldn't be happy to see him. But there was nowhere and no one else for him to go back to.

At various times during the year he had shared this apartment, Julian had brief, separate affairs with both the waitress/composer and the pedicab driver/dancer. But the waitress didn't really go for guys and the driver wasn't all that gay. It turned out the tour guide/filmmaker could happily accommodate both of them. They formed an ensemble and tended to ignore Julian.

He was twenty-three with no present and no future. He wasn't asleep, so it was in another of the daydream/visions that he saw a young guy about his age wearing knee pants and a wide, battered hat. He looked dumb and a bit confused. From a dimly remembered art history class, Julian guessed the historical period as maybe seventeenth century.

Then a voice right with him in the apartment said, "The young man who imagined himself to be my owner." Julian focused his eyes and saw Puss before him, standing on his hind legs. The Cat wore—with considerable panache—ornate leather boots that came up to his hips, a sheathed sword, and a wide-brimmed cavalier hat with a white ostrich feather. Julian thought of the Three Musketeers. The Cat was now the height of a man.

Julian didn't even ask how the Cat had gotten into the apartment. He was pretty sure that he'd gone crazy in a kind of baroque-circa-1700 manner.

"You will not mind my coming in uninvited when I've done for you what I intend. You are an artist, yes?" asked the Cat, "you have drawings, photos, examples of your work?"

Julian shrugged. He indicated the black portfolio case leaning on the wall next to the futon. Since he was crazed and doomed anyway, it was easiest to go along with his hallucinations.

"In your utter despair lies your complete acceptance of fate," Puss murmured as he opened the case. "And in that acceptance you will find your triumph." Julian watched impassively as the cat pulled out several sketches, some color collages: student work. He also found a headshot or two of the artist.

"These will do and will do nicely," he announced and tucked them into a boot.

"Stupid, useless stuff," Julian looked away.

"Simple! Naïve!! Elegant in their lack of artifice!!!"

Puss strode to the door, turned and bowed. "All this I do in your service, monsieur."

Julian heard the door click shut, sank back onto the futon, and fell into the vision-dream again. Except this time he saw it through his own eyes, felt it with his own skin.

He swam naked in a pond. The trees, the light looked like something out of a Watteau or Fragonard painting of a formal garden. It reminded him of nightmares he'd had as a kid of showing up at school bare-assed.

A carriage pulled up and liveried servants rushed forward, pulled him out of the water and dressed him in finery. Puss was in the dream too, cat-sized but wearing the hat and boots and looking very pleased. Julian remembered the story of the miller's son and his magical cat he'd read in his childhood.

3.

Few people on earth, and no one in New York, knew more about the Politics of Lunch than Angelica Siddons. Some said she attended as many as four luncheons in a single day. That was just spiteful rumor. But it was she who decreed where each day's significant lunch would be held and who would partake. A recent venue had been a pizza parlor in the Coney Island Safe Zone that had somehow stayed above water for a hundred years. "A darling little relic," as a commentator noted.

Anywhere else on Earth, Angelica Siddons would have been a woman of considerable wealth and some influence. In the Big Apple/

Arena she was a goddess and, like any goddess, she could bestow riches or ruin.

Daughter of billionaires, widow of the last really effective president of the United States, everyone felt safe in her presence. The bomb detection trucks and cars with armed guards outside whatever building she was in, the large people always alert and close at hand insured her protection and that of those around her.

The elite and the cameras had followed her to partly submerged Coney Island, not once or twice, but on half a dozen occasions. By the time the mobs caught on and followed, Angelica and entourage no longer found the locale exotic. Unpleasant incidents between visitors and natives followed. Suicide bombers took out the pizza parlor. When it was over Coney Island no longer had a safe zone.

By then Angelica Siddons had found other places to lunch. The most prominent was the radical new Artomat, a combination of automat and art gallery in Midtown on the West Side. The cuisine was Western Mediterranean and quite nice in its way.

But the cutting edge of the place was the rows and columns of glass windows on the walls. Each displayed an art object—a gold Scythian bracelet, an original Edward Hopper sketch, an exquisite illustrated eighteenth-century book of fairy tales.

The price of each item was displayed. One pressed an encoded palm against the window; money was deducted from one's account. The window popped open and the object was yours.

Across from Angelica Siddons that day at the Artomat, sat longtime acquaintance Jack Reynard with his sharp eyes and pointed face. Beside her was Clemenso, New York's current exemplar of the artist/sex object and acclaimed originator of Crisis Fashion.

Around the table, several members of Siddons' circle chattered on about a fan one of them had just found behind a glass window and bought, hoping to impress Angelica, at a rather healthy price. Open, the fan displayed an eighteenth century formal garden at dusk and a pair of lovers in court dress kissing. Closed, the fan was a sharp dagger.

It was something the Fox would love, and Reynard did seem amused. But Clemenso openly sneered at the purchase. Usually Angelica found his dark and sullen moods amusing as it would then please her to reassure him of his genius. But earlier that day she'd glanced briefly at Tales the Fairies Tell and found hints of things unamusing and even tiresome about Clemenso.

His exotic accent made little sense if it was true he came from New Jersey, and he'd be no genius if the source of his inspiration—in fact, the inventor of Crisis Fashion—was an unattractive boyfriend he kept carefully hidden (the article hinted at semi-imprisonment). Reynard the Fox noticed Angelica's shift in attitude even if Clemenso didn't.

At that moment neither gossip nor the conversation around her held Angelica's attention. She had just become aware of a certain Cat.

Puss walked toward her on his hind legs, more intense and fascinating than the photos on Tales That Fairies Tell, in his red leather boots and cavalier hat with a great white feather.

All conversation stopped. The bodyguards stepped forward. But the Cat halted, swept off his hat and bowed so low to Angelina Simmons that his head touched his extended leg.

Enchanted, she gestured him forward. Approaching, still bowing, Puss handed her a small sketch of a young woman under a tree with a cat beside her. "A gift from my master, the new artist Julian who goes by his own name." A quick feline glance at Clemenso, who didn't. "This reminds him of you and he wishes you to have it, my lady."

"Why, it's so . . . " she glanced briefly at the sketch, then looked at the cat, grasped for the word.

"So honestly simple," Puss suggested. "That is the way Julian describes his art. Perhaps 'simplicity' is something we should all embrace."

Mrs. Siddons looked again at the sketch and asked, "Is the cat you?"

"Perhaps," he replied, "and perhaps the young lady is you."

A groan erupted from Clemenso. "This is rubbish," he said in the unplaceable accent.

Puss caught Angelica Siddons' expression and both smiled.

She had always known in some corner of her mind that Clemenso was a fraud. But she'd always assumed he was a more fascinating fraud.

"This is student work, visual scribbles," Clemenso said. Puss shook his head and Mrs. Siddons did the same. Outright plagiarism and the financial misdeeds hinted at in *TTFT* article went without saying at that moment in this place. But failure to understand that one's time was over was simply unforgiveable.

Jack Reynard had disappeared from the table without any human noticing before Angelica invited Puss to sit beside her.

4.

Julian tried not to worry about hallucinations and nervous breakdown or to panic about what he was going to do next. He'd avoided looking at his phone. But when he opened his palm and saw the number of messages, Julian sat up.

Many were from names he didn't know. One of the first was the tour guide/filmmaker who hardly spoke to him in person.

"IS THIS YOU?" it began. Pasted in was a quote from a recent *Tales That Fairies Tell* update. "Simplicity is today's meme. And Julian is the name." With it was the drawing of the girl and the cat.

Other messages followed. One stood out: From Jack Reynard at Fox Productions. "Your name came up at lunch with Angelica Siddons," it read. "Here's a number if you're not too busy."

The Fox, producer of Macabre Dance, on his phone! Julian's head spun. How wrong he must have been about Reynard getting him fired! He called and by chance Jack Reynard turned out to be in the vicinity. "Be by shortly. I assume you have your portfolio."

As if drawn by scent or psychic power, Julian's roommates, the waitress/composer, the pedicab driver/dancer, even the tour guide/filmmaker had found his or her way back to the apartment. They showed him online updates.

The Fairy Godmothers sidebar in *TTFT* indicated The artist

called Julian, lucky boy, may just have acquired the wondrous Mrs. Siddons as Godmother and our own Puss as a Fairy Godfather!

As Julian tried to absorb all this, a buzzer sounded; a knock came at the door and the Fox entered, smiling and red haired. The light was on in the tour guide's camera as she filmed the arrival. The pedicab driver and the waitress hurried to give him their seats, offered to take his coat. The tall woman, coiled like a whip, who came in with him, stood at the door and watched everyone.

Only the whimsy was on display that afternoon. The blade was hidden. Jack Reynard chuckled, "Reminds me of my very first apartment in the city." He refused refreshments, only had time to glance at the images and portfolio.

He appraised, nodded, murmured, "Ah, I see what the Cat saw." Julian suddenly remembered Puss. As if he understood that, Jack Reynard smiled and said, "I ran into him a couple of hours ago. Puss and I are old companions . . . old partners."

He spread his palm, lifted it, and an image flashed on the wall. The waitress and the pedicab driver pulled the blinds down. Julian saw an eighteenth century park, avenues of graceful trees, summer light, figures in embroidered silk, and women seated on green grass in the background. It looked like a Watteau landscape, but it was a photograph.

In the foreground were two figures with elaborate wigs, clothes, and festive masks. At first glance they were human. But Puss and Reynard, Cat and Fox, were visible behind the masks if one looked closer. The glance they shared was predatory, like two pirates preparing to make everything they saw theirs.

Reynard had chosen a selection of Julian's work.

"Don't worry. He'll expect me to take over as your agent/advisor." The Fox made a sign, indicated Julian's phone. A contract was on the screen. "A simple agreement. Believe me, the Cat will understand." His smile was infectious.

Julian had never signed a contract before. In a daze he okayed it. The figure at the door said a single word and not in English. Suddenly

Reynard was out of the room and in the hall. The roommates asked if they could send their resumes. But, apparently, he didn't hear.

5.

For a few minutes afterwards his roommates barraged Julian with questions. "What are your plans for tonight, for tomorrow, for your life? Are you getting a personal assistant, talking to the media, doing a show? Is it possible you'll need to hire a private pedicab, a tour guide, companion? Couldn't his art tie in with music, dance, film?"

As they talked, Julian became aware of another presence. He closed his eyes and saw a huge figure that smelled of rotted meat. An ogre in clothes of fine velvet, stained with food and drink, sporting an elaborate beard and immense hairy eyebrows, stared down at him.

"When I consume a cow I have a gentle, calm disposition," it said. "When I dine on a child, I become innocent. When I eat a king (preferably simmered in a robust wine sauce from a traditional family recipe), I am majestic. You look at me and you don't believe it. Well think again, my friend! When I devour you I will be a witless young man." Julian began to scramble to his feet.

But the ogre turned into Puss. When Julian opened his eyes, it was just Puss and him in the apartment. The Cat had bribed the roommates to go away.

"One great difference between ogres and cats is that cats never talk about themselves," Puss said. "But others talk about us. You must know the story of how I dealt with the ogre.

Julian saw through cat eyes Puss challenging the monster to turn into a lion, an elephant, and finally a mouse; watched the cat kill and eat the mouse.

"Just as the ogre changed with what he ate, when I devoured him, I inherited his ability to change shapes and came into my dominion."

Right in front of Julian the cat turned first into a hawk, then a bear, and again into a fat, hairy ogre. Julian was terrified. He thought of the contract he'd signed with Reynard.

"Never fear me." Puss was once again a smiling cat. "You've met my old . . . acquaintance."

"He said . . . "

" . . . many things." The cat shook his head, "Young men are so foolish." But he seemed charmed by that fact.

The apartment door opened. "Movers," said Puss. "Ones you can trust. Show them what has to be taken from here. I'm placing you in more suitable quarters." The movers set to work and Puss disappeared.

Later that evening, Veronessa and Julian sat in the back seat of a car carrying them through Central Park to her townhouse in the East 70s. He stared, fascinated and shocked, at her vivid, barbaric vest of red fox fur.

She noticed this and gave a nod and a smile. "Jack Reynard will not be back. At least not in this incarnation," she said, patting the fur.

Julian wondered if having your dreams and ambitions realized always left you as tense and confused as he felt. "I hope my staying at your place is okay . . . with you . . . " he began.

She smiled, reached over and stroked the back of his neck like a pet. His nerves were so relaxed at her touch that it felt like he was sinking into the cushions. "Richelieu's' kittens," she said, "were treasured by those to whom the Cardinal gave them."

"If they knew what was good for them," Julian remarked and was surprised at himself.

"Ah," Veronessa said with a small frown. "It is not wise to be wise so soon."

Puss was there when they arrived. His hat bore a red fur tail with a white tip in place of the white plume. "The Fox has the strengths of the trickster: misdirection, a quick eye, and a fast tongue. But . . . " He shrugged. "Cat and Fox: when we meet it always ends like this."

He looked at Julian. "You're still confused by what's happened. You wonder about my motives." He showed Julian the goofy young man who was Puss's first owner swimming bare assed in a pond while Puss called out that the Marquis of Carabas had been robbed of his clothes and a king and his lovely daughter stopped their carriage. Because of a cat's schemes the young man married far above his station. He came close to ruining his life a dozen times thereafter. On each occasion Puss was delighted to step in.

"His antics gave me pleasure for his lifetime. When he died (mortals are given such a short span of years) I found another."

"So my being a failure . . . " Julian began. The Cat just shook his head and smiled a cat's smile.

6.

Veronessa, in an antique 1940s dress with shoulders that were almost wings, brought Julian (wearing a very nice suit Puss had bought him) to Angelica Siddons' lunch at Airmail Express where men dressed as stewardesses in long-gone twentieth century U.S. airlines brought airplane dinners and martinis. Earlier that day, *Tales That Fairies Tell* had named Mrs. Siddons "Fairy Godmother of this Epoch."

"She certainly has been for you!" Veronessa said on the drive there. "And she's so anxious to meet you," she added.

"Why all this with fairy tales?" he asked.

"The craving for fairy tales appears when a world is changing from one of magic to one of science and vice versa."

"But you don't believe in them." They'd slept together a couple of times and it had been fun, but not magic.

"My mother was part Fey." He narrowed his eyes. She waved a hand and a butterfly appeared. It fluttered around in the back seat of the car. She opened her palm and it landed. She closed her hand and opened it and the butterfly was gone. She was amused by his silence.

Julian was working on a collage and had sent Mrs. Siddons a sketch. It was his stepmother and father standing in their kitchen, Clemenso naked in the midst of his fashion show, Jack Reynard's deserted townhouse (he had been missing for weeks) but with bricks fallen off and a fox gazing out of a broken window. It was a world poised on the edge of catastrophe. But the colors were lovely, and Mrs. Siddons was especially charmed by the fox.

7.

"How do you get inside my head?" Julian asked the Cat. They sat on a small rise in what seemed to be a late seventeenth century formal garden landscaped in the Dutch manner. The Cat was his size.

"A skill I took from Cassese, the last dragon in France," was the answer. The image of the monster appeared in Julian's mind: huge, fire breathing, wings flapping. All this he saw through the eyes of the hawk Puss had become. Cassese reached out and caught the hawk's mind with his. But by then, Puss was a bee and when Cassese grabbed that tiny brain, Puss had already become a racing dove which moved faster than the dragon could think.

It was as a bat that Puss flew into the darkness of Cassese's left ear. In the eye of the Cat, Julian saw the smoldering ruin to which Cassese was soon reduced. Puss was a tiger eating the brains.

"The last but, perhaps, not the brightest dragon in France," said Puss. Julian felt a chill. "Yes, I am a monster, but never to you." A large paw with its claws carefully retracted brushed his cheek.

A pond beautifully ringed with willows lay not far from them. An avenue of cypress trees bordered a drive that curved towards a chateau. Windows caught the afternoon sun. Birds sang.

Julian had read the story of Puss In Boots a hundred times in the last couple of months. Would Puss order him out of his clothes and into the water as he'd done with his first master? Wary but unwilling to abandon the life he'd been given, Julian wondered how many afternoons he'd have to spend amusing Puss like this.

Aware of the questions Puss smiled and yawned as a cat does.

—◆—

Richard Bowes lives in Manhattan. He has won two World Fantasy Awards, a Lambda, an International Horror Guild Award, and a Million Writers Award. Even aside from *The Queen, The Cambion and Seven Others*, 2013 is a busy year. Lethe Press has just republished his

1999 Lambda-winning novel *Minions of the Moon* (now available for the first time electronically). Lethe has also published his novel-in-stories, *Dust Devil on a Quiet Street*: tales told by an aging spec fiction writer and set in contemporary Greenwich Village. In September, Fairwood Press will publish his *If Angels Fight,* a collection of recent stories and previously uncollected award nominees and winners.

Recent and forthcoming appearances include: *The Magazine of Fantasy and Science Fiction, Icarus, Lightspeed, Podcastle,* and *The Revelator*; and the anthologies, *After, Wilde Stories 2013, Ghosts: Recent Hauntings, Handsome Devil, Hauntings, Where Thy Dark Eye Glances, Weird Detectives: Recent Investigations, Fiction River: Unnatural Worlds, Daughters of Russ 2013, The Book of Apex,* and *The Time Traveler's Almanac.*

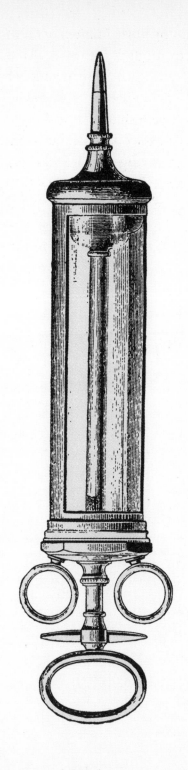

The way I understand it, fairy tales play two important roles: first, they are meant to provide us with templates of behaviors, and second, to illustrate the values of the society that produced them. When faced with a task of revamping a story to suit modern times, both templates and values had to be drastically adjusted: after all, curses are very different now, and the idea of a magical kiss seems downright reactionary. And the story of pediatric AIDS outbreak in Elista has haunted me ever since it happened—besides the heartbreak, there is nothing else I can think of that showed me that times had changed tragically, dramatically, and irrevocably. So this story is an attempt—however feeble—to extract some comfort from the terror. (I guess there's one more thing that fairy tales can do!)

Ekaterina Sedia

SLEEPING BEAUTY OF ELISTA

EKATERINA SEDIA

And this is how it begins: with a prick of a needle—a sharp point, and the children are too small to understand—infants, they just howl and squirm despite the reassuring *hush hush shhhh be quiet* of the nurse. So small that crying is just about the only thing they know how to do well. And for these children, soon enough it is the only thing—they do not sleep or eat, they only cry and fade away, they get sick and they cough, and strange white flowers bloom in their mouths and soon enough one by one by one they die. Except . . . but we will talk about her later.

It's all in a prick of the sharp point, you see; this is how curses work. Of course there is a castle there.

No, a temple. It is new, actually. Because after a curse is enacted, it will spread outward—from an injection site (vaccinations are important) and through the blood vessels and capillaries, to the translucent skin that is already covered in febrile blooms, to the very quiet ward (that just a few weeks ago was filled with weak crying), to the families standing around dressed all in black, so quiet, to the borders of the republic and all the way to the capital, to the pages of the newspaper called *Komsomolskaya Pravda*. And as people there— so far—shake their heads and whisper about the horrors of the new disease, as the newspaper is congratulating itself for its newfound freedom and bravery—because until very recently no one ever said the word "AIDS" in print, it was all some mysterious virus X—as

UNESCO and WHO get involved and outraged, the curse continues to work inside the city.

Elista never had much to brag about, apart from troubled history and the steppes surrounding it, where the grasses grew so green and then abruptly yellowed. There were no thickets to ensconce it, to hide it away from the world—it was just the yellowing of the grass and the distance, the slow falling-apart of everything inside, the hospital growing hollow and echo-filled under the curse.

It is a superstition to believe that the witch who cursed the town had meant it somehow; most curses are not manufactured out of malice or pained outrage, but rather they happen, shaped by the whims of history and coincidence, like when there are drug users dying in the hospital, dying of despair and dissolution, and when there are newborns in need of vaccinations, and when there are not enough reusable syringes because they rust and get lost and are being phased out anyway, and there are too few of the disposable ones to even talk about—things like that, the sort of things that happen in fairy tales because in real life they would be entirely too sad.

And the witch: she is in her forties and Kalmyk, the descendant of those who were once banished but returned later, slightly more frost-bitten, more cynical; the nurse wears flat shoes and has small annoying corns on the balls of her feet, and her breasts that grew heavy with age sag against her gray-buttoned coat; you would mistake her for a kindergarten teacher if you saw her in one of the dusty, sleepy streets, or walking through the parks, or craning her neck to see the face of the bronze Lenin. She looks so tired and yet placid, her dark hair misting over with gray. This is before the Buddha and before the Temple, and even before the curse—before she even knows she is a witch.

Her job is in the pediatric ward, and she loves it—she loves babies and the swirl of their hair at the very tops of their heads, black or blond, the red cheeks, dimpled fists and bent legs. She doesn't even mind when they cry. She hushes them, gently, like a mother would—with every prick of the needle their gurgling escalates to high-pitch cries which soon die, until the next one starts. She moves from crib to crib to crib, followed by the undulation of wailing. It's for their own good, she tells herself. Disposable syringes are impossible to boil, but she soaks them in alcohol between her rounds.

The floor in the hospital is blue linoleum, covered in cracks like spiderwebs, or maybe it's just the pattern. She was never interested enough to look closer. The walls are yellow subway tile, glossy and pale. There are no visitors allowed in the children's ward, lest they bring some infection with them and get all the children sick. It is only the scrubbed nurses and the doctors, and the quiet humming of the electric plate they use to boil non-disposable syringes. It is lukewarm now.

The vaccinations do not take—or take altogether too well, depending on your perspective: children develop symptoms and ulcers. At first, everyone thinks that the vaccines are defective—that instead of attenuated smallpox, scarlet fever, mumps they contain live viruses. It is the stuff of nightmares, because who wants to tell the parents? And then it gets worse. The Kalmyk nurse is fired for negligence, even though she is neither the only nurse nor the most negligent one; but such is the nature of a curse—it needs a scapegoat. Well, two: the curser and the cursed, the witch and the child, the criminal and the victim. And who is to say who gets it worse? But having one of each makes it easier to keep track: the rest of the nurses continue with their work, albeit with some extra training and the humanitarian syringes sent from overseas by the solicitous George Bush, and the rest of the children die. There is only one left by the time the scandal and the newspaper exposés fall away like dead skin; there is only one girl.

And what about the girl? Indeed, there isn't much to say about the Sleeping Beauty while she is conforming to her moniker—before or after, when she is awake, maybe. Before: she was one of the children, crying weaker, her limbs growing thinner, losing their caterpillar-like segmentation of baby fat and becoming tapered candles, waxen, melting until there was nothing but a fragile bone wick in the center, barely hidden. Her eyes grew dark as her face receded away, and her mouth filled with thrush, white fungal threads covering the red inflamed tissue underneath.

But she didn't die. Instead she slipped into a coma, and the doctors debated what to do. They decided against life support—because why extend the suffering of something too small to even understand what suffering was and there was a nobility in it—but she breathed on her own. They disconnected the glucose drip, and the thrush subsided, but the girl didn't die. She continued to breathe, sleep, and—very slowly—grow.

Her parents took her home when she was two. The hospital didn't want to keep her, and the doctors had grown uncomfortable with her failure to die despite any source of nourishment—it was as if sleep itself sustained her; and she wasn't a bad child—quiet, never fussy, never hungry. Almost pretty. She slept at home, on her older sister's cot, under the billowing of white cheesecloth curtains in the summer and heavy, silver-shot darkness in winter. They changed her clothes only as she grew out of them, because they never got soiled.

She turned sixteen in 2005, the year the Buddhist Temple was built. They don't tell you that, but she was the reason why the Dalai Lama came to Elista in the first place. The Sleeping Beauty of Elista— the only survivor out of the twenty-seven infamous pediatric AIDS patients—was a secret, but rumors travel. He came to see her when she was a mere child, but by the time the temple he had requested was finished, she had grown too long for her sister's cot. As soon as the temple was ready, her parents carried the cot with the sleeping girl on it to the hidden room, made especially for her, at the temple's center.

She sleeps in the temple from then on. Her sleep is a peculiar thing: like the curse, it spreads through the town; others do not sleep like she does, but they are stricken by a particular malaise—timelessness of sorts, the blunting of affect and feeling. It grows and it radiates through the country, where the outrage dims to smirking discontent and fear—to wary mistrust, as things continue to decay and fall into disrepair. Tractors rust. Inflation is a part of this too, I'm sure, and it is difficult not to look to the miraculous sleeping girl as some sort of salvation—and one has to wonder why didn't the Dalai Lama ever come back to see her again, or to visit the temple built for him.

They talk about practical miracles in Elista—their Buddhism tinged with the terrible shadow of Christianity and its fairy tales— they talk about how some miracles are meant as object lessons, and maybe the Sleeping Beauty is one of those. Maybe the dead children were a lesson too, maybe they were meant to remind us about proper sterilization techniques, although the price seems altogether too high for such a trivial lesson. Maybe there is something deeper in it, too. But no one can agree what the sleeping girl is meant to teach us. In fact, no one seems to agree about her either. Some say she is Kalmyk, and others insist she is Russian, the descendant of the settlers of Stepnoy—the ones for whose benefits the Kalmyk nurse's ancestors had been exiled to Siberia. There may or may not be some symbolism there, or historic justice, or whatever you want to call it. No one can ask her parents since they had passed away, and her older sister moved to some better city, possibly less decaying, leaving her cot behind. And now the Sleeping Beauty belongs to the town and the temple, floating uprooted and possibly dreaming.

The witch visits her occasionally, and it is assumed that she is there to ask for forgiveness. The more mythically minded citizens of Elista whisper when they see the nurse (the witch) walking through the park, in her flat nurse shoes, with her thick compression hose and gray coat. Her back is bent now, and people whisper about who she is. She doesn't have the advantage of the usual witch's disappearance after the curse has been cast and takes over the story; she is left to linger along with it, but with not much else to do, her historical function completed, but to crane her neck and try and discern the inanimate features of the two largest statues: the Lenin is older than the Buddha, and no less enigmatic. Neither offers her solace.

And who knows when the Sleeping Beauty will wake? (There has to be an after, so we know that she will.) There are signs now—she is stirring in her sleep and mumbling occasionally, in the soft gurgle of infants because she never learned another language. So it must be close, the citizens whisper, and disagree about what will happen then. Will she rise and walk across the land, growing gigantic, traveling from Elista to Moscow to Novosibirsk in three steps? Will she multiply herself like a true Buddha, with twin streams of water and fire shooting out of her eyes? Will she teach at the temple?

Or will the mere act of her waking shake the curse away, and the world itself, asleep since 1989, will sit up abruptly, wondering at what had become of it?

The signs are clear now, and the Sleeping Beauty's eyes are opening, and there is a terrible light behind them; the witch walks into the temple and stands, waiting, her knotted hand resting lightly on the edge of the cot, as if gently shaking the crib to wake a sleeping infant.

—　—

Ekaterina Sedia resides in the Pinelands of New Jersey. Her critically-acclaimed and award-nominated novels, *The Secret History of Moscow, The Alchemy of Stone, The House of Discarded Dreams,* and *Heart of Iron,* were published by Prime Books. Her short stories have sold to *Analog, Baen's Universe, Subterranean,* and *Clarkesworld,* as well as numerous anthologies, including *Haunted Legends* and *Magic in the Mirrorstone.* She is also the editor of the anthologies *Paper Cities* (World Fantasy Award winner), *Running with the Pack,* and *Bewere the Night,* as well as *Bloody Fabulous* and *Wilful Impropriety.* Her short-story collection, *Moscow But Dreaming,* was released in December 2012. Visit her at www.ekaterinasedia.com.

—　—

Fairy tales have informed a great deal of my fiction, both my novels and my short fiction. They're a wellspring I return to again and again, and sometimes my exploration of them is very overt—as with "The Road of Needles"—and sometimes it's only subtext. All the various incarnations of the "Little Red Riding Hood" tale, those are the ones that have most fascinated me, and so they're the ones I've gone to again and again. But I'd never done the story as science fiction, and, offhand, I couldn't recall anyone else who had, either. So, when it occurred to me, "The Road of Needles" was born.

Caitlín R. Kiernan

THE ROAD OF NEEDLES

CAITLÍN R. KIERNAN

1.

Nix Severn shuts her eyes and takes a very deep breath of the newly minted air filling Isotainer Four, and she cannot help but note the irony at work. This luxury born of mishap. Certainly, no one on earth has breathed air even half this clean in more than two millennia. The Romans, the Greeks, the ancient Chinese, they all set in motion a fouling of the skies that an Industrial Revolution and the two centuries thereafter would hone into a science of indifference. An art of neglect and denial. Not even the meticulously manufactured atmo of Mars is so pure as each mouthful of the air Nix now breathes. The nitrogen, oxygen—four fingers N_2, a thumb of 0_2—and the so on and so on traces, etcetera, all of it transforming the rise and fall of her chest into a celebration. Oh, happy day for the pulmonary epithelia bathed in this pristine blend. She shuts her eyes and tries to think. But the air has made her giddy. Not drunk, but certainly giddy. It would be easy to drift down to sleep, leaning against the bole of a *Dicksonia antarctica,* sheltered from the misting rainfall by the umbrella of the tree fern's fronds, of this tree and all the others that have sprouted and filled the isotainer in the space of less than seventeen hours. She could be a proper Rip Van Winkle, as the *Blackbird* drifts farther and farther off the lunar-Martian rail line. She could do that fabled narcoleptic one better, pop a few of the phenothiazine capsules in the left hip pouch of her red jumpsuit and never wake up again. The forest would close in around her, and she would feed it. The fungi, insects, the snails and algae, bacteria and tiny vertebrates, all of them would make a banquet of her sleep and then, soon, her death.

. . . and even all our ancient mother lost
was not enough to keep my cheeks, though washed
with dew, from darkening again with tears.
Even the thought of standing makes her tired.

No, she reminds herself—that part of her brain that isn't yet ready to surrender. *It's not the thought of getting to my feet. It's the thought of the five containers remaining between me and the bridge. The thought of the five behind me. That I've only come halfway, and there's the other halfway to go.*

Something soft, weighing hardly anything at all, lands on her cheek. Startled, she opens her eyes and brushes it away. It falls into a nearby clump of moss and gazes up with golden eyes. Its body is a harlequin motley of brilliant yellow and a blue so deep as to be almost black.

A frog.

She's seen images of frogs archived in the lattice, and in reader files, but images cannot compare to contact with one alive and breathing. It touched her cheek, and now *it's* watching *her.* If Oma were online, Nix would ask for a more specific identification.

But, of course, if Oma were online, I wouldn't be here, would I?

She wipes the rain from her eyes. The droplets are cool against her skin. On her lips, on her tongue, they're nectar. It's easy to romanticize Paradise when you've only ever known Hell and (on a good day) Purgatory. It's hard not to get sentimental; the mind, giddy from clean air, waxes. Nix blinks up at all the shades of green; she squints into the simulated sunlight shining down between the branches.

The sky flickers, dimming for a moment, then quickly returns to its full 600-watt brilliance. The back-up fuel cells are draining faster than they ought. She ticks off possible explanations: there might be a catalyst leak, dinged up cathodes or anodes, a membrane breach impairing ion-exchange. Or maybe she's just lost track of time. She checks the counter in her left retina, but maybe it's on the fritz again and can't be trusted. She rubs at her eye, because sometimes that helps. The readout remains the same. The cells have fallen to forty-eight percent maximum capacity.

I haven't lost track of time. The train's burning through the reserves too fast. It doesn't matter why.

All that matters is that she has less time to reach Oma and try to fix this fuck-up.

Nix Severn stands, but it seems to take her almost forever to do so. She leans against the rough bark of the tree fern and tries to make out the straight line of the catwalk leading to the port 'tainers and the decks beyond. Moving over and through the uneven, ever-shifting terrain of the forest is slowing her down, and soon, she knows, soon she'll be forced to abandon it for the cramped maintenance crawls suspended far overhead. She curses herself for not having used them in the first place. But better late than fucking never. They're a straight line to the main AI shaft, and wriggling her way through the empty tubes will help her focus, removing her senses from the Edenic seduction of the terraforming engines' grand wrack-up. If she can just reach the front of this compartment, there will be an access ladder, and cramped or not, the going will surely be easier. She'll quick it double time or better. Nix wipes the rain from her face again, and clambers over the roots of a strangler fig. Once on the slippery, overgrown walkway, she lowers the jumpsuit's visor and quilted silicon hood; the faceplate will efficiently evaporate both the rain and any condensation. She does her best to ignore the forest. She thinks, instead, of making dockside, waiting out quarantine until she's cleared for tumble, earthfall, and of her lover and daughter waiting for her, back in the slums at the edge of the Phoenix shipyards. She keeps walking.

2.

Skycaps launch alone.

Nix closes the antique storybook she found in a curio stall at the Firestone Night Market, and she sets it on the table next to her daughter's bed. The pages are brown and brittle, and minute bits of the paper flake away if she does not handle it with the utmost care (and sometimes when she does). Only twice in Maia's life has she heard a fairy tale read directly from the book. On the first occasion, she was two. And on the second, she was six. It's a long time between lifts and drops, and when you're a mother whose also a runner, your child seems to grow up in jittery stills from a time-lapse. Even with her monthly broadcast allotment, that's how it seems. A moment here, fifteen minutes there, a three-week shore leave, a precious to-and-fro while sailing orbit, the faces and voices trickling through in 22.29 or 3.03 light-minute packages.

"Why did she talk to the wolf?" asks Maia. "Why didn't she ignore him?"

Nix looks up to find Shiloh watching from the doorway, backlit by the glow from the hall. She smiles for the silhouette, then looks back to their daughter. The girl's hair is as fine and pale as corn silk. She's fragile, born too early and born sickly, half crippled, half blind. Maia's eyes are the milky green color of jade.

"Yeah," says Shiloh. "Why is that?"

"I imagine *this* wolf was a very charming wolf," replies Nix, brushing her fingers through the child's bangs.

Skycaps launch alone.

Sending out more than one warm body, with everything it'll need to stay alive? Why squander the budget? Not when all you need is someone on hand in case of a catastrophic, systems-wide failure.

So, skycaps launch alone.

"Well, I would never talk to a wolf. If there were still wolves," says Maia.

"Makes me feel better hearing that," says Nix. A couple of strands of Maia's hair come away in her fingers.

"If there were still wolves," Maia says again.

"Of course," Nix says. "That's a given."

Her lips move. She reads from the old, old book: "Good day, Little Red Riding Hood," said he. "Thank you kindly, wolf," answered she.

"Where are you going so early, Little Red Riding Hood?" "To my grandmother's."

Nix Severn's eyelids flutter, and her lips move. The home-away chamber whispers and hums, manipulating hippocampal and cortical theta rhythms, mining long- and short-term memory, spinning dreams into perceptions far more real than dreams or déjà vu. No outbound leaves the docks without at least one home-away to insure the mental stability of skycaps while they ride the rails.

"You should go to sleep now," Nix tells Maia, but the girl shakes her head.

"I want to hear it again."

"Kiddo, you know it by heart. You could probably recite it word for word."

"She wants to hear you read it, fella" says Shiloh. "I wouldn't mind hearing it again myself, for that matter."

Nix pretends to frown. "Hardly fair, two on one like this." But then she gently turns the pages back to the story's start and begins it over.

The home-away mediates between limbic and the cerebral hemispheres, directing neurotransmitters and receptors, electrochemical activity and cortisol levels.

There was once a sweet little maid . . .

Shiloh kisses her brow. "Still, hell, I don't know how you do it, love. All alone and relying on make-believe."

"It keeps me grounded. You learn the trick, or you washout fast."

The skycap's best friend! Even better than the real thing! Experience the dream and you might never have to come home.

The merch co-ops count on it.

"You could look for other work than babysitting EOTs," whispers Shiloh. "You've got the training. There's *good* work you could do in the yards, in assembly or rollout."

"I don't want to have this conversation again."

"But with your experience, Nixie, you could make foreman on the quick."

"And get maybe a quarter the grade, grinding day and night."

"We'd see you so much more. That's all. And it scares me more than you'll ever know, you hurtling out there alone with nothing but make-believe and plug and pray for waking company."

Make haste and start before it gets hot, and walk properly and nicely, and don't run, or you might fall.

"The accidents—"

"—the casts hype them, Shiloh. Half what you hear never happened. You know that. I've told you that, how many times now?"

"Going under and never coming up again."

"The odds of psychosis or a flatline are astronomical."

Shiloh rolls over, turning her back on Nix. Who sighs and shuts her eyes, because she has prep at six for next week's launch, and she's not going to spend the day sleepwalking because of a fight with Shiloh.

. . . and don't run, or you might fall.

The emergency alarm screams bloody goddamn murder, and an adrenaline injection jerks her back aboard the *Blackbird,* back to here and now so violently that she gasps and then screams right back at the alarms. But her eyes are trained to see, even through so sudden a disengage, and Nix is already processing the diagnostics and crisis report streaming past her face before the raggedy hitch releases her.

It's bad this time. It doesn't get much worse.

Oma isn't talking.

"Good day, Little Red Riding Hood . . . "

3.

Of course, it *isn't* true that there are no wolves left in the world. Not strictly speaking. Only that, so far as zoologists can tell, they are extinct in the wild. They were declared so more than forty years ago, all across the globe, all thirty-nine or so subspecies. But Maia has a terrible phobia of wolves, despite the fact "Little Red Riding Hood" is her favorite bedtime story. Perhaps it's her favorite *because* she's afraid of wolves. Anyway, Shiloh and I told her that there were no more wolves when she became convinced a wolf was living under her bed, and she refused to sleep without the light on. We suspect she knows, perfectly well, that we're lying. We suspect she's humoring us, playing along with our lie. She's smart, curious, and has access to every bit of information on the lattice, which includes, I'd think, everything about wolves that's ever been written down.

I have seen wolves. Living wolves.

There are a handful remaining in captivity. I saw a pair when I was younger, still in my twenties. My mother was still alive, and we visited the bio in Chicago. We spent almost an entire day inside the arboretum, strolling the meticulously manicured, tree-lined pathways. Here and there, we'd come upon an animal or two, even a couple of small herds—a few varieties of antelope, deer, and so forth— kept inside invisible enclosures by the shock chips implanted in their spines. Late in the afternoon, we came upon the wolves, at the end of a cul-de-sac located in a portion of the bio designed to replicate the aspen and conifer forests that once grew along the Yellowstone River out west. I recall that from a plaque placed somewhere on the trail. There was an owl, an eagle, rabbits, a stuffed bison, and at the very end of the cul-de-sac, the pair of wolves. Of course, they weren't purebloods, but hybrids. Both were watered-down with German shepherd genes, or husky genes, or whatever.

There was a bench there beneath the aspen and pine and spruce cultivars, and my mother and I sat a while watching the wolves. Though I know that the staff of the park was surely taking the best possible care of those precious specimens, both were somewhat thin. Not emaciated, but thin. "Ribsy," my mother said, which I thought was a strange word. One I'd never before heard. Maybe it had been popular when she was young.

"They look like ordinary dogs to me," she said.

They didn't, though. Despite the fact that these animals had never lived outside pens of one sort or another, there was about them an unmistakable wildness. I can't fully explain what I mean by that. But it was there. I recognized it most in their amber eyes. A certain feral desperation. They restlessly paced their enclosure; it was exhausting, just watching them. Watching them set my nerves on edge, though my mother hardly seemed to notice. After her remark, how the wolves seemed to her no different than regular dogs, she lost interest and winked on her Soft-See. She had an eyeball conversation with someone from her office, and I watched the wolves. And the wolves watched me.

I imagined there was hatred in their amber eyes.

I imagined that they stared out at me, instinctually comprehending the role that my race had played in the destruction of theirs.

We were here first, they said without speaking, without uttering a sound.

It wasn't only desperation in their eyes; it was anger, spite, and a promise of stillborn retribution that the wolves knew would never come.

Ten times a million years before you, we feasted on your foremothers.

And, in that moment, I was as frightened as any small and defenseless beast, cowering in shadows, as still as still can be in hope it would go unnoticed as amber eyes and hungry jaws prowled the woods.

I have wondered if my eyes replied, *I know. I know, but have mercy.*

That day, I do not believe there was any mercy in the eyes of the wolves.

You cannot even survive yourselves, said the glittering amber eyes. *Ask yourself for charity.*

And I have wondered if a mother can pass on dread to her child.

4.

Nix Severn reaches the ladder leading up to the crawlspace, only to find it engulfed in a tangle of thick vines that have begun to pull the lockbolts free of the 'tainer wall. She stands in waist-high philodendrons and bracken, glaring up at the damaged ladder. Briefly, she considers attempting the climb anyway, but is fairly sure her weight would only finish what the vines have begun, and the resulting fall could leave her with injuries severe enough that she'd be rendered incapable of reaching Oma's core in time. Or at all.

She curses and wraps her right hand around a bundle of the vines, tugging at them forcefully; the ladder groans ominously, creaks, and leans out a few more centimeters from the wall. She releases the vines and turns towards the round hatchway leading to Three and the next vegetation-clogged segment of the *Blackbird*. The status report she received when she awoke inside the home-away, what little there was of it, left no room for doubt that all the terraforming engines had switched on simultaneously and that every one of the containment sys banks had failed in a rapid cascade, rolling backwards, stem to stern. She steps over a log so rotten and encrusted with mushrooms and moss that it could have laid there for years, not hours. A few steps farther and she reaches the hatch's keypad, but her hands are shaking, and it takes three tries to get the security code right; a fourth failure would have triggered lockdown. The diaphragm whirs, clicks, and the rusty steel iris spirals open in a hiss of steam. Nix mutters a thankful, silent prayer to no god she actually believes because, so far, none of the wiring permitting access to the short connecting corridors has been affected.

Nix steps through the aperture, and the hatch promptly spirals shut behind her, which means the proximity sensors are also still functional. The corridor is free of any traces of plant or animal life, and she lingers there several seconds before taking the three, four, five more steps to the next keypad and punching in the next access code. The entrance to Isotainer Three obeys the command, and forest swallows her again.

If anything, the situation in Three is worse than that in Four. Her red gloves have to rip away an intertwining wall of creepers and narrow branches, and then she must scale the massive roots of more strangler figs before she can make any forward progress whatsoever. But soon enough she encounters yet another barrier, in the form of a small pond, maybe five meters across, stretching from one side of the hull to the other. The water is tannin stained, murky, and half obscured beneath an emerald algal scum, so there's no telling how deep it might be. The forest floor is quite a bit higher than that of the 'tainer, so the pool could be deep enough she'd have to swim. And Nix Severn never learned to swim.

She's sweating. The readout on her visor informs her that the ambient temperature has risen to 30.55°C, and she pushes back the hood. For now, there's no rain falling in Three, so there's only her own sweat to wipe from her eyes and forehead. She kneels and brushes a hand across the pond, sending ripples rolling towards the opposite shore.

Behind her, a twig snaps, and there's a woman's voice. Nix doesn't stand, or even turn to see. Between the shock of so abruptly popping from the dream-away sleep, her subsequent exertion and fear, and the effects of whatever toxic pollen and spores might be wafting through the air, she's been expecting delirium.

"The water is wide, and I can't cross over," the voice sings sweetly. "Neither have I wings to fly."

"That isn't you, is it, Oma?"

"No, dear," the voice replies, and it's not so sweet anymore; it's taken on a gruff edge. "It isn't Oma. The night presses in all about us, and your grandmother is sleeping."

There's nothing sapient aboard but me and Oma, which means I'm hallucinating.

"Good day, Little Red Riding Hood," says the voice, and never mind her racing heart, Nix has to laugh.

"Fuck you," she says, only cursing her subconscious self, and stands, wiping wet fingers on her jumpsuit.

"Where are you going so early, Little Red Riding Hood?"

"Is that really the best I could come up with?" Nix asks, turning now, because how could she not look behind her, sooner or later. She discovers that there *is* someone standing there; someone or something. Which word applies could be debated. *Or rather,* she thinks, *there is my delusion of another presence here with me. It's nothing more than that. It's nothing that can actually speak or snap a twig underfoot, excepting in my mind.*

In my terror, I have made a monster.

"I know you," Nix whispers. The figure standing between her and the hatchway back to Four has Shiloh's kindly hazel-brown eyes, and even though the similarity ends there, about the whole being there is a nagging familiarity.

"Do you?" it asks. It or she. "Yes, I believe that you do. I believe that you have known me a very, very long while. "Whither so early, Little Red Riding Hood?""

"I've never seen you."

"Haven't you? As a child, didn't you once catch me peering in your bedroom window? Didn't you glimpse me lurking in an alley? Didn't you visit me at the bio that day? Don't I live beneath your daughter's bed and in your dreams?"

And now Nix does reach into her left hip pouch for the antipsychotics there. She takes a single step backwards and her boot comes down in the warm, stagnant pool, sinking in up to the ankle. The splash seems very loud, louder than the atonal symphony of dragonflies buzzing in her ears. She wants to look away from the someone or something she only *imagines* there before her, a creature more canine than human, an abomination that might have been created in an illicit *sub rosa* recombinant-outcross lab back on earth. A commission for a wealthy collector, for a private menagerie of designer freaks. Were the creature real. Which it isn't.

Nix tries to open the Mylar med packet, but it slips through her fingers and vanishes in the underbrush. The thing licks its muzzle with a mottled blue-black tongue, and Shiloh's eyes sparkle from its face.

"Are you going across the stones or the thorns?" it asks.

"Excuse me?" Nix croaks, her throat parched, her mouth gone cottony. *Why did I answer it. Why am I speaking with it at all?*

It scowls.

"Don't play dumb, Nix."

It knows my name.

It only knows my name because I know my name.

"Which *path* are you taking? The one of needles or the one of pins?"

"I couldn't reach the crawls," she hears herself say, as though the words are reaching her ears from a great distance. "I tried, but the ladder was broken."

"Then you are on the Road of Needles," the creature replies, curling back its dark lips in a parody of a smile and revealing far too many sharp yellow teeth. "You surprise me, *Petit Chaperon rouge*. I am so rarely ever surprised."

Enough . . .

My ship is dying all around me, and that's enough, I will not fucking see this. I will not waste my time conversing with my id.

Nix Severn turns away, turning much too quickly and much too carelessly, almost falling face first into the pool. It no longer matters to her how deep the water might be or what might be lurking below the surface. She stumbles ahead, sending out sprays of the tea-colored water with every step she takes. They sparkle like gems beneath the artificial sun. The mud sucks at her feet, and soon she's in up to her chest. *But even drowning would be better,* she assures herself. *Even drowning would be better.*

5.

Nix has been at Shackleton Relay for almost a week, and it will be almost another week before a shuttle ferries her to the CTV *Blackbird,* waiting in dockside orbit. The cafeteria lights are too bright, like almost everything else in the station, but at least the food is decent. That's a popular myth among the techs and co-op officers who never actually spend time at Shackleton, that the food is all but inedible. Truthfully, it's better than most of what she got growing up. She listens while another EOT sitter talks, and she pokes at her bowl of udon, snow peas, and tofu with a pair of blue plastic chopsticks.

"I prefer straight up freight runs," Marshall Choudhury says around a mouthful of noodles. "But terras, they're not as hinky as some of the caps make them out to be. You get redundant safeguards out the anus."

"Far as I'm concerned," she replies, "cargo is cargo. Jaunts are jaunts."

Marshall sets down his own bowl, lays his chopsticks on the counter beside it.

"Right," he says. "You'll get no kinda donnybrook here. None at all. Just my pref, that's it. Less hassle hauling hardware and whatnot, less coddling the payload. More free for dream-away."

Nix shrugs and chews a pea pod, swallows, and tells him, "Fella, here on my end, the chips are chips, however I may earn them. I'm just happy to have the work."

"Speaking of which . . . " Marshall says, then trails off.

"That your concern now, Choudhury, my personal life?"

"Just one fella's consideration for a comrade's, all."

"Well, as you've asked, Shiloh is still nagging me about hooking something in the yards." She sets her bowl down and stares at the broth in the bottom. "Like she didn't know when I married her, like she didn't know before Maia, that I was EOT and had no intent or interest in ever working anything other than offworld."

"Lost a wife over it," he says, as if Nix doesn't know already. "She gave me the final notice and all, right, but fuck it. Fuck it. She doesn't know the void. Couldn't know what she was asking a runner to give up. Gets wiggled into a fella's blood, don't ever get out again."

Marshall has an ugly scar across the left side of his face, courtesy of a coolant blowout a few years back and the ensuing frostbite. Nix tries to look at him, without letting her eyes linger on the scar, but that's always a challenge. A wonder he didn't lose that eye. He would have, if his goggles had cracked.

"Don't know if that's the why with me." She says. "Can't say. Obviously, I do miss them when I'm out. Sometimes, miss 'em like hell."

"But that doesn't stop you flying, doesn't turn you to the yards."

"Sometimes, fuck, I wish it would."

"She gonna walk?" he asks.

"I try not think about that, and I especially try not to think about that just before outbound. Jesus."

Marshall picks up his bowl and chopsticks, then fishes for a morsel of tofu.

"One day not too far, the cooperatives gonna replace us with autos," he sighs, and pops the white cube into his mouth. "So, gotta judge our sacrifices against the raw inevitabilities."

"Union scare talk," Nix scoffs, though she knows he's probably right. Too many ways to save expenses by completely, finally, eliminating a human crew. *A wonder it hasn't happened before now,* she thinks.

"Maybe you ought consider cutting your losses, that's all."

"Fella, you only *just* now told me how much choice we don't have, once the life digs in and it's all we know. Make up your damn mind."

"You gonna finish that?" he asks and points at her bowl.

She shakes her head and slides it across the counter to him. Thinking about Maia and Shiloh, her appetite has evaporated.

"Anyway, point is, no need to fret on a terra run, no more than anything else."

"Never said I was fretting. It's not even my first."

"No, but that was not my point, fella," Marshall slurps at the broth left in the bottom of her white bowl, which is the same unrelenting white as the counter, their seats, the ceiling and walls, the lighting. When he's done, he wipes his mouth on a sleeve and says, "Maybe it's best EOTs stay lone. Avoid the entire mess, start to finish."

She frowns and jabs a chopstick at him. "Isn't it rough enough already without coming back from the black and lonely without anyone waiting to greet us?"

"There are other comforts," he says.

"No wonder she left you, you indifferent fuck."

Marshall massages his temples, then changes the subject. For all his faults, he's pretty good at sensing thin ice beneath his feet. "It's your first time to the Kasei though, that's true, yeah?"

"That's true, yeah."

"You can and will and no doubt already have done worse than the Kasei 'tats."

"I hear good things," she says, but her mind's elsewhere, and she's hoping Marshall grows tired of talking soon so she can get back to her quarters and pop a few pinks for six or seven hour's worth of sleep.

"Down on the north end of Cattarinetta Boulevard—in Scarlet Quad—there's a brothel. Probably the best on the whole rock. I happen to know the proprietress."

Nix isn't so much an angel she's above the consolation of whores when away from Shiloh. All those months pile up. The months between docks, the interminable Phobos reroutes, the weeks of red dust and colonist hardscrabble.

"Her name's Paddy," he continues, "and you just tell her you're a high fella to Marshall Mason Choudhury, and she'll see you're treated extra right. Not those half-starved farm girls. She'll set you up with the pinnacle merch."

"That's kind of you," and she stands. "I'll do that."

"Not a trouble," he says and waves a hand dismissively. "And look, as I said, don't you fret over the cargo. Terra's no different than aluminum and pharmaceuticals."

"It's *not* my first goddamn terra run. How many times I have to—"

But she's thinking, *Then why the extra seven-percent hazard commission, if terras are the same as all the rest?* Nix would never ask such a question aloud, anymore than she can avoid asking it of herself.

"Your Oma, she'll—"

"Fella, I'll see you later," she says, and walks quickly towards the cafeteria door before he can get another word or ten out. Sometimes, she'd lay good money that the solitudes are beginning to gnaw at the man's sanity. That sort of shit happens all too often. The glare in the corridor leading back to the housing module isn't quite as bright as the lights in the cafeteria, so at least she has that much to be grateful for.

6.

Muddy, sweat-soaked, insect-bitten and insect-stung, eyes and lungs and nostrils smarting from the hundreds of millions of gametophytes she breathed during her arduous passage through each infested isotainer, arms and legs weak, stomach rolling, breathless, Nix Severn has finally arrived at the bottom of the deep shaft leading down to Oma's dormant CPU. The bzou has kept up with her the entire, torturous way. Though she didn't realize that it was a bzou until halfway through the second 'tainer. Sentient viruses are so rare that the odds of Oma's crash having triggered the creation (or been triggered by) bzou has a probability risk approaching zero, at most a negligent threat to any transport. But here it is, and the hallucination isn't a hallucination.

An hour ago, she finally had the presence of mind to scan the thing, and it bears the distinctive signatures, the unmistakable byte sequence of a cavity-stealth strategy.

"A good quarter of an hour's walk further in the forest, under yon three large oaks. There stands her house. Further beneath are the nut trees, which you will see there," it said when the scan was done. "Red Hood! Just look! There are such pretty flowers here! Why don't you look round at them all? Methinks you don't even hear how delightfully the birds are singing! You are as dull as if you were going to school, and yet it is so cheerful in the forest!"

Oma knows Nix's psych profile, which means the bzou knows Nix's psyche.

Nix pushes back the jumpsuit's quilted hood and visor again— she'd had to lower it to help protect against a minor helium leak near the shaft's rim—and tries to concentrate and figure out precisely what has gone wrong. Oma is quiet, dark, dead. The holo is off, so she'll have to rely on her knowledge of the manual interface, the toggles and pressure pads, horizontal and vertical sliders, spinners, dials, knife switches . . . all without access to Oma's guidance. She's been trained for this, yes, but AI diagnostics and repair has never been her strong suit.

The bzou is crouched near her, Shiloh's stolen eyes tracking her every move.

"Who's there?" it asks.

"I'm not playing this game anymore," Nix mutters, and begins tripping the instruments that ought to initiate a hard reboot. "I'm done with you. Fifteen more minutes, you'll be wiped. For all I know, this was sabotage."

"Who's there, skycap?" the bzou says again.

Nix pulls down on one of the knife switches, and nothing happens.

"Push on the door," advises the bzou. "It's blocked by a pail of water."

Nix pulls the next switch, a multi-boot resort—she's being stupid, so tired and rattled that she's skipping stages—which should rouse the unresponsive Oma when almost all else fails. The core doesn't reply. Here are her worst fears beginning to play themselves out. Maybe it was a full-on panic, a crash that will require triple-caste post-mortem debugging to reverse, which means dry dock, which would mean she is utterly fucking fucked. No way in hell she can hand pilot the *Blackbird* back onto the rails, and this far off course an eject would only mean slow suffocation or hypothermia or starvation.

Nix speaks to the bzou without looking at it. She takes a tiny turnscrew from the kit strapped to her rebreather (which she hasn't needed to use, and it's been nothing but dead weight she hasn't dared abandon, just in case).

Maybe she *isn't* through playing the game, after all. She takes a deep breath, winds the driver to a 2.4 mm. mortorq bit, and keeps her eyes on the panel. She doesn't need to see the bzou to converse with it.

"All right," she says. "Let's assume you have a retract sequence, that you're a benign propagation."

"Only press the latch," it says. "I am so weak, I can't get out of bed."

"Fine. Grandmother, I've come such a very long way to visit you." Nix imagines herself reading aloud to Maia, imagines Maia's rapt attention and Shiloh in the doorway.

"Shut the door well, my little lamb. Put your basket on the table, and then take off your frock and come and lie down by me. You shall rest a little."

Shut the door. Shut the door and rest a little . . .

Partial head crash, foreign-reaction safe mode. Voluntary coma.

Nix nods and opens one of the memory trays, then pulls a yellow bus card, replacing it with a spare from the console's supply rack. Somewhere deep inside Oma's brain, there's the very faintest of hums.

"It's a code," Nix says to herself.

And if I can get the order of questions right, if I can keep the bzou from getting suspicious and rogueing up . . .

A drop of sweat drips from her brow, stinging her right eye, but she ignores it. "Now, Grandmother, now please listen."

"I'm all ears, child."

"And what big ears you have."

"All the better to hear you with."

"Right . . . of course," and Nix opens a second tray, slicing into Oma's comms, yanking two fried transmit-receive bus cards. *She hasn't been able to talk to Phobos. She's been deaf all this fucking time.* The CPU hums more loudly, and a hexagonal arrangement of startup OLEDs flash to life.

One down.

"Grandmother, what big eyes you have."

"All the better to see you with, *Rotkäppchen*."

Right. Fuck you, wolf. Fuck you and your goddamn road of stones and needles. Nix runs reset on all of Oma's optic servos and outboards. She's rewarded with the dull thud and subsequent discordant chime of a reboot.

"What big teeth I have," Nix says, and now she *does* turn towards the bzou, and as Oma wakes up, the virus begins to sketch out, fading in incremental bursts of distorts and static. "All the better to *eat* you with."

"Have I found you now, old rascal?" the virus manages between bursts of white noise. "Long have I been looking for you."

The bzou had been meant as a distress call from Oma, sent out in the last nanoseconds before the crash. "I'm sorry, Oma," Nix says, turning back to the computer. "The forest, the terra . . . I should have figured it out sooner." She leans forward and kisses the console. And when she looks back at the spot where the bzou had been crouched, there's no sign of it whatsoever, but there's Maia, holding the storybook . . .

———

The New York Times recently hailed **Caitlín R. Kiernan** as "one of our essential writers of dark fiction." Her novels include *The Red Tree* (nominated for the Shirley Jackson and World Fantasy awards) and *The Drowning Girl: A Memoir* (winner of the James Tiptree, Jr. Award and the Bram Stoker Award, nominated for the Nebula, Locus, Shirley Jackson, and Mythopoeic awards). To date, her short fiction has been collected in thirteen volumes, most recently *Confessions of a Five-Chambered Heart, Two Worlds and In Between: The Best of Caitlín R. Kiernan (Volume One),* and *The Ape's Wife and Other Stories.* Currently, she's writing the graphic novel series *Alabaster* for Dark Horse Comics and working on her next novel, *Red Delicious.*

———

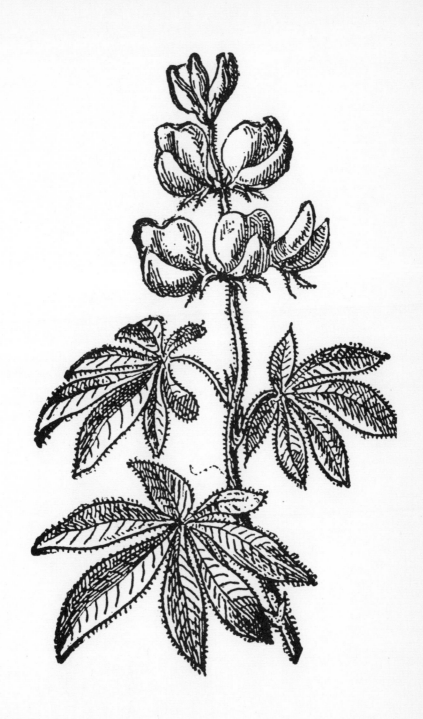

"Lupine" grew from grafts to the fairy tale rootstock most of us received as children. Here's one addition: the blue-petaled wildflower for which the heroine is named was once thought to deplete the soil, ravaging it like a wolf (there's an etymological connection); a nitrogen-fixer, lupine actually enhances it. Here's another addition: when in the company of a desperate crush we often act idiotically, in direct opposition to our own best interests. Here's a third: a character in Peter S. Beagle's awe-worthy novel *The Last Unicorn* curses another by saying: "I'll make you a bad poet with dreams!" This caused *Nisi Shawl* to think about what makes a curse truly terrible to its victims and to devise her own—strictly for literary uses.

LUPINE

NISI SHAWL

Once there was a little girl whose mother hated her. The mother was not a bad woman, but she had not wanted a child, and so she put her daughter into a secret prison and pretended she did not exist. The father was deceived, for he and the woman parted long before he would have learned she was to have a child. Soon after they separated, the mother's love for him languished and died. As for her daughter, the mother felt nothing toward her but the deepest loathing.

The little girl, on the contrary, loved her mother very much, because she was born to love, and in her prison she knew no one else. Lupine, as she was called, had not even a kitten or a cricket to love, not even a doll to play with. The wind from the mountains blew seeds into her lonely tower, and she nourished these into plants: flowers and downy herbs.

When her mother brought food and water, Lupine always lavished kisses on her; however, these only strengthened the woman's hatred of her beautiful child. "She is young and has her whole life ahead of her. My life is passing by, faster and faster, and soon I will be dead," the mother thought. To fill Lupine's years with misery was the object of her private studies, and one day she found an answer that would serve.

She gave it to Lupine as medicine, but it was really a potion containing an evil spell. Lupine suspected nothing, but complained bitterly of its awful taste. Then she coughed, her eyes rolled back into her head, and she fell to the floor as if dead.

The mother laughed with delight and eagerly awaited Lupine's return to wakefulness. When the daughter's eyes opened she no longer wore her usual sweet smile; instead, her face was ugly with disdain. The purpose of the potion's spell was to make her act hatefully toward those she loved and lovingly toward those she hated. Lupine reached up to throttle her mother's neck.

The woman easily eluded her and ran gleefully down the prison's stairs and out of the waste with which it was surrounded. She led Lupine into the thick of civilization, where her daughter would suffer the most.

So this little girl with eyes like stars and hair like the night's soft breezes grew up the plaything of bullies and the despised enemy of everyone she thought fine and fair. No one understood her inhuman passions, and she was most often left alone—except by her tormentors.

Soon after entering maidenhood, Lupine fell in love with a superior lad. Golden as the sun when it is closest to the earth, he had an unusual and endearing skill: finding things no one else knew they should look for. By now Lupine comprehended her enchantment, and so she fought every least stirring of feeling for him. But to no avail, for she found herself telling horrible lies about him, insulting his sister to her face, and spitting on his shoes whenever they met.

Kyrie, her love, being no ordinary boy, met all her stings with tenderness. This only made things worse.

One night she woke from sleepwalking under his open window, a long, sharp knife glittering in each hand. Overcome with horror, she fled back to the wilderness before her mother or anyone else could stop her.

She ran until she could only walk, and she walked until she could only stumble, and she stumbled until she could only crawl, and she crawled until she could go no farther. She had come to the top of a tall mountain. She lay so still that the vultures thought she was dead and came to feed on her, but a fierce little bird scared them away.

By and by, Lupine recovered from her exhaustion and opened her eyes. The first thing she saw was a cunning cup fashioned of leaves and filled with clear water. She drank it all and sat up. The little bird had put away its fierceness and perched on her knees, chirruping at her. She was so forlorn, she decided to confide in the beast. "Oh, Piece-of-the-Sky, if only you could tell me how to end all my sorrows," she said.

"With pleasure," the little bird replied. "I will consider it payment for your naming of me."

"You—you talk!" said Lupine, naturally amazed at this.

"Not exactly. But because of the water I gave you to drink you understand my singing. For only a short while, however, so let us waste no time.

"You need not tell me your troubles, for I have been watching you. The solution to them is simple. You must chain yourself to those rocks there—" the bird gestured with a wing "—the Rocks of Solitude, so you can do no harm to anyone. Throw the key down in the dust. I will retrieve it. Then you must wait till I return with your swain, whose kiss will release you from the spell of your mother's potion."

So Lupine shackled herself in the place where ancient princesses had sacrificed themselves to fire-breathing dragons, using for this their old, abandoned chains. The little bird flew off with the key.

Soon Kyrie strode up the path, bright as morning. Lupine hissed at him and shook her rusty chains. He was not afraid, though, for he had learned all that it was necessary for him to know from Piece-of-the-Sky.

Still, he feared Lupine would bite off his nose before he succeeded in placing his lips on hers and melting into her mouth. But at last he kissed his love.

When he stopped they were both dizzy with bliss and victory. He unlocked her, and together they rejoined the world to share their joy. Their whole lives were ahead of them, and they were free.

As for Lupine's mother, when she heard of the way in which

she had been outwitted she grew more and more anxious over her impending death. When would it come? Where would it be? How would it find her? What would be the manner of it? At last she could bear the suspense of her ignorance no longer and jumped into a fiery furnace.

Thus all concerned found peace.

——

Nisi Shawl's story collection *Filter House* was one of two winners of the 2009 James Tiptree, Jr. Award. Her work has been published by *Strange Horizons*, *Asimov's SF Magazine*, and in anthologies including *Dark Matter* and *The Other Half of the Sky*. She was WisCon 35's Guest of Honor, which Aqueduct Press celebrated by publishing *Something More and More*, a collection of stories, essays, and an interview conducted by Eileen Gunn. Nisi edited *Bloodchildren: Stories by the Octavia E. Butler Scholars*. She co-edited *Strange Matings: Octavia E. Butler, Science Fiction, Feminism, and African American Voices* with Dr. Rebecca J. Holden; with Cynthia Ward she co-authored *Writing the Other: A Practical Approach*. She is a founder of the Carl Brandon Society and serves on the Board of Directors of the Clarion West Writers Workshop. Her website is www.nisishawl.com. She believes in magic.

——

When I was working on my MA—writing reloaded fairy tales—I had two rewrites I could not make work: "The Raven" and "White Bride, Black Bride." In the end I gave up, but they've mocked me for several years. Each tale had all the elements: princesses, princes, kingdoms, magic, ill-will, bright hope, all bumping up against each other, creating tension.

But neither story was right—neither was *enough*. When asked to contribute to this anthology, I figured it was time to show those stories who was the boss. I peeled away their skins, cutting off the excess fat and flesh. I took them back to their barest basics and found—for my purposes—the core of a single story. I built a new skeleton, discarding the bones that did not fit, then layering on new flesh, new skin.

All writers working in the genre engage in the same Frankensteining process. With fairy tales, we make and remake our own pretty monsters, with their roots firmly embedded in the past. Oh, they will look new, but if you look at the shadow they cast, you'll recognize their original shape. You'll know who and what they were. That co-existence of old and new is both comforting and disconcerting.

Old storytellers used to finish with: "This is the tale you asked for, I leave it in your mouth," and I think this is the essence of the fairy tale. The words sit differently on varied tongues and each retelling changes the tale, however infinitesimally. The fairy tale is the ultimate Chinese Whisper, shifting with telling and time, its feet in the past and its head in the future—and I think that's why it's my favorite form of storytelling.

Angela Slatter

FLIGHT

ANGELA SLATTER

The feathers were tiny and Emer hoped they would stay so. Indeed, she prayed they would fall out altogether. They were not downy little pins. Small, but determined, their black shafts hardened as soon as they poked through her skin, calcifying under her touch as she stroked them in dreadful fascination.

All day she'd felt something happening beneath the gloves hastily donned after her morning's escapade. The sight of those ladylike coverings had brought approving nods from both her mother and governess, as if they were a sign she was *finally* listening to their exhortations. *A princess does not run. A princess does not shout or curse. A princess keeps the sun in her voice, but off her fair skin. A princess sits quietly, back straight. A princess smiles at a gentleman's tasteful jest, but never laughs too loudly. A princess never furrows her brow with thought. A princess does not chew her nails.*

Emer had been determined that nothing untoward was occurring; that the healing salve she'd sneaked from her mother's workroom would put everything to rights.

But that night, when Emer closed her bedchamber door and finally peeled away the doeskin gloves, she found that the wound in her palm was sprouting dark fronds around its ragged edge. They looked like the collar of her mother's favorite cloak—except those feathers with their vibrant eyes were from the palace peacocks. A great ball of fear threatened to stopper her throat.

It had been the madness of a moment, to sneak away and run through the gardens with the sky so blue, the clouds so white, the grass such a vibrant green. Trembling in the breeze, the flowers shone like delicate gems: wine-dark amethysts, sun-bright topazes, heavenly sapphires, rubies red as blood, beryl the color of a storm-tossed sea and, stranger still, the roses.

She'd danced and run, bounded and rolled like a child of five not a young lady of thirteen. Not like a princess on the eve of her fealty ceremony, someone who shouldn't frolic until her gown, once a triumph of pink embroidered with daffodils, had its hem torn and trailing, one sleeve held in place by four tenuous threads, and grass and dirt staining the pattern. Tradition decreed the heir—even if, to the regret of many, she was female—be left unattended this day, not so she could *play*, but so that she might stand vigil, alone, unsupervised and mature, meditating on her future life of state. Preparing to pledge herself to the land, to be its sovereign and its succor, now and always.

Leaving the manicured lawns upon which she was usually permitted a chaperoned stroll, Emer had wandered into unkempt areas where the demarcation between garden and myrkwood was little more than a rough boundary of aged briars. Smooth malachite stems spiked with roses' thorns—roses black as ebony!—entwined seamlessly with the gray and brittle barbs of the brambles.

A burning glow from the heart of each bloom had compelled her closer; an opalescent flash of green and red and gold, orange and azure and magenta had drawn her. She'd reached out to touch the nearest one, careful to avoid its prickles. The petals were like velvet. As she pulled away, she felt a stabbing pain in her upturned hand.

One moment the air in front of her was empty and the next, a raven, which had sat so still that it'd been invisible in the chest-high hedge, occupied the space with regal mien, its claws fixed tightly around the briar barrier. The crimson wound in the center of Emer's palm showed where it had made its mark.

Emer stared at the bird; its feathers glistened tenebrous-dark, yet radiant as if moonlight had been woven into their undersides. The raven gave a harsh cry—if she hadn't known better, she'd have said it sounded apologetic—and Emer noticed its eyes burned with the same fire as the blossoms, colors flickering and dying, only to be replaced by the next brilliant hue. The creature took off, flying higher and growing smaller until finally it dove, plummeting straight at the girl, veering at the last second and shooting into the shadowy depths of the forest.

That was when Emer's nerve had broken. Hitching her skirts, she'd fled to her rooms, changed her dress and hid the destroyed one. She'd smoothed her hair and washed her face, slipped on the snug gloves, and spent the afternoon, heart aflutter, sitting in the solar. Feigning contemplation of the book on her lap whenever her mother or governess swept past, and hoping ever so hard that nothing would come of her misadventure.

Now, Emer removed her frock slowly, fearfully, wondering why she did not feel the cold. She stood in front of the mirror and turned. An inverted feathery triangle lay across her back and shoulders. At the nape of her neck were knots and twists where her tresses had begun to tangle into a kind of plumage. Her nails had toughened, lengthened and grown points. Her thumbs and little fingers were shorter.

Yet she did not call for help.

Emer knew the price of magic—something outlawed since the beginning of her father's reign. Herbcraft was acceptable; although leechwork was a gray area, its benefits were acknowledged; but witchcraft? Enchantments had enabled the Black Bride to bring calamity, to blind the King to the one he loved, to almost ruin a prosperous land, and to leave the Queen permanently scarred. Emer, transforming as she was, must be committing sorcery, even if it wasn't her choice.

No, she would not call for help. Surely it would go away. Surely all she needed was to apply more of her mother's lavender nostrum. Surely in the morning, she thought, upending the bottle of ointment and slopping it up her arms, surely by then this would all be gone.

〜

At dawn, as the final act of her vigil the princess dressed all by herself for the first and last time.

A cream silk wimple, a veil of amaranthine gossamer, and a circlet of engraved gold hid the tight calamus cap her hair had become. Only Emer's un-feathered face remained visible. Her high-necked ruby robe had sleeves long and loose enough to conceal her glossy black body and her arms, which were rapidly knitting into wings. Stubbornly, she fumbled with gloves, but didn't bother with shoes— her legs had wizened, toughened with dusky gray skin, finished with pronged feet. Now three clawed toes *click-click-clicked* as she walked.

And so it was that the kingdom's firstborn, pride and joy (and occasional frustration) of her royal parents, entered the great hall with a strange new gait. Her eyes, once blue, were black, and her head moved this way and that, taking everything in with a darting gaze. She promenaded along the ermine carpet to where her parents sat, enthroned and enthralled by her terrible progress.

When she stood before them, dropping into the queerest curtsey ever seen, the Queen and King began to weep and wail respectively.

Emer's hands convulsed and the delicate gloves, which had been shoved onto the tips of her transmuting fingers, fell away as the flesh melded. The gown, too, was rent, and soon the princess was jiggling about on one leg then the other, kicking away the rags. Her head grew rounder, tinier, and her ears disappeared; the coronet slid down to sit around her neck like a collar. Wimple and veil hung loose until she shook them off. Emer's nose and mouth speared into a scintillating beak.

Ladies-in-waiting screamed and lords bellowed. The noise was astonishing; it swelled until the crescendo broke over the raven-girl and she tottered about, looking for escape. One of the high-reaching windows was open to allow the cool breeze in, and she half-ran, half-skipped towards it, shrinking, until the golden circlet slipped away and she leapt through the opening as if performing a circus trick. She hopped onto the sill, gave her parents one last look, and *caw-cawed*, a sound that echoed the whole sad length and breadth of the chamber.

With one swift beat of her new wings she caught an updraft. Her parents, released from their paralysis, ran to the window and watched as their daughter joined a waiting unkindness of ravens that greeted her with croaks. The sun kissed her wings and she and the birds were gone, faster than thought, faster than possibility.

They flew toward the horizon. Emer-that-was wondered how far they'd come—and when they'd stop—as they floated over fields and rivers, mountains and valleys, towers and turrets of rulers petty and great. But Emer-of-feathers did not ponder, merely obeyed instinct and followed her fellows. They flew for so long that Emer-that-was despaired of ever finding her way back.

When finally they began to descend, it was toward a huge granite edifice positioned astride a river, nothing like Emer's hilltop home of polished marble and clear glass. This was a castle fit for battle, with windows so slender they were suitable only for shooting arrows through, or sending out the occasional pigeon bearing a message to an attacking general, saying he may as well piss into the wind, for this bastion would never fall to the likes of him.

The flock aimed itself at the closed portcullis, winging precisely through the grille, Emer as lithe and light as the rest. They traversed a deserted courtyard, thence towards a great set of doors hewn from oak and banded with silver. The doors, as if sensing their approach, opened at the very last moment, but the winged host did not slow, did not hesitate, as if cooperation was to be expected.

They flew along hallways lined with threadbare tapestries and paintings of people who'd been obscured not by time but by the tearing and shredding of canvas. They flew through rooms lined with rows of weapon racks filled with rusting swords and battleaxes, unstrung bows, decaying spears and toothless morning stars. They flew through bedchambers so thick with dust they had to rely purely on intuition to navigate. They flew until at last they came to a hall as lofty and lengthy as a cathedral's nave, as cool and dim as one too, for most of the tall pointed windows were shuttered. At the farthest end sat a woman.

Bustling around the chamber was an army of servants. Here and there, valets and footmen, butlers and a majordomo, maids and ladies-in-waiting, some of them in the costume of courtiers and some of them in rustic attire, but Emer had no doubt they were all, without exception, slaves. No matter their garb, none wore human form. Each was canine, walking upright and wearing a motley mix of livery, using fans, carrying trays, bearing tea pots and saucers, one the lord of a samovar, another king of the canapés.

Emer glided onwards, unaware that her companions had dropped behind. She slowed, and descended, carefully avoiding the shifting mass of what appeared to be large rabbits—no, hares kicking at each in occasional ill-temper. She alighted on the shabby red carpet leading to the dais upon which a cushioned throne was set. Three short steps separated her from black-booted toes.

Lifting her gaze, Emer took in the woman's face, gypsy-hued, marred with long-healed scars; her hair and eyes like jet, lips like a damson plum. And the features somehow familiar, yet Emer could not place them. The woman in a long charcoal dress, with carmined nails, smiled down at the raven who was a girl. Emer shuddered deep inside her hollow-boned body. She wished to fly, to flee, but her limbs would not obey.

The dark one limped down the stairs to gather up the bird. She tucked Emer under her arm as one might a chicken, and stroked her with a hand almost entirely curled in upon itself. Emer recoiled, willing her talons to lash out and tear, her beak to stab and shred, but her body was contrary. All she could do was shiver. Clicking her fingers, the woman produced a chain as fine as thread from thin air. The thing shone and shimmered as she twisted it twice around the raven's right foot. Emer watched as the metal fused. The other end was looped through the intricately carved rose-and-briar pattern adorning the top of the throne.

The woman's voice, when she spoke, was strange, a mix of the sweet and the discordant—only later would the girl realize it came of the scars at the base of her throat.

"Now. Now you are secure, my little one, the game has begun."

Emer, finding her own voice unaffected by whatever paralyzed her body, gave an answering cry.

"Come, come—you want to help me, don't you? And if I take my fun at the same time, then what harm?" She laughed. "Would you like a story, my dear one? My sweet sister's darling child? Shall we begin thus? Once upon a time . . . "

And Emer listened as her unsuspected aunt told of two sisters, one swan-white, the other raven-dark. All the while the girl wondered how long she would be in this shape. How long before all she began to think of were bugs and beetles, worms and carrion. How long it would take for someone to find her. And Emer despaired because she knew her parents believed the Black Bride defeated and dead. They would never find their raven-daughter because they would never think to hunt for a ghost.

The girl spent many months feathered and tethered.

Each night she heard the Black Bride's version of the tale Emer's governess had told in hushed tones. Her mother had tenderly sworn it was no more than a story, and even though Emer pretended to believe her, she had seen the evidence on the Queen's very flesh: the blemishes around her neck where the gold band clutched too tightly, the left hand missing its smallest finger where her wings had been clipped so she would not flee the palace pond. By the end of her first month in captivity, Emer was acquainted with every cadence of the new account as surely as she was her own heartbeat.

How the Black Bride's mother had two perfectly serviceable husbands, one after the other, and produced one lovely daughter with each. How both girls were raised with equal affection, and how, when an exceedingly fine suitor—a king-to-be—came a-courting those very girls, this very same mother refused to choose between her daughters, so the dark girl had no choice but to make her own fate. How the prince had made his preference for the snowy girl known— and the girl of shadows had determined *her* will would prevail.

It wasn't as if she'd harmed her sister so terribly, said the Black

Bride with a shrug. Turned her into a swan, certainly, but as she was sure Emer could attest, a few feathers never hurt anyone. And hadn't the swan-sister's revenge been a terrible over-reaction?

When she came to this point in the tale, the Black Bride always fingered the scars on her cheeks, neck, breasts, where spikes hammered into the barrel had pierced her as she was rolled up hill and down dale until that barrel had finally hit a tree and burst asunder, leaving her bleeding and dying, the tiny child within her withering as surely as an ice-lily on a summer's day.

How, when she'd thought her last breath was spent, she was found by a woman, a witch—not kindly—who mended her and taught her greater things than she'd ever imagined. Marvelous magics, legends of objects that might grant every wish, but none of this imparted fast enough for her wanting or wishing. There was still much to learn when the Black Bride held a pillow over the old woman's face and stifled *her* last breath, but the girl was simply tired of waiting for her to step aside and let a new order begin.

How, after years of plotting and planning, everything she'd worked for threatened to slip from the Black Bride's grasp. Though she'd schemed and marshaled her resources so she might yet play on, she had failed to get what her heart most desired: healing. It was tricky, balancing the time she had left between revenge and recovery, but she refused to relinquish one for the chance of the other. No matter how it taxed her, she could be—*would* be—whole once more, and all scores settled with her sister and the king.

Emer listened and watched, watched and listened, although no one spoke to her but the Black Bride. She paid attention to the comings and goings of the shadowed woman's pilfered court, noting the frequency and severity of the woman's wet cough, the sweet-sour dying scent of her breath. There were suitors—for her wealth, though stolen, though dusty, was not insubstantial, and the strength of her sorcery was of great value. Aside from these charms, in certain lights, the ravages of her punishment were not so obvious. So, the willing grooms came, though none of them ever left.

In the cold hours, after the woman had talked herself out, after she'd muttered at the windows *when will she come, when will she come?*, then gone to bed, Emer would work with her sharp beak at the deceptively fragile-looking chain, more out of habit than hope, but inexorably, insistently.

Peck-peck-peck.

Peck-peck-peck.

Peck-peck-peck.

"About time."

Emer, perched on the padded armrest of the throne, was enduring the Black Bride's caress, staring out the only unshuttered window. Normally, she divided her time between eyeing the roiling mass of canine domestics, the fluttering carpet of ravens who came and went at the Bride's bidding, and the hopping, kicking sea of fur that had once been the courting princes—all now transformed to fine, fat hares. This day, though, the sky had her undivided attention. She ignored the dark woman, assuming the remark was addressed to someone else. But the Black Bride's next words—and her tone, so soft and sad—dragged the raven-girl's gaze back to the room.

"Did you think yourself forgotten?"

Emer was startled—it was precisely what she was beginning to think. She had lost track of the days, weeks, months, but the turning of the season outside told her winter was arriving for what seemed the second time. She wasn't sure—speculations about bugs and beetles had occupied her mind of late. A tentative movement at the entrance of the chamber made her head tilt in curiosity.

The figure was willowy, dressed in white furs, a hood of silver fox framing her pale face. She moved with all the grace of a bird on the surface of a lake, effortless. She hesitated as if, unable to find whom she sought, she was unwilling to commit deeper to the room.

"You should know," continued the Black Bride, her touch stilled, "that she raised an army to find you. Your father failed and wept, wasted away—trust me, my girl, I have my spies. But she, oh *she* mobilized their vassals, rode at their head, slept in the saddle, scoured all the lands that could be covered by foot and sea. I'll warrant she'd have given her very soul to take to the skies if it meant she might find you that way."

Her hand slid to the black chain. She toyed with the liquid length, unconsciously worrying at the dent Emer's beak had made. She stared at the woman hovering in the doorway and seemed to realize that there would be no further progress without some kind of carrot.

"In the end, though, I sent for her. Reports of her mourning, her burning anguish, warmed my very soul. I could *imagine* it for I know her as well as I know myself. But there is no true joy in suffering that one cannot witness, child," the Black Bride said, then she snapped scarlet-tipped fingers, and the ankle chain evaporated. Before Emer could take advantage of this freedom and make it to the open window, the Black Bride wrapped both hands around the raven's trembling form. She held the bird as if intent upon stilling her heart, then kissed the top of her head. Whispering *flux*, she threw the girl—not upward, but forward.

The raven-girl's shape became fluid, like water tossed from a bucket. Her feathers disintegrated, her beak receded to a pert little nose, legs lengthened and grew feet with soft pink toes, the tips of her wings split into fingers. Emer plummeted like a surprised stone, landing half on, half off the fusty carpet, scattering canine courtiers and confused coneys as she went. Naked and suddenly cold, she sat up slowly, feeling sick, stunned. Her mother, as if released from a cannon, sped toward her, hands reaching, lips curving, focusing entirely on her child, drawn by that agonizing relief which makes caution flee.

The Queen's hands were not as Emer remembered; once soft as silk and pale as moonlight, they were now red, the skin split and dry, callused, coarsened from gripping sword and reins. But the eyes, silvery blue, the gaze wide and wise as an owl's—those were her mother's without doubt. Emer nestled into the embrace, feeling as much as hearing a *thrum* as the White Bride crooned her love.

"Oh, sister, how sweet!" The Black Bride teetered on the edge of the dais, shuddering with the effort of her magic. "What was lost is found. You didn't look for me like that, not even to make sure I was dead."

"A mistake I will not repeat, sister," said the White Bride as she rose.

"Now, now, sister, don't be too hasty. Didn't I give her back? Isn't she safe? Isn't she lovely and whole, unlike we who still wear our battle scars? Didn't I give you hope?"

"Only as one doles out breadcrumbs, sister, for without hope, suffering tastes flat," said the White Bride, which set the Black Bride off into peals of laughter.

When she calmed, wiping spittle from her lips, she looked fondly at Emer and the White Bride. "Didn't I say so, little one? That we know each other as well as we know ourselves? You should find *this* no surprise at all then, sister dear."

And the Black Bride clapped with a noise like a lightning strike and shouted something Emer couldn't quite comprehend, a word that slipped over her ears like oil across skin, and left nothing in its wake but a slight ringing. Where her mother had stood, half-buried under the fox fur hood, was a sleek alabaster she-hare with eyes of silvery blue. Emer could do nothing but stare through hot tears as the Black Bride hobbled down the steps and scooped up the animal that made no move to run.

"No feathers for you on this occasion—I do like variety. I would we had more time for thrust and parry—I could play this game forever—but you've taken so long to find us that my time is running short. Your child must be swift if she wishes to save you."

An iron cage, which had not been there moments before, appeared at the foot of her throne. The Black Bride urged the animal in and latched the door. "Best keep her here, though I'm sure she'd be terribly popular with the boys," she cackled, then shuddered into a fit of coughing that resulted in something nasty spattering on the stone floor. A spaniel footman hurried forward to lap it up. Emer shuddered to think of her mother at the mercy of the legions of bucks, whose noses twitched at the smell of a female.

Unsteadily, the girl picked herself up and wrapped her mother's cloak around her, clinging to the warmth left within. She worried at the hood between her fingers as she tried her voice, found only a raucous sound, tried again and managed, "Why? Why all this?"

The Black Bride gave her an astonished look. "For the sport, of course. The vengeance."

Emer looked at the hare, the Queen-that-was, and quivered. "If I was the bait, then she's taken it. You win . . . What use have you for me now?"

"I thought I'd have more time," the Black Bride murmured, not to Emer, but to the ghosts, the nobodies with whom she regularly conversed. Blinking, she looked down at the girl, as if calculating fitness for purpose. "You'll have to do."

"Do what?"

"You want your freedom, don't you?"

Emer nodded. The Black Bride mirrored the movement and went on.

"Retrieve something for me, and we'll see what we shall see about *that*."

"That's hardly a bargain," Emer said, surprised at her boldness. The Black Bride ignored her.

"I've sent that lot many times." She shrugged dismissively towards the milling crowd of ravens, "and all they've brought back are excuses and complaints about the loss of this cousin or that brother. What I need can be obtained only by someone with pure intent—and we both know that's not me—once it's taken, of course, it can be handed over to whomever the acquirer pleases. It seems a fair price to me, for your liberty."

"And my mother—her life, freedom, her true form," Emer said. She had listened for so long to the Black Bride's tricksy tongue, to conditions that seemed carelessly worded but were not, to deals she'd made with all those princes who now wore fluffy tails and pointed ears.

"Very well, clever little miss." The woman frowned, curious. "What did you think about? When you were bird-brained?"

"Worms. Sky. Flight." *Home. Mother. Father.* Emer's short life had been determined by the whims and demands of others; therefore, she chose to keep some truths for herself this time.

"Ah." The Black Bride seemed disappointed, and sat back on the moth-eaten damask cushions of her throne. "So. There is a castle atop a mountain of glass, almost a day's distance. Inside is a very special crown, which you will retrieve."

"And how do I climb slopes of glass? Will you give me wings again?"

"No, I can't trust you not to fly away. You said yourself, in that form all your thoughts were those of birds—you'll lose focus, grow forgetful." She shook her head. "In the stables, there's a horse—actually there are many, but you can't miss this one. A suitable beast, but with a foul temper." The Black Bride sighed. "You're a clever girl, Emer, so listen carefully: there are no second chances for you. If you do not return here before the turning of a day and a night with the crown, I will kill your mother. Understand? I'm sick with waiting."

"Is there a map?" Emer inquired stiffly.

"Follow the river—that'll be map enough."

"What's so special about this crown?" demanded the girl, her spirit growing the longer she stood on her own two fleshy feet.

The Black Bride's eyes slid to the animal in the cage at her feet. "Enough questions. Go, and be quick about it."

The bird had spent all the time since they'd left the castle pattering across the horse's broad shoulders, up and down its neck, and making occasional forays onto saddle's pommel. In turn, the roan had not stopped whickering in irritation and shaking itself hard enough that both bird and rider were almost dislodged. The raven—Bertók by name—also kept up an unrelenting monologue.

"And *that*," he said with a meaningful look at the gingham bundle tied behind Emer, "if I'm not mistaken, is a loaf of bread and a flask of wine that will never run out. Purely magical, very valuable. The dog, I'm sure, was not meant to give you *that*."

A tired-looking Alsatian with sad eyes, green waistcoat, fawn breeches, and mauve frock coat, had been instructed to find Emer clothes and food and send her on her way. He'd led her to a room decorated with colorful arras, furniture of pale honey wood, and brightly bleached linens. An alcove housed a tub; ancient copper plumbing rattled as the valet drew a bath. In all the past months, Emer had never suspected a room like this existed here.

She was provided with trousers and shirt, highly polished leather boots, and a worsted wool cloak, all in varying shades of black. Emer ignored the cloak, keeping instead her mother's fur and hood. When she was washed and dressed, her guide took her to the stables and pointed out her steed.

The Black Bride had been right—so many princes had left many, many horses—but this one stood out. At least twenty hands high and with a burnished hide, he wore no shoes for his hooves were of spiked bronze. When Emer knelt before him, his golden gaze was measured. She held out the apple she'd kept back from her own quick meal and he deigned to sink his sharp teeth in its firm flesh. The dog, noting the beastie's compliance, swiftly—and with palpable relief—saddled him, while Emer explored some of the stalls, patted the more biddable animals.

"Ahem. Excuse me, miss?" came a voice from the shadows.

At first, Emer couldn't find the source, but when her eyes adjusted to the gloomy corners she saw a withy cage hanging from one of the rafters. Inside was a defeated-looking raven. His eyes were dull until Emer approached. Then, a flare of recognition and something else: a fire within, a swirling conflagration of green and red and gold, orange and azure and magenta.

"You!" she'd screamed, rage rushing through her, and strode forward, intent upon throttling the bird. The raven flapped wildly, shouting, "Now, don't be hasty, I can explain!"

"This is all *your* fault, with your lying in wait and your pecking. Give me one good reason why I shouldn't wring your scrawny neck."

"Well, strictly speaking, you need to shoulder some of the blame—

you were alone, wandering about outside. Well-behaved princesses—" he broke off as Emer began to shake the cage. "I'm sorry! Don't hurt me, I can help you."

The bird's terror broke through her fury and Emer suspected that the anger she felt was the sort of ire her aunt gave in to every day. She stepped back, shuddering with shame.

"No, I'm sorry I scared you." She reached for the latch and lifted it. "How is that I can understand you?"

"You were one of us for an age, it's bound to stick," he said, tentatively climbing out onto her proffered forearm. "If you're going where I think you're going, I really can help. Please let me come along."

It had seemed like a good idea at the time, but now Emer's head was fit to burst.

"When the old bat finds out what he's done he'll be a pair of slippers in the blink of an eye. Mind you, might come in handy," wittered Bertók.

"Why were you in that cage again?"

"Injustice! As always. 'Bertók, you talk too much. Bertók, you ate all the wild cherries. Bertók, you didn't bring me back that crown. Bertók, you're snoring too loudly.' It's getting so a bird can't fart let alone express an opinion without getting locked up."

In the brief respite while he took a breath, Emer used the chance to change track. "You mentioned a giant?"

"Giantess. Always hungry—I don't know if they're all like that. I wonder—"

"So, this giantess lives atop the glass mountain and has the mysterious crown and eats everyone who comes to visit?"

"Well, except us—except the ravens—not enough meat. But it doesn't stop her using us for target practice."

"And the crown can only be gained by someone with pure intent? I don't imagine that would include you." The bird didn't answer. "Raven?"

He gave a shrug of sorts. "Well, that's what we told her—the part about pure intent."

"You lied?" Emer was less scandalized than delighted by this breathtaking bit of avian bravery. "You lied to *her*?"

"She doesn't know everything, you know," the raven squawked. "She's just so . . . We couldn't bear the idea of losing more of our number every time she sent us off on one of those quests. She's crippled but she's got everything and it's never enough. Imagine her with that crown, whatever it does, still demanding more, more, more! We—I—thought if we put her off long enough, maybe she'd run out of time, so we haven't been trying too hard to do what she's asked."

"Why are you helping me? After all, you were the one who started this whole thing." She waved at him so he could see the scar still marring her palm. The bird had the good grace to look embarrassed.

"It's not easy, you know. Disobeying her takes effort and it hurts. And I had no idea of what she was planning. I'm sorry for what I did. You deserve no more torment, nor does your mother. You saved me from that cage and I owe you a boon. I'll help you retrieve what you need; what you do with it after is something you must consider carefully."

The journey had been interrupted only by the raven's chatter. They had covered leagues and leagues, the line of the river easy to follow, the roan tireless and intent. Yellow eyes gleamed from shadows and thickets, hands gnarled against tree trunks as their owners peeked out. Emer heard snuffles and snorts, snarls and grumbles, but nothing came near them. Wolves and trolls, ogres, and things with no name watched as they passed, but left them unmolested. She wondered if the Black Bride's power stretched this far, or if these brutes simply sensed her touch on Emer. Or worse, she thought, sensed that they shared blood.

Their destination was less a castle than a single stout tower of ochre-colored stone. Inside, the main chamber was topped by a stained glass dome that, on sunny days, showered the room with shafts of color. The air was icy, however; it leeched the hope from Emer's bones and she wondered if she'd ever see the sun again. She could feel the raven trembling on her shoulder. He'd been silent ever since they set foot in the bastion.

The giantess, all big bones, protruding eyes and corkscrew auburn hair, was ensconced in wingback chair, knitting, and giving Emer the same look one might bestow on a beef roast. Emer was glad she'd left the horse—who had taken the glass mountain at a canter and danced a kind of jig to show how pleased he was with himself— outside. Along the wall behind the enormous woman was a series of hooks, almost all hung with ill-made scarves. The scarf-free one held a huge bow of elm wood and a leather quiver filled with arrows longer than Emer's arm.

"How accommodating of you to arrive at lunch time," rumbled the giantess, who began to roll up her knitting. The door behind Emer shut with a *clang* and she rubbed sweaty palms against her trousers. She lifted her chin defiantly and wished she could fly away.

"My lady," she quavered and the giantess seemed taken aback to be so politely addressed. "I've come to ask—to beg with pure intent— for the crown."

They both looked to the crystal plinth in the center of the room; it was topped by a primrose cushion that held a circlet of white and black feathers.

"Ask as purely as you like, my girl, you're still going to be eaten." The amazon nodded, rose, and reached for her weapon.

"Wait!" yelled Emer, and something in her tone stayed the woman.

"And why should I? I don't like to wait and I'm starving—always starving."

"I imagine it's hard to get enough food when you're stuck up here, madam," said Emer.

The giantess loomed and Emer quaked. She hurried on. "I do not ask your bounty for free. I offer you something most valuable in return."

"What could you possibly have to interest me, you little thing?"

"What if I were able to provide a loaf of bread that is never depleted and a flask of wine that never runs dry? Would that not sate your hunger, mistress?"

The giantess crossed her arms over her mammoth chest, contemplating. "And where would you find such a treasure, little scrap?"

"Outside, on my horse," answered Emer, hoping the stallion hadn't taken it into his head to go for a run elsewhere.

"Then bring it hither. I demand proof before I agree to consider this bargain. And I am not saying I will . . . "

Fifteen minutes later, when the giantess had attempted and failed to entirely consume the loaf and the wine three times, Emer thought her troubles were over.

"And so, my dame? Do we have an accord?"

"Let's not be hasty, little speck," said the woman slyly. "What's the point of eternal food and drink without companionship? It's been decades since I've had a chat—what with my tendency to eat my guests. Stay awhile."

"My lady—" began Emer, aware of the night's hours bleeding away.

"My lady, this young one is no fit companion for you—she has not lived long enough. What stories could she possibly tell? How she once wet her bed nightly, what frocks she has worn?" The raven began to wax lyrical. "I, on the other hand, am no mere bird."

Looking into the creature's swirling, sparking eyes the giantess admitted this fact. She seemed to nod more than was necessary. It was no wonder the woman normally shot birds out of hand; it was dangerous to listen to them. Bertók's voice swooped low, its ragged edges barely discernible as he promised hours, days, weeks, months, and years of conversations. The woman, Emer thought with a tinge of sympathy, had no idea what she was getting herself into.

By the time the raven had finished, the giantess leapt to her feet, removed the delicate crown from its cushion, and held it toward Emer.

"Thank you," Emer said, as she reached out. "Thank you."

"You're welcome," growled the giantess and snatched the crown away, while wrapping one meaty paw around both of Emer's wrists. "Did you think me a fool to fall for sweet words? Anyway, what's a sandwich without meat?"

Emer's heart hammered, and her mind emptied of all thoughts but these: feathers and air, lightness and flight. Just as her memory retained the language of birds, so too her flesh kept recollection of their form. This time the shape was *her* choice—no one else's to give or take or impose. She gladly shifted, shrank, sprouted plumes. Within seconds, the giantess clutched only emptiness, for the girl had slipped the fleshy bonds and snatched the crown of feathers with her beak.

The door to the chamber remained shut. Emer flew around the room, faster and faster, higher and higher, knowing the giantess was reaching for her bow. She heard the nocking of an arrow, curses thundering from the woman, the twang of a bowstring. She braced herself, heard a thud, but felt no pain. Risking a glance, she saw another black body hurtling downwards. Resolute and determined not to waste Bertók's gift, she raised her head and aimed towards the stained glass.

The raven-girl pierced the dome, raining colored shards on the giantess. She shot upwards, a shadow against a pallid sky. With the dainty adornment gripped tightly in her beak, she flew on, tracing the snake of the river back to whence she came.

If the Black Bride had been surprised to see Emer feathered once more, she did not show it. The girl landed and transformed, steadfastly meeting her captor's gaze.

"Give it to me, girl," said the Black Bride, her tone limned by longing, and not a little desperation.

Emer shook her head. "My mother first. Restore her."

A brief, tense standoff took place while the Black Bride insisted her niece hand over the artifact before anything else occurred. Emer remained adamant. In the end, a rage-induced coughing fit tipped the balance in Emer's favor. The Black Bride was forced to concede that she did not have enough time left to indulge in a battle of wills.

When her mother at last stood beside her—shaking, dazed—Emer held the out crown. The Black Bride snatched at it greedily, turned it this way and that, held it up to the light, her eyes shining. Then she faltered, looked at her sister and niece and asked plaintively, "How does it work?"

And Emer recalled the story from her aunt's own lips, how she had done away with her mentor before full knowledge could be passed on; for all her power, the Black Bride was a half-written book—she might well know what an object did, but not *how*.

"Put it on, I'd imagine," Emer said, then asked quietly, "What does it do?"

In an equally hushed voice, the Black Bride replied, "It mends broken things," and, reverently slid the delicate diadem onto her blackavised brow. She waited, breath rattling, eyes wide and avid, a covetous child expecting a treat. Seconds stretched to minutes as she attended, with increasing impatience, for any sign of change, of *amendment*.

When it became apparent that no healing was forthcoming, the Black Bride's face seemed to split with rage.

"What have you done? Did you think to defy me?" She turned on Emer, stalking towards her, spitting out every horrible name she could muster. "I told you there would be no second chances! Both of your lives are forfeit."

Emer and her mother stumbled backwards, transfixed by the sight of the Black Bride summoning her power, watching as it coursed around her body, and sparked at the fingertips. Wanting, but not daring, to turn tail and run—for that would be certain death.

The dark woman drew back her unmaimed hand, and just as it seemed she would strike Emer down, the White Bride—in a flash of ash and silver—threw herself at her sister. The attack, so brutal and brave, so unexpected, threw the Black Bride off balance and she retreated under each enraged blow her sister rained down. The firebolt-bright magical charge around her stuttered and snuffed, but she struck back, her nails tearing furrows along her sister's smooth cheeks. The White Bride snarled and leapt, not noticing how close they had come to the windows, and the force of her bound sent them crashing into one of the shutters. The wood, brittle and ancient, splintered like twigs and both women were oh-so-briefly silhouetted against the winter sky . . . then gone.

Emer rushed to the sill and peered down, too terrified to catch enough breath to scream as she watched them fall. She clung to the hope that her mother's flesh would remember the shape of wings, that she might fly; but it did not.

Flames erupted when the Brides hit the cobbled courtyard. Emer waited. The fire burned down quickly, leaving a cloud of dust and cinders that swirled and circled and, finally, found form.

Where two women had fallen, only one remained, unfurling like a lily, her hair a mix of light and dark, skin a creamy melding of the two extremes, limbs intact, unharmed. A single woman, lovely and *whole*. The mother-aunt raised her head, looked at Emer and beamed.

"Come home," she called. Emer stared, an uncertain smile on her lips, and she heard the echo of the Black Bride's voice: *She raised an army to find you.* She thought of her mother as she had always known her, the docile White Bride, so kind and loving; wise, but so bound by convention; always passive, meek, and accepting— until the loss of her daughter. It had taken tragedy to give her the strength, determination, courage the Black Bride always had but used selfishly.

And Emer reflected on her entire life, on how it was moved by the ebb and flow of others' desires. She thought of her mother and aunt remade, all their chances given to them anew. She contemplated updrafts and thermals, swooping and diving. She looked at the sky, at the horizon.

"Come home," called her mother-aunt again.

Emer shook her head, only vaguely aware of the ruckus in the chamber behind her, of hares returned to the shape of men, and dogs released from servitude.

"I shall find my way there . . . some day."

Emer-that-was thought herself weightless. She thought herself plumed, skipped onto the sill and pitched out to spiral down and hover in front of the woman. The raven-girl memorized the new face, the familiar features, so she might recognize them later, then with a powerful flap of her wings, Emer-of-feathers rose towards the dawning firmament.

—

Angela Slatter is the author of the Aurealis Award-winning *The Girl with No Hands and Other Tales*, the World Fantasy Award-shortlisted *Sourdough and Other Stories*, and the new collection/mosaic novel (with Lisa L. Hannett), *Midnight and Moonshine*. She received a British Fantasy Award for "The Coffin-Maker's Daughter" (A *Book of Horrors*, Stephen Jones, ed.), a PhD in Creative Writing, and blogs at www.angelaslatter.com. In 2014 she will take up one of the inaugural Queensland Writers Fellowships.

—

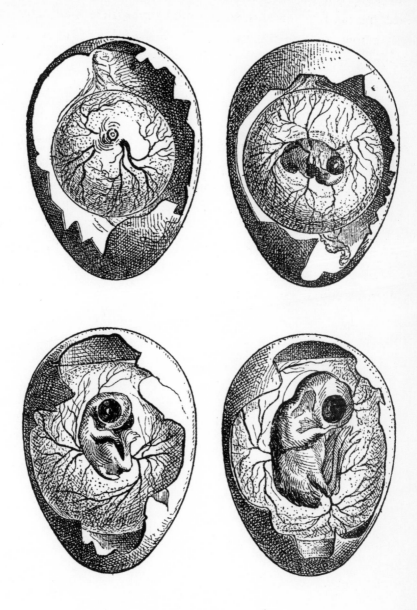

I loved fairy tales when I was a child. Hans Christian Andersen's "The Little Mermaid" and Oscar Wilde's "The Happy Prince" made me cry. As I got older I was thrilled by how grim the Grimms really were. Then came Ellen Datlow and Terri Windling's anthologies of reworkings and subversions, which led me on to "The Bloody Chamber" by Angela Carter. It contains my favorite short story, "The Tiger's Bride," her take on "Beauty and the Beast." It's dark and dangerous. It speaks of objectification, desire, and our true natures. It's important to me, not just as a reader, but as a writer. It made me pick up a pen.

So, I still love fairy tales. Not so long ago I bought a beautiful copy of *East of the Sun, West of the Moon*, Scandinavian fairy tales collected by Peter Christen Asbjørnsen and Jørgen Engebretsen Moe, and illustrated by Kay Neilson. Someone I know, who will not be named here, saw it and asked, "What are you buying children's books for?" If you're reading this anthology you're the sort of person who understands the folly of this question.

"Egg" is dedicated to my mum, Veronica Sharma. It's a very personal and important story to me for a number of reasons. It's about the difficulty of wishes. Every wish has a price. We just need to know what we're prepared to pay.

Priya Sharma

EGG

PRIYA SHARMA

I consider my egg; its speckled pattern, its curves, strange weighting, and remarkable calcium formation that's both delicate and robust.

It hurts but I'm determined. The old hag promised. I put my egg inside me.

Hot water soothes my skin. It plasters my hair to my scalp and runs in rivulets down my back. I nurse the heavy feeling in my lower abdomen with my hand. Then comes a different sort of deluge. Blood trickles down my thigh. Water carries it away and down the drain.

It's expected. I've already urinated on a stick this morning and it pronounced me *without child*. Disappointment has joined agony and blood on the same day of each month.

I drop my towel into the laundry basket and dress.

There's a sparrow on the balustrade. A blighted bird, one of many breeds decimated by predators, harsh winters, and pestilence. The public were outraged by the loss of blue tits and robins but sparrows are too nondescript to feature on calendars and cards.

Another joins it, then a third. The trio perform an aerobatic display, as if they don't already have my attention. A fourth, now a fifth. More and they're a flock.

I step onto the terrace but they don't flee. They stay earthbound and hop around, leading me down the steps to the lower garden. Past the tennis courts to the fresh green avenue of limes. Over the stile and across the fields to the crumbling farm buildings at the edge of my estate.

The barn. The sparrows enter through a broken panel. The rusty hinges whine and creak as I pull the door open.

The old hag lives on a bed of moldy hay, twigs, moss, newspaper, and woollen tufts. She squats rather than sits. Her irises are covered with a milky shroud. She wears layers of white, each stained and torn, like a demented virgin bride.

A sparrow lands on her upturned hand. The hag brings it to her face and peers at it with opaque eyes, listening intently, as if to a song I can't hear, before it flies up to the beams above.

We have an audience up there. Blackbirds, starlings, jays, sparrows, falcons, and a variety of owls jostle together for space, having set aside their differences.

"Who are you?"

"That's a rude greeting for a guest." The hag's voice has a peculiar melody, rising and falling in the wrong places.

"Guest implies an invitation."

"I'm here at your request. I'm sick of you asking."

"Request? I've never seen you before. I'll have you thrown off for trespassing."

"You've been hard to ignore. You're crying out with want."

"I want for nothing."

"Liar. The ache's consuming you."

"There's nothing *you* can give me."

"Not even motherhood?"

"You can't give me that."

"Can't I?" Then a sly smile crosses her face. "You've tried the usual way?"

"It didn't work."

"Perhaps you didn't try hard enough."

I have, not lacking in partners and willing potential fathers.

"I have fibroids and severe endometriosis." I sound bitter. My pelvis contains a tangled mess of lumps and adherences that renders my reproductive tract defunct. I'm still outraged by my body's betrayal. It's failed in the most basic of female functions.

"Can't the quacks help?"

"What do you think?"

My specialist had stressed that my conditions were benign but I couldn't see the benevolence in what's caused me so much pain and robbed me of a child. My own salvaged eggs, fertilized and implanted, failed to take as if they'd fallen on stony ground.

"Adoption?"

I shake my head.

The hag must be able to see with those white eyes. She counts something on her fingers and calculation done says, "I'll help you, but there'll be pain."

"Childbirth?" I ask hopefully.

"Much worse. Children drag you down and break your heart."

"No," I refute her jaundiced view of parenthood, "they lift you up and give you love."

"A survival trick of the young and vulnerable," the hag talks over me. "You'll love them and it'll kill you when they don't need you anymore."

"I'm strong. I'll take that pain."

"There'll be sacrifice. Your dreams will be subject to their needs."

"I've already achieved all I wanted to and more." Except this.

"Such success for one so young, but everyone looks at you as if you are unnatural. *Not having children is the price you've paid for having a man's ambition.*"

This rankles.

"I'm every inch a woman."

"Of course you are," she tries to soothe me. "I just want you to think this through. Children demand everything, even your name. You'll be mother first and last."

"And I'll be glad of it. I'll pay whatever it takes. I have the means."

"You will, never fear. There's also the thorny issue of expectation. You must love her for who she is, not who you want her to be."

"She?" I'm already enamored of the notion.

"A daughter."

"What will she cost me?"

"We'll negotiate later."

"I don't do business that way."

"I won't ask for anything you can't give."

A reckless trade. I consider the depth of my desire.

"How?"

The hag shifts on her nest, reaches under her and pulls something out. She offers it to me in her scrawny, reptilian hand. I take the egg. It's warm.

She leans over me.

"May I be godmother?"

"Is that part of the payment?"

"No," she sniffs, sounding hurt, "I just thought it would be nice."

"No child of mine will be baptized." I want to laugh. I'm clutching an oversized egg, having accepted help from a mad squatter, and am rejecting religion as a fiction.

"That's probably wise, all things considered. Now, this is what you must do."

I consider my egg; its speckled pattern, its curves, strange weighting, and remarkable calcium formation that's both delicate and robust.

More conundrums are hidden within. Viscous birth fluids designed to be consumed. The yolk, rich in unfulfilled life.

It hurts but I'm determined. I put my egg inside me. Its tip nestles into my cervix. Not for nine months. That would be ridiculous. Just long enough for my trembling DNA, fearing extinction, to permeate the shell and scramble the genes within.

Once retrieved I hold it up to the light but can't see the outline of a child inside.

Egg and I embark on a course of antenatal education. I read her Machiavelli and Chomsky. I play her Debussy and Chopin. We watch French films and listen to Cantonese language tapes. Egg will be more equipped for life than I.

Then finally.

Here she comes.

The shell cracks, the tiny life thumping its way out. Fragments come away, tethered by membrane. I pick up my featherless chick, who's pink from her labors. It *is* a girl, goose-pimpled skin as if plucked. I rub her and swaddle her in a warm towel. Her ribs are exquisite curves. Her nails miniscule and pliable.

Small for her age. Little Chick.

The hag's right. She said I'd have a mammalian response. My breasts engorge and leak. Chick's mouth puckers as she tries to plunder nourishment but she can't latch on. I prepare formula milk in a flap, fearing she'll starve. It dribbles down her chin as if it would poison her to keep it in.

I sit through the night, exhausted, waiting for the flood of love, the tugs of blood that will sustain me while she cries with hunger, but nothing comes.

Chick has dark, bulbous eyes. Her hands are drawn up before her like useless appendages. I cry as I hold her, this culmination of all my wishes, and I know that she's not right.

I go back to the hag.

"You lied." I'm not so astute. I've been duped.

"You wanted a child. I gave you one." She peers into the bundle of blankets in my arms as if to see if Chick is a child after all.

"What's her name?"

"Eloise."

The hag makes a noncommittal noise.

"She's not . . . " I struggle with the word *normal.*

"Life's a lottery," she shrugs, "you can't swap her."

"I can't bring up a child like this."

"One that requires sacrifice?"

The clouded corneas don't conceal the mockery in her eyes. I can't stand her crowing and I won't concede defeat to a mad old crone but something makes me swallow my indignation.

"Help me." I hold Chick up. "She won't feed."

The hag beckons me over with a curled talon.

There's nothing for it. I cradle Chick in one arm and dig with my free hand. My manicured nails break. Earth clogs my diamond rings.

I hate worms. Eyeless, skinless, boneless, they inch along the ground. My excavation brings one up. It writhes in protest, clamped between my thumb and forefinger.

The longer I look at it, the harder it becomes. Chick's screams have faded to a mewl. She's fatiguing without food.

I put the worm in my mouth. Then I'm sick. I find another, this time gagging as it flails against my palette. I manage to keep it in despite the spasms of my throat. I chew.

I put my mouth to Chick's and drop the masticated mess in. Her eyes brighten with excitement. She all but sings.

More. More. More please, Mummy. Chick gulps it down, her mouth open straight away in readiness the next portion. She won't be tricked by anything mashed up with a fork. It must be from my lips. I search for the bugs sheltering between the stones of the garden walls, for earthworms hiding in the flower beds. I hunt by torchlight for slugs that brave the paths by night. I retch and vomit. My little gannet's insatiable.

"Where was your daughter born?"

"Abroad."

The new pediatrician seems satisfied with this answer.

"How old is she now?"

"Seven."

"And she doesn't talk at all?"

"No."

"Toilet trained?"

Couldn't you have read her records before you called us in? I want to snap at him for his indelicate questions but I've resolved to be less prickly. He's here to help. Allegedly.

"No."

Chick trembles as I undress her. The doctor measures her height, weight, and head circumference, and then plots her poor development on a chart as if it wasn't self-evident.

"I see that no one's been able to identify Eloise as having any particular syndrome." He flicks through her file.

"No, but don't say it too loud. I haven't told her yet."

That makes him look at me. Chick, defying diagnosis, has been reduced to a list of problems in her medical records.

Poor growth. Mental retardation. Microcephaly.

"Pop Eloise on your knee."

Chick doesn't like to be held, even by me, but faced with a stranger she tries to hide her head under my arm. The doctor runs his hands around her rib cage to the hollow depression at the center of her chest.

"Eloise is more than pigeon chested. Come and see."

Chick's chest X-ray reveals the white lines of her ribs sheltering the shadow of her heart and the dark hollows of her lungs beneath.

"Look at this."

"At what?"

"A furuncle."

"Pardon?"

"Here." He points with his pen. "Her clavicles are fused together. They should be attached to either of her sternum."

"In English, please."

"She has a wishbone. Perhaps you should make a wish."

Then he looks at Chick, who's hiding under his desk and flushes.

I make up a porridge of oats, seeds, and rice milk. Chick still gorges on worms but I've coaxed her onto other things, although there's still an exhausting list of what gives her diarrhea, tummy pain, and hives.

Chick plays around my feet. *Play* is an exaggeration. She's not interested in toys. Not alphabet bricks, not the puzzles in bright plastic that are waiting to be solved, or her menagerie of stuffed toy animals. She wanders, unoccupied, then comes to stand beside me when she needs reassurance. Her tongue clicks when she wants my attention. Click, click, click. I hear the sound in my sleep.

Chick doesn't like cuddles. Once I thought she was trying to kiss me. I leaned down, eager to receive it, and got a mouthful of chewed spider instead. Her attempt at affection.

She never looks at me directly. Sometimes I want to shake her and shout, just to make her meet my gaze.

I spoon the porridge into her small mouth, set in its receding jaw. Chick's face is narrow, her eyes large, ears low, and her nose beaked. People find nothing endearing there. They either look away or simply stare.

I used to think, *Eloise will never be a business woman, a scientist, or pilot. She'll never paint or write. She'll never be friend, lover, wife, or mother.*

Now I think, *Eloise will never feed herself, she'll never take herself to the toilet, or dress herself. She'll always be at the mercy of others. She'll always need me.*

I try and imagine this life stretching out ahead of us. I'll wring the hag's neck if I ever see her again.

I wipe Chick's face and hands, sponge porridge from her hair. She hops around once freed from her chair.

Click, click, click.

The foil strip crackles as I pop out a tablet. I swallow down my daily dose of synthetic happiness with coffee, sweetened with synthetic sugar.

Click, click, click.

Chick's vocal this morning. She bumps against my legs. Her clicks have risen to a series of chirps. She hunches her shoulders and bobs her head.

I turn away. Chick's fed, watered, her nappy clean. I've met her needs.

I wonder what it would be like if I walked out. Nannies never last longer than an afternoon. *Eloise gets too upset without you. She just sits and cries. It's not fair to her.*

I imagine myself walking down the street. The luxury of going into a café to drink coffee and read a book.

Click click click click.

Even though I've folded back the kitchen's huge glass doors there's no breeze to ease the stifling heat.

Clickclickclickclickclick.

I could be picking out a dress and deciding where to go for dinner and with whom.

Chick's clicks become a sudden high-pitched squeal. I turn to see her cowering in the corner, a cat crouched before her. Scratch marks cross Chick's face. Blood wells up where the claws scored her skin.

The cat bats at her again with its paw. This hunter must have crept in while my back was turned. I shout and it looks over its shoulder, annoyed at being interrupted. It's a big, sleek tom, all black with white whiskers.

I shout again. It turns and stands its ground, back arched, spitting and hissing, unwilling to relinquish Chick. Her eyes bulge with fear, her mouth hangs open, bloodstained drool drips from her chin.

Chick's hurt cuts through my shock. I pick up a pan and fly at the cat, hissing back. I'm almost on it, screeching and stamping, when the cat decides I'm too much to take on. Its paws scramble on the tiled floor for purchase as flees between the legs of the kitchen table and chairs.

I pick up quivering Chick. Blood stains my dress. The worst thing's the sound. Her shapeless keening.

How could you let this happen to me?

The hag was right. It hurts.

At twelve, Chick still has a young child's body. There are no signs of puberty and, in truth, I'm glad that I don't have to deal with her having periods as well as everything else.

She *is* changing though.

Chick's acting strangely. Social services would have a field day if they could see her. I've delayed her hospital appointment for fear that someone might examine her and see.

She's taken to climbing onto worktops, bookcases, and tables. She leaps and lands with a heavy thud, lying on the floor looking stunned. Her bruises are a spectacular range of colors, which never fail to make me wince. I'm exhausted from the constant vigilance supervising her requires.

That's not all. She's stopped eating, just like she did as a baby, as though sickening for something. I've tried bugs and worms again but she won't take them from me. She's listless. She won't splash about in her shallow bath. She doesn't click her tongue or follow me.

I undress her for bed. She's lost more weight. I remember holding her in my hands when she was born. I resolve to take her to the doctor in the morning, regardless of her bruises.

But that's not all.

There's her skin. I slip her nightdress on, over the thick, ugly hairs on her back that are so tough that they take pruning shears to cut through them. The cotton slips down to cover the fine down on her belly.

I lock the door and lie beside her on the mattress that I've put on the floor. It's the safest way, in case she gets up at night. There's nothing left in here for her to climb.

I'm woken intermittently by Chick who spends her sleep in motion. Her arms twitch and she wakes with a jerk as if falling, followed by a dialogue of clicks as if she's telling me her dreams.

The gray light of morning comes in. There's a sound at the window, like a pebble being thrown by some lothario below. I once had a lover who did such things, imagining himself romantic. Oh, the memory of sex. Chick used to get too upset if someone spent the night, or even an hour, while she slept. Afterwards she'd shy away from me as if I was tainted by a scent that ablutions couldn't remove.

The noise comes again, a series of short, sharp raps. A pecking on the glass that chills my skin. Something wanting to be let in.

I part the curtains. A shadow flutters against the pane, its wings a blur. Not a ghost but a sparrow.

The hag's back.

I listen to Chick's ragged breathing and I want to have it out with the old bitch.

I put a coat over my pajamas and pull on boots. I put a sweater on

Chick and swaddle her in a quilt. She's a featherweight when I pick her up. Her eyelids flutter, then open and she looks through me with dead eyes before she closes them.

The barn's cold. I can see the shape of my breath. The hag's nest has been reduced by time to a rotting pile that reeks. She doesn't seem concerned. It's her throne.

"I want a word with you. You cheated me."

The hag hasn't aged, where I feel the weight of the last twelve years. She still wears a riot of once-white rags.

"She's unique, isn't she?" The hag clucks and coos like a proud parent. "You can't remake her in your own image. She's herself entirely. That's children for you."

Chick's awake now. Alert. She wriggles, wanting to be put down.

"Eloise," the hag calls.

"She only answers to Chick."

The hag smiles at that.

"Chick, come here."

I hate that Chick goes to her without hesitation.

"She'll do nicely."

"For what?"

"Our bargain. You don't want her. I'll take her back as payment."

"No."

"Don't tell me you've never thought of smothering her with a pillow or drowning her in the bath."

I can't deny it.

The hag's fingers roam over Chick.

"She's a fair payment. She has what my other fledglings don't. A wishbone."

"I've been wishing on it for years," I laugh. "It's useless."

The hag's quick as a whip. Chick's across her knee, squirming and crying to be set free. "Wishbones must be broken if the wishes are to work."

Chick's cry rises as the hag presses on her collarbone.

"Stop!"

"Really? I suppose you're right. Wishing shouldn't be an impulsive thing. And it's strongest when the bone's clean. I'll boil her in a barrel. Don't look put out. I'll be a sport. You can pull one end. That's a fifty-fifty chance on the greatest wish ever made. And Chick's hands and feet will make the finest divining bones."

"No."

"No?" The hag cocks her head on one side. "You could wish for a child. One that runs to you, arms out, when you call."

"Let her go."

"Ah, I see. You want it for yourself. Snap it and you could have a whole brood to comfort you in your dotage. Who'll hold your hand on your deathbed and bear your genes into the future. Children to praise your name and make you proud."

"I said let her go. Nothing of hers will be broken."

"Really?"

"You're hurting my daughter." I climb onto the nest.

"But you don't want her." She holds Chick out of reach.

"I do. Every inch of her is mine. I've paid in pain and sacrifice."

"Then why are you here?"

"Because you made her pay too. She's suffering and you can stop it."

"I can't make Chick different."

"That doesn't matter." I wouldn't tamper with a single cell of her. "I don't know what she's sickening for. You do."

"I can't tell you what she needs." The hag's stroking Chick now. Quieting her. "Do *you* know?"

The hag's white eyes stare through me. She's waiting.

I look at Chick. Here it is, mother's intuition, twelve years too late.

"Yes, I know."

When the hag stands she's eight feet tall, most of her length is spindly legs. She looks less haggard now. She leans down and passes Chick to me, then shakes herself out. The white tatters look like ruffled feathers. There's a sudden soft gloss about her.

"Up here."

I follow the hag up the rickety steps to the hayloft. She stoops to fit. A hole in the roof reveals clouds racing overhead. The birds have gathered up here, a panoply of breeds to bear witness to the glory of this morning. I can feel every thudding heartbeat.

Here it is. The biggest sacrifice.

There's no end of hurt.

I pull off Chick's jumper and nightdress. Her nappy. Her feathers have come in overnight. I'd be restless too if I had pinions pushing through my skin. Soft plumes cover her abdomen.

Her shoulder blades peel away from her back and unfold. Her wingspan is mighty considering she's so slight. No wonder Chick's clumsy on the ground. She's designed for flight.

Click, click, click.

Chick leaps up, her feet curling like claws around my forearm. I hold her up. She's heavy, held like this.

Click, click, click.

I'm fixed by my daughter's gaze. She's ferocious. Dignified. I bow my head. She doesn't need my limited definitions. She has her own possibilities and perfections.

Clickclickclick.

I launch my precious girl. She takes flight through the hole in the roof, going where I can't follow. She tilts and tips until she catches the wind and spirals upwards, a shadow on the sky.

How high she soars.

—◆—

Priya Sharma lives in the UK where she works as a doctor. Her short stories have been published by *Interzone*, *Black Static*, *Albedo One*, and on Tor.com, among others. Her work has been reprinted in Paula Guran's *The Year's Best Dark Fantasy and Horror: 2012* and *2013* and Ellen Datlow's *The Best Horror of the Year 2012* and *2013*. She is writing a novel set in Wales, which is taking a long time as she writes in longhand with a fountain pen and then types it up very slowly.

—◆—

I had this idea for an epic, bad-ass scene I wanted to illustrate, but as soon as I started to sketch the hero's corset, I knew he deserved a whole story. "Castle of Masks" is his story.

Cory Skerry

CASTLE OF MASKS

CORY SKERRY

It wasn't difficult for Justus to take the place of the yearly sacrifice. "Go home," he said, and when Ingrid opened her mouth to argue, he lifted his skirts to show her the stolen cutlass dangling beneath. "I've hunted fox, deer, wolf, and bear—a beast in a castle is nothing to me."

Her face was a wet moon in the chill starlight, her eyes so red that even the colorless night couldn't hide them. Her name had been drawn in the village lottery, and she'd spent the last week thinking she must die.

"Good luck, brave fool," she whispered. As Ingrid's footsteps faded behind him, the sounds of the approaching carriage grew louder. Justus smoothed his skirts and tried to pretend he was a woman.

Once in a while, when it came time for one of Justus's neighbors to give up his own daughter to the Greve, the man suddenly wanted everyone to charge the castle and slay the monster instead of sending his child to be devoured. No matter that the Greve supposedly changed into an oversized wolf in the night, or was a ghoul wearing the rotting limbs of the victims—it was high time that people risk their lives for justice. Invariably, everyone else was just as reluctant as he had been the year before when it wasn't his child being taken from him.

Justus regretted having been so complacent until last year, when his sister, Gudrun, was chosen, but he wasn't about to embarrass himself by demanding that the folk from his and other villages help with his revenge. It hadn't yet occurred to him that he might go in his sister's place—and as soon as he had the thought, he began his preparations.

The coach was black, and so were the four stout horses that drew it. Their breath ghosted through the crisp air, but the driver's didn't. Justus's heart pummeled his chest—was it true, that the Castle of Masks was served by the undead?—but after a moment he saw that the man simply had a thin wrap over his face.

"My name is Valfrid," the man's voice creaked.

"Karin," Justus said, forcing his voice into a higher register.

Valfrid offered a hand to help Justus into the carriage, and Justus took it as daintily as he had practiced for the past year. Valfrid closed the door as Justus settled on the cushioned bench. The lock clicked with finality, trapping Justus in a garish display of wealth. The carriage walls and ceiling were painted with murals of woodland beasts chasing and fleeing. Instead of simple canvas shades, there were real glass windows set in iron grids that couldn't be kicked out by desperate maidens.

Justus peered at himself in the reflection. At first he saw the captivating young lady Valfrid must see—but after only a moment his eyes adjusted and he recognized himself, shaved and painted, but the same old Justus. Even though he'd often been teased that he looked like Gudrun's younger sister, Justus was still nervous about his disguise.

Thoughts of his sister filled his belly with familiar fire. He spent the next few solitary hours fantasizing about his coming triumph, caressing the scarred hilt of the cutlass through a strategic tear in the folds of his skirt. He would look for tools he was more familiar with—he was no swordsman—but a blade this size was comforting nonetheless.

When they arrived, Valfrid helped Justus out of the carriage and led him to a small side door. Above them, the walls of the castle glared down with hundreds of green eyes. Justus prepared himself for halls lit by sickly green witchlights, but the lantern in the entry hall glowed a normal yellow.

His eyes immediately fell on the opposite wall, to a strange tapestry of pale leather, the uneven pieces stitched together by an unskilled tailor. Justus might never have realized the skin was human if not for the ghastly masks haunting every wall.

The hole-eyed faces of dozens of slaughtered women stared at him, through him, beyond him. Some of the masks were lacquered to retain the quality of the face paint; someone had painstakingly styled the hair. Justus's stomach twisted like a scared rabbit as he recognized some of the tortured faces as those of girls from his own village, now stretched over wooden frames and dried into an eternal expression of horror.

The eerily reverent display of death surrounded him on every side, even from the back of the door as it swung closed. He did not see Gudrun's face, but he had time only to glance over the collection before Valfrid set a gaunt hand on Justus's arm.

"Come," the servant said, guiding Justus into a long, dark hall.

The door at the end was plain dark wood, marred by a halo of deep slashes around the knob. It looked as if someone had tried to hack it out. Valfrid opened the door for Justus, who stepped through to meet the Greve of the Castle of Masks.

The castle's master lay curled in front of an enormous stone hearth. A pattern of scars zigzagged over the mound of shadow outlined by the flames, and as Valfrid lit the lamps, Justus could see more and more of the monstrous Greve.

Each ragged square of his motley skin was that of a different animal. A patch of silvery wolf fur covered his massive shoulder, and on his right flank was a scrap of feathers that might have come from an owl. When the Greve rose to his feet, he stretched like a cat, the firelight glistening on his pelt. Beneath a raccoon tail, his anus was surrounded by white sheep's wool.

"Valfrid?" the Greve prompted. Justus was no longer concerned that his voice would give him away; the deep, rumbling bass of the Greve's voice made any human sound dainty in comparison.

"Greve, may I present Fröken Karin, of Östbrink."

It suddenly occurred to Justus that the wolven-snouted monster before him might be able to smell the salty reek of a man's sweat, even under layers of perfume and powder.

Shaken, Justus murdered his curtsy. He rose to find the Greve scrutinizing him. The castle's master was perhaps seven feet tall.

"May I call you Karin?"

The sight of the towering Greve shattered Justus's cultivated rage, reducing it to common, cringing fear. This was not a disfigured nobleman with unclipped nails and teeth filed to points, a deranged freak who considered himself a beast, but a real monster. The Greve could have lifted the carriage outside with his bare hands and thrown it as easily as a basket.

Justus fingered the handle of his cutlass, warmed by his body heat. If the blade could even cut that thickly scarred hide, a mortal wound would take more strokes than Justus would have time to deal.

Time. Justus needed to plan, to spot a weakness in this imposing adversary and wait for a proper opportunity.

The Greve still waited for a reply. "Yes, Greve," he blurted, demurely bowing his head. Justus's mouth continued, against his better judgment. "And what shall I call you?"

The Greve grinned, baring a vicious fence of teeth. "*Monster* is fine. Would you like supper, Karin?"

Justus wanted to say no, wanted to be locked in a cell with iron bars between him and Monster, but he should study his opponent, and moreover, he should eat when he could. It would keep him alert and strong. "Yes, Monster. Thank you."

Valfrid whispered away, and Justus found himself alone with a living nightmare. Monster's muscles rippled as he settled onto his haunches, clearly a more natural position for his mutant body. "I hope the ride here was pleasant?"

"As pleasant as I imagined," Justus answered. He hadn't intended to sound bitter.

Monster laughed, rich and silky but unbearably loud. "And the castle? How did you imagine my home?"

Worse smelling. Justus shrugged, his terror getting the better of him. He did not wish to hear that laugh again, and neither did he want to hear a roar.

They sat in silence until Valfrid arrived with a tray filled with roasted pheasant, potatoes, carrots, freshly baked bread, and new-churned butter. Justus found he was hungry despite his fears. With every bite, he imagined he was eating Monster.

And I will, when I succeed. I'll carve a steak from his steaming carcass and roast it in the castle courtyard. I'll kick out one of the panes of green glass to use as a plate, Justus thought.

Valfrid did not return with a plate for Monster, and Justus's satisfaction melted away, dragging his appetite with it.

"Monster, where is your meal?"

Monster laughed again. "Don't fret, Karin. I only eat my guests if they misbehave."

Justus inhaled unexpected hope. Gudrun was always a dutiful woman—might she have survived? "Oh? Will the others be joining us?"

"They all misbehaved."

Justus closed his eyes. He should have known. He shed silent tears for Gudrun, his beautiful, vivacious sister. She was never going to paint another ink mural on the whitewashed cottage wall, never fight for the first dipper of well water or call him "Padda" again. Had this awful creature abused Gudrun before her death? Forced himself on her, hairy and cruel and wild? Did he tear out her perfect white throat with his teeth? Justus suppressed his sobs, because while the tears helped his cause, any accidental noises might betray his masculinity. He'd cultivated a habit of silencing even involuntary sounds.

"Don't be so upset," Monster coaxed. "You look obedient."

"Yes, Monster," Justus said, swallowing hard.

"I'm sure you're very tired. Valfrid will take you to your chambers."

Justus turned to find the lanky servant waiting at his elbow. Eager to leave Monster's overwhelming presence, Justus wrapped his shawl tighter and hurried after Valfrid, who locked him in his room with a sharp iron click.

A large looking glass held court on one wall, over a table with a high-backed chair; a cozy bed with a billowing silk canopy occupied one corner; tapestries of flowers and pastoral scenes obscured the walls. In this one room of the gloomy castle, the stone had been painted white. Roses withered in a vase, their table too near the fire.

Justus thought he would feel safer once he was alone, but now he was haunted by the ghosts of every lie he had told that day. This ridiculous scheme had gotten this far, but for all he knew, Valfrid had suspected his secret from their first introduction. They could be merely toying with him.

Justus padded to the window, peering out at the other lights across the courtyard. Behind one green pane, a girl carried a basket of laundry. She paused to offer a beautiful smile, and nearly dropped the linens when she waved at Justus. Her simple gesture calmed him long after she had disappeared; even in this horrid museum of death, people went about their jobs, and sometimes they were clumsy.

Justus slipped from his dress, bundled into his wool pajamas, and ducked under the covers of the massive bed. The cutlass he tucked under the pillow.

As he drifted off, he wondered if Gudrun had slept here, and before her, how many others. Tomorrow he would look for his sister among the masks in the foyer.

Justus slept poorly and was up early. He changed into his dress again, and he was shaving in front of the mirror when Valfrid knocked on the door.

"One moment," he said, hurriedly scraping off the last traces of the salve and hiding his shaving instruments. When Justus opened the door, the kohl with which he'd lined his eyes was still smeared from tears and a night's sleep, but at least he had no stubble.

"This is Rigmora," Valfrid said. "She'll help you dress for breakfast with the Greve. She doesn't hear or speak, but she'll do a better job than I would."

A girl with too many freckles watched from just behind Valfrid's shoulder. Not the cheerful laundry girl, which disappointed Justus, but Rigmora possessed an air of quiet capability. She guided Justus back to the chair by the looking glass.

The smeary, tear-stained makeup of the night before disappeared under Rigmora's careful application of a rag and cool water from the corner basin. She happily combed Justus's ringlets into a glossy cascade that poured forward over his shoulders.

When she finished, Justus looked more feminine than he had upon his arrival, and with a sigh of relief, he followed her down to breakfast.

Monster crouched at the end of an informally short table, his bulk housed in a large seat crowned in antlers. Rigmora led Justus to a much smaller chair and curtsied to Monster before disappearing.

The windows in the dining hall were among the uncolored few in the castle, and sunlight spilled in swathes across the table and floor. When Monster asked how Justus had slept, Justus had the wit to parrot his answer from the night before.

"As well as I imagined."

Monster's mismatched eyes squinted in mirth—one a golden glittering yellow, the other an entirely black orb. *A snake and an owl*, Justus thought. When Monster reached for a jug of filmjölk, he exposed a raw, red wound just below his ribs. He chugged the filmjölk, then patted his muzzle clean with a napkin. A moment later, Monster turned to grab a plate of smörgås, and Justus noticed a matching wound on the opposite side of the beast's torso.

"What happened?" Justus asked, gesturing. Monster only stared until Justus added, "You're wounded."

"Oh yes, I suppose I am. I don't feel it." Monster's grin displayed a few morsels of breakfast, but Justus didn't turn away.

"How did it happen?"

"Being a hunter is perilous."

Justus rolled his eyes, annoyed at Monster's arrogance, and said, "Matching wounds aren't a common result of hunting."

"And what would you know of hunting?" Monster asked.

"More than most," Justus said, nettled into exposing himself. Even as the fatal words escaped his painted lips, Justus cursed his pride. "My brother taught me well," he added, but he wasn't sure if made up for his slip of tongue.

Monster leaned forward, propping his chin on one massive, hand-like paw. Strawberry syrup smeared his curved badger claws.

"Oh? How intriguing. Can you prove this?"

Justus paused, and then tipping up his chin, he said, "Lend me a bow, and set me a target in the garden."

Monster's furred fingers stretched into his mane, scratching vigorously as he thought, and when he dropped them again to the table, their weight sent a shudder through the wood. "Anyone can hit a target. I have a better idea. Tomorrow, you may accompany me outside the castle walls, and we shall hunt together."

Justus wondered if he was agreeing to his own death, if he would be the prey. "Thank you, Monster."

Perhaps outside the monster's domain there would be a chance to take him unawares. An arrow might pierce an eye, throat, or belly more effectively than Justus's cutlass could pierce that variegated hide. If Monster climbed a tree or stood near the edge of a precipice, Justus could turn the creature's own considerable weight against him.

"What else do you enjoy, Karin? There are many hours to fill, on this lonely mountain. Would you like to see the library? I just enjoyed an amusing tale of the Lord of Misrule and highly recommend it."

"I like being read to," Justus said, "but I never learned to read."

"You shall be taught," Monster promised. When the meal was over, Justus was given to Valfrid for an hour's instruction in deciphering the mysteries of a book. By the end, he knew the alphabet, and hated every letter. He doubted he'd live long enough for it to matter whether he remembered it, anyway

Justus spent the rest of the day wandering the halls. He had not been forbidden to do so. The castle was clean and tidy, and Justus didn't see a single rat, though he came across three industrious female servants dusting furniture and cleaning windows. The friendly laundry girl was not among them.

So there were at least five female servants: Rigmora, the laundry girl, and these three older women. He hated that it raised his hopes— but clearly the castle still needed a staff to run it, and maybe these women were sacrifices who had been spared.

But when he asked them about Gudrun, they each shook their heads and gave the same answer: *We're sorry, fröken, but we mustn't speak of those who came before.*

He spent a long time in the entry hall, staring at the desiccated faces of the virgins who "came before." A few times he lost his breath, thinking a mask might be Gudrun's face, but each time he convinced himself it wasn't. He inspected every mask there, but they lined other halls as well. Hundreds of dead girls. If Gudrun's face hung on a wall here, it might be weeks before he found it.

The next morning, there was a sharp knock at the door. Justus's hand was under his pillow and on the handle of the cutlass before he even fully awoke. Snow-bright sunlight illuminated the room, colored a chilly green by the frosted glass of the window.

Valfrid's keys jingled and Rigmora entered with a pile of warm-looking clothes. Justus, unshaved face buried in a pillow, waved her away, pointing at the chair until she nodded, set down the garments, and left him to his privacy.

The dress was serviceable wool, double-layered with a quilted skirt. There was no unobtrusive way to slit the cloth; he must leave the cutlass behind, or resign himself to clumsily hoisting away yards of fabric to reach it. He chose the latter.

Justus shaved and then, still wearing his underclothes, climbed into the wool dress. There was a warm, fur-lined cloak as well, and Justus threw it over his arm as he descended to the main hall, where Valfrid and the Greve waited.

Justus had expected that even a beast like the Greve would have a retinue, but Valfrid was not dressed for the out-of-doors, and no other servants were present.

Valfrid presented Justus with a satchel. "A lunch, a teenage boy's bow," the dour servant said, "and ten arrows."

"Expect a gift when I return, Valfrid," Justus said, then added, "and another for Rigmora, and the remaining eight for the lord of the castle." Monster exchanged an amused, patronizing smile with Valfrid, and Justus pursed his lips. They would see.

Justus opened the satchel, unwrapping the bow and one arrow to get a look at them. The bow was of exquisitely carved yew in the shape of two fish joined at the tail; the arrow was fletched with exotic citrus-hued feathers.

Monster opened the giant front door without touching the pulley system needed by the servants.

Justus watched this feat with a dry mouth and damp palms. Monster must be mocking him with such a display of casual power. As he walked through, he imagined that any moment the beast would leap on him from behind and eat him alive. His back prickled at the thought, but when Justus turned to check, he only saw Monster heaving the door closed, the unexplained twin wounds glistening in the glare of sunlit snow. They hadn't even grown scabs.

Some of the tower windows glowed green, the bright sky shining through from the windows on the other side, and Justus gestured at the expensive colored glass. "How that must have cost!" he said.

"I wince when I think of the wasted funds," Monster agreed, catching up to Justus in three easy strides. "It was before my time."

"What would you have done instead?" Justus asked.

Monster paused, studying Justus with disturbing focus. "No one has ever asked me that. A fountain, in the center of a pond. Perhaps with lily pads, pretty little silver frogs from the south, and dragonflies."

Monster held out a hand, silently offering to carry the bag containing the bow and arrows, but Justus tightened his grip. He wasn't about to be separated from his weapons.

The path they took was lined in thick, coniferous woods and

carpeted in a crust of snow. "And you, Karin?" Monster asked after a few minutes of silence. "What would you do with such an exorbitant sum?"

Justus was caught off guard, but only for a moment. "I would buy herons to eat your silver frogs, and blackbirds to feast on your dragonflies. And a very long bandage for your disgusting wounds."

Monster howled, a twisted blend of laughter and a wolf's call, and slapped at a tree in his mirth. A shower of snow landed on Justus, and he shook it from his hair, trying not to join Monster's appreciation. He must remain aloof.

The bow was smooth and cool in Justus's hands, and he carried it under the cloak as they walked so if he saw an opportunity, he might take it. The first time he shot the bow, a hare that had been perched on the bank above them tumbled and lay still. Monster turned, surprised, and admitted he'd not even seen it hiding in a patch of snowless ground. Smugly, Justus accepted the arrow as Monster tied the rabbit by its feet to his gameline.

"Who gets this one?" Monster asked.

"Valfrid and Rigmora can wrestle thumbs for it. I'll find you something bigger."

Monster paused, then asked, "Do you enjoy killing, Karin?"

Justus shrugged. Hunting and killing weren't the same thing. "I enjoy hunting. Some women are bakers and some are gardeners. I'm a hunter."

Two wild turkeys fell with Justus's arrows in them, both under Monster's thoughtful gaze. A stupid third turkey, panicked by the unexplained deaths of its comrades, flapped straight toward them. Justus drew the bow—and then lowered it.

"We probably don't really need ten," Justus said.

Monster said nothing.

When they stopped for lunch, it was by mutual agreement, on the crest of a hill. The valley below them flowed to the horizons in a rich patchwork of colors and textures, as varied as Monster's pelt. The deep autumn air smelled like rotting apples and cold maple leaves.

"I don't hunt my own lands often," Monster said. "But every time I come through, I wonder why."

"You get enough maiden steak to satisfy you," Justus said.

Monster turned sharply to look at him. Justus regretted opening his big mouth, but Monster was quiet again. Justus sat on a stone and ate the lunch Valfrid had given him: some jam tarts and dried fruits, a rind of cheese and a skin of weak, once-warm wine. Monster devoured one of the turkeys.

"What, no salt or pepper for the cultured monster who reads?" Justus asked, when Monster finished with the organs and moved on to crunching the bones.

Monster snorted, his steaming breath raising a cloud of feather fluff from his bloodstained snout. "This turkey thoughtfully ate some herbs, so it was already stuffed."

Justus stifled a laugh and looked out into the woods. He wasn't supposed to be enjoying himself. He should have shot Monster through the eye, while the Greve was eating. Now it was too late.

"What are you?" Justus asked suddenly.

Monster met Justus's eyes. "I am this."

"But how did you become *this*? Were you a baby monster, once?" Justus persisted.

Justus's arrows were lying within Monster's reach. The Greve plucked one from the quiver and turned it over in his enormous fingers as he spoke.

"I will tell you a story," Monster said. "Long ago, there was a rich man, a magnificent hunter, who tried to impress a woman with his prowess. He told her he would bring her a thousand beasts, and so he set about killing everything he could get his hands on—never two of the same kind. Squirrel, hare, grouse, deer, wolf, even fish and snake. On the last day of his hunt, he killed an owl.

"The owl was a witch's familiar. The witch found her pet in the rich man's personal tannery, tacked up to dry on the wall. Devastated and bent on revenge, the witch set about stealing a piece from each of the thousand beasts, and sewed them into a cursed cloak."

There was a snap, and Monster looked down at the arrow, which had broken into four pieces in his mighty grip.

"She presented this cloak to the rich man and told him that only the greatest hunter should wear it. When the arrogant Greve put on his gift, it transformed him into a bulk of muscle with a thunderous voice and immense strength, indistinguishable from the human he once was. The witch thought herself clever, because now the hunter had become a great prize. Surely another hunter would make short work of him to gain such a rare and strange pelt—but she underestimated the fears of men. No one wanted to risk their life, even when it became clear it would save the lives of others."

Monster belched and got to his feet. "Forgive me, I didn't think it would be so brittle," he said, handing Justus the splinters of broken arrow. "Perhaps the head can be saved."

Justus wondered what he thought he was doing. He expected to shoot down Monster with these feathered sewing pins? To stab him with his butter knife of a cutlass? Maybe the witch should have made a tinier, weaker monster with her curse.

When Monster took to the trail, Justus followed at a short distance. Snow began to fall. It caked the hem of his dress, attracting more snow with annoying regularity, and Justus paused periodically to shake it loose so it wouldn't trip him.

He studied Monster's broad form, shaped so much like a man's in the shoulders and back, undeniably animal in the tail and bent hind legs. The unhealed wounds showed angry and red in his otherwise impenetrable pelt. If Justus could get close enough to stab into the wounds Monster already had, perhaps he could ruin Monster's guts. But if he'd already been punctured there, and he was walking around with no apparent pain, Justus did not imagine it was much of a gap in the Greve's armor.

Perhaps he could be poisoned, but then again, perhaps Monster would smell the impurity. Justus didn't want to risk it. Perhaps while Monster was asleep . . . but Justus knew better. Any hunter avoided taking a predator in its lair. It was best to catch it during a routine, when it was focused on drinking water or eating its kill—not when it had nothing better to do than wake up and savage you.

Justus was wondering if Monster would stop at a stream to drink, as his muzzle was unfit to suck at the nozzle of a water flask, when the clump of snow weighed too low and dragged the hem of his dress under his boot. Justus stumbled to the side, stepped on the hem again, and fell down the steep ravine.

He skidded over an expanse of decaying leaves and pine needles. Snow-laden branches whipped Justus's face and tangled in his hair, but every time his fingers closed on a clump of roots and leaves, his momentum ripped them free. Even after a stump knocked the wind out of him, Justus was most worried about being sliced by the hidden cutlass. He couldn't untie it any more than he could slow his descent.

The ground disappeared from beneath him. He caught a sickening flash of a rocky embankment and a foaming stream. Everything stopped.

Justus's head spun, but the grip on his ankle drew him back to safety. Monster clung to a gnarled pine with one hand, his hoof hooked behind a boulder.

Monster turned Justus rightside up before tucking him close. Monster's arm was as big around as Justus's torso, comforting and solid. Justus finally drew a shuddering breath and inhaled the musky scent of his rescuer. Monster smelled cleaner than Justus had imagined, clean and warm.

As Monster inched his way up the incline, Justus shivered, his fingers desperately clinging to clumps of mismatched fur. Tears streaked down his face, hot terror evaporating into the careless winter cold. *I almost died.*

"Why didn't you cry out?"

Justus just shook his head. Even if the rock hadn't knocked the wind out of him, he'd still been more worried that Monster would realize he was male, which would be a much slower death than a simple fall. He was already afraid Monster would finally discover him now—after all, Justus must feel different than a woman, compact and spare where a real maiden would have been light curves. Monster said nothing, though, and when they reached the top, he didn't put Justus down. Instead, he wrapped his other arm around Justus's back.

"It's all right. I won't let anything happen to you," Monster whispered.

Justus might have laughed at the irony if he did not believe the Greve meant it. Monster wanted to choose when and how his sacrifices died. Besides, he was full—he'd just eaten a turkey.

After a time, Monster fidgeted, shifting Justus to his other shoulder—and then laughed. "My, Karin, what's this?"

The cutlass. Justus tensed, waiting for Monster to squeeze him until his spine cracked and discard his broken body in the snow.

"A girl must protect her honor," Justus croaked.

Monster laughed again, and Justus relaxed against Monster's warmth. It pained him to know that he owed his life to this creature, and yet this same creature had taken Gudrun's.

"Best you don't sleep yet," Monster said, and shook Justus, who realized he had been dozing.

"Sorry."

"You've not told me what you enjoy besides hunting and being read to," Monster prompted.

Justus's skull felt like it was full of hot bees, but he understood that people with head injuries who went to sleep too soon didn't always wake up.

He forced his mouth to work through an answer. "Carving. I carve wood."

"With a sword?"

Justus's smile hurt his cold cheeks. "I'm not very good with the real tools, so perhaps I should try."

"I'm sure you just need practice," Monster decided. "You'll be given an array of carver's instruments, and any wood we have available. Could you sculpt me?"

"Perhaps," Justus said, and a thought pushed his drowsiness away, bright sunlight burning away a fog. He maintained his sleepy mumble, however, when he went on, "for a trade."

"Oh? Name a price that's not your freedom," Monster said. Each word vibrated through the Greve's chest to Justus's cheek.

"I just want a bow and arrows that won't crumble in your clumsy fingers," Justus said.

"Agreed." Monster chuckled. "When can I expect my magnificent sculpture?"

"A week," Justus said. "Maybe two, if the wood is as poor as your table manners."

"The wood will be as fine as your aim."

Justus smiled, but his heart now hurt as badly as his head.

Justus spent the next two days in bed, sipping broth through swollen, bruised lips. The injuries made his necessary shaving a painful experience, but he admired the dark ring around one eye as he looked in the mirror. In all his life, Justus had never looked tough, but now, wearing a frilly nightgown while he lay on a bank of pillows in a lady's lace-canopied bed, he looked as if he'd been in a real brawl.

When someone knocked, Justus swallowed and worked his voice into Karin's high, husky tone. "Come in."

It was Monster, carrying a small bag. "Here are your tools. I sent Valfrid to a good market for them. The wood is in the library, which has the best light. How do you feel?"

"Splendid. I told Rigmora you beat me, so she's sneaked me pastries for every meal."

"I wondered how you got so fat," Monster said.

Justus laughed his silent laugh, and Monster made up for it with his own volume.

"Your sculpture will be done in a week, but you mustn't peek until I've finished," Justus said. "I told you I'm not very good, so there's no use you thinking I'm even worse."

Monster promised not to look, and Justus ushered the Greve out so he might dress himself and begin his task.

The block of wood was as tall as Justus, of a fine grain, and it fell away as easily as snow beneath his new carving implements. Valfrid had even thought to buy paper and leads for the designs. Justus decided upon a snarling, crouching Monster, about to spring for a kill. This pose would remind Justus why he had to complete his quest.

On the third day, Monster interrupted Justus while he was carving. Justus hurriedly pulled the sheet down over his work and crossed his arms over his chest. "Yes?"

"I wasn't sure if you would be disturbed or entertained if I faced away from you and read to you as you worked," Monster said. The creature's eyes were squeezed shut.

After a pause, Justus said, "Entertained," and so they agreed upon a collection of poems. The Greve read as Justus scraped away flakes of not-Monster to expose the hulking form beneath.

Every day, Justus carved for an hour alone after breakfast. Then Monster showed up with a book, often held in his jaws as he groped his way across the room, eyes shut until he was safely in his high-backed chair. When Justus glanced up, he only saw Monster's fox ears and his hairy elbows.

Justus could tell he hadn't gotten the balance of the sculpture right; Monster leaned to the left a little, and one foot was too small. But Justus kept carving, more slowly every day, until it was the last day and he hadn't even started the head.

"I need another week," Justus said over breakfast.

"Is it more difficult than you imagined?" Monster asked.

Justus recognized his own words being thrown at him again, and he snorted. "No, your head is just so big it takes extra time."

Monster cackled and gave Justus another week, and they took up their routine once more. The statue began to take on the Greve's likeness, though it wasn't as Justus had intended.

The snarl looked more like a grin, and eyes that were supposed to be squinted with hate looked tilted in mirth. Every strong muscle was present, but Justus's hands hadn't forgotten a layer of fur and feathers to soften Monster's bulk. Justus tried to pretend the friendly cast to the carving was due to his own inadequacy as a sculptor.

Monster's company distracted Justus from fretting too much. Most of the time he let his hands work while he listened to Monster's deep voice reading poems and fairy tales, biographies and adventures, and even a hunting guide written by a clueless old nobleman a hundred years before, at which the two of them laughed themselves to tears.

"Now one of your ears is too short!" Justus complained, gasping with silent laughter.

"According to Lord Foxbane here, they'll give me away in the brush, because mounted fops have 'an eagle's eye view of their prey.' You'd best trim the other ear, too. For my safety."

That night, Justus went to his chambers with a heavy heart.

He was down to sanding away splinters and scratching unnecessary details into the mouth and stitches. It was finished, and he knew it. But if Justus stopped carving, he would be given a real weapon, and it would be time to kill his friend. Now it was no longer just an assassination; it was a betrayal. He would regret it for longer than he'd anticipated it. And yet it must be done. For the sake of Gudrun, and the sake of all who might follow her into an early and terrible grave.

His reverie was broken by the sound of female laughter in the corridor. The door was locked, as usual, but Justus had found that hairpins were a good size for tripping the tumblers.

This would be his last night. He hadn't seen anyone since the hunting trip but Valfrid, Monster, and silent Rigmora. If he wanted to change that, it must be now.

The corridor was empty. Justus lifted his skirts and hugged them close so they wouldn't rustle and give him away. Echoes led him to the right. Cold stone chilled his bare feet.

Hushed giggles threaded into the dark with curls of dead candle smoke and the hissing of drowned lamp wicks. When he was close enough to see a glow of yellow light, he could also hear gossip about a budding relationship between kitchen scullions. Just before he announced himself, one of the girls turned in profile, tucking a curtain of dark hair behind her ear. Justus's heart leaped.

It was the cheerful laundry girl.

Justus would have given anything at that moment to look like himself: his hair brushing his brow, his face bare of makeup, at least wearing some trousers. He couldn't bear to speak to her dressed like this.

The laundry girl reached up, turning the wick on a wall-mounted lamp, and Justus held his breath so he wouldn't curse. Ragged scars snaked up from her bust and over her shoulder, disappearing down her back. Her ruined skin looked like the wood around the doorknob to Monster's sitting room.

The other girl had only one arm.

Justus lost himself for a few moments, a cyclone of rage spinning in his chest. His hands tightened on his skirts, and he had to talk himself out of stomping into Monster's room and stabbing him with the cutlass that very instant.

He could at least accompany the girls to their rooms, even if they didn't know of it. If Monster showed up and attempted to savage them, Justus could draw the attention to himself. Justus was humiliated by how easily Monster had charmed him into forgetting the very atrocities that brought him here in the first place.

The girls, who called one another Pia and Annike, made their way to the northern wing of the castle. When they opened the door into the northern hall, Justus could see a line of candles, so he knew their work wasn't done. But when he caught up to them, Justus found the door bolted from the inside. His hairpin was useless.

Defeated, feeling cowardly and alone, Justus returned to his rooms.

He no longer felt torn about the murder he must commit. It wasn't that there was nothing good about Monster; it was that there was also evil.

Justus would be sure his friend didn't suffer.

~

"Will you want another week, mistakenly thinking I will eat you when you finish?" Monster asked at breakfast.

"Ha! I've seen the lard you call food," Justus said. "I'm too lean for you."

In answer, Monster passed Justus a plate of croissants slathered in butter and sweet frosting.

Justus loathed how easily he fell into their banter, how much he enjoyed it.

"Why don't you laugh aloud?" Monster asked. "You sit there and quiver like an angry porcupine. The first time, I thought you were dying."

"I don't want anyone to know what it sounds like," Justus said.

"Why not?"

"I don't want anyone to know that, either."

"Can Anyone see their sculpture, now that the lazy artist has had so much time?"

Justus shrugged. "If Anyone has a gift for me."

Monster motioned to Valfrid, who brought forth a long parcel. They cleared a place on the table, and Justus peeled away the cloth wrapping to reveal what might have been the most marvelous bow ever made. Dark-stained wood in an elegant, swooping curve, smooth and perfect, with a lightly padded grip measured exactly to Justus's hand. The arrows, fletched in shades of yellow and white, came in a variety of lengths and points, one for any animal Justus stalked.

"Thank you," he said quietly. Tears burned behind his eyes, and he rolled everything back into the cloth it came in.

"Will you reveal your masterpiece in the library today?" Monster asked.

"First I should show Rigmora," Justus lied, hoping he didn't see Rigmora at all.

He needed to prepare himself by walking through the hall with its macabre masks. He must remember Gudrun and the mutilated servant girls.

~

Justus tore the sleeves from his dress. He didn't have any men's clothes, so he was going to have to kill in this. At least he could cut away the parts that might trip him. He'd learned *that* lesson on the side of a cold mountain. Justus hacked off the skirt with his cutlass, leaving it scandalously high.

The garters holding up his stockings showed, and he allowed himself a grim smile at how foolish he must look.

Next he turned the blade to his hair, sawing painful handfuls off until it no longer trailed down his back, and only a few thin wisps remained in the periphery of his vision.

Justus had forgotten to have Rigmora help him out of his corset, but it might be better this way. It was tight, so it wouldn't snag while he shot, and he could tuck the other two arrows in the front lacing, like a quiver.

It was time.

Justus stepped into the library doorway, his weight bent to accommodate the bow, a bear-killing arrow nocked and ready to fly. Would an artist render this grand moment some day? If so, Justus knew it would be wrong. The artist would clothe Justus in a hunter's garb, perhaps even a noble's. Not a corset and the tattered remnants of a skirt, garters, and stockings. The Justus of the painting would have a beard and no lipstick. And the Monster of the painting, Justus knew, would be the snarling beast he had failed to carve.

The real Monster was already there, crouched on all fours before Justus's worst sculpture. Justus wasn't used to working on such a large scale, or with unfamiliar instruments, but Monster was admiring it with a focus that should have been reserved for a master.

"Do you like it?" Justus asked.

"I was wondering when you were going to stop torturing your voice like that," Monster said, not looking up.

"How long have you known?"

Monster smiled, still studying the lines of the sculpture. "I asked that Rigmora check your body for further wounds, and she was surprised to find you healthy in places she didn't even know you had." Monster laughed, then continued. "I love the carving. If you really were going to kill me, I should want it over my grave."

"I'll carry it there myself," Justus said, his voice breaking. "I wish I didn't have to do this, Monster. I truly call you friend, and despite this betrayal, I'll never lie: I loved you."

"If you call me friend, stay your hand but a moment. I promise I'll not move from this spot," Monster said.

"Agreed," Justus said. He blinked rapidly, shepherding tears away to keep his vision sharp. His arm ached with the need for release, and so did his heart, but he would let Monster have his last words.

Monster reached under his neck and in one fluid movement, he pulled his head off. It fell back like the hood of a cloak, revealing a breath-taking young woman with a face the color of spring petals and eyes like the sky. The laundry girl, Pia.

The rest of Monster was now only a cloak, and she casually tossed it over the statue, clad in a plain shift and woolen stockings with holes at the toes.

Justus fell to his knees on the rug, setting the bow aside and staring. Was she a witch? Enchanted?

"As it happens, Karin," Pia said, "You're worse at playing assassin than you are at playing girl. I killed the Greve five years ago."

"He came to me, in the night," Pia said, blowing the steam away from her gleg. They sat on the sofa in the library, alone but for the crackling fire.

"I sharpened the curtain rod on the stone under my bed, because after the first time I knew I couldn't stand it again. I poked a hole in the blankets, and when he came near, I harpooned him just beneath his ribs." When Justus's eyebrows rose, she nodded. "Yes, those wounds are from me. Just as these are from him," she said, rubbing a hand over her left shoulder.

"The Greve howled and tore at me, but I was quick. When I

ducked through the door, he tried to leap after me, but the curtain rod stuck across the frame, and I ran up into the attic while he tried to maneuver through. I knew he could follow the trail of blood, but perhaps if I found a small enough space, one where he couldn't reach me, I could hide there until he bled to death."

She spoke matter-of-factly, as if it was something fifty years ago rather than five. She was still too young for lines on her face, but he could see where they would appear: creases at the corners of her mouth, in her dimples, and at the edges of her eyes, which half-mooned when she smiled.

"I waited until nightfall, crammed into a dusty nook in the north tower, before I ventured back to my room. He'd died there, unable to pull the rod free—but I didn't find the beast. I found a man wearing a cloak.

"I knew better than to put it on, but I had an idea. My grandmother once said you could summon a witch if you hold an item of hers and call to the north. That night, I woke to an owl scratching at my window. When I opened the window, I found the witch in the courtyard. She was a strange and beautiful woman, with white hair longer than she was tall and billowing gray robes.

"At first I was afraid of her, but when I explained about the Greve, and told her my plan, she came inside. We had tea. It was supposed to be a curse, she said, for a terrible man that someone should have killed sooner. You know the rest of that story. She modified the cloak so I could take it off and put it back on as often as I liked. Despite what everyone thinks, for the past five years, I assure you I have not been raping and eating young women."

"What, not even the one who carved that awful wooden eyesore?" Justus gestured to his failure.

"I have other plans for her. But with the first four girls to come to me, I told each of them they were unfit to be eaten, and exiled them to higher education, apprenticeships, or suitable marriages in other countries. None of them know my secret—they cannot, or they might betray me to the common people."

"The people wouldn't kill you if they knew," Justus protested, shaking his head. "You could tell them."

"It's not about being killed," Pia said. There was diamond in her voice, hard and sharp. "It's about saving their sacrifices. They were so willing to let go of us instead of banding together and killing the Greve. Well, let them, then! If they can do without those women, so they shall, and I will continue to find better use for them elsewhere."

Justus wanted to argue with Pia; he wanted to defend the people of his village. But he remembered when he asked about hunting the Greve, how people told him to be quiet or he'd get himself killed and the rest of them in trouble.

"Of a girl called Gudrun . . . " Justus said, trailing off hopefully.

"She's in China, studying under a master painter."

Justus's soul flickered and burned like a lamp coming to life. "She's my sister."

"You look alike, though of course she's prettier. In that dress, I thought I might have a hard time marrying you off."

"And now?" Justus gestured at his clothes, spares from Valfrid. The shirt and trousers were both drab and black and had to be rolled up, but at least they wouldn't trip him in snow.

"Despite your sassy mouth and clumsiness, I don't think it will be so difficult after all. Would you like to see my notes on you?"

Intrigued, Justus nodded, and Pia rose, cupping her gleg in two hands as she strode down the hall. Justus followed her through the chilly corridor, his mug in one hand, the other guarding against his slipping waistband.

They paused at the locked door through which Pia had disappeared the other night. She let Justus through with a set of clanking iron keys.

Brilliant sunlight stabbed through the windows of Pia's workroom, illuminating a museum of shrines. Each isolated table held collections of scribbled notes, copied pages from books with underlined passages, and even a few rudimentary drawings. The ceiling arched away into darkness but for cathedral-like skylights of stained green glass.

Pia invited Justus to look closer with a swooping gesture of one arm. He skimmed the notes, looking for something he recognized. He hadn't learned enough to read well yet, but he could tell not all the words were in Swedish. Justus stopped at the fourth shrine and ran his fingers over an ink drawing of a rabbit in some reeds, carelessly scrawled on a scrap of paper. Gudrun's daisy-shaped signature curled around the rabbit's visible paw. Some of the letters here were scribbled in strange characters nothing like those he'd learned from Valfrid.

Gudrun was still gone, as much as if she'd been devoured. Justus wasn't sure where China was, but he knew what lay between: bandits and pirates, desert, sea, and jungle. His fists clenched, and he thought about telling Pia what he thought of her stealing his sister.

Her cool fingers slid over one of his fists, gentle pressure coaxing his hand open. "Her mentor says she most enjoys painting the birds, and that she makes their tails too long and refuses to change it. One is to arrive for my private collection sometime later this year. You may have it."

Justus swallowed. "I don't want her to be gone, even if she's alive."

Pia nodded. "I also dislike it when my guests leave. Yours is next," she added, indicating the next table.

Justus glanced at it. His collection was smaller than the others, and had many observations crossed out and re-written. Most of it was incomprehensible, but here and there he spotted words he knew. *Karin. Castle. Brave.*

Justus met Pia's gaze. "I can't read it," he admitted.

Pia smiled. "It says, 'I'm thinking of offering Karin a position as guardian of the castle in my absence—she's brave and skilled.' What do you think of that?"

"I don't understand. You're leaving?" Justus looked down at the paper again to mask his disappointment.

"Never for good, but I can't simply dispatch these young women off to unknown places," Pia said. "I must spend time making connections, through letters, gifts, and sometimes visits. While I'm gone, the castle staff is unprotected. I'm willing to stand for what I've done, but I don't expect them to do the same.

"I was about to ask you if you'd stay on as their protector when I found out you weren't a woman. Then I waited for proof that I could trust you, and I got it: you would even kill someone you loved if it would guard the lives of my rescued women, Justus. We'll find no better protector."

"I'm honored," Justus said. His gaze snagged on one of the notes, weighted by the two halves of his broken arrow. Sudden emotion kicked through Justus's heart like a silver frog through a murky pond. He pointed. "That paper has a heart drawn on it. What does it say?"

Pia smiled, raising one eyebrow. "When you can read that sentence, perhaps you'll find it better than you imagined."

—‿—

Cory Skerry lives in a spooky old house that he doesn't like to admit is haunted. When he's not peddling (or meddling with) art supplies and writing stories, he explores the area with his two sweet, goofy pit bulls. His retirement plan is for science to put his brain into a giant killer octopus body, with which he'll be very responsible and not even slightly shipwrecky. He promises. You can find sketches, incriminating photos, and more of his stories at coryskerry.net.

—‿—

I have a strong Norwegian lineage, so I thought it would be interesting to mine Scandinavian folklore for this story. The hard aesthetic of the Northern tales has always appealed to me: the trolls and the goblins, the brutal choices, the way night and winter feature so prominently. In "The Giant Without a Heart in His Body," found in the story "East of the Sun and West of the Moon," the giant is very much a relic of the pre-Christian story traditions; its harsh fate is emblematic of the way Christianity absorbed the relics of the pagan traditions, and turned them to its own purposes. I thought it would be interesting if the hero of the story had gotten lost in his journey, and found himself settled into a new era. How would he view his old story, if called back to it again? Would it have the same resonance for him? And what happens when it's time for the story to finally come to an end?

Nathan Ballingrud

THE GIANT IN REPOSE

NATHAN BALLINGRUD

Ivar looked through the ice-starred window of his kitchen and saw the crow perched on the fencepost near the barn, like a sharp-angled hole against the white expanse of snow. His own beard had itself become snowy since the last time he had seen the crow, his own face as weathered and creviced as earth. He watched the crow, and he felt the old feeling. The water on the range began to bubble and boil, yet he stood there, still as stone.

Olga's chin settled onto his shoulder from behind; he felt the weight of her body press against him, her breath against his cheek. "Old man," she said. "The water's boiling away."

"Is it? I'm sorry."

"What are you looking at?"

He nodded. "The crow. Do you see it?"

She put her arms around his waist, which was wider now than it once was. "You stare at it like an old enemy. Did it insult you in some way?"

"Just the opposite." He stepped away from her and walked to the door, where he fell upon the bench, pushing his feet into his boots. He stood and shouldered himself into his coat.

Olga remained by the kitchen sink, the humor in her face giving way to concern. "What's got into you, Ivar?"

"Finish the bathwater, woman. I'll be back in a moment."

It was a long trek from the front door to the barn, and though the year was old and the snow was new, a hard winter was promised, and there would be a time coming when this trek could not be made without a rope tied around your waist, lest a blizzard swallow you whole. The Minnesota plains were flat and long, not like the robust countryside of Norway, where glaciers carved bright watery roadways through the mountains. There were no hidden kingdoms in this fertile land, unless they were the kingdoms of the sown seed and the ready harvest.

The crow appeared as young as he ever was, his feathers glossy black, his beak sharp as a blade. He turned his head to the side and fixed Ivar with a bright, black glare.

"Håkon," said Ivar, coming to a stop beside the post. "I never thought to see you again."

"I've found the church," the crow said, as though countless years had not elapsed since last they spoke.

Ivar found it suddenly difficult to breathe. "Forget it," he said.

"I cannot. You rendered me a service in another age, and I am bound to repay it."

Ivar sighed. He looked over his shoulder at his little house, at the farmland stretching around it beneath the piled snow. He had come here with Olga many years ago, when he had long surrendered hope of finding the church, leaving Norway for this new world with a tide of his own countrymen. They found in the deep winters a comforting echo of home. Even if the land looked nothing like it.

He looked at the crow again. "Fine then. You've told me. Consider your debt repaid."

Håkon flared his feathers and jerked his head. He paced sideways along the fence, paced back again. "That's not how it works. You know that."

Ivar put his own hands on the wooden fence. They were old, short-fingered, broad. He was still amazed to watch the fall of his own body. He had been young, raven-haired, and strong, for the length of an age and beyond. For as long as he'd stayed true to the Story.

And then he'd come to America.

"Look at you, Håkon. Still so young. Your feathers are as black as Odin's eye. And I've grown old."

"You have abandoned the Story, and so you've aged. Everyone has aged, waiting for you to come back to it," said the crow. "Only I have not, because only I've been faithful to the tale. Return to your purpose, Ivar."

The sun hovered low in the sky. The day wore thin. How wonderful would it be, he thought, to push it up into the sky again. He remembered the directions procured for him by the princess, who whispered flattering lies into the giant's ear. "His heart is at the center of a lake, beneath a church, chained to the image of love."

Behind him Olga would be pouring the boiling water into the bath. A skirl of smoke lifted in lazy coils from the chimney, rising like a prayer into a low winter sky. He had farmed this land with her for forty years. Raised a daughter and a son with her. Together they were drifting into the strange waters of old age, and he had come to believe that they would reside together beneath the earth, in whatever realm waited for old Norwegians far from the path which God had set for them.

He was reluctant to leave, but the pull of responsibility, and more than that the pull of the old Story, were impossible to resist. If he did not come back, he could at least find consolation in the knowledge that Olga would not have to live long in loneliness. The earth would call her soon.

"Where is this church? I haven't the means to return to the old country."

"The church is in the Story, my prince. There is no need to cross a sea. Only a need to listen."

As they walked away from Ivar's house, into the field of snow, Håkon rode on the old man's shoulder, his talons gripping hard the heavy winter coat, and told the Story.

"Once there was a king with seven sons. He loved them so much that he could not bear to be out of their company. So when the time came for the sons to marry, he sent six out into the world to find seven wives, and kept the youngest at home, lest the loneliness for his children uncouple his soul from his body. The sons ranged across the land and had many adventures, at the end of which they found a palace with six beautiful princesses. After a period of courtship the sons set upon their journey home with their six beautiful wives. Transported as they were by love, they had forgotten their youngest brother."

Ivar grunted, but did not interrupt.

"They came upon the house of a giant, which was a mountain fashioned into the likeness of a cottage. The icy peaks were its shingles, the untamed countryside its porch. The chimney which released the smoke of the great kitchen fire was lost in cloud. The sons were remorseful of their forgotten promise and sought to make amends by presenting their brother with the giant's head as a trophy."

"A fine substitute for a woman's love!" spat Ivar.

"If you don't mind," said the crow.

"Continue." Ivar's stride grew longer and more sure as he listened to the old story. His breath filled his lungs more easily, and a heat grew in his blood that he had not felt in long memory.

"The brothers called upon the giant to face them. After a few moments the door swung open, and the giant stared down upon them all with a frightful face, and all six brothers and all six of their wives were so terrified that they turned to stone where they stood, and their horses beneath them. The giant left them there, and went back into his home.

"After a year had passed the king began to despair of ever seeing his sons again. 'It is well that I kept you here,' he told his youngest, 'for if I had lost you too there would be nothing left to tether me to this wretched world.' But the youth was not content to spend the rest of his days hidden away like a prized trinket in his father's castle while his brothers remained missing. He insisted that he go out and discover their fate, and bring them all safely home. Though his father protested, he wore him down in time, and at last he ventured down the same road they had embarked and been lost upon, promising his father that he would discover their fate and bring them home."

"Brash youth," side Ivar, but now there was pride in his voice.

"He had minor adventures of his own, including one in which he rescued a certain starving crow, who was then beholden to him. Eventually, he found his way to the giant's house, and in the garden he found his brothers and their six wives, their heads spattered with bird droppings and their ankles entwined by weeds. He crept secretly into the cottage at night and saw the giant talking to a girl in a suspended silver cage, who was as small to the giant as a canary would be to himself. The youth knew immediately that she would be his wife, for she was young and beautiful and she sang sweetly to the giant in a voice as delicate as the first cracking of winter's shell."

"Bergit," Ivar said, his voice full and quiet. He was walking forcefully through the snow now, unhindered by age, like a horse breaking through the surf.

"Bergit the Lovely. You remember," said Håkon, the approval plain in his voice.

"Of course I remember. Continue, crow."

"He spoke to her as the giant slept, the thin bars of the cage between them. She revealed that his heart was kept in a different place, and so he was invulnerable to death. If he would promise to free her from her imprisonment, she would help him to discover the location of his heart, so that he might slay the giant and free them all. Do you remember this part of the story?"

"She did as she promised."

"She sang sweetly to him again, on that night and on many nights thereafter, feigning love, until at last he revealed his heart's hiding place."

"In a lake. Beneath a church."

"And the hero went out to find it." Håkon fluffed his feathers, allowing himself the indelicacy of a dramatic pause. "And then he lost his way."

"I lost nothing, crow. I grew bored of a search that had no object."

Håkon nipped his ear. "How can you say that? The object was always understood!"

"Not by me," Ivar said. "Not as the years grew."

"Speak for yourself, prince. I know my function."

"What of Olga? What becomes of her now?"

"She is not part of this Story," said the crow. "She never was. Now look ahead."

Ivar did as he was told. The land in front of him rose in a sheet of rock, topped distantly with ice, and fell away on his left into a fjord, the glacial water as hard and bright in the sun as the purpose that had first stirred him from his father's castle. Along that declension of earth, rising from the grass like something grown, approached by neither trail nor road, was a small wooden church, barely bigger than Ivar's own shack, its steeple sturdy and proud, a shout of faith rendered in wood. There was no snow at this level; the land was decked in the indulgence of summer.

Ivar himself was young again, the muscles in his body gathered in his chest and arms, his hair long and black again, his beard full. He felt the full throat of the world in his chest, and breathed to fill it.

"Very well," he said. "Let us see what's inside."

The interior was warm and lit by a vast bank of candles which covered the wall behind the altar. The pews and the shelves were of polished wood, dustless, the book on the altar open and inscribed in an ancient Nordic script. Ivar paused and stared at the illumination on the page, which depicted the Angel of Death standing outside a closed door, a sword held loosely at his side.

Håkon leaped onto the altar and angled his head at the picture. His feet gripped and ungripped, repeatedly, like a nervous child. "A favorable omen," he said. "The giant's end is at hand."

"So it would seem."

Ivar turned away from the book, looking over the church's interior. A strong wind wrestled the building, and the wood creaked under its pressure, seeming to list from side to side. It felt like being in the hold of a galley, and Ivar wondered what he might see if he opened the door to the outside world.

"Who keeps this place, Håkon?"

"It is the house of the Lord, Ivar. Surely that's obvious."

"But who keeps it? Is Christ Himself dusting these shelves and lighting these candles? Does He heat soup over the fire? Will I find Him drowsing on a cot in the back?"

The crow peered at him. "You must be careful of blasphemy, my prince. You yourself have been drowsing on that prairie in the new country. The church, like the giant in his cottage and like your father in his castle, is maintained by the Story. It was a fog of dust and spiders until you looked upon it from the hill."

Ivar sat in one of the pews, and settled into thought.

"The Story awakens to you, and you to it. Look at yourself, Ivar. You're young again."

Ivar remembered hiding behind one of the chair legs in the giant's cottage, the terrible stench of cooking flesh filling his nose, the split carcass of a troll hanging from one of the rafters, its ribs pale and naked in its own exposed meat. The beautiful Bergit in her cage, dangling above the carnage on the table as the giant thrust his head suspiciously through the clotted smoke, filling his nostrils with it. "I smell a Christian's blood," it said. Its voice was old and deep, like something assembled from the rock which rooted the mountains to the earth.

Bergit had said, "A magpie flew overhead, and dropped a bone down the chimney. It went into the pot, but the smell lingers." Mollified, the giant had returned to its grisly work, and Ivar nearly sobbed in relief.

In the church, now, he passed his hand over the smooth wood of the pew in front of him. "Why would the giant hide his heart here? In a church?"

"I suppose because it's the last place anyone would look," said the crow.

Ivar was unconvinced, but could think of nothing to say. "Well. Let's find it, then."

There was only one room in the church, so it did not take long to discover the trap door behind the altar, with a ladder descending into a natural cavern. Ivar descended carefully while Håkon swooped past him and glided to a rest at the bottom. The cavern was cool, and its walls were rippled with the reflection of water. Ivar turned to see a vast lake, as black as a sky, stretching deeply into the distance. More candles were lit in small rows along its shore, illuminating a boat halfway pulled onto the sand. The crow hopped to a halt beside it.

"It doesn't make sense that it's underground," he said. "Why do you need me?"

Ivar pushed the boat into the water and settled himself inside. There was an oar lying alone the bottom, and he picked it up. "I suppose it will become clear soon enough."

"Where are you rowing it to? I can't see anything out there."

"Are you coming, crow?"

With obvious reluctance, Håkon fluttered onto his shoulder. His talons gripped his perch more tightly than perhaps was necessary.

Ivar steered them into the gloomy expanse, the small circle of candlelight receding behind them until it was only a tiny flare, a lonely flame of life in the silent, encompassing darkness. They moved through the cool air, the water trickling from the oar and lapping against the prow of the little boat. Håkon's fear was strong, and he fluttered and clucked in growing agitation.

"I think we've gone the wrong way," he said.

But Ivar had never felt stronger, or more confident in his purpose. He wanted to leap from the boat and swim the rest of the way, however far that might be, so great was his sense of strength, so great his need to spend it like an abundant coin. He wanted a foe whom he could break in his hands, he wanted a woman whose body he would open with his own. He was young and strong and the Story pulled him the way that God pulls the soul.

"We are on the right path, crow," he said. "The darkness is only a verse. To know the Story, we must know it all."

The crow settled at this admonishment.

They continued for a passage of time that neither could measure, until at last their boat nudged against something submerged, and circled around to the right, like the spoke of a wheel. Håkon cawed in alarm and took wing, becoming just a sound of muscle and feather in the dark air over Ivar's head. Ivar turned the flat of the oar to slow their momentum, and after a tense moment the boat settled into stillness.

Ivar stood, peering into the black, while the crow settled again into the bottom of the boat.

"Sit, my prince!"

"Hush."

He poked into the water with his oar until he hit something hard and unyielding.

"There."

He dropped the oar into the boat and extended his hand into the water. He had to reach deeply, leaning nearly halfway over, the water creeping up to his shoulder, before he encountered the yield of flesh, and across it heavy links of chain. Ivar grasped a link and heaved; the boat listed hideously and Håkon launched into the air, crying in alarm, but then Ivar eased himself seated again as he hauled his prize to the surface.

It was too dark to see anything, so he passed his free hand across it: an open eye as large as a wagon's wheel; a fleshy nose; an open mouth, the teeth cracked and akimbo around the chain which wrapped around the gargantuan head and extended down to the body, still hanging in the dark fathoms below.

"God in Heaven," said Ivar.

"What is it?"

"A giant. Dead."

"What?" The crow seemed outraged. "Have we been robbed of our glory?"

"I don't think so. Hold a moment." With that, he leapt over the side of the boat and into the black water. The chill of it nearly stopped his heart, and if he had been the old man he had woken as that morning, it might have done so. But he was young and strong again, a Nordic prince engaged in a mighty action, and so he pulled himself down the length of the dead giant, drifting free again, as the cold eeled its way into his brain and the increasing depth pressed against his ears, until he arrived at the bound hands and the large box they clutched. He pried the fingers free of the box with his flagging strength, and he dragged it through the water behind him, crawling up the giant's body with his free hand. It seemed to him that he ought to move with urgency, and yet his ascent was languid, almost reluctant. Never had he known such darkness, or such quietude. Something inside of him rose to it, like the ocean to the moon.

Håkon greeted his arrival with a shout of joy. Ivar wrestled the heavy box aboard the boat, then followed, where he lay gasping and exhausted. Some time passed before he had the strength to sit upright and address himself to the rescued box. He passed his hands across it, still blind in the darkness, and felt the hard wood and metal clasps, the holy cross raised in relief across its top. He felt the purpose of its construction.

"The giant did not hide his heart here," he said, after a moment. "It was taken from him. Imprisoned here."

"What difference does it make?"

"I don't know."

Ivar rowed them back to shore, where they beached beside the row of candles.

"Open it!" cried Håkon, fixing a greedy eye upon the prize.

Ivar did so. There was no lock—at least none meant for him. Inside was the giant's heart: surprisingly small, as is the way with these vast brutes, only about as large as the head of an ox. It was covered in damp soil; tiny white taproots extended from it in all directions, looking for something to root themselves into. Ivar knew that he could take it into his hands and crumble it like clumped earth. He scooped it out of the box, and felt the heat of it. It beat once, dislodging a small cloud of dirt.

He stared at it.

"What happens next?"

But even as he asked the question the heart beat a second time, and then a third, and Ivar saw not through his own eyes, nor dwelled in his own body, but discovered himself in the giant's mind, instead.

"You have me, Christian man," came the giant's voice.

The giant had lived in a cottage once. But then the world moved into another age, and his home was reclaimed by the mountain. There were no more trolls to feast on. No more villages to terrify and dismay. True, there were enough Christians now to carpet the whole earth with their crushed bones and pasted jelly—the very air stank of them, there was nowhere to draw a clean breath anymore—but age and sloth had laid the giant low, and the hills had grown over his body. His great shoulders sprouted wildflowers now, his sunken head become a precipice which little Christian children climbed upon and leapt from, landing in a clear pool of water where the river paused in leisure before continuing its seaward journey. All of his might and terror were subsumed into the ground, where he would have expired in the way of his brothers, had the spark of him not been imprisoned in a distant box, under a distant water.

Of Ivar's six brothers and their wives, there were now only twelve mossy rocks, arranged in a curious line which excited the imaginations of the locals. Perhaps it was a kind of Stonehenge, they thought, or the remains of an ancient fortification. Time and weather had erased their faces, and any indication of what they once had been.

"Tell me," said the giant. "Did you find my wife?"

Ivar thought of the huge, drowned corpse, the way it had clutched the box to itself. "I did," he said.

"Then at last I know her fate," the giant said, his voice quiet. "I am pleased that she is free of this fallen world."

"And Bergit? I do not see her. What is her fate?"

"The wench betrayed me," the giant said. "I should have eaten her as I had intended."

"Did you?"

"I could not. She was part of the wretched Story, just as I was. Just as I am. We have been waiting for you to do your part. She is buried in this hill with me, a rag and a bone, with a guttering flame still lit within her. I know this because I can hear her keening in the night."

"I am meant to force you to free my brothers and their wives. To free Bergit as well, so that she may come home with me and be my wife. I promised my father I would do these things."

"Do them then, wretch. Do them so that I may rise from this place and render you over my cooking fires."

"You are no threat to me, giant. Nor will you be ever again."

Ivar returned the heart to its box.

Håkon hopped closer, head cocked to the side. "What are you doing?"

"This was never the giant's Story, Håkon. He was imprisoned by it. He lost his wife to it. His own story ended long ago."

The crow paced, considering this. Finally he said, "I don't see how that matters. Did you tell him to free the other princes and their wives?"

"No."

"What? Why not?"

Ivar turned where he sat, resting his back against the boat, looking out onto the candlelit water, the emptiness beyond it. "Crow, I don't know what to do."

Håkon leaped onto Ivar's leg, took a step forward. He was rather a large bird, and Ivar felt some misgivings about provoking him. "You do what you are meant to do, my prince! What else? You release your brothers and fulfill your promise to your father. You marry the lovely Bergit, and you enjoy the vigor of youth. You return to the Story, as you're meant to do! What is this 'I don't know what to do' nonsense? Preposterous is what. Do this, and I will carry news of it to your father, so that he may ready the castle for your return. I'm sure that that is my function here."

"And what of Olga, my wise friend? Hm? What of my wife?"

"Well . . . " The crow seemed genuinely at a loss for a moment. "She is old, my prince. Her remaining years are so few. Bergit is young and beautiful. Just like you now! Or at least she will be when you command the giant to release her. Think of the handsome children you will have. Think of the pride in your father's eye."

Ivar did think of those things, and they were good. He thought of the promise he made to his father, which he had neglected, to his shame. He thought of his brothers, their hearts cresting as they returned home with the women they would build families with, their eyes full of life's coming bounties. And he thought of lovely Bergit, terrified and imprisoned, whose cleverness procured for him the information he needed to save her, and all the rest. It would be a sorry thing indeed to turn his back on them all.

But then at last I know her fate, the giant had said, with the sadness of long centuries alone in his voice. *I am pleased that she is free of this fallen world.*

Ivar closed the box's lid. He pushed it out into the water, where it drifted some distance before it sank.

Håkon was speechless. It is difficult to look into a crow's eye and read emotion there, but Ivar found this one to be quite expressive.

"I am quite fond of Olga," Ivar said quietly. "I think I would miss her more than I could bear."

"But the Story . . . oh, my prince . . . "

"Crow, it is time to acquaint ourselves with endings."

Håkon fulfilled his function after all. He carried Ivar's message away from the church, where the warmth of summer was already giving way to a chilly wind, across the mountains to the neglected castle of his father. The castle, like the giant's cottage, had fallen to time. A battlement here, a row of flagstones there, and a half-collapsed tower were all the remained of the once proud structure, scattered in the foliage like old teeth. The old king lived in the tower, where he rarely moved, except at night, when the moonlight would draw him to the window to watch for the return of his children.

This is how Håkon found him, his moon-kissed skull pale in the window, the cobwebs hanging from his bony shoulders like a grand cape. The crow landed on the sill beside the old king and looked thoughtfully at him, a few grey hairs still wreathed around his head, the black sockets of his eyes gazing emptily back. The crow was old himself now, the feathers around his beak thin and bedraggled, his gnarled feet scaly with age.

"My king," said the crow. "I bring news of your sons."

Upon hearing it, the king turned from the window for a final time and made his ponderous way across the room to a tumble of rocks, which, long ago, he had arranged into something approximating a throne. He reclined into it, hearing through the crow's message the voice of his youngest son: the most precious, the last to go.

I am sorry, Father. I have failed you. I cannot come back, and now you must die alone. It is unforgivable. But know that you are loved, and honored still. Your grandchildren will know your name.

And the king died at last, the sorrow of his grievous loss unanswered, but with the timbre of his son's voice to ferry him gently on.

Ivar did not look behind him as he left the church, nor did he think it was odd that the spring weather had abruptly given way to deep snow. The mountains and the fjords were gone. Before him was the austere beauty of the Minnesota plain, and there in the distance was his home, its little chimney unfurling smoke into the icy-starred twilight, while his fields slept beneath the snow until their season came upon them again.

His old joints creaked in the cold; the winter was going to be hard on him.

He opened the door and stamped the snow from his boots, slid the coat from his shoulders and set it on its hook. He passed a hand over his weathered face, rubbing warmth into his cheeks. There was a splash from the kitchen, and he entered it to see dear, round Olga, naked as a nymph, reclining in the tub with the steam rising around her as though she were taking her constitutional in some Icelandic spring.

"Horrible woman," he said. "That was my bath."

"The water was getting cold while you were out there chasing birds, you old fool. I wasn't going to let it go to waste. Did you catch it?"

"I did. We had a wonderful conversation, and then I let it go."

"One bird brain to another. It doesn't surprise me one bit."

"Ach," he said. "Have you used up all the heat yet? By God, I need some heat."

"As it happens, I'm about finished," she said. She rose from the tub, this plump old woman, this mother to his children and companion of his life, glistening like some bright mineral wrested from the earth, steam rising from her wet body as though she were a creature of some fabulous mythology, filling his home with heat as the snow fell softly beyond the glass.

—

Nathan Ballingrud is the author of *North American Lake Monsters*, from Small Beer Press. Several of his stories have been reprinted in Year's Best anthologies, and "The Monsters of Heaven" won a Shirley Jackson Award. He's worked as a bartender in New Orleans, a cook on oil rigs in the Gulf of Mexico, and a waiter in a fancy restaurant. Currently he lives in Asheville, NC, with his daughter, where he's at work on his first novel. You can find him online at nathanballingrud. wordpress.com.

—

Author *A. C. Wise* grew up obsessively reading and re-reading fairy tales from a lovely phone book-sized and phone book-style compendium containing several volumes of Andrew Lang's fairy tale series with appropriately color-coded pages. Ever since discovering Ellen Datlow and Terri Windling's retold fairy tale anthologies, Wise has aspired to writing (or rewriting) fairy tales of her own.

Fairy tales are a gateway, they hint at larger possibilities and worlds begging to be explored. They are skeletons wanting skin. Why did the heroine/hero/witch/evil step-relation/magical talking animal *really* take that course of action? Fairy tales, as brilliant as they are in their own right, are also fresh stories waiting to be told. "The Hush of Feathers, the Clamor of Wings," was born of the desire to give a voice to the cursed birds of the original story, while suggesting that not all of them might be innocent victims.

The Hush of Feathers,
the Clamor of Wings

A. C. Wise

It's Liselle's pain that brings me back.

I've been gone a long time. Sky-drunk, back to belly with the clouds, it's easy to forget. With the city all small and gray, laid out quilt-wise below me, why would I ever touch the ground?

For Liselle. Because her pain smells of nettles, pricked fingers, and blood. Because it sounds like patience and silence. Because it feels like ice forming a skin across the pond, like winter coming too soon. And I'm afraid I'm too late.

"What do you want more than anything in the world?" the witch asks.

She plants a foot on my shoulder, holding me at the bottom of the bed. She told me to call her Circe, and said it wasn't her name.

"You." I try to move, but she shifts her foot, ball planted against my collarbone, toes curled to dig in.

"Too easy."

Light slants across the bed, pools at her throat, slides between her breasts, and drizzles, crisscrossed by shadow, over her belly like honey.

"Can't you tell?" I grasp my cock, grin.

Just the edge of a frown tries her lips. They're dark, darkened further as she sips wine from a goblet by the bed. Her eyes are the color of lightning-struck stone, ever watchful. I can't tell her age. Maybe older than the world. She is beautiful, and terrifying, and if I don't give her the answer she's looking for, she'll burn me to ash without ever raising her hand.

She pushes me back, setting me off balance. "Try again."

Bells chime at her ankles. She swirls the wine in her glass, never taking her eyes from my face. She dips a finger into the glass, sucks ruby droplets from its tip, then slides it between her legs.

Blood pounds, deafening me; my cock aches. I say the first thing that comes to mind.

"Freedom?"

"Hmm." The witch arches an eyebrow, weighing me.

The words tumble now, a babble that may or may not be a confession. I don't know what I *want*; right now, I can't think past desire.

"I'm sick of George controlling the purse strings. Our parents left the money to all of us, but he acts like he's in charge."

I'm breathing hard, harder than I should be.

"Seven brothers in all, yes? And you're the seventh?" Even phrased as such, it's not exactly a question, but I nod. "And a sister?" I nod again. I haven't told her anything she doesn't already know.

At last, Circe relents. She lowers her leg, tracing her toes down my chest, and through the hair on my stomach. When she plants her foot on the bed, her legs are slightly parted, welcoming.

I crawl to her, ashamed of myself, and not caring. Thirsty, hungry, eager, I suck the lingering ghost of wine from between her legs. Her sex tastes of cinnamon and copper—a penny placed on my tongue for silence. The witch winds her fingers in my hair.

"Interesting," she says. "When I asked your brothers the same question, they all wanted power."

Folding wings tight, I dive, trading the clean smell of cloud and wind for smoky, roasted nuts, horse shit, and overflowing trashcans. Whatever else I may be, whatever else I've done, there's always this: I will come when she calls. What kind of brother would I be otherwise? Not the brother she deserves, certainly. I took her gift, and threw it back in her face. All because I fell in love with the sky, and when she came to save me, I refused.

Just before I hit the ground, I pull the trick the witch taught me and change. It's not a rational thing; it's just a different way of thinking—trading feathers for skin. But it gets harder every time.

It hurts more each time, too. Bones splinter and twist, going from hollow to full. Feathers draw blood, pulling out of my skin. The weight of my body nearly crushes me. Then I'm standing, panting, in gray clothing the same color as pigeon feathers. Which, if you look at them just right, are so many colors it will break your heart.

"Hi, Sis." I lower myself to the bench beside her.

My voice is rough. It cracks on human sounds, my lips, too, and I lick blood.

Liselle doesn't say anything. She hasn't spoken in at least fourteen years. Maybe more.

Her down coat is too big. Inside it, her wrists are thin, and her shoulders hunched. She reaches into one of the pockets, and it almost swallows her hand before she pulls out a note pad and a stub of pencil. She scribbles, tears off the sheet, and hands it to me. Her eyes, too large in her face, remind me of ice creeping in around the edges of a pond, freezing toward the center.

Liselle's scrawl is childish, unapologetic. Even cruel. Or maybe it's just because her fingers are stiff with the cold.

I'm dying.

I turn the note over, read it again. There's nothing else, just the stark words, charcoal as the sky.

"What?"

Liselle doesn't sigh, doesn't make a sound, but I see the impatience as she scribbles again, and passes another ragged sheet my way.

Cirrhosis. No transplant=dead.

Liselle turns away, and scatters a handful of breadcrumbs from the bag in her lap. Pigeons squabble at her feet.

"We'll get you help. We'll fix this." I grab her wrist.

She shakes me free, and this time she nearly tears the sheet in half handing the paper to me.

NO.

I stare at the blocky capital letters. "What do you mean, *no*?"

She snatches the paper from my fingers, underlines the word, and thrusts it back at me. Her eyes are all ice now, the black water at the pond's center swallowed up and the summer girl she used to be, drowned.

I don't know how long I've been gone; I can't tell how old Liselle is, but in this moment, she might be as old as the world. If I don't answer carefully, she will freeze my heart, and shatter it with a touch.

"Liselle . . . "

But I get no farther. My sister stands, scattering the last crumbs from her lap. The birds at her feet take flight, filling the air with the startled sound of their wings. The wind catches the empty bag, swirls it up to snag in the branches stretched over the pond. There is rage in every line of Liselle's body. Rage she has never spoken aloud.

The sound of all that silence is ice cracking, deep in the heart of winter. It's a vast oak, snapping under the weight of snow. Thin as a twig, Liselle is hard as stone.

I know exactly how hard she is, exactly how strong.

Seven years of silence, one for each brother. That was the witch's price. And Liselle paid it, laying a sister's love against the lure of sex, sweat-slick skin, and the taste of cinnamon, copper, and wine. The taste of freedom and power, against summer sunlight and raspberries picked from the brambly wilds of our parents' backyard, against woven daisy chains, and scrapes healed through the magic of Band-Aids.

Seven years, she swallowed her voice, her love and fear; seven years, she pricked her fingers to the bone sewing nettle shirts, one for each of us. Seven shirts, seven years, seven brothers who had become dirty, gray pigeons by a witch's curse.

And one who chose to stay that way.

It's too late to tell her I'm sorry. Besides, she'd know it was a fucking lie.

I reach for her, but she's twisting, gone. She can't fly, but she can still run.

"This is freedom," the witch says.

Circe stands me in front of the mirror. I'm naked, sweat cooling on my skin, but hard again the instant she touches me. She ignores my need, and runs her fingers down my chest, down the center of my body, nails catching ever so lightly on my skin.

"I'll show you what you are," she says. "Inside your skin, what you've always been."

My skin splits; it isn't blood that pours out, but feathers. There's no pain, but that doesn't mean I'm not horrified, terrified, as my flesh peels from my bones. I try to scream, but it emerges a strangled, rusty coo.

Panicked, I flap wings. My heart hammers against hollow bones, reverberating to deafen me. I want to ask her what she's done, how she could betray me. The witch only smiles, and bends low to gather me in her hands.

She holds me in cupped palms, wings pinned to my sides.

"Hush," she soothes. Her breath smells like wine; her lips skim my feathers.

The kiss stills me—not with desire this time. But, because she is predator, and I am prey. If I move to displease her, those lips will reveal white teeth, and like a carnival geek, she'll snap my head off, and crunch up my bones.

Holding me against the warmth between her breasts, so I can feel her heartbeat, Circe goes to the balcony and opens the doors wide. Her apartment, the jewel in a spire of green glass, a needle thrust up from the city, overlooks Central Park. Naked, she stands at the railing, and puts her lips close to my feathered body again.

"I'll tell you a secret," she says. "You can change back any time you want. It's only a different way of being, a different way of thinking.

You're free; no one can tell you what to do, or what to be. It's up to you to choose."

The witch leans over the rail, stretches her arms out and me with them.

"But," she says, and even though my body is suspended over the city, I still hear her as though her lips brush against me. I still feel the stir of hot breath over feathers. "If you tell anyone, it won't work anymore.

"This," she says, "is freedom."

She opens her hands, and casts me into the sky. It is flat gray. It threatens to swallow me whole. The city is too many colors, spinning up as I plummet down. Panic snaps my wings wide. Feathers arrest my fall. Chill as it is, the wind catches me, whips me over the park.

Winter-stripped branches reach for me, and grasp nothing. Far below, the pond winks with cold light, molten silver, spilled on the ground. The clouds kiss my back, smooth my fear away. People move below me, small as ants, small as I used to be. I never want to land.

I remember the sky, performing the witch's trick in reverse. It's easier than calling weight into my bones, stitching my feet to the ground. I let the aching wind knife open spaces inside me, let desire suck me upward, and fill those wounds with blue.

I'll show you what you've always been.

I know what the witch meant by those words. She didn't mean this—wings snapped wide, drinking the sky. She meant the selfishness, the desire that keeps me flying, that makes it easier to take to the sky than remember the land.

George's office has its own balcony, the prick. But it lets me bypass his personal assistant, and gives me the satisfaction of knocking on the glass, and giving him half a heart attack as I change.

He slides open the door, but blocks me, keeping me out of his office, which smells of expensive leather furniture, and Turkish rugs, hand-picked by an overpaid design consultant.

My brother doesn't look happy to see me. And why should he? I give him a big old grin, just to spite him.

"How ya been, Georgie?"

The frown lines around his mouth deepen. They're the only lines on his face. Botox, or good luck? Even with November coming on, his skin is perfectly tan, too. If his lips weren't pressed tight over them, his teeth would likely show even and white. George's hair is still dark, only the faintest threads of silver here and there, probably carefully worked in by a stylist for effect.

"What do you want?"

"Do you miss it?" The words fly out of my mouth, not at all what I meant to say. I've never been too good at humility. Circe was the only one who could make me beg.

But with my big brother, instead of getting on my knees to grovel, all that comes out is bile.

"Bran." He manages to make my name sound like a warning.

I hold up my hands, peace. "It's Liselle."

What happens to George's face when I say our sister's name is complicated. Guilt, yes, and some kind of brotherly love. But the affection is more remembered than felt, and the corners of his lips turn down in distaste. Liselle is an embarrassment to his current life. She's a reminder of feathers, squabbling after garbage, of filth and mites, and being no better than a rat with wings.

I wonder, even once, in all these years, has he checked on her? Invited her for a family dinner? Stopped by just to see how she's doing? Does he even know where she lives? Do any of them? Among all of my brothers, is anyone looking out for Liselle besides me?

"Make it quick," George glances at his watch; it's heavy and expensive, like everything else in this room. "My driver will be here with the car at precisely six o'clock. I've never had to make him wait, and I don't intend to start today."

"Liselle is dying. She needs a new liver," I say.

George's face goes through its complicated range of emotions again. Finally, he settles on impatience. "What am I supposed to do about it?"

"She needs money for a doctor, you lousy shit. It's the least you could do." I clench my jaw on the rage.

"I think you've got a lock on that." George's lips twitch, but there's genuine pain in his eyes. He must remember the raspberries, too.

Satisfied he's won, no matter how hollow the victory, George turns on his heel. I follow him into his office, and he retrieves his checkbook from a desk drawer. He comes back with the check in his hand, but plucks it back before my fingers close, and a cruel little smile turns up the corner of his mouth.

"She's still going to need a compatible donor, you know."

Shit. Of course, I didn't think of that. Smug, George puts the check into my palm, and folds my fingers over it.

"Good luck."

It isn't about Liselle for him, it's about me. What would I give up to save her? George and the rest, they forsook the sky, and now they're done as far as they're concerned. They paid their dues. In their minds, they don't owe Liselle seven years of her life back; it's enough to know they didn't steal another seven, or more. They didn't waste her blood, and stitch closed her mouth with silence for the rest of her life. Only I chose to stay a bird. In the face of a sister's love, only I chose the sky.

"Asshole."

The word doesn't wipe the smirk from George's face. Still, I leave it trailing behind me as I slip the check into my pocket, step onto the balcony, and take wing.

"What would you give," the witch asks, "to have them back again?"

To each of us seven brothers, she asked what we wanted. Of Liselle, she asks what she can take away. And as she asks it, the witch looks at me.

If I speak now, I can save my sister, but it would mean giving up the sky. The witch's penny, her copper secret, lies heavy on my tongue. I should change, shed feathers, grab my sister's hand, and take her far away from here. I wouldn't be able to fly anymore, but we'd both be able to run.

This is what the witch meant by freedom. Freedom to choose

cruelty over kindness. Freedom to choose my heart over Liselle's. *This* is freedom. It knifes me open, and I fill the wound with the taste of wind, and the blue of the sky. I keep my feathers, and hold my tongue.

Liselle's mouth forms an "O," her breath steaming in the air. She trembles, her eyes wide and frightened, her skin winter pale. The summer girl is there, as she looks at each of us in turn—seven dirty birds ranged around her feet. I watch the ice close in; I watch her drown.

"Anything," Liselle says, "I'll give anything."

"Hmm." Circe looks disappointed as she steps back.

Did she hope for Liselle to fight, to refuse, and demand power of her own? The witch's lightning-struck eyes seem to say that Liselle could have been so much more. Of all of us, Liselle might actually have been worthy of the witch's gift, and she declined.

"This is what you must do to save them," the witch says.

She puts her lips against Liselle's ear. I feel that whispered-hot breath against my own skin. I cannot weep, only let out a mournful pigeon's sob. Liselle's fingers curl, tightening against her palm, but she nods.

Circe puts her hand against Liselle's throat. Liselle looks up, her eyes going wider still. When the witch lowers her hand, Liselle puts her fingers against her lips, not to stop her voice slipping away, but to seal it inside. The witch didn't take anything from our sister, save a promise. Liselle could speak any time, if she chose.

Choice: That's the witch's gift. And her curse. Giving you what you already have, taking what you willingly give. Showing you what you are inside your skin.

When Liselle lowers her hands, already her eyes are turning dark, ice creeping around the edges toward the center of everything. Seven brothers, seven years; no matter what it takes, she will set us free.

And so, after seven years of silence, Liselle comes back to Central Park with her pricked fingers and nettle shirts, just as the witch asked. Seven years of weight drags at her bones and frost-dulls her eyes.

She is pale and ghost-thin. Seven years bound to the earth while her brothers drank the sky.

Even in these feathered bodies, we are still her brothers, and she knows us still. But I barely recognize her. Where is the little girl who ran with us in the sun, who kissed our wounds, and fed us raspberries from her thorn-pricked hands? It is already too late for her, I tell myself. There is nothing left to save.

Liselle casts the nettle shirts, stitched with her silence and her pain, into the air. They snag feathers, pulling my brothers to earth one by one. They scream with the change, cry out in agony, and weep. Liselle weeps, too, tears rolling from eyes like ink and ice. But she makes no sound. She puts a hand over her mouth, and holds all the sorrow in as her nettles tear my brothers raw, and they change.

Then there is only one shirt left. Liselle turns to me, and through the sorrow, I see the beginning of a smile. After this, she will be free. All the pain, all the silence, will be worth it, and she'll have her brothers back again.

Sunlight comes to break through the clouds. She tosses the last shirt into the air, and I snap my wings wide and fly as fast as I can. Instead of catching me, the nettles sail past me, and hit the ground.

Sometimes, in my memory of that day, I collide with Liselle's voice, winging back to her like a bird. The force of my betrayal shatters it in the air; it breaks, but never her promise. We are each bound to our choice—me, to my freedom; Liselle to her silence.

There's no sound, of course. No cry of rage from Liselle. As I spiral up, I see the ice finally cover her eyes, sealing away the summer girl. I beat my wings, lifting farther and farther away from her, fleeing the gift she tried to give me—staying drunk and in love with the sky.

My brothers, crouched bloody on the ground, feathers in their hair, and nettles buried in their skin, stare at me wide-eyed. I see shock, anger, not for Liselle, but for themselves, because they weren't clever and cruel enough to hold onto the witch's gift, the witch's curse.

~

Flying away from George, the sky soothes me, as always. Like a sister's touch, a hand on a fevered forehead, an encouraging smile at just the right time. The witch took all that away from me; broke me. Or, I threw it away. I gave up Liselle and everything—traded laughter and the taste of raspberries for blood-copper sex, for cinnamon and wine. For the freedom that was always mine.

And Liselle paid the price.

I could keep flying, leave George to his smugness and Liselle to her dying. She doesn't want my help anyway. I wouldn't let her save me; why should I expect anything different from her?

Below me, the city smears bright, red spattering the pavement where brakes slam. Horns blare. Impatient men and women shout. Babies cry. How does Liselle subsist among so much noise?

From the corner of my eye, I catch sight of the witch's tower. Fourteen years later, and it's unchanged—a needle of emerald, daring the sky. It glints in the setting sun.

I could go to Circe. I could beg. I tried it once before, and it gained me nothing. After I refused my sister's gift, I fled to the witch, sobbing, and asked her to give Liselle back her voice again.

"Would you give up the sky?" she asked me.

I couldn't answer her, as though she had stolen my voice, too.

"Then how can you ask her to give up her promise? Her heart? Her silence?"

And today, my answer would be the same.

Suddenly, the witch's tower is in front of me, as though my memories have called me back to her. I snap my wings wide to avoid striking the glass. Blood and feathers, a broken body falling from the sky.

What would you give to have her back again?

Summer sunshine. Liselle's smile. Her fingers pricked by thorns and smeared red with berries, instead of pricked by nettles and red with blood.

I chose once, I could choose again. I could break my body against the glass. I'm not a card-carrying organ donor, but could a doctor refuse a dying man's last wish?

I bank away from the witch's tower, circling. Do I have the courage to fly straight, and not break away this time?

Is it too late? Can I pull Liselle from the ice?

My reflection wavers in the witch's glass, as I turn again, skimming the tower so the window scrapes my feathers. Another thought occurs. George's car arrives at his office at six o'clock every evening. How hard could it be for a dirty, gray pigeon to startle a driver, to cause an accident? Surely George has an organ donor card in that fat wallet of his, along with all his cash.

And if not, I still have six other brothers.

What *would* I give to have Liselle back again? My blood? Theirs?

I can't give her back her voice. I can't give her back the seven years and more I stole from her, but I can give her something better—the choice I had, to take my gift, or refuse. It's the least I can do.

Liselle's pain brings me back again, the way it always has. I let it carry me through the sky, wound around my useless heart. I wonder what Liselle will choose—accept a brother's gift, or refuse it out of spite. I know what I would do, but I'm not Liselle. I can only hope that, in this sense at least, it isn't too late, and her heart is still stronger than mine.

--~--

A. C. Wise was born and raised in Montreal and currently lives in the Philadelphia area. Her fiction has appeared in publications such as *Clarkesworld, Lightspeed, Apex,* and *The Best Horror of the Year Volume 4,* among others. In addition to her fiction, Wise co-edits *Unlikely Story*, publishing three themed issues of unlikely fiction per year. You can find her online at www.acwise.net.

--~--

Retellings are a common approach to the art of writing fairy tales, but often the tales that get retold over and over are those that originated from the Grimm Brothers, Hans Christian Andersen, or Charles Perrault. Other fairy tales exist without having necessarily been classified as such, for a variety of reasons. Sometimes it's because of the form they take, like Christina Rossetti's famous poem, "Goblin Market," from which I took my inspiration. When I first read that poem, it was clear to me that it was a fairy tale, but told in the form of a poem. In my retelling, I transport the poetry into a prose story form, and also attempt to illuminate a story hidden within Rossetti's original version. That's truly the most beautiful thing about retellings, I think: the way that one author can illuminate or reveal what the original author either couldn't see or did their best to conceal.

Christopher Barzak

Eat Me, Drink Me, Love Me

Christopher Barzak

Days, weeks, months, years afterwards, when we were both wives with children of our own, our mother-hearts beset with fears and bound up in tender lives, I would call the little ones to me and tell them of my early prime, those pleasant days long gone of not-returning time. I would tell them of the haunted glen where I met the wicked goblin men, whose fruits were like honey to my throat but poison in my blood. And I would tell them of my sister, Lizzie, of how she stood in deadly peril to do me good, and won the fiery antidote that cured me of the goblin poison. Then, when my story came to end, I would join my hands to their little hands and bid them cling together, saying, "For there is no friend like a sister in calm or stormy weather; to cheer one on the tedious way, to fetch one if one goes astray, to lift one if one totters down, to strengthen whilst one stands."

And when afterward the children went on their ways to create their imaginary worlds in the afternoon sunlight, or under the shadows of the willow tree at the bottom of the garden, I would weep, silently, from where I sat on my bench, for I had lied in telling them the story in that particular fashion. It was told in that way for their own good, really, with a sound moral embroidered within it, but none of it was true. Except the part about the fruit, and the goblins, and how my sister saved me from a terrible fate.

What I did not tell them was how my sister also destroyed me. A part of me, I should say. Perhaps the best part. But stories for children never hang a broken heart upon the mantle for all to witness and to fear. Instead it is a lively heart, and it is beautiful, isn't it? Thudding away like a fine instrument! The stories one tells children always mean: Life will be happy, my dear ones, even though you will struggle within the world's fierce embrace.

Perhaps I should begin with the day when everything truly went awry, the day Lizzie and I were walking down by the brook near our family's farm on the outskirts of town, arguing, as we had been doing for much of that summer, and I first came to spot the goblin merchants as they erected their marketplace in the glen across the water. At the time I did not know it was a market they had set themselves to making in such a hidden place, outside of town, where the idea of patrons lining up to buy their goods was an unlikely gamble; but I could hear their voices float toward us, and when I looked over the swaying reeds by the gently flowing water, I could see their tables laden with fruit so lushly colored it shined like precious gems beneath the waning red sun.

It was their faces, though, that charmed me more than anything. Some wore the features of a red fox with sharp ears, charcoal-tipped. Others had long white whiskers that drooped, like a cat who has just lapped a satisfying bowl of cream. One bore the snout of a pig, another peered through the round golden eyes of an insect. Before I could realize what I was doing, I had stopped my progress on the path and Lizzie, who now stood a few steps ahead of me, had turned back to say, "What is it, Laura? Why must you always allow your heart to flap as if it does not belong to you but is possessed instead by the wind?"

I wanted to laugh, and laugh I do now, when I think of Lizzie's frustration over my displays of emotion. After all, we had been arguing that day about how it had been she who had stirred my emotions like a spoon of milk into a cup of tea. "How can you now wish that I not be stirred after having stirred me?" I had asked, just before I heard the goblin voices. But Lizzie had only shaken her head with disgust and refused to answer.

"What is it, Laura?" she asked again, with more concern this time, as I stood on the path by the river, entranced as if in a waking dream.

"Over there," I said, lifting my chin in the direction of the goblin merchants as they set about their queer business. Now they had begun to play music, a bow on a fiddle, with a long reed pipe settled upon the lips of a rat-faced goblin, and as their notes weaved toward us, the other goblins began to dance, arm in arm, with sweat on their brows, circling one another, switching partners.

"They're horrid," said Lizzie. "Do not look at them, Laura. Come. Let us be on our way."

On our way. I looked at Lizzie, who stood half-turned to me, half-turned in the direction of home, and blinked. It was not *our* way. It was *her* way. It had been her way for the entirety of the summer. It had been her way since she first kissed me in late spring, when everything was in riotous flower. It was she who held me close in our bed and told me not to say a word of this to her father, for it would break his heart to know his daughter and his oldest friend's child had been so twisted from what should have been a sisterly bond, as they had raised me in my parents' stead these last few years since my mother and father had died from consumption. It had been Lizzie who said, "We must never tell anyone what we have done, and we must stop ourselves from doing it ever again, Laura."

"But why?" I asked. "It does not feel twisted, as you name it, Lizzie. Is it not love we are feeling?"

"My father would not call it love," said Lizzie. "And if your mother and father were still here instead of with the angels, they would not call it love either."

"What do *you* call it?" I had whispered in the dark of our room, my hand resting near hers, my fingertips barely brushing her tender wrist.

But Lizzie would not answer. She simply turned her back to me, as she did now on the path, turning to lead us the rest of the way home.

"No," I whispered, and turned toward the music instead, turned toward the goblins and the fruits they had assembled upon their tables under the trees in the glen. "This is my way," I said, and stepped off the path to join them.

Behind me, Lizzie gasped. I could imagine her hand, too, delicately flying to cover her mouth as it did whenever she was shocked or frightened. "Laura!" she said, but I continued on my way. At the edge of the brook, I took off my shoes, parted the reeds with my hands, and stepped down into the water. It was ever so cold, but on a day as hot as that one had been—both from the sun and from the strong words we'd exchanged—I welcomed the shiver.

The water rose no higher than my knees, and it took only nine or ten strides before I had reached the other side and could release my dress, which I had bunched within my fists as I crossed over. Immediately, as I came to stand on the other side of the brook, the goblin's music came to an abrupt halt, and they all turned in unison to stare at me.

At first I worried they would not welcome my intrusion, so I began to apologize profusely for interrupting, but even as I unrolled my pleas for forgiveness like a long scroll before their strange faces, the cat-whiskered goblin man lifted his palm and said, "My lady, no apologies! You are our first patron of the evening, and you are welcome to our party. Come, look at our fruits, so succulent, and so deliciously dripping with juices! You will not find such fruits sold in any town. Will you try a pear or an apple or a melon? Won't you taste this peach?"

He produced a perfectly golden peach in his hand, and stretched it across the space between us. At first, he had seemed to be standing too far away to reach me, but in the next moment he stood inches before me, the peach already lifted halfway to my mouth. I could smell its ripeness, and my mouth watered, hungering for its juices.

"I have no money to buy your fruit, sir," I said, turning my face to the ground to hide my embarrassment. Here I had come in order to hurt Lizzie, here I had come to join the goblin festivities, and yet I was not prepared to purchase their goods at all.

The cat-whiskered goblin's fingertips found my chin, and lifted ever so gently, so that I stared up into his yellow-green eyes, which seemed to sparkle in the fading light, and in that moment I saw that his whiskers and his fur were no more than a mask he had placed upon his face. "You need no money here, my lady," he said. "That is the currency of humans."

"Are you not human, then?" I asked, and could not help but hear a quiver enter my voice.

The cat-masked goblin shrugged, pursing his lips as if he'd tasted something sour. "I have not lived as those in towns live for a long time now, and I do not miss their ways. They are ever so proper, don't you think? And ever so dull-witted with their cordial and celebrated proprietary agreements."

He sighed, grinning with only one corner of his mouth as he removed his fingertips from my chin, and offered me the peach again. "I would take a lock of your hair as payment," he said, almost breathless. "No coin could contain the value of the gold in those locks."

I blushed, for more reasons than I would have liked to. I blushed because he had found a way into my center, into the soft and tender part of me that wished others to see me as valuable, as something beautiful, as something that could not be ignored or forgotten as Lizzie ignored and forgot me. And I blushed because I had let him see my weakness. No woman who sets her sights on a better life should be so visibly vulnerable, yet there I was, blushing as though I were worth nothing.

A tear fell from my eye as I stood there. He caught it on the edge of his finger, then lifted it to his lips to sip at it.

"Exquisite," he said, after swallowing the tear in a theatrical gesture, and I laughed a little in nervousness, but his eyes never strayed from mine during our entire exchange. Not even when he put out his hand to offer me a pair of scissors, and said, "One lock, my dear, and you may join us."

I took the cold metal in my hands and lifted it to my head, pinched a long strand between thumb and forefinger, then slid the blades of the scissors closed. The lock shorn, I dropped it into his outstretched palm, and he closed his hand upon it.

"Your peach, fair maiden," he said, and then placed the fruit into my palm. He held my hand between his own for a long moment, lingering, still holding my gaze steady. Eventually he lifted my hand, and the fruit with it, up to my mouth for me.

I hesitated, but then opened my mouth to take the fruit between my teeth, and when I bit through the downy skin, juice sweeter than any honey from the rock, juice stronger than any man-rejoicing wine, juice clearer than any water flowed into me. Within a moment I was dizzy, but I could not resist the taste, and so sucked and sucked and sucked at the peach, until only its wrinkled pit remained, which I let fall to the ground as I turned toward the cat-masked goblin man's table, to pluck up another and another and another of his fruits, sucking and tearing at the flesh, swallowing as if my life depended upon it, and could not tell night from day any longer, as strange lights filtered through the canopy of the trees, spreading leafy shadows across the masked faces, and the goblins again struck up their music and began to dance around the glen.

One took me by the arm and twirled me into the center of them, where yet another took me up and I gasped to see her long yellow hair and soft round lips before me, the rise of her breasts beneath her tunic. We danced and danced and danced, she and I, spinning and twirling until I could no longer see anything but her face, until I was spun out of the circle like a whirlwind, and only by chance did I catch hold of a tree trunk, where I braced myself against its sturdy body and breathed heavily for a long time while the fireflies fired their bodies around me.

The female goblin left the dancing circles when she noticed I had not been able to continue twirling, and came to find me at my steady tree, still gathering my wits, as if I had just awoken from a deep dream.

"More fruit?" she asked, switching the tail she wore on her bottom back and forth. "I have fruit of my own you have not yet tasted, mistress."

She leaned down and placed her lips upon mine, and sucked at my flesh as I had sucked at the flesh of the fruits. I nearly fell into her arms as she took me into her mouth—I felt myself collapsing a little more with each kiss—but I managed to pull away before she stole my last breath from me.

"I must be going," I said, wiping my lips clean of her, blinking, in shock a little. Beneath the white moonlight, the smear of juice I had wiped away glistened on the back of my hand.

"So early?" the female goblin said, raising one sharply angled eyebrow. "But the moon has just now risen."

"My sister Lizzie," I said. And as soon as her name left my mouth, I began to remember myself, to recollect the argument Lizzie and I had had that afternoon, to remember my love for her, the love she said no one would call love should they ever discover it.

"You may find other sisters here, if you join us," the goblin woman said, trailing a fingertip down my cheek.

"But that is not love," I said, as if I knew what love was wholly from my feelings for Lizzie, as if that were the only love that could ever be.

"Love," the female goblin whispered. She smiled with what might have been sympathy, had I been able to see her entire face behind the mask and know what the rest of her features might tell me. A mask, I thought, was perhaps what I had needed when facing the cat-whiskered man. A mask would have hidden my weakness. "Love," the female goblin said, "comes in many different shapes, my dear. Why approve of only one? Particularly when no one else would approve of the shape of your love anyway?"

I stood, trembling, wishing for an answer, but her question pierced my reasoning through and through.

I turned quickly, and began to run, taken over by a fear that grew in me like a dark tide. I had come to the brink of something. A great chasm of darkness lay before me in the glen, an uncertainty that invited one to throw oneself into it, to lose my self, if I so wanted. But I ran from the sight of it, ran to rejoin the world I knew, regardless of its limitations.

Behind me, the goblin woman shouted, "Do not forget us!" But I did not look over my shoulder or give her a word in return, and only once did I stop to pick up the hard pit of a peach I had dropped earlier that evening, the first fruit I had tasted, which in the momentary madness of my fleeing I thought I might plant and grow into a tree of my own, to have that fruit available to me forever.

Lizzie. Oh how Lizzie will hate me for what I've done, I thought as I crossed the brook and took the path home. And I was right. As I approached the gate, she was already there, waiting for me with her arms folded beneath her breasts, her form a daunting silhouette in the silver moonlight, a guardian spirit to her father's cottage.

"Laura," she said, shaking her head, her voice filled with what seemed like loathing for me. "Do you know what time it is? Do you know how worried you've made my father and mother? Do you not care what others might think? Don't you remember Jeannie, after all, and what happened to her? The fate she suffered for going into the night?"

I put my head down, shamed, and began to tear up a little. Jeannie. Of course. Jeannie. I had forgotten about Jeannie, young Jeannie, who had gone off one night with a dark-skinned young man who they said lived in the woods, and had returned home some days later, a broken woman. The lovely, poor, ruined Jeannie, who withered like a plucked flower until she died from either heartbreak or, as I secretly believed, from the coldness she was forced to endure from others after returning from the woods. This was what concerned Lizzie, then. What others thought of her.

"It was not as you think," I murmured, preparing to explain myself. But Lizzie's sharp voice rose up again, barring me from speaking.

"I will not hear any of it, thank you very much," she whispered, shrill, in the late summer night air. "Do not speak a word. And do not return to the glen again, Laura, ever, or you will not be able to live here thereafter."

I nodded, and wiped my face with the back of my hand, wishing Lizzie might take my tears upon her finger as the cat-whiskered goblin man had done and relieve me of my regret and sorrow, wishing she would at least be kinder.

After my acquiescence, though, she only turned and went into the cottage without another word.

What would I have done without Lizzie and her parents? I would have been an orphan in some other house, I'm sure. I might have been given over to an innkeeper and his wife, or I might have been placed as a worker in a factory, at the ripe age of sixteen, when my own parents fell ill and began to pass away before my eyes. Instead, Lizzie's father promised my father, his oldest friend, a friend he called brother, that I would not fall into the hands of strangers and be left alone in the world to fend for myself.

And yet there I was, latching the gate to their cottage behind me, alone, and latching the door of the cottage behind me, alone, and creeping over the creaking floorboards until I could latch Lizzie's and my bedroom door behind me, as if I were a stranger stealing through their property in the middle of the night. Lizzie had already put on her bedclothes and pulled the covers up to her chin. She lay with her yellow hair streaming out on the pillow like an aura of light, her body curled into itself in the same way babies are born into the world. I changed my own clothes and slid into bed beside her, felt the heat of her body warming her half of the bed, and nearly put my hand upon her waist as I had grown used to doing all that spring and summer, before Lizzie grew afraid of our passion and told me it must end or we would burn in hell like poor Jeannie, upon whose grave no grass would grow. I had once planted daisies for poor Jeannie, who everyone shook their heads about whenever her name was mentioned, but no blossoms ever came to bloom. Everything wilted and withered, as Jeannie herself had wilted and withered after she returned from the woods without her dark-skinned suitor.

"Are you awake?" I whispered into the dark that separated us.

Lizzie groaned and told me to be quiet.

"You shall see," I told her. "Tomorrow, I will bring you the most delicious fruit—peaches, melons, fresh plums still on their mother twigs, and cherries worth getting—and then you will no longer feel such anger with me."

Golden head by golden head, we lay in the curtained bed, like two pigeons in one nest, like two blossoms on one stem, like two flakes of newly fallen snow, like two wands of ivory, tipped with gold for awful kings, and heard nothing more from the night but the sound of our own hearts beating, and fell asleep without having reconciled.

Early in the morning, when the first cock crowed, we rose together and, sweet like bees, began our work for the day, neat and busy. We fetched in honey from the combs, milked the cows, flung open the shutters to air the house, and set to rights all that had fallen out of place the day before. With Lizzie's mother, we kneaded cakes of whitest wheat, churned butter, whipped up cream, and then went on our way to feed the chickens before, in the late afternoon, we broke from our duties to sit and sew together for a while, and talk a little about nothing of importance, as we used to do, as modest maidens should, which I could see from the placid smile on Lizzie's face, bent over her needlework, gladdened her. But no matter what we did that day, my thoughts were with the night to come, with the fruits my teeth would meet in, with the music and the dancing, and the goblin men and women who would spin me within their embrace.

When at length the evening reached us, Lizzie and I took up our pitchers to fetch water from the reedy brook, and did not speak of goblins or of fruit, but went along peacefully, as we did at the end of each day. Kneeling by the brook, we dipped our pitchers into the water to fill them with the brook's rippling purple and rich golden flags, and when we stood again, the crags of a nearby mountain were flushed red with the setting sun.

"Come, Laura," Lizzie said. "The day is ending. Not another maiden lags. The beasts and birds are all fast asleep, and soon too shall we be."

I loitered by the reeds, listening for the sound of their voices, waiting to hear a bow eke a tune from the strings of a violin, or a first rush of breath fill the pipes and bring the glen alive with music. "It's early still," I said. "The dew is not yet on the grass, no chill has settled into the wind."

Lizzie, though, was not having any of my excuses. "It's them you're waiting for," she said, "isn't it?"

I turned to face her, and said, "Yes," and said, "If you but tasted their fruit, you would understand me as you once did."

"Then why do you wait?" Lizzie said. "Go to them. They are there, after all, calling for us to join them. *Come buy, come buy!* It is an ugly sort of commerce, Laura. I don't know what you are thinking."

"Wait?" I said. "I wait to hear those voices. You hear them?"

"Yes," Lizzie said, and lifted her chin to gesture toward the glen across the flowing water. "They are there already, waiting for you to return to them."

I nearly spun on my feet like a top to look where Lizzie gestured, but when I faced the glen, I saw nothing but the empty pasture where I had danced and eaten the night before. I heard nothing but the sound of the brook flowing by me. "Where, Lizzie?" I asked. "I see nothing, I hear nothing."

"Good, then!" Lizzie said with a glee that angered me. "Come home with me. The stars rise, the moon bends her arc, each glowworm winks her spark. Let us get home before the night grows dark, for clouds may gather though this is summer weather, put out the lights and drench us."

I stood still as stone, and felt cold as stone through and through. "Really, sister?" I said, my eyes wide with fear. "Do you hear them truly, or are you trying to hurt me?"

"*Come buy, come buy!*" Lizzie said again, mocking their voices, making them sound like terrible creatures. "It is good that you cannot hear them," she said. "It means your heart is still your own."

She held her hand out then, and curled her fingers inward. "Come, Laura," she said. "Let us be home again."

I did not want to take her hand—I wanted to take the hand of the goblins whose voices I could no longer hear, whose masked faces I could no longer see—but in the end it was the hand offered me, and it was the hand I took.

We went to bed that night and curled around each other as we used to, and for a while I thought that I was better off for not hearing the voices of goblins. But before our twistings and turnings could reach a satisfactory moment, I felt all passion leave me, like a cork released from its bottle, and lay in the dark, wondering about the strange people who had shown me a glimpse of a life I would now never know. Lizzie patted her kisses upon my cheek, upon my shoulders, and stroked my side and waist with her nimble fingers, but the fingers I had longed for in the past few weeks when she had kept them from me, those fingers and their touch no longer held me in the spell they once cast over me.

When Lizzie finally fell asleep, I sat up and looked out the window at the moon hanging low, caught up in the branches of a tree. I cried, silently, and gnashed my teeth like a starved animal, and held the howls of yearning inside my body so Lizzie would not wake and ask me what was the matter.

She should have known. She'd been the matter. Now it was something else taken from me.

For days, weeks, months afterward, I waited in the sullen silence that accompanies exceeding pain, hungering for another glimpse, wanting the sound of their music to find me, eager for the taste of their fruit upon my lips, desiring only to dance within their circle once more. But I never spied the goblin merchants again. Instead, I began to wither, the way Lizzie had warned me poor Jeannie had after returning from the woods without her young man. And as I withered, Lizzie seemed to grow brighter, as if she held a warm fire within her.

In all the months that passed, I had only one brief period of hope, which came when spring returned to us and I recalled the peach stone I had brought home from the goblin revels. I had placed it in a drawer and, upon remembering it, I quickly took it out to set it on a wall that faced south, and soaked it with my tears, hoping it would take root, or grow a green shoot after I planted it in the garden. No shoot ever came, though I dreamed of melons and trees full of ripe apples; and sometimes, as I came to see if the peach kernel was growing, I would be deluded by visions of ripe berry bushes, the way a thirsty traveler in the desert will see water where no water flows.

No more did I sweep the house, no more did I tend to the fowl or cows. No more did I join Lizzie and her mother to knead cakes of wheat, no more did I gather honey. Instead, I sat in the nook by the chimney and nursed my sorrow. And never did I fetch water from the brook, for going there reminded me too much of what I could no longer see, hear, touch, taste.

"Poor Laura," Lizzie said one day in late spring, while I was at my worst. I had stopped eating, because no food set before me tasted of life, and even when I tried to eat for the sake of Lizzie and her parents, I could not take more than two bites before my stomach turned and revolted. "Poor Laura," said Lizzie, coming to sit beside me. She lifted my cold hand from my lap and held it between her burning palms. "I cannot stand to see you suffering like this, sister. Tonight I will put a penny in my purse and go to the goblin merchants for you."

I was too feeble in mind and in body to say anything to stop her, and could only watch as she slid the coin into her purse and went on her daily mission to fetch water from the brook.

What occurred down there, in the glen near the flowing water, beneath the newly leafed trees and the shadows they cast upon the ground beneath them, I could only imagine from my own experiences. But Lizzie was a smart girl, and always prepared to get what she wanted without giving herself over in return. So later, when she returned at moonrise, and spilled into our room, slathered in the juice of goblin fruit from top to bottom, I could not believe the words she sang out to me.

"Laura, oh Laura, did you miss me? Come and kiss me. Never mind my bruises, hug me, kiss me, suck my juices, squeezed from goblin fruits for you. But I did not let them touch me, only you. Only you. Come, Laura. Eat me, drink me, love me. Make much of me. For you I have braved the glen and had to do with goblin merchant men."

With a start I leaped from my chair, already concerned that Lizzie had tasted fruit that would destroy her. I clutched at her, and kissed her, and held her to me, as we once did with great passion. Tears sprang from my eyes, burning as they fell from me. And as the juice from the goblin fruit smeared upon my sister's body filled my mouth, I felt my youth and vigor being restored to me, and tore at my robe, and then at Lizzie's, and we tumbled toward our bed like two awkward dancers, parting the curtains as we fell onto the pillows, and then began to touch each other as we were meant to.

Life out of death. That long night, after we had made love as we used to, I slept with the peace I once knew in life. The shades of gray that had colored me for months began to fade, and in the morning when I awoke, it was as if from a nightmare that I returned to the world, where color and scent and the feeling of Lizzie's skin as I stroked her bare, cream-colored shoulder had returned as well.

When Lizzie rose from sleep as my touch lingered, she yawned, then smiled, and quickly slipped out of bed to dress herself. "Honey, then butter, then the chickens, then the house," she murmured, grinning to herself as she sat in a chair and laced her bodice.

"And after the house," I said, sitting up on one elbow, "the brook. And after the brook, here again, beneath these curtains, where I wish we could stay forever."

Lizzie's grin turned sour the moment I said those words, though. She lifted her face to me and said, "Laura, it was for you that I did that. It was to save you. But it cannot be more. It cannot be what you are thinking. It cannot go on like that between us forever. I will be married one day. I will have children. So, too, will you, if you know what's best for you. But clearly you do not, or we would never have found ourselves in this predicament to begin with."

And at that she rose from her chair and left me there, alone.

~

It was like a curse she threw upon me with those last statements, for as the days and months began to grind beneath my feet, it all came to be true. Lizzie married a young man from a farm just down the way, past the glen; and some time later, after I fully realized we would not be together as I wished, I married too. He was a sweet man, a blacksmith with a sharp black beard and kind blue eyes, and with him I had two children, a boy and a girl to match Lizzie's pair. He was not long for this world, though. A spark flew up one day and blinded him in one eye, and soon the skin there turned an awful red, and then began to fester. The doctor said there was nothing to be done but to help ease him out of this world with the least amount of pain possible, which we did.

Lizzie helped me during that trying time. She came daily with bread and milk and honey, and cleaned my house for me, to save me the work while I tended to my husband. His passing was slow at first, and then he ran toward his end very quickly.

The house and his hearth were sold afterward. I went to live again in the house where Lizzie's parents had once raised us. They were gone by then, too, and Lizzie said it would be better if my children and I were closer, so she could look in on me more often.

She'd bring her own children with her, to play with my Tom and Lily, and we would sew together and try not to speak of the past. Only the present, only daily items and routines would be topics. Any hint of love long past, of passion hidden for the sake of others, and Lizzie would gather up her things and leave.

Sometimes she'd bring her children over and ask me to look after them when she needed to go into town for something. It was during those times that I would tell them the story of the goblin glen, about how my sister had stood in deadly peril to do me good, to save me from an awful fate. The children would listen, rapt and eager to hear the parts about the goblins, and about the fruits, and the music, and the dancing. And afterward they'd run off to play under the shadows of the weeping willow at the bottom of the garden, where once I tried to plant a peach stone out of desperation.

After they were off on their own, I would weep, silently, for having lied to them. The entire tale I told was true, yet none of it was honest. But the stories one tells children always mean: Life will be happy, my dear ones, even though you will struggle within the world's fierce embrace.

When they grow older, I decided long ago—as the days, months, and years come to pass—I will tell them a different story. A story with a good moral of its own to benefit them when they are ready. I will tell them everything they need to know about this world to find or make their happy endings. And if the world cannot provide them with the love they require for happiness, I will tell them to leave it, to join another if one is ever offered. I will tell them to not go back up the path to what they already know. Eat, drink, love without caution. Within this world's fierce embrace, they need not struggle so.

Christopher Barzak is the author of the Crawford Fantasy Award-winning novel, *One for Sorrow,* which is currently being made into the feature film *Jamie Marks is Dead.* His second book, *The Love We Share Without Knowing*, was a finalist for the Nebula and Tiptree Awards. His short fiction has appeared in a variety of venues, including *Asimov's Science Fiction, Realms of Fantasy, Lady Churchill's Rosebud Wristlet*, and several "year's best" anthologies. His most recent books are *Birds and Birthdays*, a collection of surrealist fantasy stories, and *Before and Afterlives*, a collection of supernatural fantasies. He grew up in rural Ohio, has lived in California and Michigan, and has taught English in suburban and rural communities outside of Tokyo, Japan. Currently he teaches at Youngstown State University.

"The Mirror Tells All" was inspired during a lecture at a fairy tale conference I attended in which "Snow White" was described as a story about mother-daughter competition. My immediately reaction was, *yes, but what if it isn't?* The voice of a young woman flitted through my mind, a young woman with a different interpretation. That is the beauty of fairy tales—they can be read in any number of ways, and the meanings that can be culled from them are as relevant now as they were when the stories were first written. For me, "Little Snow White" is a story of triumph in the face of those who would, by envy or other means, try to stifle a young woman's spirit.

Erzebet Yellowboy

The Mirror Tells All

Erzebet YellowBoy

Listen. Here's the story you wouldn't let me tell.

I know, I know. You're dying. Leave you to it. Let you rest in peace. You'll have all the peace you need, in a day or two. That's what the doctor told me, anyway. Did he tell you that? No? Oh well. I'm sure he'll get around to it eventually.

I read somewhere the other day that this story is about competition. Daughters growing up, mothers growing old, that sort of thing. I don't buy it. There was never any of that stuff between us. No, this is a story about love, not competition. Maybe if you'd pried your face away from that mirror . . . Nah. You didn't. So that's where this story begins.

I tried to break that thing once, did you know? I saw you go into the bathroom and I seized the moment. I threw your silver hairbrush at that mirror with all the power in my scrawny little arm. I hurled it so hard! Nothing. Not a scratch. The damned hairbrush bounced off like it'd hit rubber. *Boing.* Nearly came back to smack me in the eye. I thought about taking a hammer to it, but by then you'd locked up all of Dad's tools in the shed out back, and I couldn't find the key.

So. The story. There was this woman who couldn't stop looking at herself in the mirror. That's you, that is. Thought I'd better spell it out. This woman had everything a woman could ever want: a loving husband, more money in the bank than she could ever spend, more clothes in the closet than she could ever wear, a fantastic stone house with a turret—a turret! Who has that these days? She did. She had it all, and then some. I should point out that it wasn't like this woman had all of this stuff and then still felt unfulfilled. No, it wasn't like that at all, not as far as anyone could tell. It was just that she couldn't stop looking at herself in the mirror.

The first time I saw her (that's you, got that?) staring into the mirror I thought nothing of it. I must have been seven; school had started and I'd just been let off the bus. That was a great bus, the driver was always cracking jokes and he really liked kids so it was kind of like our own mini-party twice a day. I opened the front door and the house was quiet. I remember the silence because it was so unusual. This woman used to have the radio on all the time, couldn't get enough of it. It was nice, I liked the house full of sound. And when it wasn't, I got a little afraid that something bad had happened.

I went up to my room to dump my backpack. God, that was a horrible thing, all purple and gold with glitter. Guess it suited me at the time. So anyway, I put it on my bed and then crept out into the hall. Your bedroom door was open. When I first saw you in front of the mirror I was relieved. Everything was okay, I remember thinking. You were there. It was just that for some reason you didn't have the radio on. Well, what did I know? I was just a kid. I figured maybe there'd been nothing good playing. Come to think of it, I don't even know where that mirror came from. I don't think it was there the day before. Did Dad buy it for you? Did you order it out of a catalog? Fingerhut or something? No, that stuff would have been too cheap for you.

When this happened again the next day, I was curious but still didn't really think much of it. When I realized it was going to happen every day, that's when I started to worry. I asked Dad about it, but he was already sick by then and he wasn't really up to pondering the imponderables with me.

I mean honestly, what was it? Did you see a wrinkle? Did you hope to stare it away? Don't look at me like that. I'm joking. You never had a wrinkle in your life.

So here's this woman, and for some reason she's doing this crazy thing. Every day, morning to night, face in that mirror. And there's this kid who doesn't understand why suddenly her mom isn't fixing breakfast, or lunch or supper for that matter, who isn't putting out clothes for her to wear to school, who isn't taking her shopping for new clothes when she grows out of the old, who isn't bitching about a messy room, who isn't asking about homework, who doesn't show up to parent-teacher conferences, who isn't doing a damned thing except standing in her bedroom, in front of a piece of glass on the wall.

You'd think someone would have called Children's Services, but they didn't. It was like magic, the way the teachers and even the principal believed me when I said you were busy. They all knew Dad was sick, so they didn't ask about him. He was sick, but it was you I had to make excuses for.

This kid, right, after a couple years of this, she's kind of learned to accept that things will never go back to the way they were. She understands that she can't invite friends over because then she'd have to explain to them what her mother is doing, and she doesn't know what her mother is doing so how can she explain it? She realizes that the other kids' mothers aren't like this, so she doesn't go visit them because she can't stand the sight of their moms in the kitchen, or coming in from work, briefcase in hand, or calling them into the house to wash up before supper.

This goes on for about three years. I know, it's hard to believe, but it's true. The kid is around ten years old when finally, she's worked up the nerve to do something about it. I mean, she wants her mom back, right? It can't be like it was before the mirror, but it could be something else, something better than having a mom who does nothing but this one stupid thing. Almost anything would be better than that. And then, as if all this isn't bad enough, Dad dies. You remember that, I'm sure. That makes the kid even more determined.

This kid thinks and thinks about her mom, about all the things her mom used to enjoy, about all of the things they did together before the mirror, even though she can hardly remember some of them because she'd been so young. She thought, Mom liked shoes, but I don't know what size she wears. Mom liked steak, but I don't know how to cook one. Mom liked music, but the old radio was gone. And then she remembered how, before the mirror had appeared on the wall, her mother used to sit at her dressing table in the morning doing her hair.

Her mother had liked to do her hair. Now, this little girl had since grown out of purple ponies and glitter, and in fact she was as much of a tomboy by then as a girl could be. She didn't know anything about how to do hair—she put her own in a ponytail in the morning and then forgot about it. That was *doing hair*. Then she remembered this old doll she used to have, and how its hair had been braided, and the braids had been laced through with ribbons. Not just any ribbon either. This ribbon had been embroidered with colorful, detailed scenes of animals frolicking, flowers blooming—all sorts of wonderful, tiny things had been sewn into that ribbon. When her mother had given her the doll she'd said, "This is very old. It's been in our family for a long time, and it was my doll when I was a girl, just like you. It's your turn to take care of her now, just like I've done for all these years."

The girl remembered this because, at the time, she thought that doll was the most beautiful thing she'd ever seen. And now she thought, that is what I'll do. I'll get my mother a beautiful ribbon to weave through her hair. It'll give her something to do in front of that mirror.

Problem was, the girl had no money. Oh sure, she was always provided for, but no one thought to give her cash. Why would they? So one day, after school, instead of getting on the bus as she'd done every day, she walked the two miles or so into town. She'd never been into town, but that didn't stop her. She needed a ribbon, and that was the only place she'd find one.

Yeah, you didn't know I did that, did you. Well, you wouldn't.

She knew the way; every kid knew the way. It's all the girls talked about in class—how their mothers had taken them to the boutiques, to the mall, to wherever it is mothers take their daughters to buy them pretty baubles and bras and whatever else it is that mothers buy. Well, after a lot of walking and searching for just the right shop, she found it. It was three floors of sparkling handbags, row upon row of shoes, a lingerie section in which she could have got lost for days. It was utterly and completely filled with stuff—the kind of stuff you loved, once upon a time.

The girl found the perfect ribbon, embroidered and with the extra bonus of having beads sewn into the seams. And without a second thought, she stole that ribbon, put it in her pocket and walked out.

That night she brought the ribbon to her mother. The room was dark, but for one small lamp lit on the nightstand. Dad's side of the bed was made up tight, but yours was a mess. I remember that. It made me sad. So this girl brings her mother the ribbon, stands in front of her mother with the thing in her hand and says, "Mother, I brought you something."

Did you look down? No. Did you respond in any way? No. You just stood there, like a damned statue, saying nothing.

Fine, I thought. I left the ribbon on your dressing table and left the room. Do you know how that felt? Do you? You may as well have ripped my heart out and fed it to the wolves. I almost hated you then.

Don't wince. What do you expect? Jesus. You can't be that far gone.

Don't worry, I didn't hate you. That's funny, me telling you not to worry. As if you would.

It took the girl about three years to get over that one. She felt pretty dumb for having tried in the first place, but eventually—you know how resilient kids are—she decided to try again.

By this time (you won't have known this either), she'd got a job. It wasn't much of a job, and it wasn't a legal job, but a kid has to have some cash on hand, you know? You won't remember Mr. Spinner. He was the janitor at the middle school. He used to tell these great stories to any kid who would listen. This girl was pretty starved for attention and interaction, so she listened. And maybe he listened to all the things she didn't say, because, one day, he offered her a job helping him mop and buff the floors after all the other kids had gone home.

I saved up every penny I earned for a whole year. I realized my mistake, see, with the ribbon. It was too cheap for your tastes. I knew this time I had to do better. So when the girl—yeah, that's still me, in case you'd forgotten—had saved up enough money, she went into town again.

Quit squirming. I know there's no action in this story. What do you expect? Not much can happen when the main character is just standing there.

The girl thought she was on the right track with the hair thing, even though the first time she'd got it wrong. And maybe she was feeling a little guilty for having thrown her mother's good hairbrush at the mirror. That hairbrush was like something out of the court of some French king. Unbelievably ornate, with bristles tough as the day they were plucked from the boar. So very you. What I wanted was to find a matching comb. That, I thought, would bring you out of your stupor. Because sometimes, if I stayed up late enough at night, I'd catch you brushing your hair.

The girl found a comb, a perfect, silver comb that maybe wasn't as ornate as the hairbrush, but was still eye-catching and breathtaking in its beauty. She didn't even know they made stuff like that. It cost her every cent she had, but she didn't care. Her mother would have to be *blind* to ignore this gift, she was certain.

This time she didn't take silence as an answer. She held the comb out to her mother, and nothing happened. She waved it in front of her mother's face, and nothing happened. She started shouting, "Mom, look! I brought you this comb! Look at it, take it, will you?" and nothing happened. Her mom just stood there with that dead look on her face, staring into the mirror.

The girl wanted to cry, she wanted to sit down on the floor right then and there and wail her heart out. Do you remember what she did instead? No? She moved around behind her mother, and started combing her mother's hair. That's what she did. Gently, so as not to pull on the tangles, she combed out every strand until they lay, soft and shining, against her mother's back. Then she put the comb on the dressing table with the brush and left the room.

Getting bored, are you? I bet. All right well, I'm nearly done. I'll pick up the pace a little, if that will help.

Fast-forward two years; the girl is now sixteen. Sweet sixteen, and her mother is still there, in front of that mirror. Do you know how awful puberty is when you have to go through it alone? At sixteen the girl, now a young woman really, was in the throes of it. All sorts of stuff was going on in her body and in her mind. All sorts. She's trying to achieve some kind of independence, to be her own person, that kind of thing, and here she's got this monster in the closet, right, this dirty secret that she can't share with anyone. Because how, really, do you tell someone that your mother has been standing in front of a mirror for years on end? It's ridiculous. No one would believe you anyway even if you did tell. They'd think you were making it up.

That's what you'd become to me by then. A monster. A horrible dragon clutching its treasure in a dark room. I had to do *something*. Anything, I thought, would be better than this.

But what? I didn't know. I didn't know until one day, who knows why, Mr. Jonet—he was the English teacher that year—started talking about apples. All of a sudden, out of nowhere, apples. He went through every story that ever had an apple in it, he went on and on about the health properties of apples, the symbolism of apples, all of this stuff about apples. It drove the class nuts. Rumor had it that he'd fallen in love with Miss Hayton, the biology teacher. We made jokes about him bringing her an apple, like some pet schoolboy. We got sick of hearing about apples.

Then he told a story about a woman named Eve. She was apparently the first woman, ever, on earth. She was good, pure good, no evil in her at all. Kind of like you used to be, before the mirror came. Or at least how I remember you to be. Rose-colored glasses and all that. So anyway, this Eve lady was brought low by an apple. The fruit of evil, it was, and she took a bite and then she wasn't so good any more. Cast out of the garden, I think it was a garden, by a serpent or something. But basically, Mr. Jonet said, what had happened was that Eve's eyes had been opened to everything that was around her, to all of the nuances of life, to all of the little details that she couldn't have seen before, because pure good can't see anything but good, and that's unhealthy. That, he said, is what leads us to a fall. When we can't see and appreciate the bad in something as well as the good, we're in trouble. Rumor had it Miss Hayton had turned him down.

And the girl thought, maybe if I take my mother an apple, her eyes will open, too, and she'll look at something other than that mirror.

It couldn't be just any apple, though, could it? It had to be the best apple, the ripest apple, the reddest apple, because for her mother, only the best would do. The girl didn't really know anything about apples, which were good for what, which were sweet, which were sour, none of that. She'd just eaten whatever apples were offered her. But she learned, and that autumn she went into town again and brought home the best apples she could find.

Oh, right. I said I'd speed it up. You do look a little uncomfortable. You can probably guess what happens next.

The girl takes her mother the apple, and the woman doesn't blink an eye. Doesn't acknowledge the girl standing there beside her with an apple in her hand. The girl can't take it any more, she starts shouting and cursing and crying and making a real scene. She throws the apple against the wall and slams the door on her way out of the room. The next morning, she packs a bag and is gone.

What happened to you anyway? The doctor said the delivery boy found you lying on your bedroom floor. I didn't even know you let those kids have a key to the house, but I guess the groceries had to come from somewhere. One year I've been gone, and not a word from you. Not a call, not a question about how I was doing, and then the next thing I know Mr. Spinner is crying and telling me you're in the hospital. I called the hospital and they told me you wouldn't be going home. They told me I'd better get here as soon as I could.

I know, finish the story already. Okay. The girl hears that her mother is in the hospital, right, and her first reaction is *good, let her rot*. Then she thought, the house is empty, here's my chance.

I went to the house yesterday, Mother, to collect a few things. Do you know what I found? I could hardly believe it. You picked that apple up after I left, didn't you? You picked it up and put it on your dressing table. It's still there, all rotten, right beside the tarnished comb. I saw that apple and how you'd moved it, and I finally figured out what I could do.

Here. I brought you something. This is the story you wouldn't let me tell, and this is how it ends. I smashed your mirror, Mother. I brought one of Mr. Spinner's hammers with me to the house, was going to break open the door of the shed and get some stuff out of there. Instead, I used it to break your mirror. Don't be mad, there was no way I could have carried the whole thing.

Here, mom. Uncurl your fingers, let me put this in your hand. Be careful, I taped the edges but they might still be sharp.

Look. It's a piece of your mirror. I brought it for you. That's right, take it. Can you hold it up? Okay, good, now you can see yourself. Surprised, aren't you. Well, I told you, Mother. This is a story about love.

──

Erzebet YellowBoy was born in America, but now lives in a tumbledown cottage in rural France with her husband and a posse of wild cats. She is the co-founder and long-time editor of *Cabinet des Fées*, an online journal of fairy tales, and the founder of Papaveria Press, a micro-press specializing in hand bound, limited editions of mythic prose and poetry. Her work has appeared in *Fantasy Magazine, Not One Of Us, Electric Velocipede*, and *Clarkesworld Magazine*, and in the anthologies *Japanese Dreams, Running with the Pack*, and *Haunted Legends*. Her novel *Sleeping Helena* was released by Prime Books in 2010, and she has several novellas forthcoming from Masque Books. Erzebet is also an artist and a bookbinder. Her work can be found at www.erzebet.com.

──

"Blanchefleur" was inspired by one of my favorite fairy tales, Madame D'Aulnoy's "The White Cat." In D'Aulnoy's version, or the translation of it that I read as a child, a king wishing to pass his kingdom to his sons asks each of them to find the smallest dog, the finest linen, and the most beautiful woman in the world. Each of the princes goes on this quest, but of course it is the youngest who succeeds, with the help of a mysterious white cat who rules a cat-kingdom. She gives him the small dog and the fine linen in walnut shells, and in the end, she herself becomes the most beautiful woman. They are happily married and go back to rule over her kingdom, where all the cats have turned back into her subjects.

I'm not sure how that fairy tale turned into mine: I only know that the Lady of the Forest and Blanchefleur were both inspired by the cat queen, and that I was more interested in writing about a miller's son than a prince. Of course he had to go through three ordeals and gain a kingdom in the end. The modern—and what I hope are humorous—touches came from E. Nesbit, another one of my favorite fairy-tale tellers, who often included such touches in her versions. We often associate fairy tales with male writers such as Charles Perrault and the Brothers Grimm: I'm rather proud, in this story, of having been influenced by two important female writers in the fairy tale tradition.

Theodora Goss

BLANCHEFLEUR

THEODORA GOSS

They called him Idiot.

He was the miller's son, and he had never been good for much. At least not since his mother's death, when he was twelve years old. He had found her floating, facedown, in the millpond, and his cries had brought his father's men. When they turned her over, he had seen her face, pale and bloated, before someone said, "Not in front of the child!" and they had hurried him away. He had never seen her again, just the wooden coffin going into the ground, and after that, the gray stone in the churchyard where, every Sunday, he and his father left whatever was in season—a bunch of violets, sprays of the wild roses that grew by the forest edge, tall lilies from beside the mill stream. In winter, they left holly branches red with berries.

Before her death, he had been a laughing, affectionate child. After her death, he became solitary. He would no longer play with his friends from school, and eventually they began to ignore him. He would no longer speak even to his father, and anyway the miller was a quiet man who, after his wife's death, grew more silent. He was so broken, so bereft, by the loss of his wife that he could barely look at the son who had her golden hair, her eyes the color of spring leaves. Often they would go a whole day, saying no more than a few sentences to each other.

He went to school, but he never seemed to learn—he would stare out the window or, if called upon, shake his head and refuse to answer. Once, the teacher rapped his knuckles for it, but he simply looked at her with those eyes, which were so much like his mother's. The teacher turned away, ashamed of herself, and after that she left him alone, telling herself that at least he was sitting in the schoolroom rather than loafing about the fields.

He learned nothing, he did nothing. When his father told him to do the work of the mill, he did it so badly that the water flowing through the sluice gates was either too fast or slow, or the large millstones grinding the grain were too close together or far apart, or he took the wrong amount of grain in payment from the farmers who came to grind their wheat. Finally, the miller hired another man, and his son wandered about the countryside, sometimes sleeping under the stars, eating berries from the hedges when he could find them. He would come home dirty, with scratches on his arms and brambles in his hair. And his father, rather than scolding him, would look away.

If anyone had looked closely, they would have seen that he was clever at carving pieces of wood into whistles and seemed to know how to call all the birds. Also, he knew the paths through the countryside and could tell the time by the position of the sun and moon on each day of the year, his direction by the stars. He knew the track and spoor of every animal, what tree each leaf came from by its shape. He knew which mushrooms were poisonous and how to find water under the ground. But no one did look closely.

It was the other schoolboys, most of whom had once been his friends, who started calling him Idiot. At first it was Idiot Ivan, but soon it was simply Idiot, and it spread through the village until people forgot he had ever been called Ivan. Farmers would call to him, cheerfully enough, "Good morning, Idiot!" They meant no insult by it. In villages, people like knowing who you are. The boy was clearly an idiot, so let him be called that. And so he was.

No one noticed that under the dirt, and despite the rags he wore, he had grown into a large, handsome boy. He should have had sweethearts, but the village girls assumed he was slow and had no prospects, even though he was the miller's son. So he was always alone, and the truth was, he seemed to prefer it.

The miller was the only one who still called him Ivan, although he had given his son up as hopeless, and even he secretly believed the boy was slow and stupid.

This was how things stood when the miller rode to market to buy a new horse. The market was held in the nearest town, on a fine summer day that was also the feast-day of Saint Ivan, so the town was filled with stalls selling livestock, vegetables from the local farms, leather and rope harnesses, embroidered linen, woven baskets. Men and women in smocks lined up to hire themselves for the coming harvest. There were strolling players with fiddles or pipes, dancers on a wooden platform, and a great deal of beer—which the miller drank from a tankard.

The market went well for him. He found a horse for less money than he thought he would have to spend, and while he was paying for his beer, one of the maids from the tavern winked at him. She was plump, with sunburnt cheeks, and she poured his beer neatly, leaving a head of foam that just reached the top of the tankard. He had not thought of women, not in that way, since his wife had drowned. She had been one of those magical women, beautiful as the dawn, slight as a willow-bough and with a voice like birds singing, that are perhaps too delicate for this world. That kind of woman gets into a man's blood. But lately he had started to notice once again that other women existed, and that there were other things in the world than running a mill. Like his son, who was a great worry to him. What would the idiot—Ivan, he reminded himself—what would he do when his father was gone, as we must all go someday? Would he be able to take care of himself?

He had saddled his horse and was fastening a rope to his saddle so the new horse could be led, when he heard a voice he recognized from many years ago. "Hello, Stephen Miller," it said.

He turned around and bowed. "Hello, Lady."

She was tall and pale, with long gray hair that hung to the backs of her knees, although she did not look older than when he had last seen her, at his wedding. She wore a gray linen dress that, although it was midsummer, reminded him of winter.

"How is my nephew? This is his name day, is it not?"

"It is, Lady. As to how he is—" The miller told her. He might not have, if the beer had not loosened his tongue, for he was a proud man and he did not want his sister-in-law to think his son was doing badly. But with the beer and his worries, it all came out—the days Ivan spent staring out of windows or walking through the countryside, how the local farmers thought of him, even that name—Idiot.

"I warned you that no good comes of a mortal marrying a fairy woman," said the Lady. "But those in love never listen. Send my nephew to me. I will make him my apprentice for three years, and at the end of that time we shall see. For his wages, you may take this."

She handed him a purse. He bowed in acknowledgment, saying, "I thank you for your generosity—" but when he straightened again, she was already walking away from him. Just before leaving the inn yard, she turned back for a moment and said, "The Castle in the Forest, remember. I will expect him in three days' time."

The miller nodded, although she had already turned away again. As he rode home, he looked into the purse she had given him—in it was a handful of leaves.

He wondered how he was going to tell his son about the bargain he had made. But when he reached home, the boy was sitting at the kitchen table whittling something out of wood, and he simply said, "I have apprenticed you for three years to your aunt, the Lady of the Forest. She expects you in three days' time."

The boy did not say a word. But the next morning, he put all of his possessions—they were few enough—into a satchel, which he slung over his shoulder. And he set out.

In three days' time, Ivan walked through the forest, blowing on the whistle he had carved. He could hear birds calling to each other in the forest. He whistled to them, and they whistled back. He did not know how long his journey would take—if you set out for the Castle in the Forest, it can take you a day, or a week, or the rest of your life. But the Lady had said she expected him in three days, so he thought he would reach the Castle by the end of the day at the latest.

Before he left, his father had looked again in the purse that the Lady had given him. In it was a pile of gold coins—as the miller had expected, for that is the way fairy money works. "I will keep this for you," his father had said. "When you come back, you will be old enough to marry, and with such a fortune, any of the local girls will take you. I do not know what you will do as the Lady's apprentice, but I hope you will come back fit to run a mill."

Ivan had simply nodded, slung his satchel over his shoulder, and gone.

Just as he was wondering if he would indeed find the castle that day, for the sun was beginning to set, he saw it through the trees, its turrets rising above a high stone wall.

He went up to the wall and knocked at the wooden door that was the only way in. It opened, seemingly by itself. In the doorway stood a white cat.

"Are you the Idiot?" she asked.

"I suppose so," he said, speaking for the first time in three days.

"That's what I thought," she said. "You certainly look the part. Well, come in then, and follow me."

He followed her through the doorway and along a path that led through the castle gardens. He had never seen such gardens, although in school his teacher had once described the gardens that surrounded the King's castle, which she had visited on holiday. There were fountains set in green lawns, with stone fish spouting water. There were box hedges, and topiaries carved into the shapes of birds, rabbits, mice. There were pools filled with water lilies, in which he could see real fish, silver and orange. There were arched trellises from which roses hung down in profusion, and an orchard with fruit trees. He could even see a kitchen garden, with vegetables in neat rows. And all through the gardens, he could see cats, pruning the hedges, tying back the roses, raking the earth in the flowerbeds.

It was the strangest sight he had ever seen, and for the first time it occurred to him that being the Lady's apprentice would be an adventure—the first of his life.

The path took them to the door of the castle, which swung open as they approached. An orange tabby walked out and stood waiting at the top of the steps.

"Hello, Marmalade," said the white cat.

"Good evening, Miss Blanchefleur," he replied. "Is this the young man her Ladyship is expecting?"

"As far as I can tell," she said. "Although what my mother would want with such an unprepossessing specimen, I don't know."

Marmalade bowed to Ivan and said, "Welcome, Ivan Miller. Her Ladyship is waiting in the solar."

Ivan expected the white cat, whose name seemed to be Blanchefleur, to leave him with Marmalade. Instead, she accompanied them, following Ivan through the doorway, then through a great hall whose walls were hung with tapestries showing cats sitting in gardens, climbing trees, hunting rabbits, catching fish. Here too there were cats, setting out bowls on two long wooden tables, and on a shorter table set on a dais at the end of the room. As Marmalade passed, they nodded, and a gray cat who seemed to be directing their activities said, "We're almost ready, Mr. Marmalade. The birds are nicely roasted, and the mint sauce is really a treat if I say so myself."

"Excellent, Mrs. Pebbles. I can't tell you how much I'm looking forward to those birds. Tailcatcher said that he caught them himself."

"Well, with a little help!" said Mrs. Pebbles, acerbically. "He doesn't go on the hunt alone, does he now, Mr. Marmalade? Oh, begging your pardon, Miss," she said when she saw Blanchefleur. "I didn't know you were there."

"I couldn't care less what you say about him," said Blanchefleur, with a sniff and a twitch of her tail. "He's nothing to me."

"As you say, Miss," said Mrs. Pebbles, not sounding particularly convinced.

At the back of the great hall was another, smaller door that led to a long hallway. Ivan was startled when, at the end of the hallway, which had been rather dark, they emerged into a room filled with sunlight. It had several windows looking out onto a green lawn, and scattered around the room were low cushions, on which cats sat engaged in various tasks. Some were carding wool, some were spinning it on drop spindles, some were plying the yarn or winding it into skeins. In a chair by one of the windows sat the Lady, with a piece of embroidery in her lap. One of the cats was reading a book aloud, but stopped when they entered.

"My Lady, this is Ivan Miller, your new apprentice," said Marmalade.

"Otherwise known as the Idiot," said Blanchefleur. "And he seems to deserve the name. He's said nothing for himself all this time."

"My dear, you should be polite to your cousin," said the Lady. "Ivan, you've already met my daughter, Blanchefleur, and Marmalade, who takes such marvelous care of us all. These are my ladies-in-waiting: Elderberry, Twilight, Snowy, Whiskers, and Fluff. My daughter tells me you have nothing to say for yourself. Is that true?"

Ivan stared at her, sitting in her chair, surrounded by cats. She had green eyes, and although her gray hair hung down to the floor, she reminded him of his mother. "Yes, Ma'am," he said.

She looked at him for a moment, appraisingly. Then she said, "Very well. I will send you where you need not say anything. Just this morning I received a letter from an old friend of mine, Professor Owl. He is compiling an Encyclopedia of All Knowledge, but he is old and feels arthritis terribly in his legs. He can no longer write the entries himself. For the first year of your apprenticeship, you will go to Professor Owl in the Eastern Waste and help him with his Encyclopedia. Do you think you can do that, nephew?"

"It's all the same to me," said Ivan. It was obvious that no one wanted him here, just as no one had wanted him at the mill. What did it matter where he went?

"Then you shall set out tomorrow morning," said the Lady. "Tonight you shall join us for dinner. Are the preparations ready, Marmalade?"

"Almost, my Lady," said the orange cat.

"How will I find this Professor Owl?" asked Ivan.

"Blanchefleur will take you," said the Lady.

"You can't be serious!" said Blanchefleur. "He's an idiot, and he stinks like a pigsty."

"Then show him the bathroom, where he can draw himself a bath," said the Lady. "And give him new clothes to wear. Those are too ragged even for Professor Owl, I think."

"Come on, you," said Blanchefleur, clearly disgusted. He followed her out of the room and up a flight of stairs, to a bathroom with a large tub on four clawed legs. He had never seen anything quite like it before. At the mill, he had often washed under the kitchen spigot. After she had left, he filled it with hot water that came out of a tap and slipped into it until the water was up to his chin.

What a strange day it had been. Three days ago he had left his father's house and the life he had always lived, a life that required almost nothing of him: no thought, no effort. And now here he was, in a castle filled with talking cats. And tomorrow he would start for another place, one that might be even stranger. When Blanchefleur had taunted him by telling the Lady that he had nothing to say for himself, he had wanted to say—what? Something that would have made her less disdainful. But what could he say for himself, after all?

With a piece of soap, he washed himself more carefully than he had ever before in his life. She had said he smelled like a pigsty, and he had spent the night before last sleeping on a haystack that was, indeed, near a pen where several pigs had grunted in their dreams. Last night, he had slept in the forest, but he supposed the smell still lingered—particularly to a cat's nose. For the first time in years, he felt a sense of shame.

He dried himself and put on the clothes she had left for him. He went back down the stairs, toward the sound of music, and found his way to the great hall. It was lit with torches, and sitting at the two long tables were cats of all colors: black and brindled and tortoiseshell and piebald, with short hair and long. Sitting on the dais were the Lady, with Blanchefleur beside her, and a large yellow and brown cat who was striped like a tiger. He stood in the doorway, feeling self-conscious.

The Lady saw him across the room and motioned for him to come over. He walked to the dais and bowed before it, because that seemed the appropriate thing to do. She said, "That was courteous, nephew. Now come sit with us. Tailcatcher, you will not mind giving your seat to Ivan, will you?"

"Of course not, my Lady," said the striped cat in a tone that indicated he did indeed mind, very much.

Ivan took his place, and Marmalade brought him a dish of roast starlings, with a green sauce that smelled like catmint. It was good, although relatively flavorless. The cats, evidently, did not use salt in their cooking. Halfway through the meal, he was startled to realize that the cats were conversing with one another and nodding politely, as though they were a roomful of ordinary people. He was probably the only silent one in the entire room. Several times he noticed Blanchefleur giving him exasperated looks.

When he had finished eating, the Lady said, "I think it's time to dance." She clapped her hands, and suddenly Ivan heard music. He wondered where it was coming from, then noticed a group of cats at the far end of the room playing, more skillfully than he had supposed possible, a fife, a viol, a tabor, and other instruments he could not identify, one of which curved like a long snake. The cats who had been sitting at the long tables moved them to the sides of the room, then formed two lines in the center. He had seen a line dance before, at one of the village fairs, but he had never seen one danced as gracefully as it was by the cats. They wove in and out, each line breaking and reforming in intricate patterns.

"Aren't you going to ask your cousin to dance?" said the Lady, leaning over to him.

"What? Oh," he said, feeling foolish. How could he dance with a cat? But the Lady was looking at him, waiting. "Would you like to dance?" he asked Blanchefleur.

"Not particularly," she said, looking at him with disdain. "Oh, all right, Mother! You don't have to pull my tail."

He wiped his mouth and hands on a napkin, then followed

Blanchefleur to the dance floor and joined at the end of the line, feeling large and clumsy, trying to follow the steps and not tread on any paws. It did not help that, just when he was beginning to feel as though he was learning the steps, he saw Tailcatcher glaring at him from across the room. He danced several times, once with Blanchefleur, once with Mrs. Pebbles, who must have taken pity on him, and once with Fluff, who told him it was a pleasure to dance with such a handsome young man and seemed to mean it. He managed to step on only one set of paws, belonging to a tabby tomcat who said, "Do that again, Sir, and I'll send you my second in the morning," but was mollified when Ivan apologized sincerely and at length. After that, he insisted on sitting down until the feast was over and he could go to bed.

The next morning, he woke and wondered if it was all a dream, but no—there he was, lying in a curtained bed in the Lady's castle. And there was Blanchefleur, sitting in a nearby chair, saying, "About time you woke up. We need to get started if we're going to make the Eastern Waste by nightfall."

Ivan got out of bed, vaguely embarrassed to be seen in his nightshirt, then reminded himself that she was just a cat. He put on the clothes he had been given last night, then found his satchel on a dresser. All of his old clothes were gone, replaced by new ones. In the satchel he also found a loaf of bread, a hunk of cheese, a flask of wine, and a shiny new knife with a horn handle.

"I should thank the Lady for all these things," he said.

"That's the first sensible thing you've said since you got here," said Blanchefleur. "But she's gone to see my father, and won't be back for three days. And we have to get going. So hurry up already!"

The Lady's castle was located in a forest called the Wolfwald. To the north, it stretched for miles, and parts of it were so thick that almost no sunlight reached the forest floor. At the foot of the northern mountains, wolves still roamed. But around the castle it was less dense. Ivan and Blanchefleur walked along a path strewn with oak leaves, through filtered sunlight. Ivan was silent, in part because he was accustomed to silence, in part because he did not know what to say to the white cat. Blanchefleur seemed much more interested in chasing insects, and even dead leaves, than in talking to him.

They stopped to rest when the sun was directly overhead. The forest had changed: the trees were shorter and spaced more widely apart, mostly pines rather than the oaks and beeches around the Lady's castle. Ahead of him, Ivan could see a different sort of landscape: bare, except for the occasional twisted trees and clumps of grass. It was dry, rocky, strewn with boulders.

"That's the Eastern Waste," said Blanchefleur.

"The ground will be too hard for your paws," said Ivan. "I can carry you."

"I'll do just fine, thank you," she said with a sniff. But after an hour of walking over the rocky ground, Ivan saw she was limping. "Come on," he said. "If you hate the thought of me carrying you so much, pretend I'm a horse."

"A jackass is more like it," she said. But she let him pick her up and carry her, with her paws on his shoulder so she could look around. Occasionally, her whiskers tickled his ear.

The sun traveled across the sky, and hours passed, and still he walked though the rocky landscape, until his feet hurt. But he would not admit he was in pain, not with Blanchefleur perched on his shoulder. At last, after a region of low cliffs and defiles, they came to a broad plain that was nothing but stones. In the middle of the plain rose a stone tower.

"That's it," said Blanchefleur. "That's Professor Owl's home."

"Finally," said Ivan under his breath. He had been feeling as though he would fall over from sheer tiredness. He took a deep breath and started for the tower. But before he reached it, he asked the question he had been wanting to ask all day, but had not dared to. "Blanchefleur, who is your father?"

"The man who lives in the moon," she said. "Can you hurry up? I haven't had a meal since that mouse at lunch, and I'm getting hungry."

~

"He's an owl," said Ivan.

"Of course he's an owl," said Blanchefleur. "What did you think he would be?"

Professor Owl was in fact an owl, the largest Ivan has ever seen, with brown and white feathers. When they entered the tower, which was round and had one room on each level, with stairs curling around the outer wall, he said, "Welcome, welcome. Blanchefleur, I haven't seen you since you were a kitten. And this must be the assistant the Lady has so graciously sent me. Welcome, boy. I hope you know how to write a good, clear hand."

"His name is Idiot," said Blanchefleur.

"My name is Ivan," said Ivan.

"Yes, yes," said Professor Owl, paying no attention to them whatsoever. "Here, then, is my life's work. The Encyclopedia."

It was an enormous book, taller than Ivan himself, resting on a large stand at the far end of the room. In the middle of the room was a wooden table, and around the circular walls were file cabinets, all the way up to the ceiling.

"It's much too heavy to open by hand—or foot," said Professor Owl. "But if you tell the Encyclopedia what you're looking for, it will open to that entry."

"Mouse," said Blanchefleur. And sure enough, as she spoke, the pages of the Encyclopedia turned as though by magic (*although it probably is magic*, thought Ivan) to a page with an entry titled *Mouse*.

"Let's see, let's see," said Professor Owl, peering at the page. "The bright and active, although mischievous, little animal known to us by the name of Mouse and its close relative the Rat are the most familiar and also the most typical members of the Murinae, a subfamily containing about two hundred and fifty species assignable to no less than eighteen distinct genera, all of which, however, are so superficially alike that the English names rat or mouse would be fairly appropriate to any of them. Well, that seems accurate, doesn't it?"

"Does it say how they taste?" asked Blanchefleur.

"The Encyclopedia is connected to five others," said Professor Owl, turning to Ivan. "One is in the Library of Alexandria, one in the Hagia Sophia in Constantinople, one in the Sorbonne, one in the British Museum, and one in the New York Public Library. It is the only Encyclopedia of All Knowledge, and as you can imagine, it takes all my time to keep it up to date. I've devoted my life to it. But since I've developed arthritis in my legs,"—and Ivan could see that indeed, the owl's legs looked more knobby than they ought to—"it's been difficult for me to write my updates. So I'm grateful to the Lady for sending you. Here is where you will work." He pointed to the table with his clawed foot. On it was a large pile of paper, each page filled with scribbled notes.

"These are the notes I've made indicating what should be updated and how. If you'll look at the page on top of the pile, for instance, you'll see that the entry on Justice needs to be updated. There have been, in the last month alone, five important examples of injustice, from the imprisonment of a priest who criticized the Generalissimo to a boy who was deprived of his supper when his mother wrongly accused him of stealing a mince pie. You must add each example to the entry under Justice—Injustice—Examples. The entry itself can be found in one of the cabinets along the wall—I believe it's the twenty-sixth row from the door, eight cabinets up. Of course I can't possibly include every example of injustice—there are hundreds every hour. I only include the ones that most clearly illustrated the concept. And here are my notes on a species of wild rose newly discovered in the mountains of Cathay. That will go under Rose—Wild—Species. Do you understand, boy? You are to look at my notes and add whatever information is necessary to update the entry, writing directly on the file. The Encyclopedia itself will incorporate your update, turning it into typescript, but you must make your letters clearly. And no spelling errors! Now, it's almost nightfall, and I understand that humans have defective vision, so I suggest you sleep until dawn, when you can get up and start working on these notes as well as the ones I'll be writing overnight."

"Professor," said Blanchefleur, "we haven't had dinner."

"Dinner?" said Professor Owl. "Of course, of course. I wouldn't want you to go hungry. There are some mice and birds in the cupboard. I caught them just last night. You're certainly welcome to them."

"Human beings can't eat mice and birds," said Blanchefleur. "They have to cook their food."

"Yes, yes, of course," said Professor Owl. "An inefficient system, I must say. I believe I had—but where did I put it?" He turned around, looking perplexed, then opened the door of a closet under the stairs. He poked his head in, and then tossed out several things, so both Ivan and Blanchefleur had to dodge them. A pith helmet, a butterfly net, and a pair of red flannel underwear for what must have been a very tall man. "Yes, here is it. But you'll have to help me with it."

"It" was a large iron kettle. Ivan helped the owl pull it out of the closet and place it on the long wooden table. He looked into it, not knowing what to expect, but it was empty.

"It's a magic kettle, of course," said Professor Owl. "I seem to remember that it makes soup. You can sleep on the second floor. The third is my study, and I hope you will refrain from disturbing me during daylight hours, when I will be very busy indeed. Now, if you don't mind, I'm going out for a bit of a hunt. I do hope you will be useful to me. My last apprentice was a disappointment." He waddled comically across the floor and up the stairs.

"These scholarly types aren't much for small talk," said Blanchefleur.

"I thought he was going out?" said Ivan.

"He is," said Blanchefleur. "You don't think he's just going to walk out the door, do you? He's an owl. He's going to launch himself from one of the tower windows."

Ivan looked into the kettle again. Still empty. "Do you really think it's magic?" he asked. He had eaten the bread and cheese a long time ago, and his stomach was starting to growl.

"Try some magic words," said Blanchefleur.

"Abracadabra," he said. "Open Sesame." What other magic words had he learned in school? If he remembered correctly, magic had not been a regular part of the curriculum.

"You really are an idiot," said Blanchefleur. She sprang onto the table, then sat next to the kettle. "Dear Kettle," she said. "We've been told of your magical powers in soup-making, and are eager to taste your culinary delights. Will you please make us some soup? Any flavor, your choice, but not onion because his breath is pungent enough already."

From the bottom, the kettle filled with something that bubbled and had a delicious aroma. "There you go," said Blanchefleur. "Magical items have feelings, you know. They need to be asked nicely. Abracadabra indeed!"

"I still need a spoon," said Ivan.

"With all you require for nourishment, I wonder that you're still alive!" said Blanchefleur. "Look in the closet."

In the closet, Ivan did indeed find several wooden spoons, as well as a croquet set, several pairs of boots, and a stuffed alligator.

"Beef stew," he said, tasting what was in the kettle. "Would you like some?"

"I'm quite capable of hunting for myself, thank you," said Blanchefleur. "Don't wait up. I have a feeling that when the Professor said you should be up by dawn, he meant it."

That night, Ivan slept on the second floor of the tower, where he found a bed, a desk, and a large traveling trunk with *Oswald* carved on it. He wondered if Oswald had been the professor's last apprentice, the one who had been such a disappointment. In the middle of the night, he thought he felt Blanchefleur jump on the bed and curl up next to his back. But when he woke up in the morning, she was gone.

Ivan was used to waking up at dawn, so wake up at dawn he did. He found a small bathroom under the stairs, splashed water on his face, got dressed, and went downstairs. Blanchefleur was sitting on the table, staring at the kettle still set on it, with a look of disdain on her face.

"What is that mess?" she asked.

"I think it's pea soup," he said, after looking into the kettle. It smelled inviting, but then anything would have at that hour. Next to the kettle were a wooden bowl and spoon, as well as a napkin. "Did you put these here?" he asked Blanchefleur.

"Why would I do such a stupid thing?" she asked, and turned her back to him. She began licking her fur, as though washing herself were the most important thing in the world.

Ivan shrugged, spooned some of the pea soup into the bowl, and had a plain but filling breakfast. Afterward, he washed the bowl and spoon. As soon as he had finished eating, the kettle had emptied again—evidently, it did not need washing. Then he sat down at the table and pulled the first of Professor Owl's notes toward him.

It was tedious work. First, he would read through the notes, which were written in a cramped, slanting hand. Then, he would try to add a paragraph to the file, as neatly and succinctly as he could. He had never paid much attention in school, and writing did not come easily to him. After the first botched attempt, he learned to compose his paragraphs on the backs of Professor Owl's notes, so when he went to update the entries, he was not fumbling for words. By noon, he had finished additions to the entries on Justice, Rose, Darwin, Theosophy, Venus, Armadillo, Badminton, and Indochina. His lunch was chicken soup with noodles. He thought about having nothing but soup, every morning, noon, and night for an entire year, and longed for a sandwich.

He sat down at the table and picked up the pen, but his back and hand hurt. He put the pen down. The sunlight out the window looked so inviting. Perhaps he should go out and wander around the tower, just for a little while? Where had Blanchefleur gone, anyway? He had not seen her since breakfast. He got up, stretched, and walked out.

It had been his habit, as long as he remembered, to wander around as he wished. That was what he did now, walking around the tower and then away from it, looking idly for Blanchefleur and finding only lizards. He wandered without thinking about where he was going or how long he had been gone. The sun began to sink in the west.

That was when he realized that he had been gone for hours. Well, it would not matter, would it? He could always catch up with any work he did not finish tomorrow. He walked back in the direction of the tower, only becoming lost once. It was dark when he reached it again. He opened the door and walked in.

There were Professor Owl and Blanchefleur. The Professor was perched on the table where Ivan had been sitting earlier that day, scribbling furiously. Blanchefleur was saying, "What did you expect of someone named Idiot? I told you he would be useless."

"Oh, hello, boy," said Professor Owl, looking up. "I noticed you went out for a walk, so I finished all of the notes for today, except Orion. I'll have that done in just a moment, and then you can sit down for dinner. I don't think I told you that each day's updates need to be filed by the end of the day, or the Encyclopedia will be incomplete. And it has never been incomplete since I started working on it, five hundred years ago."

"I'll do it," said Ivan.

"Do what?" said Blanchefleur. "Go wandering around again?"

"I'll do the update on Orion."

"That's very kind of you," said Professor Owl. "I'm sure you must be tired." But he handed Ivan the pen and hopped a bit away on the table. It was a lopsided hop: Ivan could tell the owl's right foot was hurting. He sat and finished the update, conscious of Blanchefleur's eyes on him. When he was finished, Professor Owl read it over. "Yes, very nice," he said. "You have a clear and logical mind. Well done, boy."

Ivan looked up, startled. It was the first compliment he ever remembered receiving.

"Well, go on then, have some dinner," said Professor Owl. "And you'll be up at dawn tomorrow?"

"I'll be up at dawn," said Ivan. He knew that the next day, he would not go wandering around, at least until after the entries were finished. He did not want Blanchefleur calling him an idiot again in that tone of voice.

~

Summer turned into winter. Each day, Ivan sat at the table in the tower, updating the entries for the Encyclopedia of All Knowledge. One day, he realized that he no longer needed to compose the updates on the backs of Professor Owl's notes. He could simply compose them in his head, and then write each update directly onto the file. He had not learned much in school, but he was learning now, about things that seemed useless, such as Sponge Cake, and things that seemed useful, such as Steam Engines, Epic Poetry, and Love. One morning he realized Professor Owl had left him not only a series of updates, but also the notes for an entry on a star that had been discovered by astronomers the week before. Proudly and carefully, he took a blank file card out of the cabinet, composed a new entry for the Encyclopedia of All Knowledge, and filed the card in its place.

He came to write so well and so quickly that he would finish all of the updates, and any new entries the Professor left him, by early afternoon. After a lunch of soup, for he had never managed to get the kettle to make him anything else, however politely he asked, he would roam around the rocky countryside. Sometimes Blanchefleur would accompany him, and eventually she allowed him to carry her on his shoulder without complaining, although she was never enthusiastic. And she still called him Idiot.

One day, in February although he had lost track of the months, he updated an entry on the Trojan War. He had no idea what it was, since he had not been paying attention that day in school. So after he finished his updates, he asked the Encyclopedia. It opened to the entry on the Trojan War, which began, "It is a truth universally acknowledged that judging a beauty contest between three goddesses causes nothing but trouble." He read on, fascinated. After that day, he would spend several hours reading through whichever entries took his fancy. Each entry he read left him with more questions, and he began to wish he could stay with Professor Owl, simply reading the entries in the Encyclopedia, forever.

But winter turned into summer, and one day the professor said,

"Ivan, it has been a year since you arrived, and the term of your apprenticeship with me is at an end. Thank you for all of the care and attention you have put into your task. As a reward, I will give you one of my feathers—that one right there. Pluck it out gently. *Gently*!"

Ivan held up the feather. It was long and straight, with brown and white stripes.

"Cut the end of it with a penknife and make it into a pen," said Professor Owl. "If you ever want to access the Encyclopedia, just tell the pen what you would like to know, and it will write the entry for you."

"Thank you," said Ivan. "But couldn't I stay—"

"Of course not," said Blanchefleur. "My mother is expecting us. So come on already." And indeed, since it was dawn, Professor Owl was already heading up the stairs, for he had very important things to do during the day. Owls do, you know.

The Castle in the Forest looked just as Ivan remembered. There were cats tending the gardens, where the roses were once again blooming, as though they had never stopped. Marmalade greeted them at the door and led them to the Lady's solar, where she was sitting at a desk, writing. Her cats-in-waiting were embroidering a tapestry, and one was strumming a lute with her claws, playing a melody that Ivan remembered from when he was a child.

"Well?" she said when she looked up. "How did Ivan do, my dear?"

"Well enough," said Blanchefleur. "Are there any mouse pies? We've been walking all day, and I'm hungry."

Really it had been Ivan who had been walking all day. He had carried Blanchefleur most of the way, except when she wanted to drink from a puddle or play with a leaf.

"Wait until the banquet," said the Lady. "It starts in an hour, which will give you enough time to prepare. It's in honor of your return and departure."

"Departure?" said Ivan.

"Yes," said the Lady. "Tomorrow, you will go to the Southern

Marshes, to spend a year with my friend, Dame Lizard. She has a large family, and needs help taking care of it. Blanchefleur, you will accompany your cousin."

"But that's not fair!" said Blanchefleur. "I've already spent a year with Ivan Idiot. Why do I have to spend another year with him?"

"Because he is your cousin, and he needs your help," said the Lady. "Now go, the both of you. I don't think you realize quite how dirty you both are." And she was right. From the long journey, even Blanchefleur's white paws were covered with dirt.

As they walked upstairs, Ivan said, "I'm sorry you have to come with me, Blanchefleur. I know you dislike being with me."

"You're not so bad," she said grudgingly. "At least you're warm." So it had been her, sleeping against his back all those nights. Ivan was surprised and pleased at the thought.

That night, the banquet proceeded as it had the year before, except this time Ivan knew what to expect. Several of the female cats asked him to dance, and this time he danced with more skill, never once stepping on a cat paw or tail. He danced several times with Blanchefleur, and she did not seem to dislike it as much as she had last year. Tailcatcher, the striped cat, was there as well. Once, as they were dancing close to one another, Ivan heard a hiss, but when he turned to look at Tailcatcher, the cat was bowing to his partner.

At the end of the evening, as he was wearily climbed the stone stairs up to his bed, he passed a hallway and heard a murmur of voices. At the end of the hallway stood Tailcatcher and Blanchefleur. The striped cat spoke to her and she replied, too low for Ivan to hear what they were saying. Then she turned and walked on down the hallway, her tail held high, exactly the way she walked when she was displeased with him. Ivan was rather glad Tailcatcher had been rebuffed, whatever he had wanted from her.

As he sank into sleep that night, in the curtained bed, he wondered if she would come to curl up against his back. But he fell asleep too quickly to find out.

$\sim$

The next morning, they started for the Southern Marshes. As they traveled south, the forest grew less dense: the trees were sparser, more sunlight fell on the path, and soon Ivan was hot and sweating. At midafternoon, they came to a river, and he was able to swim and cool himself off. Blanchefleur refused to go anywhere near the water.

"I'm not a fish," she said. "Are you quite done? We still have a long way to go."

Ivan splashed around a bit more, then got out and dried himself as best he could. They followed the river south until it was no longer a river but a series of creeks running through low hills covered with willows, alders, and sycamores. Around the creeks grew cattails, and where the water formed into pools, he could see water lilies starting to bloom. They were constantly crossing water, so Ivan carried Blanchefleur, who did not like to get her feet wet.

"There," she said finally. "That's where we're going." She was pointing at one of the low hills. At first, Ivan did not see the stone house among the trees: it blended in so well with the gray trunks. Ivan walked through a narrow creek (he had long ago given up on keeping his shoes dry) and up the hill to the house. He knocked at the door.

From inside, he heard a crash, then a "Just a moment!" Then another crash and the voice yelling, "Get out of there at once, Number Seven!"

There were more crashes and bangs, and then the door opened, so abruptly that he stepped back, startled. He might have been startled anyway, because who should be standing in front of him but a lizard, who came almost up to his shoulders, in a long brown duster and a feathered hat askew over one ear.

"I'm so glad you're here!" she said. "They've been impossible today. But they are dears, really they are, and the Lady told me that you were a competent nursemaid. You are competent, aren't you?" Without waiting for a reply, she continued, "Oh, it's good to see you again, Blanchefleur. Did you like the shrunken head I sent you from Peru?"

"Not particularly," said the white cat.

"Splendid!" said the lizard. "Now I'll just be off, shall I? My train leaves in half an hour and I don't want to miss it. I'm going to Timbuktu, you know. Train and then boat and train again, then camel caravan. Doesn't that sound fun? Do help me get my suitcases on the bicycle."

The bicycle was in a sort of shed. Ivan helped her tie two suitcases onto a rack with some frayed rope that he hoped would hold all the way to the station.

"Such a handy one, your young man, my dear," said the lizard to Blanchefleur.

"He's not—" said Blanchefleur.

"Kisses to you both! Ta, and I'll see you in a year! If I survive the sands of the Sahara, of course." And then she was off on her bicycle, down a road that ran across the hills, with her hat still askew. As she rode out of sight, Ivan heard a faint cry: "Plenty of spiders, that's what they like! And don't let them stay up too late!"

"Don't let who stay up too late?" asked Ivan.

"Us!" Ivan turned around. There in the doorway stood five—no, six—no, seven lizards that came up to his knees.

"Who are you?" he asked.

"These are her children," said Blanchefleur. "You're supposed to take care of them while she's gone. Don't you know who she is? She's Emilia Lizard, the travel writer. And you're her nursemaid." Blanchefleur seemed amused at the prospect.

"But the Lady said I was supposed to help," said Ivan. "How can I help someone who's on her way to Timbuktu? I don't know anything about taking care of children—or lizards!"

"It's easy," said one of the lizards. "You just let us do anything we want!"

"Eat sweets," said another.

"Stay up late," said yet another.

"Play as long as we like," said either one who had already spoken or another one, it was difficult to tell because they kept weaving in and out of the group, and they all looked alike.

"Please stand still," he said. "You're giving me a headache. And tell me your names."

"We don't have names," said one. "Mother just calls us by numbers, but she always gets us mixed up."

"I'll have to give you names," said Ivan, although he was afraid that he would get them mixed up as well. "Let's at least go in. Blanchefleur and I are tired, and we need to rest."

But once they stepped inside, Ivan found there was no place to rest. All of the furniture in the parlor had been piled in a corner to make a fort.

"If I'm going to take care of you, I need to learn about you," said Ivan. "Let's sit down—" But there was nowhere to sit down. And the lizards, all seven of them, were no longer there. Some were already inside the fort, and the others were about to besiege it.

"Come out!" he said. "Come out, all of you!" But his voice was drowned by the din they were already making. "What in the world am I supposed to do?" he asked Blanchefleur.

She twitched her tail, then said in a low voice, "I think it's the Seige of Jerusalem." Loudly and theatrically, she said, as though to Ivan, "Yes, you're right. The French are so much better at cleaning than the Saracens. I bet the French would clean up this mess lickety split."

Ivan stared at her in astonishment. Then he smiled. "You're wrong, Blanchefleur. The Saracens have a long tradition of cleanliness. In a cleaning contest, the Saracens would certainly win."

"Would not!" said one of the besiegers. "Would too!" came a cry from the fort. And then, in what seemed like a whirlwind of lizards, the fort was disassembled, the sofa and armchairs were put back in their places, and even the cushions were fluffed. In front of Ivan stood a line of seven lizards, asking, "Who won, who won?"

"The Saracens, this time," said Blanchefleur. "But really, you know, it's two out of three that counts."

Life in the Lizard household was completely different than it had been in Professor Owl's tower. There were days when Ivan missed the silence and solitude, the opportunity to read and study all day long. But he did not have much time to remember or regret. His days were spent catching insects and spiders for the lizards' breakfast, lunch, snack, and dinner, making sure that they bathed and sunned themselves, that they napped in the afternoon and went to bed on time.

At first, it was difficult to make them pay attention. They were as quick as seven winks, and on their outings they had a tendency to vanish as soon as he turned his back. Ivan was always afraid he was going to lose one. Once, indeed, he had to rescue Number Two from an eagle, and Number Five had to be pulled out of a foxhole. But he found that the hours spent working on the Encyclopedia of All Knowledge stood him in good stead: if he began telling a story, in an instant they would all be seated around him, listening intently. And if he forgot anything, he would ask the pen he had made from Professor Owl's tail feather to write it out for him. Luckily, Dame Lizard had left plenty of paper and ink.

He gave them all names: Ajax, Achilles, Hercules, Perseus, Helen, Medea, Andromache. They were fascinated by the stories of their names, and Medea insisted she was putting spells on the others, while Hercules would try to lift the heaviest objects he could find. Ivan learned to tell them apart. One had an ear that was slightly crooked, one had a stubby tail, one swayed as she walked. Each night, when he tucked them in and counted the lizard heads—yes, seven heads lay on the pillows—he breathed a sigh of relief that they were still alive.

"How many more days?" he would ask Blanchefleur.

"You don't want to know," she would reply. And then she would go out hunting, while he made himself dinner. Of course he could not eat insects and spiders, or mice like Blanchefleur. On the first night, he looked in the pantry and found a bag of flour, a bag of sugar, some tea, and a tinned ham. He made himself tea and ate part of the tinned ham.

"What in the world shall I do for food?" he asked Blanchefleur.

"What everyone else does. Work for it," she replied. So the next day, he left the lizards in her care for a couple of hours and went into the town that lay along the road Dame Lizard had taken. It was a small town, not much larger than the village he had grown up in. There, he asked if anyone needed firewood chopped, or a field cleared, or any such work. That day, he cleaned out a pigsty. The farmer who hired him found him strong and steady, so he hired him again, to pick vegetables, paint a fence, any odd work that comes up around a farm. He recommended Ivan to others, so there was soon a steady trickle of odd jobs that brought in enough money for him to buy bread and meat. The farmer who had originally hired him gave him vegetables that were too ripe for market.

He could never be gone long, because Blanchfleur would remind him in no uncertain terms that taking care of the lizards was his task, not hers. Whenever he came back, they were clean and fed and doing something orderly, like playing board games.

"Why do they obey you, and not me?" he asked, tired and cross. He had just washed an entire family's laundry.

"Because," she answered.

After dinner, once the lizards had been put to bed, really and finally put to bed, he would sit in the parlor and read the books on the shelves, which were all about travel in distant lands. Among them were the books of Dame Emilia Lizard. They had titles like *Up the Amazon in a Steamboat* and *Across the Himalayas on a Yak*. He found them interesting—Dame Lizard was an acute observer, and he learned about countries and customs that he had not even known existed—but often he could scarcely keep his eyes open because he was so tired. Once Blanchefleur returned from her evening hunt, he would go to sleep in Dame Lizard's room. He could tell it was hers because the walls were covered with photographs of her in front of temples and pyramids, perched on yaks or camels or water buffalos, dressed in native garb. Blanchefleur would curl up against him, no longer pretending not to, and he would fall asleep to her soft rumble.

In winter, all the lizards caught bronchitis. First Andromache started coughing, and then Ajax, until there was an entire household of sick lizards. Since Ivan did not want to leave them, Blanchefleur went into town to find the doctor.

"You're lucky to have caught me," said the doctor when he arrived. "My train leaves in an hour. There's been a dragon attack, and the King has asked all the medical personnel who can be spared to help the victims. He burned an entire village, can you imagine? But I'm sure you've seen the photographs in the *Herald*."

Ivan had not—they did not get the *Herald*, or any other newspaper, at Dame Lizard's house. He asked where the attack had occurred, and sighed with relief when told it was a fishing village on the coast. His father was not in danger.

"Nothing much I can do here anyway," said the doctor. "Bronchitis has to run its course. Give them tea with honey for the coughs, and tepid baths for the fever. And try to avoid catching it yourself!"

"A dragon attack," said Blanchefleur after the doctor had left. "We haven't had one of those in a century."

But there was little time to think of what might be happening far away. For weeks, Ivan barely slept. He told the lizards stories, took their temperature, made them tea. Once their appetites returned, he found them the juiciest worms under the snow. Slowly, one by one, they began to get better. Medea, the smallest of them and his secret favorite, was sick for longer than the rest, and one night when she was coughing badly, he held her through the night, not knowing what else to do. Sometimes, when he looked as though he might fall asleep standing up, Blanchefleur would say, "Go sleep, Ivan. I'll stay up and watch them. I am nocturnal, you know."

By the time all the lizards were well, the marsh marigolds were blooming, and irises were pushing their sword-like leaves out of the ground. The marshes were filled with the sounds of birds returning from the south: the raucous cacophony of ducks, the songs of thrushes.

Ivan had forgotten how long he had been in the marsh, so he was startled when one morning he heard the front door open and a voice call, "Hello, my dears! I'm home!" And there stood Dame Lizard, with her suitcases strapped to her bicycle, looking just as she had left a year ago, but with a fuchsia scarf around her throat.

The lizards rushed around her, calling "Mother, Mother, look how we've grown! We all have names now! And we know about the Trojan War!" She had brought them a set of papier mâché puppets and necklaces of lapis lazuli. For Blanchefleur, she had brought a hat of crimson felt that she had seen on a dancing monkey in Marakesh.

Blanchefleur said, "Thank you. You shouldn't have."

Once the presents were distributed and the lizards were eating an enormous box of Turkish Delight, she said to Ivan, "Come outside." When they were standing by the house, under the alders, she said, "Ivan, I can see you've taken good care of my children. They are happy and healthy, and that is due to your dedication. Hercules told me how you took care of Medea when she was ill. I want to give you a present too. I brought back a camel whip for you, but I want to give you something that will be of more use, since you don't have a camel. You must raise your arms, then close your eyes and stand as still as possible, no matter how startled you may be."

Ivan closed his eyes, not knowing what to expect.

And then he felt a terrible constriction around his chest, as though his ribcage were being crushed. He opened his eyes, looked down, and gasped.

There, wrapped around his chest, was what looked like a thick green rope. It was Dame Lizard's tail, which had been hidden under her duster. For a moment, the tail tightened, and then it was no longer attached to her body. She had shed it, as lizards do. Ivan almost fell forward from the relief of being able to breathe.

"I learned that from a Swami in India," she said. "From now on, when you give pain to another, you will feel my tail tightening around you so whatever pain you give, you will also receive. That's called *empathy*, and the Swami said it was the most important thing anyone can have."

Ivan looked down. He could no longer see the tail, but he could feel it around him, like a band under his shirt. He did not know whether to thank her. The gift, if gift it was, had been so painful that he felt sore and bruised.

After he had said a protracted farewell to all the lizards, hugging them tightly, he and Blanchefleur walked north, along the river. He told her what Dame Lizard had done, lifting his shirt and showing her the mark he had found there, like a tattoo of a green tail around his ribcage.

"Is it truly a gift, or a curse?" he asked Blanchefleur.

"One never knows about gifts until later," said the white cat.

Marmalade met them at the front door. "I'm so sorry, Miss Blanchefleur," he said, "but your mother is not home. The King has asked her to the castle, to consult about the dragon attack. But she left you a note in the solar."

Blanchfleur read the note to Ivan.

My dear, Ivan's third apprenticeship is with Captain Wolf in the Northern Mountains. Could you please accompany him and try to keep him from getting killed? Love, Mother.

This time, there was no banquet. With the Lady gone, the castle was quiet, as though it were asleep and waiting for her return to wake back up. They ate dinner in the kitchen with Mrs. Pebbles and the ladies-in-waiting, and then went directly to bed. Blanchefleur curled up next to Ivan on the pillow, as usual. It had become their custom.

The next morning, Mrs. Pebbles gave them Ivan's satchel, with clean clothes, including some warmer ones for the mountains, and his horn-handled knife. "Take care of each other," she told them. "Those mountains aren't safe, and I don't know what the Lady is thinking, sending you to the Wolf Guard."

"What is the Wolf Guard?" Ivan asked as they walked down the garden path.

"It's part of the King's army," said Blanchfleur. "It guards the northern borders from trolls. They come down from the mountains and raid the towns. In winter, especially . . . "

"Blanchefleur!" Tailcatcher was standing in front of them. He had stepped out from behind one of the topiaries. "May I have a word with you?" He did not, however, sound as though he were asking permission. Ivan gritted his teeth. He had never spoken to Blanchefleur like that—even if he had wanted to, he would not have dared.

"Yes, and the word is no," said Blanchefleur. She walked right around him, holding her tail high, and Ivan followed her, making a wide circle around the striped cat, who looked as though he might take a swipe at Ivan's shins. He looked back, to see Tailcatcher glaring at them.

"What was that about?" asked Ivan.

"For years now, he's been assuming I would marry him, because he's the best hunter in the castle. He asked me the first time on the night before we left for Professor Owl's house, and then again before we left for Dame Lizard's. This would have been the third time."

"And you keep refusing?" asked Ivan.

"Of course," she said. "He may be the best hunter, but I'm the daughter of the Lady of the Forest and the Man in the Moon. I'm not going to marry a common cat!"

Ivan could not decide how he felt about her response. On the one hand, he was glad she had no intention of marrying Tailcatcher. On the other, wasn't he a common man?

This journey was longer and harder than the two before. Once they reached the foothills of the Northern Mountains, they were constantly going up. The air was colder. In late afternoon, Ivan put on a coat Mrs. Pebbles had insisted on packing for him, and that he had been certain he would not need until winter.

Eventually, there were no more roads or paths, and they simply walked through the forest. Ivan started wondering whether Blanchefleur knew the way, then scolded himself. Of course she did: she was Blanchefleur.

Finally, as the sun was setting, Blanchefleur said, "We're here."

"Where?" asked Ivan. They were standing in a clearing. Around them were tall pines. Ahead of them was what looked like a sheer cliff face, rising higher than the treetops. Above it, he could see the peaks of the mountains, glowing in the light of the setting sun.

Blanchefleur jumped down from his shoulder, walked over to a boulder in the middle of the clearing, and climbed to the top. She said, "Captain, we have arrived."

Out of the shadows of the forest appeared wolves, as silently as though they were shadows themselves—Ivan could not count how many. They were all round, and he suddenly realized that he could die, here in the forest. He imagined their teeth at his throat and turned to run, then realized he was being an idiot, giving in to an ancient instinct although he could see that Blanchefleur was not frightened at all. She sat on the dark rock, amid the dark wolves, like a ghost.

"Greetings, Blanchefleur," said one of the wolves, distinguishable from the others because he had only one eye, and a scar running across it from his ear to his muzzle. "I hear that your mother has sent us a new recruit."

"For a year," said Blanchefleur. "Try not to get him killed."

"I make no promises," said the wolf. "What is his name?"

"Ivan," said Blanchefleur.

"Come here, recruit." Ivan walked to the boulder and stood in front of the wolf, as still as he could. He did not want Blanchefleur to see that he was afraid. "You shall call me Captain, and I shall call you Private, and as long as you do exactly what you are told, all shall be well between us. Do you understand?"

"Yes," said Ivan.

The wolf bared his teeth and growled.

"Yes, Captain," said Ivan.

"Good. This is your Company, although we like to think of ourselves as a pack. You are a member of the Wolf Guard, and should be prepared to die for your brothers and sisters of the pack, as they are prepared to die for you. Now come inside."

Ivan wondered where inside might be, but the Captain loped toward the cliff face and vanished behind an outcropping. One by one, the wolves followed him, some stopping to give Ivan a brief sniff. Ivan followed them and realized the cliff was not sheer after all. Behind a protruding rock was a narrow opening, just large enough for a wolf. He crawled through it and emerged in a large cave. Scattered around the cave, wolves were sitting or lying in groups, speaking together in low voices. They looked up when he entered, but were too polite or uninterested to stare and went back to their conversations, which seemed to be about troll raiding parties they had encountered, wounds they had sustained, and the weather.

"Have you ever fought?" the Captain asked him.

"No, sir," said Ivan.

"That is bad," said the Captian. "Can you move through the forest silently? Can you tell your direction from the sun in the day and the stars at night? Can you sound like an owl to give warning without divulging your presence?"

"Yes, Captain," said Ivan, fairly certain that he could still do those things. And to prove it to himself, he hooted, first like a Eagle Owl, then like a Barn Owl, and finally like one of the Little Owls that used to nest in his father's mill.

"Well, that's something, at least. You can be one of our scouts. Have you eaten?"

"No, sir," said Ivan.

"At the back of the cave are the rabbits we caught this morning," said the Captain. "You may have one of those."

"He is human," said Blanchefleur. "He must cook his food."

"A nuisance, but you may build a small fire, although you will have to collect wood. These caverns extend into the mountain for several miles. Make certain the smoke goes back into the mountain, and not through the entrance."

Skinning a rabbit was messy work, but Ivan butchered it, giving a leg to Blanchefleur and roasting the rest for himself on a stick he sharpened with his knife. It was better than he had expected. That night, he slept beneath his coat on the floor of the cave, surrounded by wolves. He was grateful to have Blanchefleur curled up next to his chest.

The next morning, he began his life in the Wolf Guard.

As a scout, his duty was not to engage the trolls, but to look for signs of them. He would go out with a wolf partner, moving through the forest silently, looking for signs of troll activity: their camps, their tracks, their spoor. The Wolf Guard kept detailed information on the trolls who lived in the mountains. In summer, they seldom came down far enough to threaten the villages on the slopes. But in winter, they would send raiding parties for all the things they could not produce themselves: bread and cheese and beer, fabrics and jewels, sometimes even children they could raise as their own, for troll women do not bear many children. Ivan learned the forest quickly, just as he had at home, and the wolves in his Company, who had initially been politely contemptuous of a human in their midst, came to think of him as a useful member of the pack. He could not smell as well as they could, nor see as well at night, but he could climb trees, and pull splinters out of their paws, and soon he was as good at tracking the trolls as they were. They were always respectful to Blanchefleur. One day, he asked her what she did while he was out with the wolves. "Mind my own business," she said. So he did not ask again.

As for Ivan, being a scout in the Wolf Guard was like finding a home. He had learned so much in Professor Owl's tower, and he had come to love the lizards in his charge, but with the wolves he was back in the forest, where he had spent his childhood. And the wolves themselves were like a family. When Graypaw or Mist, with whom he was most often paired, praised his ability to spot troll tracks, or when the Captain said "Well done, Private," he felt a pride that he had never felt before.

"You know, I don't think I've ever seen you so happy," said Blanchefleur, one winter morning. The snows had come, and he was grateful for the hat and gloves Mrs. Pebbles had included in his satchel.

"I don't think I ever have been, before," he said. "Not since—" Since his mother had died. Since then, he had always been alone. But now he had a pack. "I think I could stay here for the rest of my life."

"We seldom get what we want," said Blanchefleur. "The world has a use for us, tasks we must fulfill. And we must fulfill them as best we can, finding happiness along the way. But we usually get what we need."

"I've never heard you so solemn before," said Ivan. "You're starting to sound like your mother. But I don't think the world has any tasks for me. I'm no one special, after all."

"Don't be so sure, Ivan Miller," said Blanchefleur.

Suddenly, all the wolves in the cave pricked up their ears.

"The signal!" said the Captian.

And then Ivan heard it too, the long howl that signaled a troll raid, the short howls that indicated which village was being attacked.

"To the village!" shouted the Captain.

"Be careful!" said Blanchefleur, as Ivan sprang up, made sure his knife was in his belt, and ran out of the cave with the wolves. Then they were coursing through the forest, silent shadows against the snow.

They saw the flames and heard the screams before they saw any trolls. The village was a small one, just a group of herding families on the upper slopes. Their houses were simple, made of stone, with turf roofs. But the sheds were of wood, filled with fodder for the sturdy mountain sheep. The trolls had set fire to the fodder, and some of the sheds were burning. The sheep were bleating terribly, and as wolves rushed into the village, the Captain shouted to Ivan, "Open the pens! Let the sheep out—we can herd them back later."

Ivan ran from pen to pen, opening all the gates. Mist ran beside him and if any sheep were reluctant to leave their pens, she herded them out, nipping at their heels.

When they reached the last of the pens, Ivan saw his first troll. She was taller than the tallest man, and twice as large around. She looked like a piece of the mountain that had grown arms and legs. Her mottled skin was gray and green and brown, and she was covered in animal pelts. In her hand, she carried a large club. In front of her, crouched and growling, was Graypaw.

"Come on, cub!" she sneered. "I'll teach you how to sit and lie down!"

She lunged at Graypaw, swinging the club clumsily but effectively. The club hit a panicked ram that had been standing behind her, and the next moment, the ram lay dead on the snow.

Mist yipped to let Graypaw know she was behind him. He barked back, and the wolves circled the troll in opposite directions, one attacking from the left and the other from the right.

What could Ivan do? He drew his knife, but that would be no more effective against a troll than a sewing needle. To his right, one of the sheds was on fire, pieces of it falling to the ground as it burned. As Graypaw and Mist circled, keeping away from the club, trying to get under it and bite the troll's ankles, Ivan ran into the burning shed. He wrenched a piece of wood from what had been a gate, but was now in flames, then thrust its end into the fire. The flames licked it, and it caught. A long stick, its end on fire. This was a weapon of sorts, but how was he to use it?

Graypaw and Mist were still circling, and one of them had succeeded in wounding the troll—there was green ichor running down her leg. The troll was paying no attention to Ivan—she was wholly absorbed in fending off the wolves. But the wolves knew he was behind them. They were watching him out of the corners of their eyes, waiting. For what?

Then Ivan gave a short bark, the signal for attack. Both Graypaw and Mist flew at the troll simultaneously. The troll swung about wildly, not certain which to dispatch first. *Now*, thought Ivan, and he lunged forward, not caring that he could be hit by the club, only knowing that this was the moment, that he had put his packmates in danger for this opportunity. He thrust the flaming stick toward the troll's face. The troll shrieked—it had gone straight into her left eye. She clutched the eye and fell backward. Without thinking, Ivan drew his knife and plunged it into the troll's heart, or where he thought her heart might be.

A searing pain ran through his chest. It was Dame Lizard's tail, tightening until he could no longer breathe. It loosened again, but he reeled with the shock and pain of it.

"Ivan, are you well?" asked Mist.

"I'm—all right," he said, still breathless. "I'm going to be all right." But he felt sick.

The troll lay on the ground, green ichor spreading across her chest. She was dead. Behind her was a large sack.

"That must be what she was stealing," said Graypaw.

The sack started to wriggle.

"A sheep, perhaps," said Mist.

But when Ivan untied it, he saw a dirty, frightened face, with large gray eyes. A girl.

"You've found my daughter!" A woman was running toward them. With her was the Captain.

"Nadia, my Nadia," she cried.

"Mama!" cried the girl, and scrambling out of the bag, she ran into her mother's arms.

"This is the Mayor of the village," said the Captain. "Most of the trolls have fled, and we were afraid they had taken the girl with them."

"I can't thank you enough," said the woman. "You've done more than rescue my daughter, although that has earned you my gratitude. I recognize this troll—she has been here before. We call her Old Mossy. She is the leader of this tribe, and without her, the tribe will need to choose a new leader by combat. It will not come again this winter. Our village has sustained great damage, but not one of us has died or disappeared, and we can rebuild. How can we reward you for coming to our rescue, Captain?"

"Madame Mayor, we are the Wolf Guard. Your gratitude is our reward," said the Captain.

On the way back to the cave, Graypaw and Mist walked ahead of Ivan, talking to the Captain in low voices. He wondered if he had done something wrong. Perhaps he should not have told them to attack? After all, they both outranked him. They were both Corporals, while he was only a Private. Perhaps they were telling the Captain about how he had reeled and clutched his chest after the attack. Would he be declared unfit for combat?

When they got back to the cave, Blanchefleur was waiting for him.

"Ivan, I need to speak with you," she said.

"Blanchefleur, I killed a troll! I mean, I helped kill her. I want to tell you about it . . . "

"That's wonderful, Ivan. I'm very proud of you. I am, you know, and not just because of the troll. But it's time for us to leave."

"What do you mean? It's still winter. I haven't been here for a year yet."

"My mother has summoned us. Here is her messenger."

It was Tailcatcher. In his excitement, Ivan had not noticed the striped cat.

"The Lady wishes you to travel to the capital. Immediately," said Tailcatcher.

"But why?" asked Ivan.

"You are summoned," said Tailcatcher, contemptuously. "Is that not enough?"

"If you are summoned, you must go," said the Captain, who had been standing behind him. "But come back to us when you can, Ivan."

Ivan had never felt so miserable in his life. "Can I say goodbye to Mist and Graypaw?"

"Yes, quickly," said the Captain. "And thank them, because on their recommendation, I am promoting you to Corporal. There is also something I wish to give you. Hold out your right hand, Corporal Miller."

Ivan held out his hand.

The Captain lunged at him, seized Ivan's hand in his great mouth, and bit down.

Ivan cried out.

The Captain released him. The wolf's teeth had not broken his skin, but one of his fangs had pierced Ivan's hand between the thumb and forefinger. It was still lodged in his flesh. There was no blood, and as Ivan watched, the fang vanished, leaving only a white fang-shaped scar.

"Why—" he asked.

"That is my gift to you, Corporal. When I was a young corporal like yourself, I saved the life of a witch. In return, she charmed that fang for me. She told me that as long as I had it, whenever I fought, I would defeat my enemy. She also told me that one day, I could pass the charm to another. I asked her how, and she told me I would know when the time came. I am old, Ivan, and this is my last winter with the Wolf Guard. I believe I know why you have been summoned by the Lady. With that charm, whatever battles you have to fight, you should win. Now go. There is a storm coming, and you should be off the mountain before it arrives."

Ivan packed his belongings and made his farewells. Then, he left the cave, following Tailcatcher and Blanchefleur. He looked back once, with tears in his eyes, and felt as though his heart were breaking.

The journey to the capital would have taken several days, but in the first town they came to, Ivan traded his knife and coat for a horse. It was an old farm horse, but it went faster than he could have on foot with two cats. The cats sat in panniers that had once held potatoes, and Tailcatcher looked very cross indeed. When Ivan asked again why he had been summoned, the cat replied, "That's for the Lady to say," and would say nothing more.

They spent the night in a barn and arrived at the capital the next day.

Ivan had never seen a city so large. The houses had as many as three stories, and there were shops for everything, from ladies' hats and fancy meats to bicycles. On one street he even saw a shiny new motorcar. But where were the people? The shops were closed, the houses shuttered, and the streets empty. Once, he saw a frightened face peering at him out of an alley, before it disappeared into the shadows.

"What happened here?" he asked.

"You'll know soon enough," said Tailcather. "That's where we're going."

That was the palace.

Ivan had never seen a building so large. His father's mill could have fit into one of its towers. With a sense of unease, he rode up to the gates.

"State your business!" said a guard who had been crouching in the gatehouse and stood up only long enough to challenge them.

Ivan was about to reply when Blanchefleur poked her head out of the pannier. "I am Blanchefleur. My mother is the Lady of the Forest, and our business is our own."

"You may pass, my Lady," said the guard, hurriedly opening the gates and then hiding again.

They rode up the long avenue, through the palace gardens, which were magnificent, although Ivan thought they were not as interesting as the Lady's gardens with their cat gardeners. They left the horse with an ostler who met them at the palace steps, then hurried off toward the stables. At the top of the steps, they were met by a majordomo who said, "This way, this way." He reminded Ivan of Marmalade.

They followed the majordomo down long hallways with crimson carpets and paintings on the walls in gilded frames. At last, they came to a pair of gilded doors, which opened into the throne room. There was the King, seated on his throne. Ivan could tell he was the King because he wore a crown. To one side of him sat the Lady. To the other sat a girl about Ivan's age, also wearing a crown, and with a scowl on her face. Before the dais stood two men.

"Ivan," said the Lady, "I'm so pleased to see you. I'm afraid we have a problem on our hands. About a year ago, a dragon arrived on the coast. At first, he only attacked the ports and coastal villages, and then only occasionally. I believe he is a young dragon, and lacked confidence in his abilities. But several months ago, he started flying inland, attacking market towns. Last week, he was spotted in the skies over the capital, and several days ago, he landed on the central bank. That's where he is now, holed up in the vault. Dragons like gold, as you know. The King has asked for a dragon slayer, and I'm hoping you'll volunteer."

"What?" said Ivan. "The King has asked for a what?"

"Yes, young man," said the King, looking annoyed that the Lady had spoken first. "We've already tried to send the municipal police after him, only to have the municipal police eaten. The militias were not able to stop him in the towns, but I thought a trained police force—well, that's neither here nor there. The Lady tells me a dragon must be slain in the old-fashioned way. I'm a progressive man myself—this entire city should be wired for electricity by next year, assuming it's not destroyed by the dragon. But with a dragon sitting on the monetary supply, I'm willing to try anything. So we've made the usual offer: the hand of my daughter in marriage and the kingdom after I retire, which should be in about a decade, barring ill health. We already have two brave volunteers, Sir Albert Anglethorpe and Oswald the—what did you say it was?—the Omnipotent."

Sir Albert, a stocky man with a shock of blond hair, bowed. He was wearing chain mail and looked as though he exercised regularly with kettlebells. Oswald the Omnipotent, a tall, thin, pimply man in a ratty robe, said, "How de do."

"And you are?" said the King.

"Corporal Miller," said Ivan. "And I have no idea how to slay a dragon."

"Honesty! I like honesty," said the King. "None of us do either. But you'll figure it out, won't you, Corporal Miller? Because the dragon really must be slain, and I'm at my wits' end. The city evacuated, no money to pay the military—we won't be a proper kingdom if this keeps up."

"I have every confidence in you, Ivan," said the Lady.

"Me too," said Blanchefleur.

Startled, Ivan looked down at the white cat. "May I have something to eat before I go, um, dragon-slaying?" he asked. "We've been traveling all morning."

"Of course," said the King. "Anything you want, my boy. Ask and it will be yours."

"Well then," said Ivan, "I'd like some paper and ink."

~

Sir Albert had insisted on being fully armed, so he wore a suit of armor and carried a sword and shield. Oswald was still in his ratty robe and carried what he said was a magic wand.

"A witch sold it to me," he told Ivan. "It can transform anything it touches into anything else. She told me it had two transformations left in it. I used the first one to turn a rock into a sack of gold, but I lost the gold in a card game. So when I heard about this dragon, I figured I would use the second transformation to turn him into—I don't know, maybe a frog? And then, I'll be king. They give you all the gold you want, when you're king."

"What about the princess?" asked Ivan.

"Oh, she's pretty enough. Although she looks bad-tempered."

"And do you want to be king too?" Ivan asked Sir Albert.

"What? I don't care about that," he said through the visor of his helmet. "It's the dragon I'm after. I've been the King's champion three years running. I can out-joust and out-fight any man in the kingdom. But can I slay a dragon, eh? That's what I want to know." He bent his arms as though he were flexing his biceps, although they were hidden in his armor.

Ivan had not put on armor, but he had asked for a bow and a quiver of arrows. They seemed inadequate, compared with a sword and a magic wand.

The dragon may have been young, but he was not small. Ivan, Oswald, and Sir Alfred stood in front of the bank building, looking at the damage he had caused. There was a large hole in the side of the building where he had smashed through the stone wall, directly into the vault.

"As the King's champion, I insist that I be allowed to fight the dragon first," said Sir Albert. "Also, I outrank both of you."

"Fine by me," said Oswald.

"All right," said Ivan.

Sir Albert clanked up the front steps and through the main entrance. They heard a roar, and then a crash, as though a file cabinet had fallen over, and then nothing.

After fifteen minutes, Oswald asked, "So how big do you think this dragon is, anyway?"

"About as big as the hole in the side of the building," said Ivan.

"See, the reason I'm asking," said Oswald, "is that the wand has to actually touch whatever I want to transform. Am I going to be able to touch the dragon without being eaten?"

"Probably not," said Ivan. "They breathe fire, you know."

"What about when they're sleeping?" asked Oswald.

"Dragons are very light sleepers," said Ivan. "He would smell you before you got close enough."

"How do you know?"

"It's in the Encyclopedia of All Knowledge."

"Oh, that thing," said Oswald. "You know, I worked on that for a while. Worst job I ever had. The pay was terrible, and I had to eat soup for every meal."

Another half hour passed.

"I don't think Sir Albert is coming out," said Ivan. "You volunteered before me. Would you like to go next?"

"You know, I'm not so sure about going in after all," said Oswald. "I can't very well rule a kingdom if I'm eaten, can I?"

"That might be difficult," said Ivan.

"You go ahead," said Oswald, starting to back away. "I think I'm going to turn another rock into gold coins. That seems like a better idea."

He turned and ran up the street, leaving Ivan alone in front of the bank. Ivan sighed. Well, there was no reason to wait any longer. He might as well go in now.

Instead of going in by the front door, he went in through the hole that the dragon had made in the side of the bank. He walked noiselessly, as he had done in the forest. It was easy to find the dragon: he was lying on a pile of gold coins in the great stone room that had once been the vault. Near the door of the vault, which had been smashed open, Ivan could see a suit of armor and a sword, blackened by flames. He did not want to think about what had happened to Sir Albert.

An arrow would not penetrate the dragon's hide. He knew that, because while he had been eating at the palace, he had asked Professor Owl's tail feather to write out the entire Encyclopedia entry on dragons. He had a plan, and would get only one chance to carry it out. It would depend as much on luck as skill.

But even if it worked, he knew how it would feel, slaying a dragon. He remembered how it had felt, killing the troll. Could he survive the pain? Was there any way to avoid it? He had to try.

He stood in a narrow hallway off the vault. Keeping back in the shadows, he called, "Dragon!"

The dragon lifted his head. "Another dragon slayer? How considerate of the King to sent me dessert! Dragon slayer is my favorite delicacy, although the policemen were delicious. I much preferred them to farmers, who taste like dirt and leave grit between your teeth, or fishermen, who are too salty."

"Dragon, you could fly north to the mountains. There are plenty of sheep to eat there."

"Sheep!" said the dragon. "Sheep are dull and stringy compared to the delicious men I've eaten here. Just the other day, I ate a fat baker. He tasted of sugar and cinnamon. There are plenty of teachers and accountants to eat in this city. Why, I might eat the Princess herself! I hear princess is even better than dragon slayer."

The dragon swung his head around, as though trying to locate Ivan. "But you don't smell like a man, dragon slayer," said the dragon. "What are you, and are you good to eat?"

I must still smell like the wolves, thought Ivan.

He stepped out from the hallway and into the vault. "I'm an Enigma, and I'm delicious."

The dragon swung toward the sound of his voice. As his great head came around, Ivan raised his bow and shot an arrow straight up into the dragon's eye.

The dragon screamed in pain and let out a long, fiery breath. He swung his head to and fro. Ivan aimed again, but the dragon was swinging his head too wildly: a second arrow would never hit its mark. Well, now he would find out if the Captain's charm worked. He ran across the floor of the vault, ignoring the dragon's flames, and picked up Sir Albert's sword. It was still warm, but had cooled down enough for him to raise it.

The pain had begun the moment the arrow entered the dragon's eye, but he tried not to pay attention. He did not want to think about how bad it would get. Where was the dragon's neck? It was still swinging wildly, but he brought the sword down just as it swung back toward him. The sword severed the dragon's neck cleanly in two, and his head rolled over the floor.

Ivan screamed from the pain and collapsed. He lay next to the dragon's head, with his eyes closed, unable to rise. Then, he felt something rough and wet on his cheek. He opened his eyes. Blanchefleur was licking him.

"Blanchefleur," he said weakly. "What are you doing here?"

"I followed you, of course," she said.

"But I never saw you."

"Of course not." She sat on the floor next to him as he slowly sat up. "Excellent shot, by the way. They'll call you Ivan Dragonslayer now, you know."

"Oh, I hope not," he said.

"It's inevitable."

The King met him with an embrace that made Ivan uncomfortable. "Welcome home, Ivan Dragonslayer! I shall have my attorney drawn up the papers to make you my heir, and here of course is my lovely Alethea, who will become your bride. A royal wedding will attract tourists to the city, which will help with the rebuilding effort."

Princess Alethea crossed her arms and looked out the window. Even from the back, she seemed angry.

"Forgive me, your Majesty," said Ivan, "but I have no wish to marry the Princess, and I don't think she wants to marry me either. We don't even know each other."

Princess Alethea turned and looked at him in astonishment.

"Thank you!" she said. "You're the first person who's made any sense all day. I'm glad you slayed the dragon, but I don't see what that has to do with getting my hand in marriage. I'm not some sort of prize at a village fair."

"And I would not deprive you of a kingdom," said Ivan. "I have no wish to be king."

"Oh, goodness," said Alethea, "neither do I! Ruling is deadly dull. You can have the kingdom and do what you like with it. I'm going to university, to become an astronomer. I've wanted to be an astronomer since I was twelve."

"But . . . " said the King.

"Well then, it's decided, " said the Lady. "Ivan, you'll spend the rest of your apprenticeship here, in the palace, learning matters of state."

"But I want to go back to the wolves," said Ivan. He saw the look on the Lady's face: she was about to say no. He added, hurriedly, "If I can go back, just for the rest of my apprenticeship, I'll come back here and stay as long as you like, learning to be king. I promise."

"All right," said the Lady.

He nodded, gratefully. At least he would have spring in the mountains, with his pack.

Ivan and Blanchefleur rode north, not on a farm horse this time, but on a mare from the King's stables. As night fell, they stopped by a stream. The mountains were ahead of them, glowing in the evening light.

"You know, before we left, Tailcatcher asked me again," said Blanchefleur. "He thought that my time with you was done, that I would go back to the Castle in the Forest with my mother. I could have."

"Why didn't you?" asked Ivan.

"Why did you refuse the hand of the Princess Alethea? She was attractive enough."

"Because I didn't want to spend the rest of my life with her," said Ivan. "I want to spend it with you, Blanchefleur."

"Even though I'm a cat?"

"Even though."

She looked at him for a moment, then said, "I'm not always a cat, you know." Suddenly, sitting beside him was a girl with short white hair, wearing a white fur jacket and trousers. She had Blanchefleur's eyes.

"Are you—are you Blanchefleur?" he asked. He stared at her. She was and she was not the white cat.

"Of course I am, idiot," she said. "I think you're going to make a good king. You'll have all the knowledge in the world to guide you, and any pain you cause, you'll have to feel yourself, so you'll be fair and kind. But you'll win all your battles. You'll hate it most of the time and wish you were back with the wolves or in Professor Owl's tower, or even taking care of the lizards. That's why you'll be good."

"And you'll stay with me?" he asked, tentatively reaching over and taking her hand.

"Of course," she said. "Who else is going to take care of you, Ivan?"

Together, they sat and watched the brightness fade from the mountain peaks and night fall over the Wolfwald. When Ivan lay down to sleep, he felt the white cat curl up next to his chest. He smiled into the darkness before slipping away into dreams.

— ❧ —

Theodora Goss's publications include the short story collection *In the Forest of Forgetting* (2006); *Interfictions* (2007), a short story anthology coedited with Delia Sherman; *Voices from Fairyland* (2008), a poetry anthology with critical essays and a selection of her own poems; and *The Thorn and the Blossom* (2012), a novella in a two-sided accordion format. She has been a finalist for the Nebula, Crawford, Locus, and Mythopoeic Awards, and on the Tiptree Award Honor List. She has won the World Fantasy Award.

— ❧ —

❧ ABOUT THE EDITOR ❧

This volume and the just-released *Halloween: Magic, Mystery, and the Macabre* are the third and fourth "original" anthologies edited by Paula Guran; her twenty-second and twenty-third anthologies altogether. As senior editor for Prime Books and Masque Books she also edits novels and collections. Guran has a website (www.paulaguran.com) that she has yet to actually do much with, but you can find out more about her there.

❧ ILLUSTRATIONS ❧

17: Year of Dragon © 2013 Avian / Shutterstock

31: Black Hellebore or Christmas Rose or Helleborus niger. Old engraved illustration of a Black Hellebore showing flowers. "Trousset encyclopedia" (*Nouveau dictionnaire encyclopédique universel illustré*), Paris 1886-1891 / Shutterstock

49: 1790: An old English spinning wheel for spinning yarn. (Photo by MPI/Getty Images) / iStockphoto

57: The Muse of Dance, vintage engraved illustration from *La mosaique* edited by A. Bourdilliat, Paris, 1875 / Shutterstock

91: Newfoundland or Canis lupus familiaris. Old engraved illustration of a Newfoundland. "Trousset encyclopedia" (*Nouveau dictionnaire encyclopédique universel illustré*), Paris 1886-1891 / Shutterstock

117: Engraving, bread and rolls with corn flax, vintage / Shutterstock

127: Illustration (1901) from *Tales of Mother Goose* by Charles Perrault; translated and edited by Charles Welsh; "The Marquis of Carabas is drowning!" Illustrating "The Master Cat, Or Puss in Boots." Adapted from by Gustave Doré's "Puss in boots" (*Le chat botté*). Date: Unknown, 1883 at the latest. (Public Domain) (modified)

147: Syringe, vintage engraved illustration from *Manuel des hospitalière et des garde-malaldes*, edited by Librairie Poussielgue, Paris, 1907 / Shutterstock

157: Eurasian Wolf, Canis lupus lupus; European, Common or Forest Wolf or Altaicus or lycaon or Grey wolf. Old engraved illustration of a Eurasian Wolf. "Trousset encyclopedia" (*Nouveau dictionnaire encyclopédique universel illustré*) Paris, 1886-1891 / Shutterstock

183: Lupinus or lupins or lupines, vintage engraved illustration. *Dictionnaire francais illustré des mots et des choses*, Larive and Fleury, Paris, 1895 / Shutterstock

189: Raven drawing © 2013 Silver Tiger / Shutterstock

215: Development of a Chicken Egg, vintage engraved illustration. *Dictionnaire francais illustré des mots et des choses*, Larive and Fleury, 1895, Paris / Shutterstock (modified)

233: Corset, vintage engraved illustration, *La mode illustrée* by Firmin-Didot et Cie, , Paris, 1882 / Shutterstock

263: Norwegian village in the mountains, an illustration from *The Encyclopedia Publishers Education*, St. Petersburg, Russia, 1896 / Shutterstock

283: Annual Nettle (Urtica urens), *Meyers Konversations-Lexik*, Berlin, 1897 / Shutterstock

299: Peach or Prunus persica, vintage engraved illustration. "Trousset encyclopedia" (*Nouveau dictionnaire encyclopédique universel illustré*), Paris, 1886-1891 / Shutterstock

319: Old mirror, vintage illustration from *Meyers Konversations-Lexik* Berlin, 1897 / Shutterstock

333: Cat Art Drawing © Silver Tiger 2013 / Shutterstock